Love is
a time of enchantment:
in it all days are fair and all fields
green. Youth is blest by it,
old age made benign:
the eyes of love see
roses blooming in December,
and sunshine through rain. Verily
is the time of true-love
a time of enchantment — and
Oh! how eager is woman
to be bewitched!

THE DIVIDED HEART

For a teenage girl like Rosaleen, growing up in the mid-fifties, Belfast had its compensations — even if they went against everything a nice convent girl like her had ever been told. There was the music, the urgent rhythms of Elvis, Fats Domino and Bill Haley. There were the Teddy boys, with the slick DAs and tight drainpipes. And there was first love — the kind of loving that only a handsome, arrogant rebel like Colin could offer, the kind that, with he a Protestant and Rosaleen a Catholic, would find many obstacles in its path . . .

EILEEN SHERMAN

THE DIVIDED HEART

Complete and Unabridged

ULVERSCROFT
Leicester

First published in Great Britain in 1985 by
Warner Books, London

Published in the United States of America
under the title of 'The Celtic Heart'

First Large Print Edition
published 1998
by arrangement with
Little, Brown and Company (UK) Ltd, London

British Library CIP Data

Sherman, Eileen
  The divided heart.—Large print ed.—
  Ulverscroft large print series: romance
  1. Catholic Church—relations—Protestant churches
  —Fiction
  2. Teenagers—Northern Ireland—Belfast—Fiction
  3. Love stories 4. Large type books
  I. Title
  813.5'4 [F]
  ISBN 0–7089–3910–4

Published by
F. A. Thorpe (Publishing) Ltd.
Anstey, Leicestershire

Set by Words & Graphics Ltd.
Anstey, Leicestershire
Printed and bound in Great Britain by
T. J. International Ltd., Padstow, Cornwall

This book is printed on acid-free paper

This book
is dedicated
to the people of Belfast

Acknowledgements

Special thanks to Houghton Mifflin Company and P. F. Collier for their kind assistance.

Very special gratitude to International Korwin Corp. for their overly generous contribution of 'Come To Me' and 'It's Not For Me To Say'.

Heartfelt thanks to Denise Catrone and Grace Miele, whose interest in what I was doing gave untold encouragement; to Judy Jusinski and Margaret Sherman, whose assistance in research I could not have done without.

Countless thanks to my three children, Margaret, Elizabeth, and Tommy, who in no way hindered me, but whose young lives bore the brunt of a writer's urge to create.

And above all, I give bountiful and everlasting acknowledgement to Tom Sherman, my husband, whose optimism kept me going during *The Divided Heart*'s two years in limbo, and without whose love and devotion this book may never have been written . . .

. . . and in loving memory of my father, Edward Canavan, whose great love for work, art, learning, and God provided me with four very necessary ingredients for living.

1

THE glow from the oil lamp spilled like liquid gold over the table and across the paper on which Rosaleen was writing a letter home to her mother and father, and its mellow charm found its way across the room and warmed the handmade quilts on the bed, across which Rosaleen's two school friends had draped themselves. But it did little to waylay the impatience brooding there, for its infectious relay merely provoked one of the girls, Mary, into shouting across to Rosaleen.

"Hey, Rosaleen, hurry up. That ceilidhe starts at nine o'clock."

Rosaleen turned in her chair and looked at the girl.

"Ssssh . . . If they hear you talking in English they'll send you home."

"Well, at least, then, I'd be doing something. What's taking you so long, anyway? You said you were only writing to your parents."

1

"I'll just be a few more minutes," Rosaleen said, attempting to put her friend's mind at ease, "I want to post this on the way." And taking the letter in her hand, and holding it closer to the lamp, she reread what she had just written.

Rannafast
Co. Donegal
6 July 1995

Dear Mammy and Daddy,

Donegal is just lovely. It is serene and tranquil, and a far cry from Belfast. The little cottage in which I am staying looks like it was planted here between the hills, as indeed all of them do, for they are as much a part of the countryside as the ploughed potato fields and the turf bogs, which, incidentally, as I am sitting here writing to you, the smell of the smoke from the turf fire is drifting in under the door, along with the music of *Roisin Dubh*, which the man of the house is playing on some kind of old stringed instrument that sounds almost like a mandolin, both of which fill me with such a sense of how I, and all of us have missed by not being more familiar with these parts of Ireland. In fact, this whole experience has shown me how much we've lost our Irishness as a whole. The man asked me just yesterday, if I had been named after 'Roisin Dubh', which means 'Dark Rosaleen', the secret name given to Ireland during one of the many times she was being persecuted.

The people who own the cottage are very good to us. Mr Green is a farmer, and Mrs Green helps out in the fields, along with taking care of the house and their five children (and now, with the three of us, the poor woman has twice the work to do, especially with Mary, as she eats like a horse). But these people are very rugged and really wonderful. I am so proud to be living under the same roof as those who have retained their Irish heritage. When I first arrived here, I felt as though I had come from another world and was intruding upon their civilization. But, when I came face to face with the

Greens and the rest of the villagers, I felt as though I had come face to face with a breed of people who strongly resembled my ancient ancestors, for they aroused my Irish tribal blood, which I shall carry in my veins back to Belfast.

Today, at the college, we only had classes in the morning due to the exams being held tomorrow. So, after lunch, I went to the village to buy some stamps and instead of returning to the cottage, I walked out along the cliffs that overlook the adjoining waters of the North Atlantic and the Irish Sea. It was wonderful being there all by myself. There was a wind blowing in from the sea and, as it came, it caught the waves and carried them halfway up the rock walls, and it lashed the spray and the smell of the ocean onto everything within reach, and I had to run for shelter behind some large rocks until it subsided. But all it did was make this place more wild and beautiful than ever, and standing there, looking all around me, I somehow got the feeling that this was the last place on earth because, looking beyond the cliffs and the sea, the only thing left were the clouds, and whatever lies beyond them.

I have to close now, as we are going to a ceilidhe, so give my love to Joseph and Peter, and baby Christine (please tell the boys to write, as I miss them very much). Also, give my love to Maureen and Dominic and tell them I miss them too, and tell grannie and granda I send my love, and also Aunt Hetty and Uncle Jackie, and wee John and Michael . . .

Mary's endurance to hold still while time passed was next to impossible and she whined coaxingly across to Rosaleen again.

"Oh, c'mon, Rosaleen. It's a mile or more to the college, and all the best looking boys will have chosen their partners for the entire evening, and I'm going to be stuck with big Gabriel McGrath again. Yuk! He's nothing but a big, long drink of water."

The third girl, Kay, laughed, and Rosaleen smiled as she continued with her letter. But this time it was Kay who interrupted.

"Are you all set for the big day tomorrow, Rosaleen? That's when they separate the women from the girls, heh, heh, heh."

"And from the men," Mary interjected. "Did you know that we are going to be tested separately, Rosaleen?"

Smiling, Rosaleen nodded while continuing to write.

. . . but, most of all, I miss you very, very much. But I want you to know that I am studying hard and the Irish is starting to roll off my tongue as though I had been born speaking it. As I mentioned before, tomorrow will be the true test to see if I qualify as a speaker of the native tongue, and, if I do pass, I won't tell you, you'll know soon enough when you see the silver *fainne* in my lapel.

During the writing of this last paragraph, Mary and Kay had been putting on their cardigans and were preparing to leave, and, in one last plea, Mary cried,

6

"Rosaleeeeen!" And Rosaleen, quickly bringing her letter to a close, signed off with,

> Goodbye, and God bless you both.
> Your loving daughter,
> Rosaleen

Quickly placing the letter in the already stamped-addressed envelope, she licked the flap and sealed it shut, and then, grabbing her own cardigan off the bed, she heard Mary again.

"Oh, c'mon, c'mon."

"Alright, alright, I'm coming." And Kay, putting a finger to her lips in caution as they opened the bedroom door, whispered,

"No English, remember."

Upon leaving, the girls passed through the big kitchen and called out to the family in Irish, and the man still playing, waved a hand in acknowledgement, and his music followed the girls long after they had left and were running across the hills, and one of the youngsters, who had jumped on to a seat by the window to look after them, watched their silhouettes, which were outlined against the not-quite-darkened sky.

Their laughter was heard as they found their way across the unfamiliar terrain, one behind the other, and, as they came closer to their destination, they heard the distant sound of Irish-dance music, which only tended to quicken their pace even more. The louder the music became, the harder they ran to meet it, until, bursting through the big, green wrought-iron gates that opened onto the courtyard of the college, they greeted the music with breathless laughter and entered the great, big hall.

Standing on the verge of the dance-floor to watch the dancers, Mary, who was carried away by it all, started clapping her hands and stomping her feet in time to the music, at which point, both Rosaleen and Kay stepped back without her knowing, and leaving her there by herself, they stood choking with laughter as Gabriel McGrath swept her onto the floor. But, before long, both girls were approached by none other than two fellows who they, themselves, had hoped to avoid, and, who continued to pursue them for the rest of the night.

The next day, Rosaleen stood in a classroom in the midst of about twenty other girls who were seated around her, and faced the examiner. Pacing back and forth at the opposite end of the room, the examiner pursed his lips in non-commital and listened while she told him a story in Irish. When she had finished, he merely nodded and said,

'Gura maith agat.' ('Thank you.') Seeing the apprehension so plainly visible on Rosaleen's face, and knowing the tension they'd all been under throughout the past several hours of oral examination, Mary tugged Rosaleen's dress in a vote of confidence as she sat down. And it wasn't until the evening of the next day did they know the result of their gruelling ordeal. Seeing the list of names posted on the college bulletin, Rosaleen, Mary, and Kay discovered that they had made the grade, and, in an open expression of pure accomplishment, they hugged each other, jumping up and down, at the sheer joy of winning.

It was not easy returning anywhere after having spent a month in the remote, west-part of Northern Ireland, especially not to the hustle and bustle of Belfast, with its big, red double-decker buses. But Rosaleen, who was looking forward to seeing her family, waved goodbye to her friends in the city's centre and eagerly hailed a taxi-cab that would take her directly to her door. But, as the taxi pulled into her street, she got the driver to let her off half a block from the house, and paying him, and shrugging off his offered assistance, she struggled up the remainder of the block with her big, trunk-like suitcase. Just before she entered the hallway of the small, Victorian row-house, she put her suitcase down for a moment, and looking at the silver emblem encircled in her lapel, she rubbed it with her cuff, and smiling, she picked up the suitcase and went inside.

2

THE new school year began. One rainy day, towards the end of September, during the lunch recess, when such a day cancelled all outside activities, and the various classes took turns offering either a scene from Shakespeare or a poem by Wordsworth, Tennyson, or Robert Burns, Mary, Kay, and Rosaleen, seated about a third of the way up the room, found themselves in a very precarious position; it was the fourth form's responsibility to present the entertainment that day, and not only had the trio not made any preparations, but Mary was in one of her devilish moods and Rosaleen and Kay were having a hard time keeping it under cover from the watchful eye of Sister Mary Josephia, the lunch director, as she patrolled the aisles.

Having just finished lunch, and as the entire school awaited in hushed expectancy for the opening performance, Rosaleen and Kay, who were still bearing the brunt of one of the several pranks that Mary had pulled during lunch, could hardly look at one another without the threat of falling into convulsions. While Mary, herself the picture of innocence, displayed a tendency known only too well by the other two, which told them that she was cooking up something that would outdo her latest episode.

Attending such a prestigious school, which, until recently, was strictly a private academy for the daughters of the rich and the very rich, the lack of which, now, due to the decline in student contribution, had forced the academic doors open to government subsidy, and ultimately to the growing multitudes from the working-class areas, afforded one the opportunity of meeting those, who while being of average means, were, nonetheless, endowed with snobbish minds; two of whom were now seated directly in front of the girls. It was these two who had been the recent victims of Mary's gad-about behaviour, and although Rosaleen was feeling a little remorse, it was of the ludicrous kind, for she couldn't deny that these two had it coming to them.

Although Rosaleen, Mary, and Kay were among the many who were scholarship students, there were several girls, Mary being one of them, who, if their brains had not met the stiff, scholastic standards of the school, as well as that of the Ministry of Education, their parents' economic positions would have done just as well. Except, judging Mary, who was madcap, foolhardy, loving, and brilliant, and who had given neither Rosaleen nor Kay a sane moment from the instant all three had met, it would never be known that she, the youngest of three, was the only daughter of a very wealthy Sligo merchant, and who, with approaching maturity, appeared to be getting worse, and that day, during lunch, was only one more indication of such.

Always bringing her lunch to school in a big, silver-metal box, much like the type a hard-working labourer might have carried, Mary never missed a day of devouring two large, thick sandwiches, the first of which would come unwrapped just around Latin period, when the mounting pressure and excitement brought about by the translations of the

13

Helvetian Wars would goad Mary into taking large chunks into her mouth, at which untimely points she would be called upon by sister to contribute her efforts. So it was that the wars of 58 B.C., fought between the Romans and the Helvetians, had been undistinguishably unfolded by Mary through mouthfuls of bread, tomatoes, and Swiss cheese.

Hence, so it was, on this particular day, when upon having suffered a setback during Latin, with the Helvetian States being linked to Rome, by means of the Romans building roads between the two territories, Mary, the great liberator, ate one and a half sandwiches by mistake, all of which resulted in a foul mood at lunch time and a lookout for something on which to vent her fury, which didn't take long to find. Spotting Helen and Martina sitting coyishly apart up the bench, and away from the bulk of the girls, Mary furtively uncorked the top of her big, silver thermos and immediately concocted her scheme.

Calling the girls by name, and receiving a wide smile in united acknowledgement, Mary offered them her thermos of coffee, telling them that her father had had it imported from South America, but that she'd had so much of it lately, she'd grown tired of the flavour. Filled with delight, the two girls showed great pleasure in accepting the coffee and who, under Mary's scrutiny, demolished the contents; the last cup becoming a small matter of deciding who had the most, and ending with Martina carefully dividing the remainder and Helen more carefully making sure that the amounts were equal.

"Mary!" Kay had asked curiously, but with a trace of suspicion. "What kind of coffee was that you gave those two?"

"South American," Mary had answered innocently, but with a trace of mischief, and Rosaleen, who knew better, had said with a slight reprimand:

"Mary, we know it's South American, sure, we've been drinking it 'til it's been coming out of our ears, and we know it's not *that* good." Then Kay, recognizing the gleam in Mary's eye, had asked hesitantly,

"Mary, what did you put in that coffee?" and she and Rosaleen exchanged glances, expecting the worst.

"Salt," was all Mary had said, and which was repeated by Rosaleen and Kay, as it passed between them in one word. Then, as if they needed to know the brand, Mary had said, "Saxa," and then, as though she were giving them the required ingredients for a special recipe, she threw in, "Two to three ounces," which had sent Rosaleen and Kay into hysterical laughter, and, in the midst of it all, Martina had come down the bench to return the thermos. Thanking Mary, she had told her that it was the exact same kind of coffee that her uncle had brought her mother from South America. In which instant, Mary had engaged her in great detail, inquiring into the percentages of the different blends, with Martina taking it all very seriously, and with Kay and Rosaleen like two *mental cases* between the benches.

But for all Mary's 'benevolence' towards the two girls, it was soon forgotten. With the rearrangement of the benches turned now towards the stage, Helen and Martina had pushed ahead of Mary, Rosaleen and Kay to take the last seats in the last row of the front section, which had been set up especially with nice, comfortable chairs, instead of benches, to accommodate several of the sisters who had come over from the convent for the programme. Now seated behind the pair, Rosaleen and Kay could almost hear the machinations of Mary's mind.

Meanwhile, Rosaleen had managed to quell her internal state with the receptive mood of the audience, and, now, as the curtain parted, she settled back, curious to see who and what was being offered from amongst her peers.

Starting with a run-down of the general programme, Rosaleen heard the announcer mention that the balcony-scene from 'Romeo and Juliet' was to be performed by Helen (Lafferty) and Martina (Duffy), and she heard Mary's snicker, and she heard Kay's agonized gasp, and she felt her own teeth sink into her bottom lip.

But there was one name on the programme which sparked Rosaleen's interest, and it was that of a quiet, little English girl who had come to the school

17

towards the end of their first year, and who, despite the uniform of the school-body, had still maintained her individual appearance and managed to stand out amongst the many. Her name was Bernadette Dove, and she had appeared in last year's Christmas production of 'The Scarlet Pimpernel', and, in which Rosaleen had admired her performance. She was slated now to recite William Wordsworth's 'The Solitary Reaper', and was, in fact, scheduled to open the programme.

Standing alone in the centre of the stage, her presence, alone, commanding the respect of the audience, and when she began to speak, her voice had the strength to capture even the least attentive, and Rosaleen noticed that Mary, for all her scheming, had set it aside for the moment and had focused all her attention on the stage.

Upon hearing the familiar lines, which Rosaleen herself had had to memorize at one time, she realized that never had they held such meaning as right then, and listening to the manner in which they were being pronounced, she felt the gentle ringing of a response within her and she knew that this girl was destined for a life in the theatre.

'Behold her, single in the field,
Yon solitary Highland Lass!
Reaping and singing by herself,
Stop her, or gently pass!
No nightingale did ever chaunt
more welcome notes to weary bands
of travellers in some shady haunt,
Among Arabian sands . . . breaking
the silence of the seas
among the farthest Hebrides.
Will no one tell me what she sings?
Perhaps the plaintive numbers flow
for old, unhappy far-off things,
And battles long ago?
Or is it some more humble lay,
Familiar matter of today?
Some natural sorrow, loss, or pain
That has been, and may be again
Whate'er the theme, the maiden sang
As if her song could have no ending . . .
. . . I listened, motionless and still;
And, as I mounted up the hill,
The music in my heart I bore,
Long after it was heard no more.'

During the outburst of applause which followed, Mary brought Rosaleen and Kay's attention to the fact that the two girls in front had alternately been making short trips in and out of the row; one leaving, and, then, returning with water for the other. Then, Mary, finding the following acts, readings from Chaucer's *Canterbury Tales,* in *olde* English, yet, to be too dull for entertainment, brought the girl's further attention to the fact that the two chairs in front were being vacated more and more frequently, with both girls leaving and returning at various intervals, with their trips becoming longer and their timing at odds with each other; with one going out, and blocking the way for the other coming in, which highly amused Mary and left her to query whether it was all due to the quantity of water they'd been taking or if it was in anticipation for their big scene, and she retreated into snickering. Until, finally, they were gone so long that Mary suggested that maybe they had drifted afloat, upon, at which remark, they both returned dressed in what what was supposedly the style of sixteenth-century England; with Helen's 'period costume' consisting of two braided, nylon stockings pinned under her school beret, which was turned backwards, with the badge of *veritas* staring Mary straight in the face; and Martina wearing a cardboard vest made from the two ends of a *Sunlight*-soap box and sewn together with black yarn, with the letters U-LIT-SOP printed across her back, which prompted Mary to tap her on the shoulder and proclaim the message to be most profound, for which Martina graciously thanked her, all of which threw Rosaleen and Kay into fits of hysteria and into a state of near helplessness, and one which no water nor stage-fright was needed to induce.

And, now, the girls were in fine shape for the 'Romeo and Juliet' scene; with Kay and Rosaleen dreading it and Mary looking forward to it with great relish.

But first, there was another sobering prelude through which Rosaleen sat, and watched, and listened and felt herself gain a sense of composure. The performer was the class's prefect, Yvonne McGuire, who was going to recite Tennyson's very intense 'The Charge of the Light Brigade', and, as Rosaleen and Kay both raised their brows in anticipation, Mary sat forward on the edge of her seat, for it was her all time favourite poem.

"Half a league, half a league,
Half a league onward
All in the Valley of Death
Rode the six-hundred
'Forward the Light Brigade!
Charge for the guns!' he said
Into the Valley of Death
Rode the six-hundred . . . "

Rosaleen and Kay suddenly sensed Mary's anticipation, as she recited the lines right along with the prefect, and they smiled at her enthusiasm.

"Someone had blundered
Theirs not to make reply
Theirs not to reason why
Theirs but to do or die
Into the Valley of Death
Rode the six-hundred
Cannons to the right of them
Cannons to the left of them

22

Cannons in front of them
Volley'd and thundered
Stormed at with shot and shell . . ."

Rosaleen nudged Kay with her elbow and brought her attention to Mary, whose enthusiasm had grown into a fever and who, in keeping time to the words by slapping the knuckles of one hand against the palm of the other, was almost into the next row between Helen and Sister Mary Unity.

" . . . Into the mouth of hell
Rode the six-hundred . . ."

At this point, Sister Mary Unity turned in her chair and told Mary that if she wanted to recite, the proper place was on stage, and that that's where she should be. Mary, throwing sister a sullen look, sat back on the bench and folded her arms resolutely across her chest. But it wasn't for long, for as the prefect proceeded without her, Mary, completely unnoticed by Rosaleen and Kay, unobtrusively took one of 'Juliet's' nylon braids and tied it to the girdle around

'Romeo's' school tunic. Then, she took the other braid and affixed it to Sister Mary Unity's chair, and, then, quietly sat back and waited for the prefect to finish.

"... They that had fought so well
Came through the jaws of Death
Back from the mouth of hell
All that was left of them
Left of six-hundred ..."

The applause was very warm as the prefect took her leave of the stage, and Mary looked at Helen and Martina as they exchanged glances; both girls and Mary having the same thought, but with different intentions: one more act and then ...

The next girl up was Ann Muckian. She was not from the girls' class, but from 4B, and, who just happened to have been absent on the day her class performed, and she was dying to get on stage. Now standing in front of the entire school, the dark, red curtains closed behind her, the large assembly was silent, waiting for her to begin.

All eyes were glued to the solitary

figure on stage, as she stood tall, with head held high, and hands clasped in front, the right inside the left, as was the rule, and the lunch director, catching the girl's eye, nodded slightly as a cue to begin, and she did: but, instead of the regular, scholarly material, which had been the school's fare for years, and years upon years, the girl, breaking her pose, spread her feet and, with arms flagellating above her head, belted out American pop-singer, Kay Starr's, 'She Wears Red Feathers and a Huly, Huly Skirt.'

The girls, of course, all broke into laughter, but, the lunch director turned and stared. When her fiery temper, which followed in the wake of the outburst of song, boiled over, the girl had already made no less than half a dozen wide-legged stances across the stage, inter-mingled with her halting every so often to bring her knees together several times on the words, 'huly, huly skirt'. The lunch director clapped her hands to stop the performance, but she did it in such a way that it was in the exact, same tempo as the song, and with her back to the audience, the girls thought that she was clapping in time for her own enjoyment and they joined in. And the girl, delighted to have such a vast accompaniment, acknowledged it by bowing and continued with more of the same. Abhorred, the visiting sisters got up to leave and, as they made their exit, the entire assembly was on its feet, howling uncontrollably. The lunch director was on the stage in a flash and after having grabbed the first thing on hand, which happened to be a pole with a hook on the end for opening and closing windows, she grabbed at the girl with it who, completely taken aback by the seeming change in attitude, danced about the stage to avoid the threatening end of the pole. The whole scene became reminiscent of the dud acts of the old English Hall genre, and rocked the audience into more laughter.

Within minutes, Mother Superior had been sent for and the girl was removed, until whatever steps would be taken to chastise her for her actions.

Mother Superior, addressing the school from the stage, was enraged.

" . . . And furthermore, there will not even be a hint of vulgarity, such as has been demonstrated here today. If there is such a recurrence, those of you who are involved will leave me no option than to call in the Ministry of Education and have it rescind your scholarships . . . "

All at once, as though singularly directed to look in the same direction, Rosaleen and Kay were horrified to discover 'Romeo' and 'Juliet' to be completely 'wrapped up in each other', and, without further ado, set immediately to undo the imminent catastrophy, and without either of the actresses becoming aware of what was going on behind their backs.

" . . . There will be absolutely no tolerence shown towards these trashy, modern lyrics, which pass for music . . . " Rosaleen was having trouble disentangling Helen's nylon braid from the back of the chair and her fingers fumbled with the stubborn knot, as she heard Mother drawing in her breath and releasing it with the words: "You are dismissed. Please leave quietly, two by two."

Rosaleen still hadn't succeeded, not even with Kay helping by holding the chair steady, and she panicked, as the entire roomful of girls rose to their feet, as Mother Superior stepped down from the stage and made her way down the centre aisle. But, she hadn't counted on the one facet of the entire episode which turned out to be mercifully advantageous to the predicament at hand, and that was, that 'Romeo' and 'Juliet' had been unwittingly, but undeniably cancelled, which, thus, explained the present inertia of the would-be-thespians. Then, while Rosaleen was still diligently trying to untangle the chair from Helen's 'hair', she overheard her attempting to console Martina, who let loose with an expletive, which should have made the fair 'Juliet' blush, but didn't; but it made everything that Mary had done to date seem almost charitable.

Between classes, that same afternoon, the trio was approached by another two girls, Rubino and McMurray (known as Maxie). These two were known as 'women of the world', by their class-mates; having attended modern dances and for having been caught twice with traces of make-up on their lips and eyes.

"Muckian had her nerve, didn't she?"

Rubino said, "You'd think butter wouldn't melt in her mouth. I wouldn't be surprised if she got expelled for this one." Then parking herself on top of a desk, she wet the ends of her hair between her fingers and arranged them in little spitcurls across her forehead.

"In that case, you should have been expelled a long time ago." Maxie threw at her friend, and to the others, she added, slyly, "You should have seen her at the Kingsway on Sunday night, she was jiving the whole night with a big geek from Manchester; she even let him take her home."

"The Kingsway?" Kay asked. "I thought you had to be eighteen to get in there?"

"You do, my dear, you do," Rubino cracked, sticking out her chest. "When you have it, you have it." Then, turning to Rosaleen, she chided, "Don't tell me that you're still going to those namby, pamby dances, with the fiddle and bow, and with those big bokes from St Gerard's, yuk!" and she threw a distasteful look, which included all three girls.

"Oh, they're not all that bad."

Rosaleen smiled amusingly.

"Hey, I've made the rounds," Rubino was quick to throw in, "and let me tell you, I'd sooner have a man's arms around me," she said, adding a sultry tone to her voice, "than dance like some fruitcake," and jumping off the desk, she held out a pinkie to Maxie who, grabbing it with her own, two-stepped down the aisle. This exaggeration caused the girls to snicker, until someone yelled that Miss Parfait was on her way down the corridor, a warning that sent every last girl rushing to her seat.

Coming home on the bus, later that same day, Rosaleen, who was sitting on the top deck with Mary and Kay, was surprised to find herself witness to a very enchanting scene. The bus was stopped in traffic, and not more than ten feet away, from where she was sitting, was a young man and woman performing ballroom steps. Nudging Mary and Kay to take a look, Mary opened a window and the strains of the dance-music reached them. Awed by the graciousness of their movements, Rosaleen was unable to take her eyes off them, and even as the bus pulled away, she continued to watch, and a thoughtful look crossed her face and she looked down at the brass plate by the door of the building and she read:

MARTIN SPECKY
BALLROOM DANCE INSTRUCTOR
Classes Mon. Wed. Fri. & Sat. Eves.
8pm. — 10:30pm.

and her expression turned to one of pensive amusement as she left the dancers behind.

Over the next few days, Rosaleen, who had been unable to completely shake the dance scene from her head, had a compulsive curiosity to see more. Yet knowing that neither Mary nor Kay would be caught dead in an English-style dance-studio, Rosaleen asked two of her neighbourhood chums, Ann and Phyllis if they would go to Specky's the following Friday night.

Friday night came and Rosaleen, with her friends, entered the tiny ballroom; her first attendance at any kind of dance other than the ceilidhes; the latter, which were always well-lit and boisterous, she felt the difference more so than seeing it and hearing it. She was mesmerized by the coloured-lit ballroom, which seemed to float on its airlight atmosphere. But, most of all, she was completely enchanted by the instructors, as the crowd, eager to learn, gathered around the edge of the dance-floor to await their first lesson.

The same man, who Rosaleen had seen from the bus window, walked gentlemanly into the centre of the floor with the same, young lady in tow, except now, he was handsomely dressed in black tie and tuxedo, and black, patent-leather shoes; and she was wearing a calf-length ball gown, covered with tiny sequins, that shimmered when she moved under the tiny, coloured lights, as did her silver, high-heeled slippers.

The dance-team went through a couple of beautiful steps together a few times, and Rosaleen couldn't help but admire the grace and ease with which they moved. The instructor then began to repeat the steps to music and, as he flicked the switch of the record-player, the little ballroom was filled with the music of England's most popular dance band, Victor Sylvester.

As the couple glided across the floor, almost as though they were being carried by some unseen force, Rosaleen, watching them, was fascinated, and even as she felt Ann's hand on her arm, she could hardly tear her eyes away from the floor.

"Don't you know who that is?" Ann asked, but then answering her own question, she went on. "I knew she looked familiar, and now, with the gown and the dance music, and all . . . that's Betty McCarron."

"Who?" Rosaleen asked, her gaze never leaving the dance-floor.

"You know the McCarrons who live at the back of us." Ann offered to enlighten her. "Well, that's Betty. You know, she's on television, and everything." And snapping her fingers, she added, "I knew it! As soon as I heard Victor Sylvester . . . and the way she moves, and all, I knew it was her. You know, she's won three gold cups for dancing." Then grabbing Phyllis's arm, she said, "You know that television show, 'Come Dancing': Well, she's been on that." Rosaleen looked pensive.

"Wait a minute. That can't be the same Betty McCarron I know. Sure, she works in a shirt factory, and just the other day I saw her going to work with her hair in clips and a scarf on her head . . . No, that can't be the same girl."

"Yes, it is. That's the same one. But she's sure not making shirts now, is she? Just look at her."

But Rosaleen was unable to accept the fact that this was the same girl she knew, and Ann, watching her expression, nudged her with her elbow.

"She sure has something going for her on the side, doesn't she? So much for dreams coming true! Our Patricia said, that she was always dancing out in the street when they were kids."

Just then the music came to a stop and the instructor and his partner took a bow, and then, in the midst of the applause, he invited the men to take partners and to come onto the dance-floor.

A man who was practically the same size as Rosaleen, herself, asked her to dance, and Ann and Phyllis snickered as he led her onto the floor. Rosaleen began very awkwardly and was very unsure of herself, but, after several more dances with various partners, and, then, one, who seemed born to the steps, she started to loosen up a little.

Now as she moved around the floor, she could afford to pay attention to the other dancers and to the decor of the ballroom itself. But more than the primrose-coloured walls, which were covered with dancing awards, or the accompanying gallery of black and white pictures, portraying such presentations, caught Rosaleen's eye, for she was more taken with the placards posted at intervals, which read: 'NO JIVING', 'NO MOODY DANCING' and 'GENTLEMEN MUST WEAR TIES'.

Much taken with this little ballroom studio, Rosaleen looked forward to going again and again, until, within a matter of a few weeks, she had learned all of the beginning steps given by the instructor, which, in turn, brought many partners.

But there was one in particular who kept seeking her out — the one who had seemed born to the steps — and, who, because of the tweed jackets and suits he wore, which when revealed he bought at discount from the shop where he worked in 'haberdashery', made him a real character in the girls' eyes, ultimately became known as 'Tweedy'.

One night, after leading Rosaleen around the floor in a waltz, Tweedy enquired as to where she had been the previous evening.

"Here it was, Friday, and I was so looking forward to an entire evening of quicksteps and foxtrots, and you didn't show up." Rosaleen gave him a funny look at the idea that he should suggest that he had a claim on her as *his* dance-partner, but she told him.

"Oh, yesterday was my birthday and my family gave me a party; just a small one, though."

"Oh!" Tweedy exclaimed, raising an eyebrow, "And what age were you yesterday?"

"Fifteen," Rosaleen replied, looking at him, and half-expecting him to make some remark, she heard him say.

"And what age are you today?"

"Fif . . . " she began and then realized she'd fallen for what she'd come to feel was his queer sense of humour, and at

36

which Tweedy gave a hearty laugh, visibly taken with himself, and, in the midst of it all, he managed to hold Rosaleen a little more firmer about the waist; a move she couldn't help but notice.

"I say, Rosaleen," Tweedy said, in a way that suggested he'd suddenly struck a brilliant idea, "how about if you and I celebrate your birthday by me walking you home and stopping on the way for two ice-cream cones."

"Oh, I can't, Twee . . . Grahame, my chums, what about them?" Rosaleen, taken by surprise at his proposal, offered the best excuse she could think of in a moment. But not to be put off, Tweedy said, though somewhat begrudgingly,

"Oh, they can come too." But, when Rosaleen put the offer to Ann and Phyllis, Ann's response was a loud giggle.

"Oh, I couldn't, Rosie. I couldn't eat an ice-cream in front of him; not after all the joking we've done about him. I think I'd choke on the ice-cream." At this she and Phyllis broke into more giggling. "No harm to you, love," Ann told her, "but you and Tweedy go on ahead, Phyllis and me'll just mosey on ourselves. Cheerio, love."

Hearing them still laughing, Rosaleen shook her head at her own dilemma, and taking a deep breath, went to face Tweedy, who had already got his coat from the cloakroom and was waiting for Rosaleen by the door.

Standing with Tweedy on the corner of a street several blocks from her own, lest Ann and Phyllis should see them, Rosaleen, who had long since finished her ice-cream cone, watched Tweedy with amusement making the most of his. He had bitten a hole at the pointed end, and holding the cone above his head, took all the ice-cream through the tiny opening, making loud, sucking noises as he did so. Then, shoving the deflated remains in his mouth, he pulled out a large, folded handkerchief, but not the one from his breast-pocket, which was a perennial part of his attire, but from his trouser pocket, and, while wiping his mouth, he patted himself on the chest, telling Rosaleen,

"See, I have one for blowing and one for showing." And, then, laughing at his own profundity, he shoved the handkerchief back into his trouser pocket, and moving against Rosaleen, he gave her, what could hardly be called, her first kiss, throughout which she felt the very uncomfortable bulk of his handkerchief against her thigh.

3

CHRISTMAS and New Year's Day passed and 1956 saw Rosaleen back at school after the holidays, but less involved now with Mary and Kay, who, up until now, had shared her academic interests, than she was with Ann and Phyllis, who had not had her educational and cultural background, for while she was still involved with her studies, they had both been working for several years in a local factory, with Ann's wages going mostly towards clothing and popular records. In fact, Rosaleen had gone to several parties over the holidays with Ann and Phyllis, where nothing but popular music was played: and so it was, upon returning to school, she felt something other than an interest in her studies take hold of her. Subsequently, she spent a good deal of her evenings, and Sunday afternoons, at Ann's, where she found listening to records more interesting than doing homework, and it wasn't long before such singing stars as Eddie Fisher, Rosemary Clooney, Nat King Cole, and Billy Eckstine became as much a part of her sabbath as Mass and Communion.

About the middle of January, the newspapers released the headlines chronicling the Belfast engagement of the one and only, Nat King Cole. The city was in a frenzy, and the downtown Hippodrome became a forum mobbed by hundreds of eager fans anticipating the personal appearance of a star of such magnitude.

Rosaleen, Phyllis and Ann were no exceptions, and they looked forward to seeing Nat King Cole in the flesh.

From early in the morning of the Saturday on which the star was appearing for one night only, the area around the theatre was like bedlam. Most of the kids had been congregating since six am., including Ann and Phyllis. But Rosaleen had morning classes each Saturday, and she had to come home, eat lunch, just to appease her mother, and change from her uniform to street clothes, and then, leave the house before her mother could ask any questions, and run all the way downtown.

Running without a breather, she arrived at the theatre, and for a frenzied fifteen minutes, fought the crowds to get through to her friends, much to the annoyance of many who'd been waiting for hours themselves. It was many more hours before the doors finally opened and as the crowds surged forward, rope-barriers, which had been set up, restrained them and they were admitted a few at a time through the open half of the big, double doors. With much anticipation, Ann and Rosaleen and Phyllis, who were next in line, moved forward, but, as Ann passed through and Rosaleen about to follow, a big, surly attendant, in uniform, pushed her back and addressed her in a gruff tone.

"Okay there, hold it just a minute. Nobody under eighteen allowed." Rosaleen, completely taken by surprise, looked at the man, dumbfounded, as he continued to let those behind her in line through the barricade. She looked at the other attendant, but he merely gave her a futile shrug of his shoulders.

"Okay, out," the first attendant commanded. "C'mon, you . . . you're blockin' the line here." Rosaleen and Phyllis looked at each other in the hopes that one of them would come up with an answer, and, unable to find one, they both looked at Ann. But she'd already been admitted and was now being carried away by the onrush of excited fans, and her disappearing, waving hand was the last they saw of her, as she was swallowed up by the crowd.

Rosaleen turned, pleading to the attendant for both herself and Phyllis.

"Mister, we are eighteen. We've been waiting here all day. You can't turn us away now." But the attendant was adamant and, without even looking at her, he said,

"Sorry. Rules is rules. Nobody under eighteen permitted, and that's that." At this, the other attendant turned, and throwing a compassionate look in Rosaleen's direction, cried,

"Oh, for God's sake, let the childer in." The chief attendant turned on his subordinate in anger.

"What? And lose my bloody job?" Then, turning on Rosaleen and Phyllis, with venom in his voice, he yelled at

43

them. "Git away with ye, ye wee scitters, yees. Yees should be home scrubbin' the floors. Aye, that's where yees all should be, alright." Then, blocking Rosaleen off completely with his outstretched arms, he pushed her back into the crowd with his chest, forcing her to give up her coveted place at the barricade.

Left with no alternative but to leave, Rosaleen choked back the tears of frustration and disappointment, and she bit back those which had arisen from the sheer embarrassment of the entire episode, not wanting anybody to see them, especially not Phyllis, who didn't seem to be half as affected as she was over the whole experience.

The next day being Sunday, Rosaleen went over to Ann's, after coming from Mass, and listened to her litany of praises, as she reported every little detail of the previous night's concert, all of which brought back much of the disappointment that Rosaleen had felt before.

Between classes the following Monday, as Rosaleen was walking down the corridor with Mary and Kay, and with the conversation passing between the latter two, and not holding Rosaleen's interest at all, they were approached by their Irish language sister.

"Girls! I would like a word with you before you go to your next class." The girls, stopping, surrounded the little sister as she brought them the news that Mary and Kay had been waiting for. "As you know, it is that time of the year again when we start preparation for the disbursement of scholarships for Donegal. I assume you are all eagerly anticipating what your chances will be?" Beaming, Mary and Kay answered in one voice, as Rosaleen smiled weakly,

"Oh, yes, sister."

"Good!" sister beamed back, looking from one to the other. "Now, let me inform you that you three girls have been accepted whole-heartedly again this year," and then, seeing both Mary and Kay's excited faces, she turned to Rosaleen, and her own face grew grim. "Why, Rosaleen, you don't look too happy about the news. Aren't you looking forward to going this year?" Rosaleen looked uncomfortably at the ground.

"No, sister, I don't think I'll be going

to the Gaeltacht this year," and fumbling for an excuse, though hating to lie, she told sister, "You see, my family is going to England this year, and I'm expected to go with them."

"England!" Sister's eyebrows disappeared into her wimple. "Why, of all places, would your family want to go to England? Sure, there's nothing there. Look at all the beautiful places to visit right here on your own native soil. Tell me, Rosaleen, what on earth is taking your family to England?" Rosaleen, looking at sister and unable to come up with a suitable answer, muttered,

"Excuse me, sister," and leaving the little group looking after her in bewilderment, she ran off down the corridor and into the bathroom.

Later, that same day, she was sitting on the embankment of the school's tennis court, watching a double-set in progress.

It wasn't the season for tennis, but this was no tennis game; rather, the four girls, seniors, were in hard training for the summer tournament. Preparing themselves in advance, and with complete indifference to the wintry, inclement weather, the intensity with which the girls approached the net and their total abandonment to everything but getting the ball to the opposite end of the court, had caused Rosaleen to abandon her solitary walk through the grounds. There was something compelling in the determination with which the girls moved about the court. Rosaleen felt a certain empathy rise within her, yet, not having any real interest in the sport itself, it was not directly with the players; it had more to do with the unification of the individual wills, which, becoming the real strength on the court, was the essence that had made Rosaleen stop and watch.

It was here, then, in this part of the school grounds, that Mary and Kay, having looked every place else, finally found her.

"Rosaleen! Where were you at lunch time?" Mary asked, her voice filled with surprise at finding Rosaleen so far removed from the normal activities of this hour. "Everyone was asking where you were." Throwing them a look over her shoulder, Rosaleen's attention returned to the court. "Well! Where were you?" Mary persisted. Taking time to

47

answer, Rosaleen replied,

"Oh, no place. I wasn't hungry, so I just went for a walk," and shrugging her shoulders, she gave a slight nod in the direction of the players, their activity alone suffice for her excuse. An awkward silence fell between the once-friendly trio, and Kay, in an attempt to break it, asked Rosaleen,

"Have you changed your mind about Donegal?" Rosaleen looked at her with a look of disbelief on her face.

"When have you ever known me to change my mind? I said I wasn't going, didn't I? Well, I'm not going, and that's that." And getting up, she ran off, leaving the two girls with an embarrassed silence between them.

Arriving home from school that same day, and going upstairs to change out of her school-uniform, Rosaleen, without taking off her coat, stood looking at herself in the mirror for a long time. Then, her eyes fell on the reflection of the little, silver *fainne*, the emblem of Irish speakers, and carefully removing it from her lapel, she placed it in a box at the back of the bottom drawer of her dresser.

4

ROSALEEN, Phyllis and Ann entered the powder room at Martin Specky's and as they each started to prepare themselves; Rosaleen applying the make-up, which she was forbidden to wear, Phyllis combing her eyebrows into two fine arches and Ann lighting her usual cigarette, a girl with whom they'd become acquainted burst through the door and greeted the girls with obvious excitement.

"Hey, have you heard the news?"

"What news?" all three asked in unison, turning from their various tasks to look at the newcomer.

"Billy Eckstine is coming to the Hippodrome next month." Watching and waiting for their reactions, she went on, "February twenty-fifth, I think it is," and, as Rosaleen, Ann and Phyllis crowded her for more news on the subject, they heard another girl turn to another, a rather sophisticated type, and ask,

49

"Who is Billy Eckstine?" Which brought a bored shrug of the shoulders along with the complacent response,

"Who knows," which caused Ann and Rosaleen to glare into the mirror at both of them.

Instead of going home from school, the day of the concert, Rosaleen went straight to Ann's house, where the latter had an array of everything waiting for her. There was an outfit belonging to one of her older sisters, which, when Rosaleen put it on, made her appear older, and even more so after Ann applied heavy make-up to her eyes, cheeks and lips. Then, pulling her hair into a ponytail, and taking her sister's 'jigger' coat from the wardrobe, she made Rosaleen put it on, and then she turned her towards the full-length mirror to see the result.

It was in the midst of all this excitement that Rosaleen suddenly became aware that Phyllis was not there, and she asked Ann where she was.

"She's not coming." Ann told her. "Not after what happened the last time; she said it wasn't worth it."

Hurrying downtown, Rosaleen and

Ann pushed their way into the crowd for the long wait until the doors opened. Exactly at half-past six, the two attendants appeared at the entrance, opening only one of the double doors, and letting the fans in a couple at a time. As it neared their turn, Rosaleen took a lighted cigarette, and holding it between her lips, shoved her way past the uniformed attendant, and entered the theatre.

Hours later, still glowing from the magic of the live performance, Rosaleen waited in line to receive a warm handshake and a magnificent wink from the sparkling star himself.

In the days that followed, Rosaleen's pre-occupation with Billy Eckstine was only a foreshadow of what was yet to come: exactly a week after the concert, a neighbour of Rosaleen's, who was an avowed Frank Sinatra fan, asked her to pick up some records at a friend's house, as he had to meet his girlfriend downtown; she was then to bring them to an address where the party was being held.

Later, as Rosaleen lifted the brass knocker and the door was opened to her, she got an earful of music, and, as she handed the records over to a somewhat dusky, frizzy-haired redhead, she saw several couples doing a kind of dance she'd never seen before, and very expertly they did it too.

Standing there mesmerized, Rosaleen heard the girl say,

"Will that be all, love?" and as the front door closed behind her, the music followed her down the garden passage, and, hidden from the street by the tall, privacy hedges on both sides, she was overcome by it and by the desire to imitate what she had just witnessed.

The following Friday night, Rosaleen, Ann and Phyllis entered Specky's and were confronted immediately by the addition of new placard signs, which had been posted along with the old ones, and warned, 'NO JIVING'

'ABSOLUTELY NO JIVING' and, further along, 'JIVING STRICTLY PROHIBITED'. Almost immediately, Tweedy pounced on Rosaleen and, in a fit of excited anticipation, pulled her onto the floor.

"Where have you been?" he demanded, "You should have been here.

They announced the Junior Championships that are to take place in April, and," he added, through clenched teeth, "on the Isle of Man." Rosaleen looked at him with a puzzled look on her face.

"What does that have to do with me?"

"What does that have to do with you?" Tweedy mimicked, and then looked around furtively to make sure no-one was within earshot. "It has everything to do with you," he confided, looking around again, and, then, he told her secretively, "You are going to be my partner," and he withdrew a folded paper from his inside pocket. "See here, I already have the entrance form for the tryouts. All you have to do is sign your name." Getting only a glimpse of the paper before he shoved it back into his pocket, Rosaleen, looking dumbfounded, stared at him.

"Me? Are you kidding?" But Tweedy, ignoring her question, continued.

"Just think, going to the Isle of Man," and, again, through clenched teeth, "And it's going to be televised." Then, throwing his head back, he cried, "Just think of it, Rosaleen. I can get my firm of

Bradbury Limited to give me an evening suit from their formal collection; think of the publicity!" and, then, giving her a determined look, he told her, "And you, my dear, could buy the most splendid gown, completely covered with . . . " But Rosaleen didn't let him finish.

"Just a minute, Grahame. You're sort of putting the cart before the horse. You want me to be your partner in the Junior Ballroom Championships? You must be kidding. I'm only a beginner."

"Nonsense!" Tweedy said, putting her off. "With practice, we can make it."

"But it's only a few weeks away," Rosaleen reminded him.

"So, Rome wasn't built in a day," he told her, and Rosaleen, frowning at his odd choice of cliché, heard, as he went on, "You can meet me here early four nights a week, from now until then: we will dance rings around them!"

For the next several weeks, Rosaleen met Tweedy on the four prearranged evenings, getting there an hour or so before the normal time. Tweedy was determined to be footwork perfect; but for Rosaleen, the practice was gruelling, and each night, by the time the doors opened at eight o'clock, she was exhausted. Finally, one night, in the middle of a very strenuous quickstep, she came to a complete halt. Arms dead at her sides, and unable to hold her head upright for another second, she told Tweedy.

"Grahame, stop. I can't go on. I can't dance anymore."

"Of course you can," he told her. "Here. I'll support you. Just hold on to my shoulder with a good, tight grasp."

"No!" Rosaleen said, completely breathless. "No. Grahame, no more," and she pulled away from him and headed for one of the chairs that lined the wall, and limped down into it. Tweedy followed her, still dancing, and he held his arms as though Rosaleen was still in them.

"Alright, then, five minutes, if that's the way you want it. But look at my feet. Keep watching now and picture in your mind that you are following me. Are you watching?"

"Yes, Tweedy . . ."

As Tweedy continued around the floor,

alone, strictly intent on time control, the door to the ballroom swung open and the first patrons of the evening burst into the room, and, standing agog, they stared at the sight that they saw on the dance-floor. At first, Tweedy was unaware of his audience, and continued on. But, upon hearing the murmur of voices and a laugh or two, he displayed annoyance.

"Blast!" he muttered under his breath, as he unwillingly left the floor.

Rosaleen, somewhat less enthused than Tweedy, and tired of the whole gruelling hours of practice, looked for some respite from it all by inviting Ann and Phyllis along the following evening. Upon their arrival, the girls saw that Tweedy was in top form, and he was anxiously awaiting Rosaleen's appearance. As soon as she entered, he dragged her over to a corner to where a black evening suit, covered with a canvas garment-bag, was hanging on the same nail as the sign, 'JIVING STRICTLY PROHIBITED'.

"See," he told Rosaleen, "I got Bradbury's to donate the suit by promising them that I'd drop their name after I receive the prize; the shoes, now, they're another story: I think I'll ask Martin Specky to loan me a pair. After all, just think what it will do for business here." He hung the suit back on its nail, over the sign, and over his shoulder he threw a request to the two onlookers. "Would one of you people be so kind as to start the record." Then, without further ado, he held out his arms in invitation to Rosaleen. But, unbeknownst to either Phyllis or Rosaleen, Ann had brought along a popular recording of Rosemary Clooney's, 'Come On-A My House', and, as Tweedy was already in place to commence the quickstep; feet in starting position, hands exactly where they were supposed to be, arms correctly extended, head perfectly poised, and with an air of anticipatory expectancy on his face, the words and music of the pop record blared out of the speakers and filled the tiny ballroom.

Tweedy was shocked into stupified suspension. Without moving a muscle throughout his entire frame, he became polarized into frozen disbelief by what he was hearing. Only his face took on a change, and it became that of an old man who had just been executed, without first having faced the firing-squad. After the realization dawned on him, he spun around in a delayed reaction, still in the same position, and faced his 'executioners'.

"What in blazes . . . "

But, Ann, wasting no time on him, shouted across to Rosaleen.

"C'mon, Rosie, let's show them how the real stuff is done." Phyllis exploded with laughter, and Rosaleen, infected by the unexpected humour of it all, couldn't resist. Imitating what Ann was doing, the two of them danced towards each other, Tweedy pulled his handkerchief from his breast-pocket and wiped his eyes in disbelief. Just then, the door from the adjoining office burst open, and in charged Martin Specky himself, followed by his dance-partner.

"Just what the devil do you think you're doing?" His tone brought the girls to an immediate halt, and his partner rushed to shut off the record. Specky advanced towards the wall to where the sign that said, 'NO JIVING' was hanging.

"Do you see this?" he pointed, and,

without waiting for an answer, he advanced on the second one that said, 'ABSOLUTELY NO JIVING', and pointed to this, and, finally, to the one that demonstrated,

'JIVING STRICTLY PROHIBITED'

He grabbed Tweedy's garment-bag, containing his evening suit, and threw it to the floor.

"And do you see this!" he demanded, flinging out his whole arm to the wall. Meanwhile, Tweedy, retrieving his garment-bag, hugged it to his body, determined to free himself from all blame.

"Mister Specky, I assure you, I had no idea . . . This is their crazy idea of a joke, I had no idea . . . "

"Oh, shut up!" Specky shouted, looking threateningly at Rosaleen and pointing an accusing finger in her direction, as he approached her.

"In my fifteen years as a ballroom instructor, and the time I have spent nurturing some culture into you little good-for-nothings, I have never, NEVER," he stressed, "witnessed such hooliganism. You can be assured, miss, that you are subsequently barred and disqualified from any and all contests which my good name sponsors. Why if the Amalgamated Association of Ballroom Dancers got wind of this sort of conduct, it would blacken my good name forever . . . I would probably lose my licence to dance," he spluttered. Then, somewhat regaining whatever composure he had left, he continued to address Rosaleen. "I suggest you leave my premises immediately, miss," and, as she started to move across the room, he added, "And take your trash with you."

"Hey, watch it, fairy feet." Ann threw at him, getting ready to move in.

"I was talking about the record, miss," Specky retorted, backing up, and, then, snapping his fingers, his partner handed Ann the record as though it had the mange.

During all this, Tweedy, completely recuperated from his experience, had already replaced his garment-bag back on the nail, and, as the girls exited, the last thing Rosaleen heard was Tweedy hurrying after Martin Specky into his office, with the request,

"I say, Marty, I'd like to talk to you about a pair of shoes for the Championship . . . " and she smiled, as she closed the door on that part of her life.

5

DURING the week preceding Easter Sunday, although the school had been preparing for the feast days with daily, hymnal processions across the grounds, ending in outdoor benediction, despite the constant drizzle, there was a hub of excitement on Holy Thursday, the last day before spring recess.

While walking through the tree-lined avenue to the bus, Rosaleen, Mary and Kay found their topic of conversation wind its way to the period after Easter, which was the time for academic scrambling, culminating in the Junior Certificate Examination, for which the three girls were candidates. Mary was telling the others how she was going to get the most out of the coming week so as to get her nose to the grindstone when classes resumed. Kay felt the same way, because both girls realized that this was to be their last year for any laxity that might have crept into their studies: They knew that it would be a hard grind to achieve the certificate, especially since it determined two pre-college years, when they returned to school in the autumn — both girls were considering either the training college afterwards, or the university. Rosaleen, who at one time had shared their ambition, was her unusually quiet self, just as she had been lately.

"What about you, Rosaleen?" Kay asked her. "Do you have any plans for Easter week, before the roof caves in on us?" Rosaleen was slow to answer.

"Not really. I'll probably just stay at home. I haven't planned on going any place." At which point, Mary piped in.

"Oh, yes, just watch; she'll stay at home and work hard and come in exam week with the brains busting out of her head."

"Oh, sure," Rosaleen said, smiling. "Not a chance. Anyway, we still have about nine weeks to cram; it won't be too bad."

The girls boarded the waiting bus that would take them to the centre of the city, where each would then catch her own individual bus for home, and it was on the way that Rosaleen dropped the bomb about not returning to school after she received her Junior Certificate. Mary and Kay were aghast, and Mary said incredulously,

"You must be joking, Rosaleen. I mean, to have come all this way and then to chuck it all up. Why, in two years you'll have reached Senior, and you'll certainly have no trouble getting into Queen's."

"I can't believe I heard you right, Rosaleen." Kay said, astounded. "What brought this about? You were always so studious; so eager to learn." Rosaleen, looking away from both of them, concentrated on the passing traffic.

"Oh, it's just that I don't see very much opportunity here. We don't have too many choices, do we?" Then, focusing her gaze on one and then the other and, as though she were hearing her own philosophy aloud for the first time, she went on. "I mean, we can't all be teachers, and, yet, that's about as far as we can go. There's not much else, and I really don't want to teach."

"We could become nuns," Mary offered facetiously, and Kay threw her a wicked glance, and then gave her own suggestion.

"Well, there's always marriage," she said, and then pausing momentarily, she directed herself to Rosaleen specifically, "And a good education is never wasted."

Arriving in the city centre, and emerging onto the traffic-island, Mary turned to Rosaleen, saying in a sentimental tone,

"Well, whatever you do over the Easter holidays, if nothing else, please, please try and talk yourself into coming back after Junior. Well, there's my bus. Cheerio, Kay; Rosaleen! Good luck."

"Yes, Rosaleen, I'll be praying for you to make the right decision," Kay said, and leaning over, gave her a peck on the cheek. "I must be going. I see a queue a mile long and I hate it when I have to stand all the way home. Well, love, cheerio."

"Cheerio, Kay," Rosaleen said with an uncharacteristic-like trace of sadness in her voice. "Have a nice Easter."

Left alone on the traffic-island, Rosaleen was forced to stay there until the onrush of traffic came to a halt, and a passing motorist, a respectable-looking, middle-aged man, wearing a felt-trilby, stuck his head out of the window and said, quite casually,

"Them's a nice set of tiddies you have there, love."

Castle Street cut into the heart of the city like a main jugular, bringing big, red buses loaded with people from the various Falls Road areas. As one arrived at the Castle Junction every three minutes and one left on the same schedule, there was always an overflow of humanity from every walk of life. But recently, after a big, new record shop opened its doors to the arriving and departing traffic, there seemed to be more people than ever milling around these particular crossroads of the city.

On this, Holy Thursday, the record shop was doing fantastic in sales, despite the sobriety of such an austere day, and its music, loud and inviting, spilled its American flavour out onto the sidewalks, and the young people lapped it up.

As Rosaleen crossed the junction, the week-long drizzle which had grayed the city, draining it of all colour, though had failed to put a damper on Easter shopping, started to ease off, and the first rays of sunlight, which had not been seen in days, began to creep over the antiquated, architectural parapets of Belfast's many department stores.

On the other side of the junction, a recording that had birthed a rock'n'roll sensation by the name of Elvis Presley, was being played for the benefit of a prospective customer and, as Rosaleen came closer to her bus, which was loading just a little bit before the record shop, her proximity to her destination was in keeping with the rising tempo of the music.

Coinciding with Rosaleen's approach, and at an equal distance from the record shop, was a group of youths coming in the opposite direction, and, as they entered the musical realm of sound, their swaggered walks picked up in rhythm to the record's beat.

But it was not this alone that caused passers-by to turn and look after them; it was their overall appearance, from head to toe: their clothes; velvet-collared suit jackets that fell way beyond the conventional length; leg-tight trousers, referred to as 'drain-pipes'; thick sponged, suede shoes, that not only added inches to their height, but were also an aid in producing the deliberate self-assured swagger; and, last but not least, their hairstyle — it was coiffured after the backside of a duck, the anatomy part that proffered its name — the DA. Of all the menaces that threatened to shatter the existing morals of Belfast youth, it was this hairstyle that caused the most concern amongst conservative parents. For it was this long-lengthed, greased-back style, with its overhanging eye-level lock of curls, which created a cocky exterior, that seemed to stimulate an almost reverent response in the opposite sex, which, in turn, produced repercussions of masculine macho that oozed every bit as thick and smooth as the stuff that held the very hairstyle in place. These were the Teddy Boys, casually referred to as 'the Teds'.

The music greeted Rosaleen upon entering the neck of Castle Street, and the rain seemed to have come to a complete stop. A glimmer of sunlight, caught in the darkened windows of the Bank Buildings, escaped and danced its way along the pavement, preceding Rosaleen all the way to the bus, and, directly ahead of her, although not yet within her visibility, was a magnificent rainbow whose colours had not yet reached their peak of hue.

The youths reached the record shop as Rosaleen joined the bus queue, and while she moved slowly towards the platform, the youths paused momentarily before the large plate-glass window to look at the life-size poster of Elvis Presley holding his guitar in one of his pelvis poses. Their smiles reflected in the window and, as the bulk of them moved on, one lagged behind and, in time to the record, strummed an imaginary guitar while he imitated Elvis's pelvic and leg movements.

Rosaleen was the last to board the bus, and seeing that the lower deck was crowded, with people standing in the aisle, she took to the stairs. Her ascent, together with her short school-uniform, caught the youth's attention and he hurried over to get an eyeful. Simultaneously, the bus conductor, standing inside the lower deck, reached out and pulled the bell that set the bus in motion.

Rosaleen had just reached the top step and, although the bus was pulling out, the youth was clinging to the rail, and, the conductor, overseeing that no passengers were standing in the upstairs aisle, by way of a convex mirror, realized, at once, what the youth was up to and he made a swipe at him, shouting,

"Get away on with ye, ye cheeky wee bugger, ye."

As the bus picked up in speed, the youth jumped off, and watching it disappear up the street, he raised his right hand, much like a puppy would hold its paw, and shook it in the air, and, raising his eyes to heaven, he shook his head.

When Rosaleen's stop came, she got off and had just reached her street when she ran into Ann.

"I must say," Ann said, facetiously, "some people really know how to get out of working."

Used to this sort of slagging by now,

Rosaleen retaliated jokingly, "Oh, and talking about non-workers; what did they do, give you the sack over at Clarence's?"

"Not a chance. I just told auld Robertson I had cramps."

"Are you still using that as an excuse?" Rosaleen smiled, bemused.

"Ach, sure what does he know? I gave him the same yarn last week and he swallowed it," Ann retorted. Then, dropping the subject for more important matters at hand, she said, "Where are you going on Saturday night?"

"Saturday night?" Rosaleen mused, " . . . Oh, I have to go to confession," and seeing Ann's raised brows, she added, "For Easter, you know."

"Aye, me too," Ann smirked. "Do you want to go anywhere on Sunday night?"

"Where to?"

"Anywhere, just to get out. Maybe we'll go up to the Hibs; might as well give them a break."

Smiling, Rosaleen said, "Aye, alright with me."

"Listen," Ann said, moving closer to Rosaleen and pretending to look cautiously around, "nothing against your

71

school-uniform, or nothing, but I don't want your reputation to rub off on me. See you around, kid," and she went off, leaving Rosaleen smiling to herself as she entered the house.

6

THE Hibs, short for 'The Ancient Order of Hibernians', was a well-known spot on the Falls Road for two reasons. First, while it was the club-rooms for an American-founded organization for the promotion of independence, individual as well as national, it was also a dance-hall for the youth of the area, opening its doors Sunday nights, as well as Sunday afternoons, Tuesday, Friday and Saturday nights. The dance-hall was not lavish by any means, far from it. In size, it was a mere fifty feet by a hundred, with a couple of deep corners to catch the overflow from the dance-floor. But it did have the unique distinction of boasting a space-saving record corner which jutted down out of the ceiling. Actually, it was a wooden platform with two walls about four-feet high and was built catty-corner three-quarters of the way up the walls. There was a ladder going up to a trapdoor in the floor, through which the record-jockeys, and only the record-jockeys had access — the A.O.H. having very strict rules about this — and as soon as the jockey on duty climbed the ladder, he pulled it up into the box behind him.

And so here, in this little corner, were stacked by the hundreds, recordings of music, which, long after the turntable at the Hibs had stopped, would continue to live, like so many memories, in the recesses of people's lives, waiting to haunt, or taunt them at the turn of a switch.

Easter Sunday night saw Rosaleen, Phyllis and Ann climbing the stairs to the second-storey dance-hall. Waves of Cogi Grant's 'The Wayward Wind' were drifting down to greet them, and, as they arrived on the landing, the girls got their first visual implication of what Martin Specky's 'NO MOODY DANCING' signs were all about. For, inside, the little dance-hall was crowded with couples; young men and women clinging to each other; cheek to cheek, they danced without barely moving, on a semi-darkened floor.

Rosaleen, having second thoughts, pulled at Ann's coat, but she and Phyllis were already paying their way in to a man seated behind a table, and Rosaleen, holding back for a second, reluctantly handed over her shilling. Up one more flight of stairs was the ladies 'powder-room', which boasted of one small room, one toilet cubicle, a yellow mirror, a heavily scarred, wooden table that was nailed to the wall, having only two front legs, and a wooden chair to match, that had no back to it.

"Not exactly Martin Speckly's, is it?" Ann said, grimacing.

"Nothing's exactly Martin Specky's." Rosaleen answered, and all three laughed, as though sharing a secret, and a girl, who was combing her long ponytail, made a face in the mirror to her companion, who was applying a bright, pink lipstick to her mouth for the third time.

"I don't know if I fit in here or not," Rosaleen whispered to Ann, as a very bosomy girl in a red, v-neck sweater pushed her way past them.

"Who does?" Ann winced, letting the girl through. The three girls waited until the room had emptied before taking off their coats. Then, Ann, fussing a little before the mirror, drew in her breath and murmured,

"Well, girls, this is it."

Fats Domino's 'Josephine' was playing, as the girls entered, and the dance-floor was palpitating with jiving couples. Being both mesmerized and suffering pangs of intrepidation at the same time, Rosaleen followed Ann and Phyllis to a wide corner under the record box where they mingled with a large crowd of girls. Feeling less conspicuous and taking advantage of the fact that the majority of people were dancing, and holding the attention of the onlookers, helped her to relax somewhat. When the dance ended, she was halfway to feeling composed, enough anyway to refuse the cigarette offered to her by Ann.

As her two friends lit up, Rosaleen saw that there was a division of 'turf' here, and that the males resorted to the two adjacent corners, while the girls occupied the one wide expanse under the records; a policy for which she was secretly grateful, for now she and the others were practically unnoticeable; but not for long. As the next record began, Phyllis was asked to dance, and Ann, who for some insecure reason couldn't bear to be left standing when one of the others had been chosen over her, nicked her cigarette, and stepping on the glowing ash with the toe of her shoe, turned to Rosaleen.

"Come on, let's stag it."

The Diamonds' 'Little Darlin' was playing, which prompted some couples into a slow jive, while most of them still moody-danced. Dancing casually around the floor, as girls usually do when they danced with each other, Rosaleen began to unwind and started to enjoy the music. It aroused a certain response to a rhythm she was not accustomed to dancing to, and, while the beat was striking this responding rhythm throughout her body, moving her with an adept coordination, she was intent on watching the talent with which some couples jived, and who did so without leaving the spot in which they were dancing.

Suddenly, and completely unexpectedly, Rosaleen saw a fellow coming up behind Ann, and putting his hand on her arm, took her away from her. Rosaleen was momentarily at an odds what to do and her first impulse was to flee the floor. But, as she turned to do so, she slammed head-on into the arms of a tall, young man who had been standing directly behind her. Then, realizing that his intention had been to step in and replace Ann, she was at once embarrassed. The young man, looking down at her with a smile on his lips, spread his arms in a gesture of mock helplessness.

"Well, this is a first; usually they're running away from me."

This first utterance was a clue to the strain of insolence that was as much a part of Colin Murdoch's sex-appeal, as were his other attributes, but Rosaleen, caught too unexpectedly off guard, and being too flustered to notice it just yet, was to be confronted with it, face to face, before the evening was over.

Then, as he took her hand in his and placed the other at her waist, he began to move in slow, rhythmic, yet subtle gyrations, which were immediately disturbing to Rosaleen. Unable to pick up any of the rhythm that she had felt before, she remained motionless as she looked up at him.

"I don't jive," she told him, feeling her tongue dry against the roof of her mouth. Colin stopped, as though frozen, and looked down at her intently.

"You don't jive!" and, then, revealing that smile on his lips again, he slowed his pace, and bringing her near him, he enclosed her in his arms.

As far as Rosaleen was concerned, he might just as well have drawn her into a black, bottomless pit, for she was just as lost, with nothing more to guide her than Martin Specky's signs screaming, 'NO MOODY DANCING'.

"Where are you from, anyway? Venus?" he asked, looking down at her, and without waiting for an answer, "You can't live around here and not know how to jive." And, unexpectedly, his look deepened, as he waited for an answer.

Rosaleen could have been in another world, because she was completely alienated from her own self, and, now with him looking down at her like that, she felt as though she were, because she couldn't find the right words to answer him. What she did find was that the sparkle in his deep, blue eyes and the gleam of his hair under the soft, overhead lights were having a very unnerving effect on her.

"Well, do you? Do you live around here?" Rosaleen heard his voice coming at her as though she really were in the pit, and when she opened her mouth to speak, she heard herself echoing and re-echoing as though against the walls of the pit itself.

"I . . . yes . . . I do live around here," and then, realizing that she had mouthed him almost word for word, she added, but at a much-too-fast-pace, "I live in Balaclava Street," but it came out sounding like 'Bal-la-kill-ava Street'.'

Repeating it exactly as Rosaleen had said it, Colin remarked, sounding quite serious,

"I don't think I've ever heard of that street."

Fully aware that he was being facetious, yet not wanting him to see that she was, while still hoping to end the conversation on an intelligent note, Rosaleen cleared up the 'confusion' by repeating the name in a normal voice.

"Oh, *that* street!" he said, "Oh, yes, I know where that is. But why haven't I seen you here before, then, if you live around here?" But Rosaleen, not wanting to sound like a novice, answered,

"There was nowhere else to go tonight, with it being Sunday, but, then, with it being Easter, and all, we decided to come here."

"Oh? And where do you usually go?" he asked, displaying an interest, as if it really mattered to him where she went. Feeling flustered again, and afraid of it showing on her face, Rosaleen looked past him as she answered.

"Oh . . . we usually go to the . . . Plaza."

The Plaza, a downtown ballroom, which catered to a more mature crowd, and which, because of its location, received a lot of international visitors and such who came off the ships that temporarily docked in the Belfast harbour; the staffs, as well as the crews, which included Scandinavian sailors, as well as foreign students attending the university. But, most of all, it was a favourite spot for American soldiers, sailors and air-force men.

Raising an eyebrow, and in a voice an octave lower than what was normal, Colin retorted,

"The Plaza? And what does a girl like you do at the Plaza?"

"What everybody else does, dance," Rosaleen said.

"And what night . . . or is it *nights* do you go?" Catching that sparkle again, Rosaleen replied,

"Fridays and Saturdays," guessing them to be as good as any.

"Oh, I've heard that those are the best nights to go; plenty of action, I hear." Rosaleen detected the coy streak in his tone, which if coming from someone else, would immediately have put her on the defensive, but from him, she had no defences; they all seemed to have disappeared before him, like strong oaks before a forest fire, and now, while there was a moment of silence between them, which she used to collect her wits, he unravelled her in less time by asking,

"Are you going tonight?"

"Tonight?" Rosaleen repeated, completely at a loss for an answer.

"Yeah, you know, the big midnight dance," and looking closer at her, "For Easter."

"Oh, no. We're not going," she told him, as straightforward as possible, and was glad when he dropped the entire subject altogether. Drawing her closer, he was silent until the record ended, and the next one being a fast one, she excused herself. But, as she started to push her way through the crowd to the door, she realized that he was going to escort her there personally. Upon reaching the brightly-lit hallway, she nodded a token of appreciation, though barely looking at him, and, then, fled upstairs to the ladies room, if for nothing else except to get beyond his gaze.

She was glad to find it deserted and went immediately into the toilet. Leaning against the wall, she tried to recall everything she had said in the hopes that she hadn't sounded as stupid as she had felt. But more unsettling was her attempt to recall everything he had said, and when she became aware of this, she left the cubicle, catching her reflection in the mirror as she did so.

"Oh, God," she said to herself, when seeing her flushed face, and she attempted to wipe it away with the back of her hands, which were oddly cold.

Feeling it safe to return to the dance-hall, as the same fast record was still playing, Rosaleen found a bench in the corner under the record box and lit a much-needed cigarette. Sitting there all alone, separated from the dancers by a line of onlookers, she thought of them out there on the darkened floor, under the soft lights, and she found a certain empathy with them, even though she knew that they were completely oblivious to her. All too soon the music stopped and loud talk broke into her reverie. Phyllis and Ann rejoined her and thankfully collapsed onto the bench beside her, as they, too, went for their cigarettes. But, before they could light them, the same two fellows who they had danced with before beckoned them onto the floor. Phyllis went, but Ann, feeling more secure now with this demand on her, motioned for the fellow to wait while she took Rosaleen's cigarette from her, and drawing deeply, a satisfied look reached her face, as the nicotine found its way to her lungs. Still engrossed with this, she then opened her eyes only to see Rosaleen being led onto the dance-floor, and when it dawned on her that she was the last remaining, she abruptly dropped the cigarette to the floor, and crushing it with her foot, she hastened to the dance-floor.

Feeling Colin Murdoch so close behind her, Rosaleen walked to the dance-floor much like a non-seasoned swimmer might approach the ocean, wading out to its depth, and facing it for the first plunge, fearings its effect, yet seeking the excitement of its eternal power, she turned to Colin, and he, as though the old man of the sea himself, held out his arms to her, and taking her hand, he drew her to him.

The record playing was 'Come To Me' and the singer, Johnny Mathis; the first in a long succession of Johnny Mathis recordings that spoke to a young girl's heart and stirred up her deepest and most human emotions and brought them to the surface.

Colin Murdoch was the first man with

whom Rosaleen had the experience of being close to accompanied with emotion; and it was an emotional closeness that created a whole new experience; like the uncontrollable thudding of her heart, which felt as though it were pumping every drop of blood from her neck down and rushing it to her head, to cause it to throb at the temples and to fill her cheeks and set them on fire. Then, lest he might hear the thumping speed of her heart, or feel the flame of her cheek against his own, she withdrew a little from his embrace. But, as slight as her movement was, Colin detected it, and looking down at her, he pulled her even closer.

"Come to me, now that I have found
    you
Come to me, wrap my love around you
Look in my eyes, hear what they say,
Don't run away, stay, stay, stay.
I'm on fire, let your lips caress me
My desire is that you possess me,
Don't be afraid for love to come to you
My lover come to me, lover come to
    me,
Come to me."

Rosaleen's overall emotions at this point were just like those of the swimmer, who, having gone blindly into the deep, looks back too late to find entwined, the steadfast arms of the old man of the sea and with no foreseen sign of escape, is tempted to throw all hope to the wind and care to the waves. Only Rosaleen couldn't let go and the waves that continued to engulf her and constrict her breathing were the words of Johnny Mathis that kept beckoning her to succumb.

And so it was, with the incredible paradox of being on fire and of drowning at the same time, Rosaleen managed to maintain a composure of external normality and finished the dance. A few seconds pause between records and Rosaleen, aware that Colin's arm had remained where it was, and of his eyes watching her, was also aware of a growing determination within her to keep her distance this time around.

Trying to dance against a force was no easy task, but persisting to resist even when the tide of Johnny Mathis's 'No Love' was threatening to gain momentum, was the first of two hardest things that Rosaleen was to do before the night was over.

As the dance progressed, Rosaleen started to feel the muscles pulling at the back of her neck, and her left arm, touching, but not daring to feel the shoulder beneath its flesh, soon became like a wooden limb, and even the hand which was enclosed in his had become like clay; but not the substance that could be softened by the touch and becomes pliable between the warmth of the fingertips, but more like the unyielding kind which, when refusing to relent, hardens to a petrified lump, and Rosaleen, not quite sure what to do about it all, maintained this posture and continued to bear the strain, until, passing in front of the record box, she happened to glance up and saw the record jockey looking down at her. Motioning to her, but she not getting his meaning, he then signalled to her to look around. Able to do this without moving her heard, she saw couples that were but shadows, each fusing into the other, and she raised her eyes again, and he, leaning over the box on his elbows, as though overseeing that she did his bidding, threw her a do or dare look. Continuing to see him watching her, Rosaleen detected the hint of goading in his eyes slowly change to a gleam of encouragement, which brought a frown from her, as she threw him a disapproving look. Then, catching a ghost of a twinkle, as his face broke into a grin, and she, unable to suppress a smile, but attempting to hide it from him, moved her arm along Colin's shoulder and turned her head, and, suddenly, she found her hand resting on the back of his neck, and felt her forehead brush against his face, and Colin, without further encouragement, tightened his hold on her and brought her face closer to his.

Gone now was the strain of trying to resist him, as the touch of him, warm beneath her fingers, sprung life back into her arm, and she felt the comfortable support of his shoulder, and the hand, once turned to stone, melted now beneath his fingers, like the wax of a candle beneath the flame.

Now looking up at the record jockey, a secretive look of appreciation in her eyes, she received the approving nod of his head, along with the added blessing of his thumb and forefinger brought together victoriously, all of which created the semblence of a bishop in his pulpit conferring his blessing on his flock below.

Without wasting any time between records, the jockey immediately put on another Johnny Mathis record. Making little or no attempts at conversation, Rosaleen, too intent on her own thoughts, and Colin, apparently having deep thoughts of his own, failed to notice just how many songs by the same singer had been played; nor were either of them aware that it was all for their benefit: all Rosaleen knew was that Johnny Mathis was, for her, like the ebb and flow of the tide that kept sweeping her into the eternal depths of the sea and, then, with gathering force, deposited her back on sands that were without bottom. And then his 'Twelfth of Never' stung her with the impact of the words.

The words created butterflies in the pit of her stomach that stirred up emotions which continuously flooded her entire system, but, yet, came to a halt behind her eyes, where they managed to get caught up in knots and caused a stinging sensation that made her feel as though she were about to uncontrollably break into tears.

The words and the music and the voice made Rosaleen want to dance on forever. And that's exactly how it felt, for she was unaware of where one song began and another ended. For Rosaleen, there was no beginning and no end; there was just one magic-filled moment that went on and on.

So it was with as much surprise and annoyance that jeers and boos broke into her thoughts and disturbed her mood, and the record was jarred to a screeching halt. Not knowing what was happening, Rosaleen soon found out, as voices, mildly raged, shouted up at the jockey concerning the unfairness of five slow dances in a row. They wanted one to which they could jive, and amidst the arguing that followed, some couples split, leaving the floor, and Colin and Rosaleen, passing an intense look between them, did the same.

Rejoining Ann and Phyllis in the corner, Rosaleen made a half-hearted attempt to listen to their conversation, until she felt a hand on her arm, and turning around, she came face to face with the freckle-faced, curly-haired record jockey. His position at the turntable had been replaced and now the hall was jumping to Bill Haley's 'Rock Around the Clock'.

Against Rosaleen's protests, the jockey persuaded her to dance. Telling him that she didn't know how to jive, he brushed it aside with a cheeky grin, saying, "You're never too old to learn," and with a good-natured wink, he proceeded to give her her first lesson right there in the corner, behind the crowd.

He started the rhythm for both of them and Rosaleen, unable to resist the beat, soon found herself responding, and, before the music was over, she was able to keep up with him in steps she had never seen before, much less performed.

"Good girl!" the record jockey told her, "I knew you had it in you." Then, before she had time to catch her breath, he pulled her out onto the floor, saying as he did so, "Now you're ready for the big time."

Leading her into a slow jive, to Paul Anka's 'Diana', he set a pace which she found easy enough to follow, and without feeling the least bit conspicuous out there on the floor with all the rest of the jivers, she began to feel right at home with this freckle-faced youth, who had deemed himself her mentor.

When the record stopped, and while they waited for the next one to begin, he placed a friendly elbow on her shoulder, and, in a brotherly manner, teased her about the 'big Ted' she'd been dancing with.

"You know, I did that on purpose, playing all those Mathis records."

Rosaleen gave him a wide-eyed look, "Why did you do that?"

"Oh, you and that big fella looked so good together; besides, I wanted you to have a good time."

"Why me? You don't even know me."

"Well, I do know that this is your first time here and I just wanted to make sure you'd come back again." Then he added,

"Although I'm not sure I'll be back. I'll probably get suspended for what I did."

"What? For playing too much of the same kind of music?" Rosaleen asked, as the jockey grimaced.

"No. For playing more than three records in succession without a break in between. The A.O.H. has very strict rules about that. The only time they make an exception is for the big jiving contest."

"Oh?" Rosaleen felt her interest sparked, "What's that?"

But the next record starting up interrupted them, and shouting over the full volume of it, he told her, "I'll tell you about it later."

Smiling, Rosaleen nodded her head. Feeling happy all over, glad that she had come here tonight, she realized that she was happy with the place, the music, the people in general, and especially one in particular.

"Now remember those three steps I showed you?" the jockey was saying, as he grabbed her hand and pulled her out of a swing and close so she could hear him talking. "After this, we break away again, do the steps, come together, swing twice and repeat the steps again. Now, have you got that?"

The first set of steps went perfectly and the jockey gave her a nod of approval and grabbed her hand for the first swing. But the second time around, Rosaleen was caught up short by Colin Murdoch standing just a few feet away. Leaning with his back to the wall, with one foot drawn up behind him and his arms folded across his chest, he watched her with interest. A sudden warmth flooded her body when she saw him, but, avoiding his eyes, she focused all her attention on the jockey.

By the time the record ended, they had jived their way out of sight of Colin, and the jockey, still holding her hand, led her to a bench onto which they both collapsed, laughing, side by side. When they had time to draw their breath, Rosaleen turned a smiling face to him.

"So, tell me. What is this 'big jiving contest' all about?"

Offering her a cigarette, which she declined, he lit one for himself, and blowing the smoke down through his nostrils, he turned and placed a friendly arm around her shoulders.

"Well, it's like this: Everybody's on the dance floor, see; fellas and girls together only. Just rock'n'roll records are playing, I mean anything you can jive to. But, as the contest progresses, the records get faster. The judging comes from who can hold out the longest."

"Oh, you mean, then, that that's the couple who wins the contest?" Rosaleen interrupted.

"No, no. This is strictly a male thing. It works like this: Everyone's sitting, see? After a while, if the girl gets tired, she sits down and another comes and takes her place. Then, when she falls out, in comes another one to replace her, and it goes on like that 'til the men drop themselves: though many's a time it's the men who are ready to quit before some of the women even get warmed up, and more's the shame, 'cause some of the women here can really dance. But now what they do is this: the better ones sit out the start of the contest and don't come in 'til the end. This way the fellow is a cert to have a partner for the finish."

"Have you ever won it?" Rosaleen asked him.

"Oh, yeah, last time I did, but that was on account of 'wee' Andy not bein' here."

"Who's 'wee' Andy?"

"The best f . . . , oh, excuse me. 'Wee' Andy's one of the greatest jivers ever to walk through that door. I mean he doesn't do much except dance. I don't think he ever put in a full week's work in his life, but he could jive anybody blind."

"So, then, you've only 'wee' Andy to worry about and if he doesn't show up, then you're certain to win?"

"Oh, no. I'm out of it now. Ever since I became an A.O.H. member, I can't participate. I mean, I can dance in it, but I can't compete, if you know what I mean."

"Are there very many good jivers? It wouldn't be much of a contest if 'wee' Andy was a sure bet."

"Oh, aye, there's plenty of good jivers, alright. Let's see now . . . " He started to count them off on his fingers, which meant that he had to pull the arm that

97

was around Rosaleen even tighter, which made them look like a very cosy couple. " . . . there's big Albert McGahy, who's a terrific jiver, then, there's Bo Bo Gillen, he's not too bad, there's Frankie Falooney, and his brother Jackie, there's 'Dirty Eyes' McGeown, and, let me see now, oh, aye, there's Manuel Lochern, Jerry Coogan, Terry Malcomson, and then there's . . . "

"All right." Rosaleen stopped him, laughing, "I'll just take your word for it." Then looking around, as though just by learning their names she could spot them. "Are they all here tonight?"

"Oh, no. Tonight's one of our bad nights, believe it or not; you should be here when the whole gang's here, you can hardly get in through the door." Pausing here, he sucked in his breath, signalling that what he was about to tell her was worth the breath it was spoken on. "No, I'm afraid there was some other attraction on for tonight."

"Oh?" Rosaleen asked, curious, "Is there a party on somewhere?"

"Oh, aye, some party!" he told her, rolling his eyes. "There's a midnight dance at the Plaza, from twelve to five in the mornin'."

He grinned, as though the very thought of it was enjoyment enough. "That's when the 'tarts' come in for breakfast behind the bandstand," and he looked at Rosaleen from the corner of his eye, but seeing her quizzical expression, he added, "Never mind, you're too young." And he continued. "But there are a lot of nice birds there — some of them too nice, if you ask me," which drew another curious look from Rosaleen. But, this time, he went on. "Married ones out for a lark, some of them have husbands away on the boats." And, as though seeing the sheer irony of the situation, he gave a deep, satisfactory laugh. "They like the sailors, I hear. And can you blame them? Their men are probably in some foreign port doing the very same thing . . ." Suddenly distracted by the sight of Phyllis on the dance floor, he broke off. But she, deeply engrossed in conversation with her partner, passed by, unaware of Rosaleen sitting there, or of the record jockey looking at her.

"I've been meaning to ask you about

99

your mate. What's her name?"

"Phyllis Donegan," Rosaleen told him. "Why?"

"Oh, she's a nice looking wee 'tart'. I couldn't help noticing her when she came in."

As though beginning to see the light, Rosaleen withdrew his arm from around her shoulders, and narrowing her eyes, she told him, "Oh, so Phyllis is the reason why you want me . . . " she stressed the last word and pointed to " . . . 'to have a good time' and 'to come back again'," and she punched him playfully.

"I want youse all to come back," he said, laughing, and grabbing her, he wrestled with her playfully. "Honest, youse are all nice wee 'tarts' . . . " Then, all at once, sobering up, he nodded to the dance floor, to where Colin Murdoch was dancing with his back to them. And Rosaleen couldn't help but feel a twinge upon noticing that the girl he was with had both her arms up tight around his neck. " . . . Jesus!" the jockey gasped. "How could I've forgotten to count him — the 'big Ted'. Now, there's a smashing

100

jiver. One of the best. Has a style all of his own . . . a Protestant, but a hell of a good jiver."

It was a while before Rosaleen set eyes on Colin again, but about ten minutes before the end of the night, she saw him coming towards her, and her pulse started racing even before he reached her, but, before this happened, someone, a fellow from behind, touched her elbow, and, unable to do anything else, she went out onto the floor with him.

For two records Rosaleen danced with the fellow she had never seen before till then, and it was with much disappointment. And more so when she heard the jockey, who was now back in the box, announce,

"This is it folks, the last dance for tonight. I hoped you all enjoyed yourselves. See you all on Tuesday night."

The microphone went dead, but the room came alive with Johnny Mathis singing 'It's Not For Me To Say'. Resenting the fellow she was with, she went unwillingly into his arms, and the words and the music, which should have been a caress to her heart, were wasted by

101

the position she found herself in: For beyond the crowd she could see the back of Colin's head, the lights gleaming in his hair added a certain halo-like glow to it. Then, suddenly, in the unpredictable freedom of the dance-floor, she was at once confronted with his gaze, but simultaneously she saw too who his partner was.

Seeing Phyllis, she immediately knew why he'd been heading in her direction; it was Phyllis he'd been coming for, not her; it had been only coincidental that this fellow she was now dancing with had approached her, as Colin himself was crossing the room — something for which she was at least thankful — she couldn't bear it if he had asked Phyllis to dance right in front of her — nonetheless, this didn't alter her disappointment nor the mood that this had created in her and especially now that he and Phyllis were out of sight.

Assuming that they had left together, Rosaleen felt the disappointment well up in her throat and form a dry lump, the weight of which she carried around the floor until the record came to an end.

Then, almost miraculously, she saw them. It was the very least that they were still there, and Rosaleen, watching him, filling her eyes with his image, not knowing when, or even if she would ever see him again, much less dance in his arms, saw him make a subtle, yet meaningful gesture up at the record jockey, which, if she hadn't been watching so intently, she would have missed.

Seeing the jockey leaning over on his elbows, Rosaleen knew, just by his very pose, that he was up to something, yet, without knowing exactly what was going on between them, she suspected that it had something to do with Phyllis.

And now, as the record hit the last note, Rosaleen, finding herself exactly adjacent to them, curtly nodded to her partner and started to walk away. But, as she did, two things happened that changed the course of the entire evening. Though not quite sure which came first — the sound from the record box that a needle makes when it slips off a record, or on to it, or Colin Murdoch's hand on her arm, pulling her back. Whichever, the two blended in perfect harmony and made Rosaleen feel like she was in a beautiful dream.

It was all there as before; the wonderful feeling of him holding her, her hand in his; that is, until he withdrew his and brought it to rest on her waist. Now, with both his arms around her, she had no choice but to bring her other arm up to his shoulder and around his neck, and Johnny Mathis did the rest.

"It's not for me to say, you love me
It's not for me to say, you really care
But, oh, for the moment I can hold you fast
And press your lips to mine and dream that love will last
It's not for me to say, this is heaven
But speaking just for me, it's ours to share
Perhaps the glow of love will grow with every passing day
Or we may never meet again, but then, It's not for me to say."

Somewhere in the middle of the song, Rosaleen heard him ask if he could take her home. But now, with the song over the hall flooded with light, she wasn't at all sure that he had asked her. Somewhere in her mind, his words had gotten mixed up with those of Johnny Mathis, making it all come out as one beautiful melody, and now she didn't know what to do, so she asked Ann.

"What do you mean, you don't know if he asked to take you home?" And then, after a feeble explanation from Rosaleen, "Well, all you can do now is walk down the stairs, if he's hanging around, smile at him, then leave the next move up to him."

"But what do I do?" Rosaleen persisted, wishing she had just taken her coat and fled.

"You don't do nothing. Just walk kind of slow to give him a chance to catch up with you, and, if he does, you got him."

"Oh, Ann!" Rosaleen said, her tone telling her friend that she'd just as soon forget the whole thing.

"Look! Do you want me to go and ask him if he asked you if he could take you home? Jesus!"

"All right, I'll do it, but, for God's sake, wait for me outside."

"Oh, Jimmy Reed asked us to go over to Moloccos for fish and chips," Ann told her.

"Who's Jimmy Reed?" Rosaleen asked.

"You know, the one who plays the records. Well, we'll be there if nothin' happens. Good luck, kid."

Upon leaving the ladies room, Rosaleen reached the second landing, which was filled with waiting youths, and not wanting to appear obtrusive, yet with her heart in her mouth, she ran down the remaining flight of stairs and into the street.

Directly across the street, Moloccos fish and chip shop was catching the youngsters coming out of the Hibs faster than it could handle them and the pavement outside was crowded. Over the heads of the crowd, music, that someone had coined from a jukebox, was playing loudly, but the pavement around the A.O.H. hall itself was deserted, and it was with a sinking heart that Rosaleen, ignoring the action across the street, turned in the direction of home.

"What's the rush?" His voice stopped her dead on the spot, and, with her heart beating somewhere in her throat, she turned and saw him waiting for her by the darkened doorway of the little shop that was next to the A.O.H. hall.

Without moving, she waited in anticipation for him to come to her, and when he did, she started walking and he fell into step beside her. After an awkward silence, Rosaleen said, not daring to look at him, "I wasn't sure where you'd be." And without any further remarks, he put an arm across her shoulder and they crossed the street, the music from Moloccos following them.

A bit further on, leaving the Falls Road and going down through the darkened side-streets, his voice came out of the darkness beside her.

"What's the matter, did you lose your tongue?"

"Well, you're not too talkative yourself."

"No, I'm not. But then, I never am. But you were doing alright back there with Jimmy Reed."

Grasping his meaning, she turned and looked at him, and, although his features were barely visible in the dark, she had no trouble focusing on his eyes, nor on the sparkle that she saw there.

"Oh, you mean the fellow that plays the records?"

"Is he a good friend of yours?"

"No, I never saw him before tonight."

"You'd never know it. But, then, again, maybe he'd like to know you better."

Suddenly it dawned on her the direction from which the conversation was coming from, and, better still, where it was heading, and she hastened along. "Yes, could be, but maybe he'd like to know my chum even better."

"Oh? And which one is that?"

"The one you were dancing with." And getting no reply, "The one you asked up for the last dance."

"You mean after that fellow who asked you beat me to the punch?"

And Rosaleen, smiling to herself in the dark, answered, "Yes, that's the one."

More sure of herself now that the ice had been broken between them, Rosaleen was more relaxed during the rest of the way home.

"Well, this is it," she said, slowing down, as they turned the corner, a block before her street.

Looking up at the building in front of them, Colin repeated, "This is it? You live in a school?"

"No," Rosaleen said, "I mean . . . I . . . live around the corner from here."

"Oh, you mean you want to say goodnight here," he said, looking down at her. "Is that it?"

"If you don't mind," she heard herself saying, none too steady.

"I don't mind one bit," Colin said, his smile gleaming through the darkness, and he drew her into the deep well of the doorway. His arms around her and his mouth dangerously near, she felt his warm breath on her cheek.

"Now, tell me, what were you thinking about all that time you were dancing with me?"

Her breath constricted in her throat, accompanied by the stinging behind her eyes, Rosaleen was finding it impossible to say anything. She felt his lips gently on her cheek, on her forehead, and she closed her eyes against the onrushing tide of emotions, and he, as though sensing the helplessness within which the very centre of her being was threatened, brought his lips to her closed eyelids in kisses that took hold of the tide itself and subdued it, but just enough to enable her to reassure herself that her feet were still on solid ground.

"What's the matter?" he whispered to her, "Did you lose your tongue again?"

In a voice that was like that of a stranger's, Rosaleen told him, "I . . . I don't know what I was thinking about, I just . . . "

"Ssh . . . " he told her, his breath warm against her ear, "Let me say it for you." And he brought his mouth down fully against hers in a kiss that felt like he had dredged every bit of earthly life from her soul.

"Is that what you wanted to tell me?"

Feeling both confused and elated at the same time, Rosaleen could just look at him through the darkness and, as their eyes met and held, she felt his arm tighten around her waist, and he pulled her to him in a kiss that gave her a sensation of falling head first through endless clouds.

"Tell me more," he gently demanded

against her ear, and Rosaleen, in an act of faith, gave him her lips in a kiss filled with so much emotion she was sure that her entire life had been spent leading up to it.

But to a young man who had long since crossed the threshold of his first kiss, he took her response to mean only one thing. But he found his move blocked and, as Rosaleen broke away from him, she told him, and almost too innocently, "I don't do things like that."

"Oh, no? You also told me you don't jive." And he pulled her back to him and kissed her with all purpose and intent.

But he was disappointed, for she pulled him up short once more, her own disappointment far surpassing his own, and her voice came at him from out of the darkness, as though the question had been hurled from a great distance.

"What do you take me for?" she asked him.

And now it was he who appeared to have lost his tongue, for he was silent, and she, feeling the security of solid ground under her feet, threw at him, "I'm sorry, but I must have misinterpreted your intentions . . . " she stopped, and, biting her lip, couldn't continue.

"But not as much as I misinterpreted yours," he said. "Why did you let me go so far?"

Rosaleen, embarrassed, choked out at him, "Where did I let you go? I kissed you. I thought that's what you wanted me to do."

Colin's eyes softened somewhat, as he looked down at her, and realizing that he had definitely made a mistake, tried to iron things out. "Look, so alright, you're not the bird I took you for . . . "

Rosaleen looked at him with something in her eyes that wasn't at all familiar to him, and her voice stung him through the darkness. "Bird?" she said, angrily. "What's a bird? A bird is something that flies. You better look again, mister, because I'm no bird. Next time you want a bird go to the park, I'm sure you'll be lucky enough to catch one of the pigeons."

With this, she pushed past him and ran down the street. But, as she ran, the emotions that had been tied up behind her eyes all night finally broke loose, and bursting with the force of a dam, they blinded her to where she was going and caused her to stop.

Coming to a big gable wall, that was a block from her house, she turned to it, and, as though it had arms to hold her and ears to hear her, she took comfort in it by laying her face against its big, stone bosom, finding its coldness a balm to her steaming cheek, and crying tears from the heart, she poured its secrets into the structure, where they'd be lost forever. She then ran the remaining block and into the house.

7

ALTHOUGH she was determined never to set eyes on Colin Murdoch again, Rosaleen was persuaded to go to the Hibs with Ann and Phyllis the following Tuesday night. But she was sorry she did. Because, instead of being confronted by Colin, she found him with a girl — a good-looking, long ponytailed blonde, with whom he not only danced every dance, but sat out with throughout all the intervals in between, and he was completely oblivious to Rosaleen even being there.

Feeling miserable, Rosaleen went through the entire evening with a variety of partners, her misery relieved only by Jimmy Reed who, when not dancing with Phyllis, spent some of his own free time away from the record box giving her jiving lessons. And later, she and Ann and Phyllis went with him to Pocky Moloccos. Grabbing the last booth before the biggest part of the crowd came in, they gave their orders to the little, dark-haired waitress.

Phyllis and Ann left Rosaleen and Jimmy to go to the confectioners on the corner for cigarettes, and Jimmy, going to put money in the juke-box, returned to join Rosaleen, where the two of them were alone.

Looking at him, as he sat down across the table from her, she smiled,

"They just can't keep you off the job, can they, Jimmy?" Jimmy gave her a wide grin and then, leaning across the table to talk above the noise of the crowd, he asked her, a serious tone in his voice.

"What's with you and the 'big Ted'? Did he get his walking papers already?" Rosaleen sensed the ominous tone in his last word, which brought a slight blush to her cheeks, and she looked away.

"Too rough on you?" Jimmy asked, and his words, on account of their bluntness, forced her to look at him, and he saw the answer to his question in her eyes. There was an embarrassed silence between them as he preoccupied himself with an imaginary spot on the table. "Ah, well, he has a reputation for

115

that sort of thing." Rosaleen threw him a quick look.

"What do you mean by 'that sort of thing'?"

"Well, he's well-known amongst the ladies. It goes without saying, that he has them wrapped around his finger, if you get my meaning."

"And that blonde?" Rosaleen asked, without looking at him. "Who is she, his number one?"

"Thirty-eight's more like his number." Jimmy told her. "But, you know, love, I think that that big fellow's lost on . . . " Ann and Phyllis, returning with the cigarettes, cut him short, and, as Ann passed them round, Rosaleen took one, glad of the diversion.

Someone had been keeping the juke-box well supplied and the place was jumping with one record after another. The waitress brought their orders, and while they were eating, Jimmy had a proposition for them.

"Why don't you all come to the Clonard picture-house on Thursday night. You know, the Hib crowd takes over the entire pit every Monday and

Thursday. I guarantee you'll all get a good laugh." Deciding there and then, all three agreed to go, and in the middle of it all, the door opened and a little fellow with a black, curly-topped DA and dressed immaculately in a black suit, white shirt and black string-tie entered and the whole place burst into applause, and the fellow, bowing from the waist, then walked to the counter midst cat-calls and whistles.

"That's 'wee' Andy," Jimmy told the girls. "King of the rock n' rollers, second only to Elvis. Wait till you see *him* jiving," he threw at Rosaleen.

Thursday night the girls went to the local picture-house and met Jimmy, and Rosaleen, seeing the pit crowd up with the now-familiar faces, while the back-stalls and balcony remained empty, could understand why. The noise was almost deafening and the majority of the crowd, rather than being permanently seated, chose, instead, to walk around, continuously changing seats, as though it were one big game of musical chairs. She and the others had seats in the side aisle, herself next to Ann, who was seated next

117

to Phyllis, who was seated next to Jimmy, their location far removed from most of the central action, something for which Rosaleen was glad.

The show, about to start, began first with a cartoon, which brought cheering, stomping and loud whistling from the audience. Sitting there in the dark, her thoughts anywhere but on the screen, Rosaleen was startled to see Colin's unmistakable frame silhouetted against the light from the projector as he passed down the middle aisle, and, as if her thumping heart needed any confirmation, a loud-voiced girl, sitting in the middle of a row several feet in front of her, called out to him that there were empty seats beside her and her mates. One of Colin's companions, stopping to check it out, shouted back at her.

"Aye, an' I can see why." At this half the theatre pit exploded into laughter. Then, apparently unable to find suitable 'seats' in the centre aisle, Colin and his mates came up the side on which Rosaleen and the others were sitting and just two rows in front of them, his second mate stopped, and cupping his mouth with his hand, he yelled into the darkness,

"Hey, Susie!" And a girl's voice replied,

"Yes?" and loud enough for even the people in the balcony to hear, he yelled,

"Are you wearing any knickers tonight?" and again the place went into an uproar.

Glad of the darkness, Rosaleen felt her face burning. Suddenly, from behind them, a middle-aged, uniformed usher came charging with a brightly shining flashlight. Apparently incensed by the behaviour, he hurried to get the trouble-makers seated, and, much to Rosaleen's chagrin, he shone his flashlight down her row.

"Alright, alright now, move along there!" he called out, ushering his beam in such a manner as though it could actually shift people from their seats to the empty ones further along the row. And, as several people did him the obligation of moving, Rosaleen saw that it was Colin who was first into the row, which meant, that when she moved, he would be seated next to her. Seeing no way out of her predicament, she didn't know what to do about it. But, the problem resolved itself, for, as the usher's light fell on Rosaleen, Colin remarked,

"Forget it, Barney, we've already seen this one," and he left through the side exit-door, his mates in tow.

Rosaleen, Ann and Phyllis went to the Hibs that Friday night, and Jimmy Reed, having some free time before the crowd came in, took Rosaleen into the corner to teach her the 'passing technique' in jiving. Practically obsessed with this form of dancing, which was responsible for bringing her back to the Hibs more than anything else, she particularly enjoyed these sessions with Jimmy, and she was really beginning to get the hang of all that he was teaching her. And, now, she felt the rhythm strongly take hold of her and the faster the music, the faster Jimmy's feet moved, encouraging her to quicken her own pace. Then, before she realized what was happening, a third person joined them, and looking with wonderment from his feet to his face, Rosaleen saw that it was 'wee' Andy. Yet, expert that he was, he set his pace to hers, for he no doubt saw the earnestness of her efforts.

Now, as they were well into the steps, Jimmy unobtrusively stepped out and left Rosaleen strictly to Andy. Soon the circle of onlookers widened, but Rosaleen was unaware of everything except her partner, her feet, and the beat that was synchronizing their steps; she didn't see Colin Murdoch and his mates come to the edge of the crowd, only to disappear just before the record ended.

Everyone applauded when they'd finished and Rosaleen knew that it was for Andy's benefit and not hers, for he was surrounded by his 'fans' while Jimmy alone came to her side.

"He's terrific, Jimmy." Rosaleen beamed, "You were right."

"You didn't do too bad yourself, Rosie. I bet with a bit more practice you could probably be a partner of his in the jiving contest."

"Aye, in about ten years," she laughed, flushed and perspiring, and Jimmy handed her his handkerchief.

"Here, I'll get it later. I have to get up in the box before Leo up there ties himself in knots."

Standing with Ann and Phyllis and still

glowing in the after-effects of dancing with Andy, Rosaleen saw him throw her a nod from the not-yet crowded floor, and handing Jimmy's handkerchief to Phyllis, she went to join him.

Rosaleen had taken an instant liking to Andy and she soon learned that he had more than one admiral quality for he now spoke to her in a serious tone.

"You did great back there, love. But, always remember, a good dancer never looks at his feet. It's alright to look at your partner's . . . " Somehow his words grew reminiscent of her old Irish dancing teacher, who had been a stickler on that very point. " . . . but it's a definite rule, a good jiver never looks at his own feet. Now, in that one step . . . "

"I'll tell you what, love," he told her, as the record came to an end, "A couple of the mates'll be here tomorrow night, bein' Saturday's jivin' night, an' all. I'll get them to take you around. That'll give you your jivin' legs."

Rosaleen saw very little of Colin Murdoch that night, in fact, she wouldn't even have known if he was there if Ann hadn't told her. Although she did become aware, that, despite everything, she was looking out for him. But once she saw him in the company of two distasteful companions, she put him out of her mind for the rest of the night. But it was with great difficulty that she tried to avoid eye contact with him, for, on one occasion, while she was dancing, she came upon him unexpectedly. He was standing in a corner, other than the one she was used to seeing him in, and he was with another fellow, an older one, one of the A.O.H. men, and they seemed engrossed in deep conversation, seemingly, with the older fellow doing most of the talking, and Colin, standing with his arms folded across his chest, gave her the full benefit of his gaze, as she came towards him. She saw the sparkle take birth the minute their eyes met, and, although she looked away almost immediately, she could still feel his eyes on her and she was aware of the effect he had on her; and, then, again she saw him, when they were both dancing. Trying to avoid looking at him, she felt his presence to be even more disturbing, for he was too close for comfort. She felt him tower over her, almost threateningly, as though his very nearness could command that she look at him, and so she shut him out by closing her eyes. But, even then, as he and his partner passed by, she overheard the girl say something, which was followed by a very insinuating giggle,

"Oh, Colin!" All of which convinced her that it had been strictly her imagination that he'd been purposely watching her, and a kind of grief settled in on her.

Therefore, it was a tremendous shock to her to feel a hand on her arm for the next to last dance and to turn and see him. Wishing that none of this were happening the way it was, she, nonetheless, went to the dance-floor with him. And now, with the determination not to let him rattle her one bit, it was still very hard not to feel some response, not only in his mere presence, but even more in his arms.

Feeling a bit weak at the knees, Rosaleen kept up her resolve and was proudly and safely home free as she walked away from him at the end of the dance. But just as she reached the door, she felt him once more take her arm, and drawing her into the corner and away from the crowd, he looked earnestly into her face. Rosaleen's heart started doing strange things again, as she never expected ever being with him eye to eye again.

"I'd like to take you home," he said, his hand taking a somewhat firmer hold on her arm. "Let's leave now before the rush." Not believing that she was hearing right, Rosaleen said to him,

"You want to take me home? What for? A repeat performance of last Sunday night? No thank you," and she walked away from him. But he pulled her back a second time, only now his grip was stronger, and when he looked at her, his eyes were cold and his voice distant.

"What performance?" He pulled her closer yet, until her face was next to his own. "Don't make me laugh, you don't even know what the word means. But, then, again, how could you, when you're not a woman yet, baby." He spat the last word at her, the tone of which surprised her with its impact, and she knew he didn't mean it endearingly.

Rosaleen took his hand and removed it

from her arm as though she'd just been contaminated, and, then, looking up into his face, she told him,

"You might as well know this now. I don't go with boys who are only out for one thing," and leaving him standing alone in the corner, oblivious that others had heard, and were looking at them, she got her coat from the cloakroom and fled the Hibs; once more the tears blinding her way until she got to the comfort of her own street.

Almost reluctant to go to the Hibs that Saturday night, she eventually did so at the last minute. She and Ann, jiving in the corner beyond sight of the dance-floor was not enough to perk up Rosaleen's spirits and there was a disinterested expression on her face, but, which soon vanished as soon as Andy came towards them, along with two others.

"This is the wee girl I was telling you about," he told the others, as he threw Rosaleen a nod. Then, moving his head towards the fellow on his right, "This here's 'Dirty Eyes'," and with a nod to the left, "and this is Manuel."

'Dirty Eyes' was a big brute of a fellow, though not so much in height as in muscle and brawn. There was a slight suspicion of a broken nose, which, rather than detracting from the rest of his less than tough, good-looking features, especially his eyes, which, although narrow, were very deep brown and the exact same shade as his thick, beautiful hair, which managed to convey the popular style, but without a trace of grease to take away from its rich, natural lustre, provided the necessary ingredient to his otherwise gentle face.

The other boy, Manuel, had the darkest eyes that Rosaleen had ever seen. They were coal-black with a deep fierceness, which disappeared as soon as he opened his mouth to the nicest smile she had ever received, and she knew then what was meant by the expression 'teeth like pearls'. As she returned the acknowledgement with a half-shy smile herself, 'wee' Andy continued.

"She has the basics as far as jiving itself goes; what she needs to learn is hand control, she's way off on that, but, as far as holding her own to the beat itself, I'd say she has that goin' for her more than anybody I've ever seen," — a remark which drew a look of amazement from Rosaleen herself. "She has a good ear, so concentrate on that. Now let me see," he said, pausing, turning his eyes on Rosaleen in a way that made it seem possible that he could gather inventory on her just by looking at her. "I think that's it," he said and in a manner that made her feel like she was his pet protégé, and that he was reluctant to hand her over until making absolutely sure that those taking over from him knew exactly that what they were supposed to do was to be of valuable consequences to her. "Aye . . . " he said, obviously satisfied with his conclusions, " . . . just run through every step you know. The learning of them will be the easiest, since it's all memory. The rest is just practice, so see she gets plenty." With this last statement, he went off without so much as a word or a nod, and, as he disappeared into the crowd, 'Dirty Eyes', making the first move, closed in, and Manuel held his hand out to Ann.

During the next to last dance, and

dancing now to a slow number with Jimmy Reed, Rosaleen rested her forehead against the coolness of his cheek, and with her last bit of remaining strength, submitted the entire burden of her weight over to him, for she was that tired after her strenuous workout. Her eyes closed, and lulled now to the soothing melody, and seemingly floating along with the notes that made it so. Rosaleen was suddenly mindful of the fact that Colin Murdoch had not been an unnecessary distraction to her during the course of the night. Apart from the mood she had been suffering from in the beginning, she had worked up a determination not to give him a second thought, and she hadn't; well hardly: and she purposely hadn't looked for him, for two reasons: First of all, going on the assumption that he was out with Blondie, it being Saturday, and all, she'd rather not look for his absence, which would only verify it; and secondly, if he were there, he was more likely to be with her, and so, preferring not to seek his presence accompanied by hers, she simply took it upon herself to completely concentrate on what she had to do, which she more than halfway accomplished.

"What do you think of 'Dirty Eyes'?" Rosaleen heard Jimmy ask, his voice breaking into her mood.

"Fabulous," she said, her own voice erupting from her melancholy of thought, and then brightening to the memory of him. "He's a marvellous dancer, Jimmy. Moves like his name should be Achilles, though, instead of 'Dirty Eyes'. How'd he ever get a name like that anyhow?"

"Ho, ho! Dancin's not the only thing 'Dirty Eyes' does well. Don't let that baby-face fool you for a minute. He has the same kind of co-ordination in his fists as he does in his feet, which, by the way, he probably learned in the street. As fast as he'd give you a kind look, he'd give you a boot that would ruin you for life." Rosaleen listened intently, as Jimmy continued. "And very moody. Jesus, never be the first to look his way, always wait and see what he does first. He has a whole lot of different talents in him. You see, he thinks that he's a whole lot of different people, like actors, for instance, you know what I mean? For a while there he thought he was James Dean, you know, sullen and silent, nobody could get through to him, not even his old lady, God help her, her with her bad ticker, an' all. Then came that film with Richard Widmark; the one where he pushes the old cripple down the stairs, wheelchair, an' all? Well, one day, a neighbour's kid was cryin' and didn't shut up for a half an hour, or more. So what does 'Dirty Eyes' do? Takes the friggin' pram and shakes the kid out into the street. The kid's mother runs out an' there's 'Dirty Eyes' grinnin' from ear to ear, pleased as punch with himself, as if he'd done his good deed for the day. Now he's in his Brando mood," Jimmy continued, stopping only to draw his breath. "Nothin' you can do right now'll get to him, unless you plan on corruptin' the dockers; 'Dirty Eyes' works on the docks, and ever since he saw 'On The Waterfront', he's very big on fightin' labour control."

Choking back the laughter, accepting everything that Jimmy was telling her without question, Rosaleen smothered her outburst in his shoulder until she was able to subdue herself. But it was several minutes before she was able to bring herself to look at him without falling back into convulsions.

"Jimmy!" she retorted finally, saying his name aloud in purposeful reproach, and then, when she could bring at least a half normal tone to her voice, she said, "But isn't there something else I can call him besides 'Dirty Eyes'? I'd feel like I was making fun of him, or something."

Jimmy gave her a long, hard look before answering,

"You want to call him Francis?"

Enjoying a cigarette in the solitude of the ladies room, while the last dance was in progress, and feeling greatly relieved from the misery with which she'd entered the Hibs, Rosaleen couldn't help but feel somewhat elated now. Recounting to herself the very pleasurable experiences she had had during the course of the night, and yet, exhausting as these experiences had been, she knew that she had learned more in those few short hours from her two very proficient teachers than she could have had otherwise from six months of successive mediocre partners.

Crushing the end of her cigarette in the lone ashtray, she went downstairs to get her coat and Ann's, as Phyllis had already left with Jimmy. Putting on her coat, and with Ann's draped across her arm, she stood alone in the darkened doorway, her frame enhanced by the light from the hall behind her, she waited for the last dance to end.

Whether it was listening to the music, or feeling the wistfulness of the atmosphere, which the last dance always created for her and filled her with a certain sadness, or seeing the dancers, moving like shadows within the embrace of the darkness, something touched Rosaleen and evoked the deep-down yearning that had been buried within her all night. And now, as it slowly surfaced, it swept up to encompass her with all its force and filled her with a great longing to see Colin Murdoch.

Suddenly, from the corner around the doorway, which was out of sight to Rosaleen, came a remark that affected her the way a stream of water effects a fire when aimed purposely.

"Jesus Christ! They're lettin' them in

younger by the minute. Next thing you know, they'll be comin' with their f . . . . babysitters."

Agitated not so much by what was said, as by the way it was said, for she being the only one there and the obvious target, Rosaleen took a step around the doorway to see who had said it, and why. But, immediately upon doing so, she was sorry she took the trouble, for it was none other than Colin's companions, and she had to go and give them the pleasure of letting them know that she had heard them. Having no appropriate response for the one who had spoken, and not even knowing which one of them had said it, Rosaleen abruptly left them to their corner and walked out into the hallway, a little beyond where she'd been standing before.

Apparently getting their jollies, and with Rosaleen herself having seemingly paved their way, they came prying for more.

"I don't know why that should bother you, Bopper," one of them said, "After all, you an' me were ten-bob richer on Sunday night. Murdoch thought he'd a 'good thing' on his hands, but what a joke that turned out to be."

Stunned by the words, yet unable to walk away from them, Rosaleen waited for their sniding to subside, and with heart thumping, and choosing her words carefully and in a very pronounced tone, she addressed the one who had just spoken.

"I hope that you spent that ten-shillings very carefully, because it will be the hardest earned money either of you will ever see," and, then to the other one, "You know, when you sidled around that door, there, you looked like something that had just crawled out of the wood-work, and I would have stepped on you, only I don't like taking advantage of any creature smaller than myself."

Turning away, Rosaleen felt the blood pounding against her cheeks, and trying to keep the lump in her throat in place, at least until she got out of the Hibs, she almost ran head-long into a girl who had been leaning against the doorway entrance to the small billiard room down the hall and listening to the verbal exchange taking place a few feet away.

135

Rosaleen mumbled an apology and the girl stepped aside to let her pass, giving her a wink and a grin that was from ear to ear, as she did so.

Rosaleen didn't go to the Hibs the following night, even though it was her last free evening before the spring term started, even against the persuasion of both Phyllis and Ann.

8

MONDAY saw Rosaleen back at school and, as if her mood wasn't bad enough, her class had to start right in with preparations for the Junior Exam. One teacher, who thought she was being helpful, brought in a pile of old exam-papers dating back some five years, and Rosaleen groaned inwards, as she was given two of them to be completed by the weekend. Believing this to be an impossible task, she couldn't see how she was going to get through them, because she couldn't shake her thoughts of Colin, nor the memory of his kisses; no matter what he appeared to be, Rosaleen was hopelessly attracted to him. Still, ironically enough, she was finished with the exam-papers by Thursday, which pleased her form-room teacher, but which caused no end of teasing from Mary and Kay in the lunch-room that day.

"See! Didn't I tell you," Mary started

off, "she spent her entire Easter holidays cramming, only to start the term off with a bang, and here I am (yawn) still making excuses for Tuesday's homework," she said, as though in a determined effort to stay awake. "Mother warned me that sooner or later my social life would catch up with me, and, you know," she said, stifling another yawn, 'she was so.o.o ri.g.h.t . . . ' and she broke off, as her head started to nod. Kay laughed and Rosaleen grimaced to herself, for she knew that, in truth, she did cram a lot of studying, but only since the past Monday, and she didn't deserve any medals, for it was the only way she could find that would help her stop thinking about Colin Murdoch. In fact, the only relief she permitted herself from her studies was to talk for a while with Ann and Phyllis the night before, when they informed her that Colin hadn't been to the Hibs on Sunday night, but, that he had shown up just before the last dance, alone, but had left almost immediately. He had been there on Tuesday night with his mates, but had spent most of the night talking to John, the A.O.H. man, and just standing by the door, watching the dancers in general, and he had left early.

Now with all the extra studying that Rosaleen had been faced with, together with the regular homework, which had gotten a lot heavier since returning after the holidays, she knew only too well that she'd have to get out of the house by the end of the week, and knowing that Phyllis had a date with Jimmy, she asked Ann if she wanted to go to the Plaza on Friday night.

The Plaza in downtown Belfast was far different, not only from the Hibs, but from every other night spot in the city for that matter. A huge palatial-like building, its interior was breathtakingly beautiful to someone who had never been in the midst of such splendour. Its deep, rich, gold-carpeted corridors led to pink-lavender powder rooms, with lush purple rugs, which spread lavishly from wall to wall, and to a ballroom that was every dancer's dream.

The dance-floor itself was sunken about two and a half feet below the level of the rest and was fully separated by wrought-iron balustrades, behind which were dozens and dozens of linen-clad tables, and chairs upholstered in dark-blue velvet. At the furthest end of the ballroom, opposite the main entrances, there was a revolving bandstand which featured a full sixteen-piece orchestra and, when it reversed, at forty-five minute intervals, a jazz trio. In the area behind the bandstand was the famous EL MOMBO ROOM, with its refreshments of soft drinks, coffee, tea, American sandwiches and Continental pastries.

People from all walks of life patronized the Plaza; shop-assistants, professional people, factory and office workers; and all the naval uniforms of Danish, Dutch and German sailors, along with those of the three branches of the American service, gave it an international flavour, which fascinated Rosaleen, visiting it for the first time.

Overcoming her initial trepidation, she started right in to enjoy herself, at least up to a point, and, after a succession of dance partners, among them a young, talkative fellow, with a clipped British accent, a black West-Indian, who was a purser on one of the sailing vessels docked in the harbour and a German, who couldn't speak a word of English, she felt a good deal relaxed and could hardly wait to see who and what the next dance would bring.

Directly behind her, seated at one of the tables, Ann was doing her best to convince a young man from Istanbul, who was a pre-med student at Queen's University that she didn't intend going up to his rooms for Irish stew made with curried rice and shish kebab. It was all Rosaleen could do to keep from bursting out laughing. So, when she felt a hand on her elbow, instead of turning to see who her prospective partner was, as she ordinarily did, she walked to the dance-floor without looking around, just in case she should catch sight of Ann with her intended dinner date-cum-chef.

Walking ahead, Rosaleen led the way to the very centre of the floor, well out of sight of both the tables and Ann, and then she turned to face the man who had followed her there. Now, as she did so, her heart stopped beating in her breast and leapt wildly to her throat, for it was none other than Colin Murdoch.

Too stunned to protest, she stared up at him, too helpless to do anything else, and, as he put an arm around her and drew her near, she closed her eyes against the onrushing emotions that were galloping from the pit of her stomach to her head. Without a word, not even an acknowledgement of any kind to her, he led her slowly through the dance, as though they had only just met.

Feeling his hand on her back, his fingers touching hers, her forehead resting against his jaw, all of her former anger was reduced to a certain shyness, the kind which she had only experienced since first meeting him. And, now, there was no other place in the world for her, but here; no other time, but now; no other person, but him. And so she was; completely wrapped up in emotions that only he could create, she couldn't even find the right words to say to him, and, contrary to the pain he had brought her, it was far exceeded by the joy she now felt, and she wanted to look at him, see his eyes, his sparkle, his smile; and she wanted him to look at her, and yet, she knew if that were to happen right then and there, he would see everything she felt for him right there in her eyes. But before she could let that happen, she would first have to hear him say something: words, which would make it alright, that it was her he wanted to be with, for herself; not for anything else. She wanted him to take her aside, right there, in the midst of all this splendour, and speak softly to her, to reassure her of a good relationship between them; one in which love had time to grow, time to flourish, and time to bloom; not one that was to be plucked at the first sign of fragrance — for then it was too soon, too fragile, too delicate, all of which would cause it to wilt before it had time to gain sustenance.

This was the song in her heart, when, suddenly, the whole ballroom was cast in darkness. At first, Rosaleen was startled, but then it became like a fairyland to her, because through the darkness came the glow of coloured lights and she saw the bandstand like a huge rainbow in a darkened sky. Then, above their heads, a big glittering ball started to revolve and it caught the dancers below in a shower of falling stars, as though they were being

143

scattered from the heavens themselves.

Turning to share all of this with Colin, she suddenly felt his lips pressing down on hers in a kiss that was long and hard on her mouth. For the moment Rosaleen could only accept what he was giving her, she wasn't aware of what she was giving him in return, and, when he pulled her closer to him, it was closer, much closer than she had ever been to him, or to any man, and she abruptly pulled away.

Thankful that the lights had come back on, even though they had just returned to their mellow glow, and trying to look as though she had been unaffected by the whole experience, she looked him straight in the eyes, unaware that her emblazoned cheeks were visible under the soft lights. But Colin Murdoch had a more tender expression, as he looked down into her eyes.

"I didn't know this was going to be a blackout dance, but it was a nice surprise, wasn't it?" Completely taken aback by his flippancy, Rosaleen responded accordingly.

"Who did you take me for there?" she asked him, "One of your blonde fillies?"

Holding her eyes with his own for a second before replying, Rosaleen could see the arrogance build and manifest itself.

"*One* of my blonde fillies?" he asked, apparently amused that she should even be aware that there were any. "There's only one blonde 'filly' in my life," he said, slightly mocking her choice of words, and then he added provocatively, "as far as I know."

"Then why are you playing the field?" Rosaleen flung at him, "Does she know you're here tonight?"

"Look, I don't let anyone keep tabs on me. I go where I please and with whom I please," he told her, his last statement very pronounced, and Rosaleen could see his insolence like sparks in his eyes. "Besides, I came here tonight for one reason and one reason only."

"Oh! And what is that?" she asked.

Starting to say something and then changing his mind, he said, instead,

"Forget it. I already got it," and stalking off, he left Rosaleen in the middle of the floor and, as the last note of music faded, so did the last remaining warmth of her emotions; and her heart, which had recently beaten its way to her throat and her temples, was now back in its normal place, performing its normal function, only now it felt cold and hard in her breast, just like the once revolving ball above her head, its previous glitter now sadly suspended in cold, brittle stillness.

9

BACK at school on Monday morning, Rosaleen threw herself fully into her studies and instead of permitting her thoughts to slip into silent reveries of Colin, to which she had previously submitted, she stopped them short and allowed nothing nor none of him to slip through the shell that was starting to build around her memories: nothing got in and nothing got out, and, as the days passed, she knew that she could take that shell and bury it in the sands of time, where it would remain forever.

However; coming home from school that Saturday at noon, and taking a usual seat on the upper deck of the bus, a girl, several years older than Rosaleen, with a DA and long, dangling earrings, took the seat directly behind her. Lighting a cigarette and about to throw the match out of the upper part of the window, she caught Rosaleen's reflection in the glass, and withdrawing her hand and looking at her profile, just to make sure, she tapped her on the shoulder.

"Hey, aren't you the one that goes to the Hibs?" she asked Rosaleen, "the one Colin Murdoch was chasing for a while?" Without moving, Rosaleen turned her head just enough to see that it was the same girl she had bumped into her last night at the Hibs. "I haven't seen you there for a while," the girl continued. "I hope you didn't let those big galoots that Colin hangs around with stop you from coming back." Rosaleen threw her a weak smile over her shoulder and shook her head, though not too convincingly, and then, she said,

"I . . . it's just that I've been too busy . . . too much studying lately." The girl stuck her head over the seat and saw that Rosaleen was wearing a school uniform.

"Shit! You're just a kid, a schoolgirl!" she exclaimed. "Though I have to say I liked the way you handled yourself that night," and she tapped a finger into Rosaleen's shoulder, as if to congratulate her. "I don't know what that was all about that night, but, knowing them, I have a pretty good idea, and by the looks on their faces, I could see that they'd been taken down a peg or two." Hesitating to inhale, she then asked, unexpectedly, but in a tone that implied she already knew the answer, "Did it have to do with you and Murdoch?" Then, sensing that she had hit a raw nerve, she got up out of her seat and went in beside Rosaleen and she spoke to her with a voice that was touchingly tender for a girl who displayed such a tough exterior. "Look, there's nothing that you can tell me that would surprise me. I've been around their type all my life, and, believe me, they think they're tough nuts to crack, and Murdoch's the toughest of all, for the main reason that to get to him directly, you first have to shovel away the shit that he surrounds himself with, namely them turds you told off that night. But them, they're nothin', they have no skin on their faces, they bounce back like their own friggin' rubber balls that make them think they're God's gift to women — heaven forbid. But Murdoch," she gave Rosaleen a long side-glance, "he's different. Tough as hell to penetrate, but, when that happens, just stand back and watch. I know," she added, "I've been living next door to him all my life."

Rosaleen was silent throughout the whole thing. They were the first positive words she had heard so far concerning Colin's character; apart, that is, from the opinions that she herself had formed about him in the beginning. But she was not about to reveal these to anyone, least of all to the girl next door to him, and, who probably saw him every day of her life.

Giving the girl a watery smile to show her that she had at least been hearing, if not heeding, everything she'd said, she then announced that the next stop was hers, and after the girl swung her knees out into the aisle to let her pass, she looked up at Rosaleen with a total look of earnestness on her face.

"You're only a wee bit of a thing, and there's not much to you, but then," she added, holding up the dead match, "I could've said the same thing about this match before I struck it."

Several weeks went by and the pressure of meeting her academic levels kept mounting, with Rosaleen devoting all her time to her studies, until . . .

"Enough!" Mary had shouted, and, on their way downtown to a Friday night film, she added, "I have had it! I told myself that I was taking this weekend off, and you!" she said, stopping and flinging a hand in Rosaleen's direction, "Look at you," she exclaimed, and, in mock dramatics, and with an American southern accent, she went into one of her acts. "You're nothin', but skin and bones. They're killin' us at that school, Rosalie," and with her hand to her forehead, "wearin' us away to nothin', gettin' too weak to hold even a pencil in our frail little hands," and, then, in her own voice, she said, "And that's why I'm going to buy the biggest and the most expensive box of chocolates they have in this place."

Rosaleen smiled at the antics of her friend, as they joined the already moving queue into the Royal Cinema. Located on the corner of two adjacent streets, with the admission box open to two different queues, the Cinema, a popular weekend spot for young couples, had the unwitting tradition of having its back-stalls

151

monopolized by these courting couples, while all other patrons occupied the front-stalls, and it was this latter queue that the girls joined. Handing Rosaleen the money for her ticket, Mary went over to the concession counter. Approaching the admission box and handing the money over to the girl, it was while she was waiting for the tickets and her change that Rosaleen heard the fellow on the other side of the booth jesting with the other ticket girl, and casually glancing over, she was suddenly surprised to see that the girl he was with was none other than Blondie, Colin's girlfriend.

Somewhat mystified, and wondering what she was doing out with this fellow and not Colin, she went over to join Mary. Standing in the small crowd gathered around the counter, she watched as Blondie and her date crossed the foyer and ascended the small flight of steps which led to the back-stalls.

Having gotten this opportunity to observe Blondie, Rosaleen could understand why Colin Murdoch was attracted to her.

What with her good looks, her great

figure, her way of dressing (her way of walking); what she didn't understand was why, having someone like Blondie, did Colin play the field the way he did. Why did he go out of his way to show a pretended interest in Rosaleen herself, when the only thing he accomplished was that he ended up hurting her? As for Blondie, if she had attracted Colin enough for him to want to go out with her, and the way Rosaleen understood it, for a couple to go openly to the Hibs together was considered more than just casual dating, which she took to mean, then, that the couple had a steady relationship, why, then, couldn't Blondie hold him? And who else, if not she, would be able to? Why was it that she was out with someone else tonight? And, Rosaleen thought to herself, was he? And she wondered just what kind of game they were playing.

Sitting there in the dark of the theatre, Rosaleen found her thoughts shifting more and more from what was going on on the screen to Colin. It was the first conscious thought she had permitted herself since that night she had encountered him at the Plaza, which was not to say that she hadn't thought of him at all, for there was always the unexpectedness of becoming aware that he was very much present on her mind, and that's when she'd shut him out. But now her feelings about him were taking a slightly different turn, for she was just really becoming aware of the ways in which people play around with one another's feelings and, God knows, Colin Murdoch, who didn't have any genuine ones of his own, had gotten the better of her's up until now. And, so it was, then, that these new feelings for him were the kind that came as a result of resentment, which, blended with a little anger, produced a need for resolvement that were spurred on by the resolution that things couldn't continue the way they had been.

Coming out of the Cinema and after being thoroughly entertained by 'The King and I', Mary and Rosaleen pushed all thoughts of school from their minds. Saturday classes had been cancelled in honour of the Mother Prioress's feast day, and tonight, being Friday, was merely a

154

prelude to the weekend, which meant, for Mary, sleeping late, an all-night party, and, to wind it all up, a date with a fellow she had been dying to go out with for the longest time; for Rosaleen, it spelt excitement, along with a couple of old scores to settle.

10

DOWNTOWN shopping in Belfast was a treat for anyone, anytime. What with the many large department stores and the arcades, with their row upon row of smaller, more intimate lingerie salons and shops selling tailored clothes. And, then, there were the monumental landmarks of the city itself — Belfast's selective shoe shops, which stood in prominence on every downtown city block.

For Rosaleen, Saturday morning downtown shopping was a rarity, because going to school six days a week hadn't left her much free time for Saturday shopping sprees, and she knew that she was going to enjoy this one. For not only was she buying some new clothes, but she was shopping with a certain someone in mind; perhaps it might even be safe to say that she was buying for herself, but that she'd be shopping with Colin Murdoch's eye.

Taking the bus downtown, Ann, paying the fares, asked the conductor for two tickets to Smithfield. As much as the centre of Belfast was a metropolis for the avid shopper, there was a perimeter between it and the Falls Road that was a haven for the ardent browser, and this area was known as Smithfield.

Composed mainly of one long, wide street, with several shorter, narrower streets cutting into it from both sides, Smithfield was devoted to novelty shops stocked with all sorts of magic tricks and illusions, antique shops, spilling out into the street and filling the pavements with all sorts of imaginary merchandise. There were also lots of fruit stands, flower carts, comic and magazine stalls and, last but not least, its first and best attraction — its record shops.

One after another filled an entire area and each with its own sound system reached the public with its musical speciality. For instance, one shop dealt chiefly in jazz records (progressive, percussion and modern) and displayed the talents of Ella Fitzgerald, Sarah Vaughn and Duke Ellington; another, selling only country music, had every star on record that ever came out of The Grand Ole Opry, while another dealt strictly in Irish music — authentic and traditional, as well as the stuff imported from abroad; another still would be pushing the big-band era, with such notables as Woody Herman, Stan Kenton, Glenn Miller, Tommy and Jimmy Dorsey, and, hanging in there with the kings of swing, none other than the one and only, unflappable Victor Sylvester.

Yet, within this megalopolis of the music world, the record shops which took precedence over all the others were those in the majority that catered first and foremost to the rock and roll crowds. It was almost impossible to get into these shops without pushing and shoving since there were top-tune lists, top of the pop indexes and top-twenty charts posted in the windows and up-dated frequently and to which the youth flocked and watched as carefully as though it were the stock market instead of a record mart. And then there were others who just came to listen to the music, or to just hang around, and these young gangs, mainly

Teddy Boys, lounged in front of the record shops all Saturday long, buying fruit from the vendors, watching the female shoppers and just hanging about the place in general.

But, as maddening as Smithfield could get some days, this day was a special one for the record fans; a new record had just been released, and the American top-twenty chart had just been replaced for the third time that day, and the record shops, having given up trying to keep their own up-to-date lists posted, soon discarded them altogether. The crowds were going wild, especially since the record that was causing all the commotion was played every time a sale was made, with all the rock and roll shops running neck and neck, each one overlapping the other in what had been the greatest record-breaker of nineteen-fifty-six, the one that was responsible for pushing Presley's 'Heartbreak Hotel' down to number two on the charts — Elvis's 'Hound Dog'.

It was into this sort of madness that Ann and Rosaleen got off the bus to start their shopping-spree — the first item on

Ann's list being the new record. And, not only were they hit with it as they entered Smithfield, but the song followed them all over town; it was playing everywhere. For starters, Rosaleen went with Ann to buy a brassiere. After they were shown into a little private fitting room, the shop-assistant closed the door, and Ann, changing modestly into the bra, asked Rosaleen to hook the back for her. But before Rosaleen got the chance to do so, they both heard a man's baritone voice within very close hearing range, and singing the new hit. Exchanging glances, Rosaleen shrugged her shoulders, unable to detect where the singing was coming from. Suddenly, the bottom half of the window was pushed up from the outside, and a man's hairy hand reached in, clutching a chamois. Screaming at the top of her lungs, Ann grabbed the closest thing with which to cover herself — the bottom of Rosaleen's dress. In the wake of Ann's screaming, a young man's bewildered face appeared at the window. Chamois in one hand and comb in the other, he was the living image of Elvis Presley.

160

While this phenomenon sent Rosaleen into pure hysterics, it caused her to abandon everything, except the illusion that had appeared at the window. Then the half-naked Ann, who was trying to hold the bra in place with one hand, and with her sweater in the other, began hitting the window-washer's hand, which was now resting on the forsaken job at hand.

Amidst all of this screaming, the shop-assistant came running in, grabbed the gray drapes on the window and quickly shut out the grinning, cheeky-faced youth, saying reproachfully to Ann, as though she herself had invited the incident and was therefore responsible for her own plight,

"These are supposed to remain closed at all times," and, with another disapproving look that included Rosaleen, she left the room.

And later, in Woolworth's, where the girls were having tea, 'Hound Dog' was blaring into the upstairs tea-room, and, upon finishing, and leaving by way of the Ann Street exit, they passed the record corner, which was jam-packed with young customers, some of them so carried away by Elvis they were even dancing in the aisles.

And much later, in one of the very sedate shoe shops, where Ann, who was trying on a pair of high-heels and was being assisted by a very respectable young lady in the uniform of shop-assistant black, walked down the shop to the full-length mirror at the other end, the squeaky newness of the leather against the thick, rich carpeting being the only noise that penetrated the stillness. Suddenly as if the quietness itself had triggered a latent reaction to the earlier episode in the lingerie shop, or whether it was due to the fact that she'd been hearing the song all day and it was all pent up inside her, playing nowhere but in her head, Ann let loose with "You ain't never caught a rabbit and you ain't no friend of mine,"; right there in the

'MESSRS. SAXON'S ROYAL AVENUE ESTABLISHMENT OF BRITISH FOOTWEAR LIMITED'

This entire staff of shop assistants were startled out of their starched, white collars, and one matron patron was so shocked that her gold-rimmed spectacles fell to the edge of her nose and the foot that she was about to put into a very expensive shoe went into the empty shoe-box instead, which caused Ann to remark, in passing,

"Aye, that seems to be a better fit, missus."

Rosaleen was mortified and stood by deeply embarrassed while Ann told the shop assistant that she thought their shoes were too old fashioned and that they should bring their entire stock up to date. And once outside, Rosaleen chided her for her behaviour, to which Ann replied,

"I couldn't help myself, Rosie. Honest to God, I just couldn't help it." And when she saw Rosaleen turn away, trying to suppress a smile, Ann, not one to waste an opportune moment to get a laugh, nudged Rosaleen with her elbow, and, then, she started throwing her meaningful glances out from the corner of her eyes, until Rosaleen, unable to hold it back any longer, broke into convulsive laughter in the middle of Royal Avenue.

Then, Ann, not content to let it rest,

hurried away and left Rosaleen to fend for herself amongst the curious stares of Belfast's Saturday afternoon shoppers.

Both girls, much sobered up after a lunch in one of Fountain Lane's quiet little cafes, made their way over to the London Mantle Warehouse, where Rosaleen tried on and then bought a full, soft, black felt skirt, a pure tweed skirt, with a boxed pleat and a form-fitting, black skirt, with a narrow slit. Retracing their steps through Royal Avenue, they next headed for Peter's Hill and the Shankill Road, where Ann knew of a little shop which stocked the finest selection of cardigans and sweaters.

Shown into a little room at the back of the shop by the friendly little proprietress, the girls found themselves with floor to ceiling shelves filled with boxes upon boxes of every style, size and colour imaginable. Going through several of the boxes which the woman set out for suggestion, Rosaleen finally settled for a fully-fashioned, long-sleeve, turtle-neck sweater, a fine, rose-coloured Prince Charles, which could be worn over a blouse, or could be modestly revealing and worn alone. She also bought an emerald-green v-neck, which Ann insisted must've been made from a mould of her, a black lumber-jacket, and, finally, a white, crew-neck sweater, with raglan sleeves. And, while Rosaleen was paying for her purchases, Ann wasn't a bit backward in telling the woman that she really knew her customers and all of the sweaters looked like they had been made for Rosaleen.

On the way back to the centre of town and upon reaching the bottom of Peter's Hill, Rosaleen looked in the window of an inconspicuous little shoe shop and saw a pair of black, Italian leather high heels, exactly the kind she'd been looking for but had not been able to find.

Now, more than satisfied with her purchases, Ann brought an easy smile to Rosaleen's lips with her dry wit. But, it wasn't dry, and it wasn't witty when she told her,

"You wear one of those sweaters tonight, and with your hair, and all, you'll look so sultry . . . " she broke off, as the thought struck her. "Oh, God," she said, "listen to me, I can't wait to see you all dressed up, but when Colin Murdoch sees you it'll only make him want to undress you."

"Ann!" Rosaleen brought her up short. "That's an awful thing to say," and as Ann tried to make a joke of it, Rosaleen looked away, for she felt the warmth that burned her cheeks flood her entire body and she realized that even in jest, Colin Murdoch had more of an effect on her than he could possibly know; more, in fact, than she could even know herself.

In crossing Royal Avenue, the two girls had become part of a small crowd of pedestrians stopped midway in the wide intersection, due to heavy traffic, and the policeman who detained them there, delayed them even further, allowing the stop-and-go passing of a succession of half a dozen or more buses. The last bus, depositing several passengers onto the pavement before clearing the pedestrian-walk, finally moved off, and Rosaleen, holding back with the others until the policeman blew his whistle, suddenly saw Colin. He was standing on the pavement directly ahead of her so that if she were to make a straight line for the curb, she'd walk right into him. But then she saw that he wasn't alone, for emerging from the midst of passengers that had just gotten off the bus, was Blondie. Holding her breath, and not wanting to walk into them, Rosaleen was then relieved to see them turn and go up Royal Avenue, but not before Blondie stopped to look in a shop window. Through the plate-glass, as though through a mirror, Rosaleen saw her admiring the mannequins' sweaters, and Colin, obviously finding the live models to be more interesting, intimately hugged Blondie's waist and smiled down at her.

Feeling every bit of her new resolve desert her, Rosaleen was at least glad that Colin hadn't seen her, and they moved off before she reached the pavement, and the last thing from her lips to Ann, before they entered Goorwiches was, "If it's all the same to you, Ann, I'd be just as well off if I wore my school uniform tonight."

11

DESPITE Rosaleen's disappointment of seeing Colin and Blondie together and without knowing why, it was with a quiet feeling of titillating expectancy that she entered the Plaza that same night. The feeling had arisen when she was getting dressed and it was still with her. Now, while she headed for the powder room, she tried to subdue the feeling of climbing anticipation that Colin would be there, and she tried, instead, to concentrate on just having a good time. But, when she took off her coat and saw her reflection in the mirror, she silently wondered if Colin would even recognize her if he were there. Ann had done such an expert job with makeup and a comb, that her hair, which she normally wore loose about her shoulders, was now softly pulled back from her face, both on top and at the sides, which created the effect of a ponytail, its thick, rich, dark tresses hung almost to her waist, all of which, combined with the effect created by her new black felt skirt and her pale-yellow turtle-neck sweater, which did complete justice to her recently developed fullness, gave her second thoughts about whether she wanted Colin Murdoch to be there or not.

But Ann was more than pleased with the results and, as the music drifted in every time the door opened, she persuaded Rosaleen to finally come out into the ballroom.

Just as mesmerized as ever with the whole scene, but before she had a minute to take it all in, Rosaleen was immediately seized by two hands, which seemed to come out of nowhere. It was Tweedy.

"Rosaleen! How are you?" Rosaleen took one look at the face framed above the tweed jacket and practically screamed in delight.

"Tweedy! . . . Grahame! What a surprise to see you here," and taking a step back to look at him and finding no change whatsoever, she exclaimed, "You haven't changed a bit." And he, returning the compliment, told her,

"And neither have you, Rosaleen; the same old two and sixpence."

Completely ignoring Ann, he beamed down at Rosaleen, and taking her by the arm, he led her out onto the floor, even though it was completely deserted.

"Grahame, don't you think we should wait until there are more people on the floor . . . I mean . . . this dance hasn't even started yet."

"Nonsense!" Tweedy told her, and without further ado, signalled the band: and the band, like any collection of musicians anywhere, not expected, nor was it accustomed to starting without the direction of its bandleader, started up immediately.

Those who had witnessed this phenomenon were not only surprised by it, but were also enticed into peals of laughter, which, in a very short time, changed to great admiration, and, as this became audible, it caught the attention of everyone else and brought them forward to watch the performance ringside, until the entire ballroom turned into one massive audience.

Non-plussed, Tweedy performed *par*

excellance, and despite the fact that there were others who also got into the act, the floor belonged to him, and so did the audience. Not to mention the management, who, entrepreneurs that they were, and recognizing an opportunity to shine when they saw one, ordered the lights dimmed and the ball rolling.

Captivated, there were many present who had never before witnessed such a spectacle live before their eyes, and their open admiration was heard again and again, as the dancers were captured under the revolving ball, which emphasized their movements.

Tweedy was in his glory. Acting as though they were alone on a distant planet and taking every advantage of surrounding space, he held Rosaleen as though she were weightless while he, mastering the task of keeping his own two feet on the ground, engaged her in conversation and shut out the rest of the world.

"You know, Rosaleen, if you had been my partner in the Junior Championships we would have won hands down." Rosaleen gave him a disappointed look.

"Oh, Grahame! You didn't win?"

"No, blast it," he told her, "But, I was nearly there. I could feel it right up to the moment that darn girl lost a shoe. I told her before, over and over, that she was not wearing the correct shoes for the contest. But the stubborn little wench that she was insisted upon them. Imagine — Rosaleen! Cuban heels for a quickstep! Have you ever heard anything so preposterous in your entire life?" Biting her lip, and afraid that her answer was going to come out in a fit of laughter, she said, as straight-faced as she could,

"I'm awful sorry you didn't win, Grahame."

"Don't be, Rosaleen, I'm not. Not really. It was the experience that counted; going off to the Isle of Man, not just to sit on the gritty sand, or get dried out by the salt air, but to have a reason for going — a real reason . . . " Looking straight over her head, as though he were talking to someone at the far end of the room instead of to her, he continued, " . . . that no matter what happened; you went, you saw, you participated. Now, an experience like that you can't beat." Then, breaking off, sudden-like, he immediately started talking again, but in a tone suggestive of a whole new topic of conversation. "Rosaleen, don't forget, there's always next year." Rosaleen looked at him as though seeing him for the first time, and she was surprised to discover that the very fact that she was looking at him brought an embarrassed flush to his face. Rosaleen could hardly believe it. She had always thought Tweedy to be one dimensional, and now she suspected that there were many sides to him that she had been completely blind to, and, that now, without being given the chance, he would never be able to redeem himself. "I don't suppose you would be interested in trying out with me for 'The Golden Slipper Award' in September?" It was a rhetorical question, requiring no answer, and, expecting none. Tweedy went on anyway. "We could attend another studio, it doesn't have to be Specky's. It will be interesting to see where the contest is being held. I heard once that one such contest was held in Belgium," he told her, and that faraway look came into his eyes again.

"What a splendid opportunity that would be: to go to the Continent itself to compete," and he looked down at Rosaleen, but his eyes were not exactly on her. "Why . . . it would be like going to the Olympics itself and coming home a crowned champ. What a splendid homecoming that would be." And, again, as though he were talking to the far end of the room, "I'd like to try my hand at that one day, Rosaleen." And, then, as if new life was being pumped into his veins, he went on, "I think I will. Great scot! I'll be damned if I don't." And with that, the music came to an abrupt end. With Tweedy having saved the best for last, he pinpointed his movements to the tempo in an incredible finish.

The ball stopped rolling, the lights went up and the audience madly applauded; some of them even jumped the balustrades to congratulate them on their performance.

Tweedy was exuberant, and with so many holding out their hands to him and he, always the social perfectionist, tossed all social amenities aside and gave both hands to his admirers. It was Tweedy's finest hour and Rosaleen used it to leave him and to seek out Ann.

But, as much as the evening had started off with an unusual twist, it ended with an even more ironic one.

With Rosaleen's predictions confirmed about Colin not being there, the attempts to convince herself that maybe he was more serious about Blondie than she took him to be, or perhaps more than he himself cared to admit, started to take seed. After all, for the two of them to do such an intimate thing as to go shopping together, which, to her, bore the same implications as going to the Hibs together, there had to be something between them.

And, so it was, with a sinking feeling, disappointment and a sense of remorse, that she chose to sit out, not caring to dance with anyone. And finding herself more and more alone, as Ann was in quick demand, Rosaleen went to the powder room.

It was here, while sitting on one of the lavender sofas and smoking a cigarette, that Rosaleen saw Blondie.

With the decor of the walls being

mostly mirrors, it was through one of these glass walls she was looking and thinking to herself of the fantastic effect they created, like looking into a room and seeing one dimension after another, without end. Then, without knowing exactly where it was the girl came from, she was suddenly aware that Blondie was heading her way. Sitting there on the sofa, in the middle of the room, Rosaleen watched as hundreds and hundreds of Blondies came at her from every direction, all of them wearing the same clothes, walking the same way; all of them identical in every way. As they came closer to her, threatening to crowd her out with their multitude, they suddenly stopped, as though suspended in animation, with only one of them, the real Blondie, continuing to show any signs of life.

"Aren't you the girl that was dancing out there on the floor earlier?" she asked from the end of the sofa, looking at Rosaleen in such a way as though afraid to miss one tiny detail. Rosaleen looked up in disbelief, thinking for a minute that the girl was joking, for despite the change in her appearance, she didn't look all *that* different; the girl must've known that she was from the Hibs, and everything else besides. But Blondie continued with the intention of telling her what was on her mind.

"You were just great out there on the dance-floor. God, what I'd have given to be in your shoes." Rosaleen's mind was racing. What was Blondie doing here? Was she with her chums? No, most girls usually came to the powder room in numbers, seldom alone. And what if she was? Where, then, was Colin? Before she could come up with a suitable solution, her question was unwittingly answered. "I was saying to my boyfriend the whole time you were dancing of how I used to love Ginger Rogers and Fred Astaire. I went to all their pictures, when I was a kid. Well, you reminded me of her the way you moved, it was just beautiful, with the orchestra and everything, it was so . . . romantic. To me, you were Ginger Rogers in the flesh, and your boyfriend . . . well . . . the two of you are so suited to each other. Now, my boyfriend," and she clicked her tongue, "you know what men are, he said that he liked your style but he thought that Ginger Rogers had better legs."

Rosaleen couldn't believe that this was taking place between her and Blondie. But the girl went on, as she started to cross the room for the door.

"Wait'll I tell him that up close you're even better looking than Ginger Rogers, legs and all," and with what seemed like a too friendly, but knowing, wink, and another click of her tongue, she exited, leaving Rosaleen with the feeling that someone was playing a joke on her.

Without moving from where she'd been sitting while the whole episode with Blondie was taking place, Rosaleen let the smoke from her cigarette eat away at the tobacco, as she smiled ruefully at the blank, grey walls.

Since she'd first entered the Plaza that night, she had been enshrouded with an explosive expectancy, without really knowing why. But now, sitting there in the solemn aftermath, the high charge having been pulled on her before it had time to go off, she knew what it was that she had intended to do: if by any chance

178

or circumstance she had come face to face with Colin Murdoch there tonight, she was going to show him, to let him see in her eyes, everything that she felt for him, and along with it, the glimmer of promise with a hint of things to come, for which, no doubt, he'd have no trouble arranging. And, when that would have happened, Colin Murdoch would begin to feel, for the first time in his life, what it was really like; but not everything — for that had not been her intention, besides, he wasn't deserving, but just enough to set him back on his ear, and, then, leave him begging for more — and that's what Colin Murdoch deserved.

But now, turning to the ashtray to crush out her cigarette, she felt the irony of it all, and she suddenly shuddered, as she sat back to wait for Ann, and it seemed like an eternity.

12

THE following day was Confraternity Sunday of the Third Order of the Redemptorists and of which Rosaleen and Phyllis were both solidarity members. Leaving the Redemptorist Monastery at half-past four, the girls had to pass the Hibs on their way home, and Phyllis having promised Jimmy, who was on duty that afternoon, that she'd stop in for the last dance, after much persistance, finally persuaded Rosaleen to go with her.

Not accustomed to seeing the A.O.H. hall in daylight, with the windows up and the open drapes fluttering in the afternoon sun, Rosaleen felt uncomfortably familiar, while, at the same time, strangely alienated, and while she and Phyllis waited for Jimmy to come down from the record box, she took a seat in the corner, whose dark recesses she saw illuminated for the first time.

Having already removed her hat and

left it on the seat beside her, and now with one high-heeled foot over the other, Rosaleen stretched her legs in front of her, and resting her head against the wall behind her, she closed her eyes and shut out the intruding sunlight.

Lost in a reverie of uncontrolled thought, she was soon enveloped in the blackness which preludes sleep. It was from within the depths of this void that she felt someone stir at her side and heard the familiar voice of Phyllis in greeting to someone, and, while she heard the music itself, it was like the kind that one heard while at a great distance from the source, for while it was still beating musically, it was lacking in melody, all of which fit appropriately into the blackness: and then, she saw Colin's face, his eyes looking directly at her, his gaze set deep and darkly pensive, and she felt herself smiling at him, which seemed to alter the expression in his eyes and they became like the sky upon the passing of a storm. Just then, her dream became a reality and there he was, holding out a hand to her, the one that had just touched her own.

Going to him as though walking through clouds and unable to find the substance beneath that will keep her from falling through, she succumbed to the mighty arm at her waist, to the shoulder beneath her head, and to the strength in the hand which she had found with her own.

Not at all certain that she was still not dreaming, for she was unable to open her eyes, which seemed nailed shut, she attempted to feel her teeth against her bottom lip, the result of which produced a numbness that convinced her she must still be asleep. Finally, it was upon hearing his voice that stirred her out of the sleep-like stupor, and she was able to open her eyes, only to have them forced shut again as the light from the windows struck them.

"That was some performance you gave last night," she heard him say, the words seemingly coming from a great distance reached her ear as though carried there on a soft current of warm air. "Though I could hardly say I recognized you, except for your figure, and I must say, you looked great." There was no reply within her control, just a ghost of a smile, then, along with it, the feeling that a beautiful dream was taking place. And then knowing for certain that she was indeed dreaming, she felt his lips against her ear in a whisper of a kiss, and she sensed the tightening of his arm on her waist, and the strengthening of his fingers entwined in her own.

But it was far from a dream, for suddenly and unexpectedly, she was jarred awake by loud shouts of laughter, followed by wild applause, and, when she opened her eyes, Colin was still there.

'Dirty Eyes' had just put in an appearance and, however he had made his entrance, it was enough to have caused an uproar. Yet when Colin and Rosaleen turned to see what had caused the commotion, all they saw was the usual 'Dirty Eyes'; the only difference in his appearance was a big cloth peaked-cap that he was wearing.

Colin and Rosaleen exchanged a puzzled look, and then, as if by some strange magnetic mechanism, their eyes became locked within each other's, with neither of them able to supply the correct combination to tear them apart. It would take an outside force, something or someone who had nothing to lose in whatever it was that bound them together in one magic moment; it had to be a strong diversion, something that had more strength than both of them combined, because neither one seemed to have any of it in his or her possession: it took the uproarious and outrageous laughter of the rest of the dancers to cause them to tear their eyes away. But, even while they were no longer looking at each other there was a very strong pull binding them one to the other, and Colin, who had placed one foot on the bench, drew Rosaleen to him until she was resting against his knee, and she felt the softness of his hand gently on the back of her neck.

What had provoked the outburst before was soon to be revealed, for as the next to the last record of the afternoon was played, it spun ignored, as all eyes focused on 'Dirty Eyes'.

Midst calls of persuasion, he removed his cap, an action which caused a fresh outburst of roars and screams of laughter, but which left Rosaleen thunderstruck.

Gone was the beautiful head of hair that Rosaleen had silently admired, upon meeting him for the first time, and now, standing but a few feet away was a young man whose skull had been shaved clean; his pink head as bald as the King of Siam's. Not knowing whether to laugh or cry, she drew in her breath, and she felt Colin's knee gently prodding the small of her back, and when she looked at him, she found his eyes filled with understanding and, in a voice that only she could hear, he told her,

"That's 'Dirty Eyes', don't go feeling sorry for him, the others don't. They have a certain respect for him, in their own way, and, besides, that's how he gets his kicks, by doing the outrageous things that most people would like to do but don't have the guts to carry out." And, then, as if to thoroughly convince her, he added, "You watch, you'll see his 'fan club' grow on account of this latest craze. He may be the first to sport a 'Yul Brynner', but I'll guarantee you, he won't be the last." And then, as though to redeem not only themselves from the sobriety brought on chiefly by Rosaleen's own mood, but also the still-spinning record, he grabbed her playfully in his arms and moved slowly around the floor.

When the record came to an end, and while waiting for the last one to begin, Rosaleen felt Colin watching her, and turning to look at him, she saw him reach out and take the lapel of her coat between his fingers.

"What's this?" he asked, referring to the pin she was wearing. Following his gaze to the little white shield, which bore a heart and a cross, encircled by flames, representing the love and sacrifice of Jesus for humanity, she told him,

"That's a pioneer pin. I just got it today."

"Oh?" Colin mused, her answer bringing a smile to his lips, and with neither of them aware of the next record starting, he went on, "You're kind of young to be a pioneer, aren't you?" and letting his eyes study her for a moment, he continued, "What are you a pioneer of?"

"I took the pledge of abstinence," she said, and seeing the question posed in his expression, she explained further, "You know, temperance against alcohol."

"Oh, that kind of pioneer," he said, "And just how long do you plan on staying away from the stuff?" And Rosaleen, sensing his mood, answered,

"I took the total pledge."

"You mean you're not going to drink at all?" and seeing her shake her head, "Never? Oh, c'mon. Not even a little drop?" Again, she shook her head. "How about at weddings? No? Parties? C'mon now, do you mean to tell me that you're never going to drink?" Then, drawing in his breath, he said, "You know, *never* is an awful long time."

"Oh, I don't think that it's going to be too hard, being as I've never had a drink. But imagine those who do already drink, some for years even, and who, then, take the pledge? Now that's giving up more than I ever could."

Remaining quiet for a moment, and letting what she had just said sink in, he then asked,

"So what else have you given up for life?" Rosaleen looked at him.

"Nothing. Why?"

"Oh, I was just curious. I mean, being

as you smoke, and all, isn't there a pledge, or something you can take for that?" Watching his eyes, Rosaleen asked, "Do you see something wrong with that?"

"Oh, I don't see anything wrong with it at all. I was just wondering that if you can give up one vice, you could probably give up another one just as easy."

"Well, *you* don't smoke . . . " Rosaleen retorted, feeling the colour in her cheeks heighten.

"No, that's true," Colin agreed, the smile in his eyes deepening, "But then, it's not for religious reasons, or anything like that." Then putting his hands behind his back, and leaning against the wall, he brought one foot up behind him, all of which added a casualness to his tone, as he remarked, "Now, you being a Catholic, and all, suppose you decided to give up smoking, I mean really make a sacrifice of it. Is there some kind of emblem you would wear that would warn people against offering you a cigarette, or of even trying to influence you?"

"Yes, there is," Rosaleen said, purposely making her tone serious to offset his own. "Just as there is one for people who are against profanity."

"Cursing!" Colin exploded. "No! Do you mean there are people who actually swear not to curse?"

"And also to stay away from the company of those who do," Rosaleen added quietly.

"Well, those people wouldn't do too well around me, because I'm terrible, especially on the job. If I hit my thumb, or something, whew, I have to express the pain, in one way or another . . . oh, I get it, maybe there's a special list of words they use," he said, "like, ah . . . sugar," and without taking his eyes off her, he held out his arms to her to dance, "or, ah . . . fiddlesticks, or something like that. What do you think?"

"I couldn't tell you," Rosaleen said, tightlipped, "You'd have to ask somebody who knows."

"Well, who would I ask? Or better yet, what kind of emblem do they wear so I'll know to stay away from those people? I wouldn't want to be the cause of their downfall."

Looking into his eyes, Rosaleen knew

189

that the question, like certain others she had received from his lips, while requiring no verbal answer, did awaken a need to respond. But simultaneous to her feeling his arm tighten around her, as they moved away from the corner in which they'd been standing, she saw 'Dirty Eyes' lift a girl's hat right off her head, and covering his baldness with it, he strutted around the floor in an exaggerated fashion, and she found that response rise within her as she felt herself laughing, as was Colin, but she more so, much, much more.

★ ★ ★

Later that night, after having bathed, and still in the process of getting dressed to go out, Rosaleen knew that it was against her better judgement. Though it was not due directly to the slightly darker than usual areas under her eyes, nor to the extreme tiredness that was within her body, it was on account of the vulnerability that accompanied such biological changes that nature demanded of her each month. That afternoon was a good example of vulnerability and she felt positive that Colin was well aware of what was going on within her and that everything that had happened between them had been the direct result of such. He surely must have sensed her weakened defenses and taken advantage of them. Even when they had parted in the dance-hall, his eyes had held the promise that he would be waiting there for her that night. Now, in an attempt to dispel some of the gaunt look from her face, she applied a touch of make-up to the darkened areas, and then she brought out the colour to her cheeks with some rouge, and she completed the job by adding a trace of lipstick to her mouth.

Fully dressed, she stood before the full-length mirror on the wardrobe door and, as she examined her reflection, she felt a sudden blush on her cheeks. Unaccustomed to wearing anything revealing at any time, she felt somewhat naked wearing the Prince Charles whose neckline was open almost, though not quite, to the point of suggestion. She then had second thoughts about wearing a blouse under it, then, thinking about it for a minute or so, she went instead to a box in her top dresser drawer, and taking a tiny gold cross on a chain, she put it around her neck. Now when she looked in her dresser mirror, she saw the light catch the chain and reflect the glimmer of its yellow gold.

Putting on her coat, but before she turned to leave, she took a bottle of perfume and while she touched its fragrance to the selected vital spots, she smiled through the mirror, knowing beforehand that the glow she expected to find there was very much present in her eyes.

The Hibs was more crowded than she had ever seen it, which meant that the jiving sessions would be fewer than usual, something for which she was grateful, because she definitely was not in a jiving mood.

Long before the record, which was playing when she entered, had the chance to run its course, she sensed, rather than saw Colin coming towards her from behind, yet, despite her high-pitched fervour, she maintained a cool exterior. With hands on her waist, he whispered his request jestingly against her ear, knowing full well beforehand that he didn't have to ask.

Being in his arms was all Rosaleen had thought about since she'd left him that afternoon, and when he drew her even closer within his embrace, she felt the anticipation climb even higher than it had already been. With one hand on her back, he reached down with the other and taking hold of hers, he drew it up and held it gently against his breast.

Now feeling the beat of his heart with her hand, Rosaleen was not as shy as she previously had been about letting her own heart convey her emotions, and she was aware of the exact moment when it was that Colin felt, for the first time, the beating that was within her own breast.

Dancing as they were, Rosaleen felt the soft strength of his jaw gently touching her forehead, and then the smoothness of his cheek against her own, until the nearness of his mouth sent signals from the base of her spine, telling her that her yearnings, if followed through, would cause havoc, but for which this was neither the time nor the place.

Reaching up to him, she brushed against his cheek with her mouth, not so much with a kiss as with a tender promise, and with the hand which had been gently guided by his own, she caressed the material beneath her fingertips, and Colin, holding her even closer, grasped the hand within his own even tighter against his heart, until Rosaleen felt that it was about to leap from his body. Then, in lieu of kissing her, he brought her hand to his mouth and pressed it to his lips; a gesture that did more to weaken whatever resistance she had left and weakened it more than anything else he could have done. And, to make matters worse, he looked down into her face with eyes so piercing that she felt they were looking into her very soul.

Inevitably, a Johnny Mathis song, 'I Look At You', was not helping matters, for as the magic of the afternoon returned to bind them together once again, and unable to tear her eyes away from him for a second, she felt rather than heard the music enter her soul, and then, creating more havoc within her, flowing out of her fingertips and into his, where it seemed to have the same effect, and then back to her own again as though in one, single, continuous, sensuous circuit, it joined them as close as two people could be in public; one in mind, one in heart, one in emotion.

After the third record stopped and couples parted, the magic between them was still there, weaving its warmth and beauty around them, not permitting one to walk away from the other. So Colin, putting his arm around Rosaleen, led her to the deepest corner of the hall, and which provided the privacy needed by two people who had so much to say to each other.

In the same soft tone with which he had spoken to her that afternoon — and which was far removed from the Colin Murdoch she thought she knew — he told her again how much he had admired her exhibition dance in the Plaza, and of how great she had looked on the floor, and of how proud he had felt that he knew her. And then, he told her how sorry he was that he had not been able to find her later, that he had wanted to talk to her, as well as to congratulate her, but, he'd realized too late that she'd gone. There was no mention of Blondie.

Colin's compliments did more for her cheeks and her eyes than any make-up could ever do, for even in the dimness of the corner, a deep blush painted her unusual pallor, and the darkness merely seemed to accentuate her eyes, that glistened and shone with the excitement of just being with him.

Looking at Rosaleen with an emotion in his eyes that she had never witnessed there before, Colin caressed her hair, though, at first, it was with a certain shyness, but then, finding a response in her eyes, the caress became strong in want and surety. And, as though finding in her expression the encouragement he was hoping for, he told her that he had never seen her look as beautiful as she did right then.

Hearing her name on his lips for the first time, brought all the emotions she had ever felt for him rushing to the surface, threatening to spill from her eyes and her lips. But quelling the storm within her, she looked at Colin, searching his eyes for the sparkle that was as familiarly as much of him that yet belonged to her, but unable to see it, she found, instead, a warm, tender glow, which was an extension of the gentle smile on his lips; a look that held her eyes captive as she watched his gaze leave hers, and like a tepid wave that had just passed over his face, left it slightly glowing in its wake. His eyes warmed her throat as they came to rest on the tiny cross at the end of the chain.

Reaching out his hand, he touched it gently. Holding it between his fingers, he caressed it with his thumb, and looking at it, he told her, "I'm not a Catholic, as you know, Rosaleen," and his eyes suddenly sought her own, as though searching for a reaction. "And I know how the Church feels about Catholics and Protestants going together. Does that bother you? Would that stop you from going out with me?"

Greatly moved by his tenderness, a side to him she had never seen before, it brought a lump to her throat. And having no answer for him, nor was she looking for one right then, she remained silent.

But Colin pursued it, keeping the low, tender quality in his tone. "Rosaleen?" His gaze was questioning.

There was no need to answer, for it was all there in her eyes, but she confirmed it anyway with her lips. "No, Colin. It wouldn't stop me from going out with you."

The rest of the night was spent between the corner and the dance-floor; the former, when they wanted to be alone, to talk about themselves, and about each other, the latter, when they wanted to hold each other, to be close; things that were acceptable on the dance-floor, but which would be inappropriate for the corner.

Leaving long before the last dance gave them ample time to walk slowly and to talk some more and to arrange for their going out together for the first time.

During the course of the night, Rosaleen's fervour had climbed, rather than diminished, and, as they approached her corner, a racing excitement gripped her as Colin put his hands on her waist and captured her eyes with his own.

"Remember the night you told me that

you didn't go with boys who were only out for one thing?"

Shy and embarrassed in hearing her own sentiments echoed aloud, Rosaleen nodded her head, unable to put an appropriate answer into words.

"Well," Colin continued, "I have never gone with a girl who had anything else to offer."

And with this, he kissed her lightly on the forehead and bid her goodnight.

13

WITH Junior Exams only three weeks away, Rosaleen's time for the past four weeks had been filled with studying and going on quiet dates with Colin, yet Rosaleen was worried. The nights which she had spent keeping up with the demands of school, what with the old exam exercises, along with the never-ending homework, were gruelling enough; it was the evenings she had spent with Colin that were causing her to worry, because, unlike her studies, he had placed no demands on her at all, and this was what concerned her most about their relationship. For while she had hoped for, in fact, yearned for, his exquisite kisses, which had sent her head spinning and her pulse racing, his warm, strong embraces that had crushed her soul into a million pieces, and the fervent whisperings in her ear, which had brought responses from her lips and which she previously didn't know she possessed, and which had set Colin, himself, on fire, were non-existent. Apart from their friendly hand-holding in the cinema and the odd times he would grab her around the waist, always playfully, and a somewhat lukewarm good-night kiss, there was nothing — no intimacy — nothing: the magic all seemed to be gone and what they were left with were three or four nights of very ordinary dates a week, that were probably just like any other couple's.

Preparing for yet another evening with him, and it being Saturday, Rosaleen silently predicted to herself that they would probably just go to the cinema or up to the Hibs. So it was without much enthusiasm that she got dressed. She had even reached the point where it was immaterial to her whether her parents found out about him. She was not even supposed to be dating, never mind having a steady boyfriend, and a Protestant one at that; her scholastic achievement was first and foremost on their minds as far as their daughter was concerned. She knew that her father would be very angry, as well as disappointed in her, if he found out she'd been deceiving them. Lenient enough as they were to let her go out dancing two or three nights with her 'friends', but if they knew that she had been going out with Colin, there would be fireworks, to say the least.

Pulling a black sweater over her head, she pulled it down over the waistband of her black skirt, and brushing her hair absent-mindedly, and aware that she should have washed it, she coiled it around her fingers and pinned it up at the back of her head. Slipping into her shoes, she dabbed on a little make-up, and grabbing her coat and bag, she went off to meet Colin.

Almost immediately, she realized that there was something different about him, and, as she got closer, she saw that whereas she had taken little care getting dressed, Colin, himself, had never looked better, for he was wearing a new suit and he had gotten a hair-trim. Rosaleen wanted nothing more but to turn around and go home, but, instead, she greeted him with an awkward smile.

Insisting upon taking her to the Plaza, Rosaleen did her best to talk him out of it, as she really wasn't in the mood for dancing. But his insistence won out.

She was unusually quiet as they rode the bus down town, but Colin's first acknowledgement of anything being different about her came as she met him outside the powder-room.

"Did somebody die in your family?" Rosaleen threw him a quizzical look. "Why the mourning clothes?" he asked whimsically, and then drawn back by the solemn look on her face, his voice took on a more serious note. "Hey, what's the matter, are you unhappy about something?" Without answering and continuing on in silence, Rosaleen remained that way for most of the night, despite all of Colin's attempts to lighten her mood. Through four entire dances, he couldn't get a word out of her, and when he took her down to the EL MOMBO ROOM, she made no effort to touch the pastry he brought her, but sat silently sipping a cup of tea and smoking cigarettes, one after the other.

Feeling as though she were about to burst into tears at any moment, Rosaleen excused herself while they were walking back to the ballroom and she went into the powder-room. In the hopes of chasing the black mood, which had been following her around all day, with a comb and a lipstick, she soon saw that it was useless and she pushed her way back out through the swinging doors, expecting Colin to be waiting for her somewhere in the hallway near the ballroom.

What she didn't expect was to see him fully engaged in what looked like a very interesting conversation with none other than Blondie. Hands behind him and leaning against one of the great pillars that graced the entrance to the Plaza ballroom, Colin had a look about him that suggested that Blondie was a very welcome relief to him on this morose, dragged-out evening. For not only did his eyes hold a smile that was definitely intended just for Blondie, but his handsome face broke into something pleasurable to behold and, as Rosaleen heard the resounding sound of his deep laugh, she saw Blondie put a hand on his shoulder and bring herself against him while telling him something that was apparently meant for his ears alone and with an intimacy that Rosaleen herself could not display under any circumstances. Then, watching both of them shake with laughter at whatever it was that Blondie had said to him, she saw Colin's arm go around her waist, as though he had a natural reflex for such things when with her, and he pulled her towards him in what looked to Rosaleen as a betrayal of their own relationship.

Not daring to intrude on their moment of whatever shared reminiscence, and not wanting to go back into the powder-room, Rosaleen slipped around the corner, to where several stone benches were set amidst a little fountain, a couple of statues and some artificial Mediterranean greenery. Lighting a cigarette, just to give her hands something to do, she sat there with her head leaning against the wall behind her. The place, deserted, except for her lone figure, was soon permeated with strains of an unfamiliar song, and the band's vocalist delivered it in such a way that it made Rosaleen take notice and made her feel that it was intended directly for her ears alone.

The words told the story of an angel, who came to earth in the guise of a human being. The one person who was able to see through the angel's disguise would win paradise and find the way to heaven in the angel's eyes.

Purposely engrossed in the words, while listening to the melody, Rosaleen watched the repetitious flow of the small fountain. Then, as if suddenly realizing it, she saw that it was the same quantity of water being used over and over again. There was no fresh water being supplied from any source, unlike a natural waterfall, and that if the little fountain were to be shut off, the water would just lie there and, in due time, grow stagnant.

With the cigarette burning ignored between her fingers, Rosaleen listened to the song as it went on to tell of the revealment of the angel's identity and of the instant attainment of heaven for the discoverer. It was then that her eyes strayed to the statues; Cupid, with his bow and arrow, and, directly across from him, Venus, without her arms, and suddenly the irony of their positions, which were probably arranged without much consideration, took hold of her, and she was seized by a fit of laughter. Aware of her own predicament, she tried to hold it back and, as she did, she felt her insides welling up in vast waves of emotion, which, the more she tried to control, the more momentum they gained, until, breaking loose from any control she might be in command of, it suddenly subsided by itself, bringing with it a flow of contentment and a sense of inner calm.

Looking once more to Venus and noticing for the first time the replicated droop of the head, Rosaleen at once felt sorry for this, the most reknowned of all mythical diety, and going over to her, she traced with her fingertips the stone cold visage. Continuing down the grey dampness of her naked shoulder, she brought her fingers to rest tenderly about her legendary deformity and whispered to her what was probably the most retrospective soliloquy ever eulogized over the sculptured remains, original or replica, of the Goddess of Love.

"Goddess of Love
Did you, too, once a love deny?
How else, a heart to turn to stone
And arms to atrophy."

Colin, who had come looking for
Rosaleen, found her in the midst of this
quiet little scene filled with silent statues
and stone benches, its very stillness
enhanced by the sound of the fountain,
and seeing her, almost as though she
were in prayer, he hesitated to intrude
upon her solitude.

Looking at her, her back to him,
unaware that he was there, watching,
observing, looking first at her small,
narrow frame, then at the curve of her
shoulders, the straight line of her back,
and where it met the indent of her waist.
Then, his eyes, continuing down to the
small of her back, paused, and there, at
the base of her spine, the lines, which had
first caught his attention, while displaying
a firmness had yet managed to retain
their softness. He looked then to the tilt
of her head, and again, a firmness, but
this time in the graceful line of her
profiled chin as she turned slightly as

though reaching for the words of the song that was being sung, and he himself listened, as he continued to look at her.

Then, as though sensing his presence behind her, Rosaleen turned, embarrassed to find him there, for she knew that he had been watching her, and she saw the question in his eyes.

"What are you doing here?" he asked, coming towards her, and putting his hands on her shoulders, he looked down into her face. "I thought you'd gotten lost on me," he told her solemnly.

"No," she told him, turning away to look once again at the fountain falling upon itself. "I just wanted to see what was back here."

"Oh?" Colin said quietly, looking at the curve of her cheek. "If I'd known, I would've come with you."

"No," Rosaleen said, her voice barely audible above the noise of the fountain, and looking up at him, she told him, "Colin, I want to go home."

Taking the cigarette from her hand, he studied her face and seeing something there he hadn't seen before, gently traced her cheek with the back of his hand, and looked seriously, but softly, into her eyes, he said, "All right, if that's what you want to do."

It had just started to rain as they left the Plaza, and now, getting off the bus, they were greeted by a steady drizzle, and Colin, turning up his collar, put a protective arm across Rosaleen's shoulder as they hurried down her street.

There had been a mutual silence between them all the way from the Plaza, and by the time they got to the corner, it had become a kind of sharing between them that neither one was willing to break. But now, standing just within the doorway of the school, Colin, his back to the street, looked down into Rosaleen's face.

"What are you thinking about?"

Getting no reply from her lips, but reading it in her eyes, he took her face in his hands, and lifting it up to his own, he kissed her tenderly on the mouth. And when he had finished, Rosaleen's voice came through the darkness to him.

"Oh, Colin." She whispered his name, and her feelings for him washed over her entire being, their intensity sweeping her up and swallowing her gave her the sense of being lost at sea, and she put her arms around his neck and clung to him more tightly than she had ever done before.

But, still, his kisses, slow and prolonged, were awakening an urgency in her that she couldn't hold back and she kissed him with a passion she never knew she had.

"Hold on, baby," Colin said against her ear. "Don't let us get carried away."

But, still, she continued, kissing him, feeling his own warmth come alive to match hers. Caressing the back of his neck, she reached up to touch his face, his hair; and his own fingers, behind her ears, caressed the flesh on her neck, and she felt him reach up and take the pins from her hair, and she felt it fall about her shoulders. And when he looked at her, she saw the whole world reflected there in his eyes; eyes that held the sparkle she had come to love, but offset, now, with something new.

Standing just within the doorway of the school, the rain behind them starting to come down harder, Rosaleen saw his hair glisten under the light of the street lamp and she felt the dampness beneath her fingers.

"Colin, your suit," she said against his chest. "It's going to get ruined."

"Sssh . . . " Colin lulled her against him, fondling the ends of her hair between his fingers with one hand, and caressing her face with the other. " . . . Don't think of anything else right now except us," and he tightened his hold on her, as though he would pull her right through his body.

"Colin," Rosaleen broke through the silence again, "we should move in out of the rain."

Releasing her enough so as to move back deeper into the doorway, Colin came to her and took her into his arms as before. But, now, holding her against him, he sensed something different; something that had not yet been resolved between them, and he looked at her.

Her head resting against the wooden door behind her, Rosaleen looked at him in a way that only confirmed what he had just felt in her embrace, and hesitating, but continuing to look at her, the unspoken remembrance of a night past, standing like a ghost between them, dissolved in the fervour of her eyes: and still, as though seeking reassurance, more for her sake than for his own, he asked her softly, "Are you sure, Rosaleen?"

And she, attempting to speak, but unable to swallow the lump in her throat, which was threatening to cut off the breath from her body, could only nod her head in golden silence.

"Oh, baby," Colin murmured against her cheek and then, cradling her in his arms, he rocked her gently within his embrace, and stroking her hair, he started to unbutton her coat.

Slowly and gently, he undid each button and, upon reaching the last one, he held her coat open, and holding her at arm's length, hesitating, first loving her with his eyes, he then pulled her close and placed his hands on her waist.

Her coat, no longer a barrier between them, now served to bring them closer, and Colin, feeling her nearness, kissed her softly on the lips. But, in so doing, he suddenly sensed that not everything was right with her, and bringing his lips to her eyes, he found them moist with tears.

"What's the matter, baby?" he asked,

looking at her, his own eyes filled with tenderness.

But Rosaleen, filled with all her old shyness, as well as with the emotion of the moment, couldn't answer him.

Sensing all of this, Colin tilted her chin up, forcing her to look at him, as he repeated the question. "What's the matter?"

"Oh, Colin."

"What is it? Tell me."

"It's just that . . . " Rosaleen began, and then broke off, and then, getting a little encouragement from him, she continued. " . . . I've never seen a boy looking at me. I . . . mean . . . it's the first time I've ever deliberately let a fellow look at me. Do you know what I mean?"

Colin's eyes softened, and putting a hand to the back of her head, he drew her over to him and touched her cheek with his own. "I know exactly what you mean, baby. This is a first for me too. I've never been this slow, I usually grab without bothering to look to see what I'm getting."

"Colin!" Rosaleen pulled her head away from him, shocked by his tone.

Realizing his mistake, Colin tried to redeem himself.

"What I mean, Rosaleen, is that . . . " But Rosaleen was looking at him with questions in her eyes that even he didn't have the answers to. " . . . well, you know what I mean?"

Buttoning up her coat, and in a voice slightly raised, Rosaleen told him in no uncertain terms, "No, I don't know what you mean. Just what kind of a fellow are you, Colin Murdoch?"

And Colin, unable to find the right words to pacify her, said, "I'm a human fellow . . . what I mean is, I'm human," and then softer, "I'm only human."

"Aren't we all," Rosaleen flung at him. "But we don't all go through life grabbing at everything we want, just because it's there. Do we?"

"No, Rosaleen, we don't," and then, leaning his elbow against the wall, he looked at her solemnly. "Sometimes we don't have to grab. Sometimes you just look, and there it is, staring you in the face. Sometimes it's hard to say no."

"Do you ever, Colin?" she asked, somewhat softened by his tone.

215

"Sometimes I do, especially if it's someone who has a son almost as old as you are yourself."

"Colin, you don't mean that?" Rosaleen said, shocked anew.

"Oh, yes, I do mean it."

"I find that hard to believe. When did this happen? and where? and how?"

Colin turned to her with a serious expression. "I had just turned sixteen at the time, and I was coming home after playing a football game. I was muck up to the eyebrows, you know how that is, so I came in the back door, and knowing the way my mother always shouts about walking through the house covered with clay, I stood at the kitchen door and took off my boots. I was in the process of taking off my jersey and had just pulled it over my head, when the kitchen door from the living room opened, and there stood this neighbour of ours, a woman, who used to sometimes keep the key to our house for us whenever my mother wasn't going to be home, and she was naked to the waist, same as I was."

Rosaleen looked away for a moment, embarrassed by the thought of such a thing taking place. "My God, Colin. And did she really have a son your age?"

"Sure she did. She lived four houses down from us and she had a son my brother's age, who was . . . is two years older than me. What I mean is that he was two years older than me at the time . . . I mean he's still two years older than me . . . oh, you know what I mean." Then his speech became more precise, and Rosaleen, doing her best to keep from laughing, suddenly realized that he was embarrassed now himself. "What I mean to say is that my brother was eighteen at the time this happened, and so was her son, which is the age I am now — that's what I meant to say."

Laughing softly now, Rosaleen told him, "I understand, Colin. But what did you do? Were you embarrassed?"

"Let's see now, what did I do?" he said, starting to grin. "Of course, I was embarrassed. What do you take me for? I asked her if she'd like a cup of tea. But she just stood there looking at me, so I got down some cups. Then, looking for a way out of there, I started searching the cupboards and I pretended that we had no sugar. But she reached up behind her and came down with the sugar bowl. Then, getting desperate, I told her we were short of milk, but realizing I had said the wrong thing, I just rushed right past her and out the door."

Rosaleen looked at him questioningly. "Why? Why all of a sudden did you run?"

"Rosaleen!" Colin said, intimating by his tone that she shouldn't have to ask that. "Here she was, all ready to supply the milk, and I hadn't even put the kettle on to boil yet."

Unable to contain herself, and moved to laughter by the way in which he had told the story, and not at all sure if he hadn't just been putting her on, she punched him playfully in the arm.

Grabbing her by the shoulders, and placing a friendly arm around her, Colin asked her, "Would you like to go for a walk tomorrow?"

Rosaleen smiled up at him, "Where?"

"Oh, maybe the Cavehill."

"I think I'd like that."

"I'll see you about half-past-one, then?"

"All right." Rosaleen nodded, starting to walk away.

"Rosaleen!"

She heard him call after her, and she turned around. "What?"

Colin pointed to her coat. "You missed a button."

"You!" Rosaleen made a playful swing at him with her arm.

Colin caught it and pulled her against him. "Goodnight." he told her, tapping her lightly on the nose with a friendly forefinger.

"Goodnight." Rosaleen said, softly, walking away.

14

AFTER Saturday's rain, Sunday dawned bright and clear, and by early afternoon, the day had become sunny and warm. Rosaleen and Colin took the bus to Bellevue, a huge, natural reserve, with a small animal zoo. Climbing the narrowly-spaced stone steps, which led up to the zoo, itself, and to the wide expanse of forest beyond, called Hazlewood, they stopped for ice cream, and then went to sit on a low, stone wall, a little way off from the vendor and the crowds.

Quietly enjoying the atmosphere, they each took delight in the splendour around them and above them, as though both were seeing it all for the very first time. Pointing to the huge promontory in the distance, which marked the end of the Cavehill, known as Napoleon's Nose, Colin asked Rosaleen if she was game to climb it. And Rosaleen, whose school lay practically at the mouth of this structural wonder, and whose magnificence she had been confronted with on her way to school every morning for the past three years, told him that she had never been one to turn down a challenge.

Finishing his ice cream, and like a boy scout impatient for his first hike, Colin, who could no longer delay his enthusiasm to show Rosaleen the view from Napoleon's Nose, grabbed her firmly by the hand; and their walk, slow at first, so as to enable her to finish, they soon broke into a run, and they left the crowds behind, amongst them, those who turned and smiled in their wake, sensing the happiness of the young couple.

But the people became fewer and fewer, the higher they climbed and now, as they left the expanse of park behind them, their path became hemmed in by hazel trees and elm trees and beechnut trees. And as they climbed higher, the sloping terrain here and there was sprouting with gorse, and further up, a few little evergreens.

"How high up are we, anyway?" Rosaleen asked breathlessly, practically falling onto a large boulder, where they had stopped to rest, and Colin, jumping up on top, and like an Indian scout with his hand over his eyes, told her,

"Oh, I'd say about six or seven hundred feet above sea-level."

"Are we really?" Rosaleen, shading her eyes from the sun, looked up at him.

"Sure," Colin said, holding out his hand to her. "C'mon up if you don't believe me," and he pulled her up beside him.

Standing there, each with an arm around the other, they looked at the country around them.

"Isn't it beautiful, Colin!" Rosaleen breathed, and turning to get his reaction, she met his eyes head on.

"And so are you," he said, kissing her, and then, jumping down swiftly, he held out his arms to her and helped her down. With his hands still on her waist, he looked deep down into her eyes with all the promise of another kiss, but then pulled away, and grabbing her hand once more, he told her, "C'mon, we still have a couple of hundred feet to go."

A little more than half-an-hour later, after climbing through endless gorse and huge boulders, their path long left behind them somewhere down the mountain side, and having encountered only two other couples the entire time, they emerged upon a clearing.

"Here it is," Colin said, as though introducing a stranger to the land, 'Napoleon's Nose!'

"Oh, Colin!" Rosaleen said, looking around her, "There's nothing up here but the sky."

"That's right, baby, we're pretty high up. Actually, this is the last peak after the Cavehill. Down there," he said, pointing to the sharp, narrow ridge, which instantly fell away below the brow of the mountain, "is Napoleon's Nose, itself. Look," he said, enticing her to come and stand on the edge beside him. "This is how we used to come up here, when we were kids; a whole bunch of us would come here of a Sunday, just to climb up and over old Napoleon's Nose."

"You must've been the kids, then, that I used to read about in Monday's *Irish News*; always falling down into blind caves and being trapped for hours until someone came to the rescue," said

Rosaleen, looking down to the dangerous depths below.

"Oh, there's plenty of those, alright," Colin assured her. "So you better come over here beside me and hold on tight, for, you see, those caves are very tricky; they just pop up out of nowhere."

Smiling, Rosaleen went to him and Colin, grabbing her in his arms, pulled her to him. Holding her for a minute, looking at her eyes, her hair, feeling the bare smoothness of her arms, he then put his hands on her waist, and turning her to face out over the wide expanse of space beyond them, he brought his arms around her from behind.

"Look, baby," he told her, close to her ear, "If you look over there, in a south-westerly direction, you can see our little corner by the school." Going along with him, Rosaleen turned her head to look.

"Where?"

"There, see it?" Colin said, pointing a forefinger off in the distance. But, Rosaleen, taking his arm, drew it back to her, placing his hand at her waist, and Colin said softly against her ear, "It has a sign posted on it that says, 'reserved for tonight'."

"Oh?" Rosaleen smiled, feeling the sun warm on her face, along with the gentle hint of a breeze. "Reserved by whom?"

"For us. For you and me."

"What for?" she asked, closing her eyes and leaning into the comfort of his shoulder behind her head. "To continue where we left off last night?"

"Would you like that?" Rosaleen felt his words against her temple, and letting the question encompass her with its emotion, she asked him softly,

"Would you?"

"More than anything in the world, baby," he told her and, she, turning to face him, to see in his eyes the emotion she had just heard in his voice, looked up at him.

"Tonight's an awful long time to wait," and Colin, looking down at her with eyes containing the whole, entire blue of the sky, reached up his hand and brushed the top of her head.

"Oh, you've kept me waiting longer than that."

Looking at him, seeing the face she had come to love, the expression of the eyes, the lines of the mouth and jaw; feeling the hands she loves about her waist, and being close to the nearness that she never wants to be apart from, she told him, "I don't want to wait anymore." Then going into his arms and in the tenderest embrace she has ever known, she tasted the warmth and passion, as well as the want, in his kiss. Then, leaving the clearing, their thoughts gravely entwined with anticipation, they looked for a secluded spot.

Taking her hand, Colin led the way into the shelter of some tall hazel trees and it was like stepping into the heart of a blaze, for the trees were aflame with reds and yellows, and browns so sombre they were almost black, and their branches, stretching far above, their colours like fiery torches touching the vivid blue, looked like they were about to set fire to the sky itself. And standing in the midst of these trees, overwhelmed by the resplendent beauty of them all, Colin saw one that was unlike the others; different because it had somehow managed to distinguish itself from the rest, its branches, long and reaching, fell almost to the ground, like great big arms bending from the sky to hug the earth.

Gently parting the delicate foliage, Colin led Rosaleen into an enclosure where the glorious curtain surrounded them like the russet walls of a room and she, eyes appraisingly filled with wonder, turned her glowing face to his, as though he had just presented her with the most handsome and sacred of all bridal suites.

Leaning with his back to the tree, he gently drew her to him, and through the cool dimness of their sanctuary, she looked at him, seeing in his eyes an expression borne out of emotions never before divulged to her and, as he bent his head to kiss her, he took her face in his hands, and looking at her, he gave her a measure of her own emotions, and she raised her face to his lips.

Now, feeling the warmth of his mouth against her own, she brought that look to mind, imprinting it upon her memory, wanting to keep it forever, for she had seen something that had never been spoken aloud, and for now, didn't have to. She could feel that expression on his lips, as they softly and tenderly sought her own, and in his hands as they embraced her, massaged her, and caressed her.

Moving now so that her back was to the tree, she felt her heart beating wildly against his own, and as though it were in his power to stop it, to calm it, to slow it down, he placed his hand across it, and only succeeded in making it beat all the harder.

Now with his mouth fully on hers, the gentility gone from it, she suddenly felt the pressure of his kiss build into a demand she knew she was not quite committed to make, and she withdrew her mouth and her arms from his in an effort to sustain herself from drowning in her own passion. But Colin, neither daunted nor surprised by this drawback, pulled her even closer to him, tighter, till it seemed the two were one, and with his mouth now on her ear, he broke down her resolve with the whisper of his voice.

"Baby, I never knew it could be this sweet," and pulling her face closer to his, he claimed her lips once more with his own and she felt his hand on her throat, on her shoulders, and then, grabbing her arms from underneath, he gently forced them around his neck, and he continued to caress her. And now, the endearment that she had longed to hear from his lips within such an embrace, fell cherishingly against her cheek.

"Baby," he whispered, "my baby. Every minute of every hour of every day was worth waiting for this; for you. I'll never let you go."

Then his kisses rained on her, and catching her in a torrent of passion, held her against the tree, and she felt the strong, supple body that was keeping her there against her own. His hands, now on her waist, fell longingly to her hips, and she felt his grip sensuous to the flesh beneath her thin dress, and Rosaleen, her heart caught like some little winged creature within her breast, struggling with the might of her will to be set free and, as it struggled right there next to her soul . . . once . . . twice . . . its wings smothered as it tempted to lift off the earth, knew she was not ready — morally — that is, physically, yes; biologically, yes; emotionally, ah, yes; she was more than able; it was her conscience that just wouldn't permit her to be willing.

"Colin! Colin! Please stop it." And then, as if her actions had to convince him of her words, she pushed him from her with a strength that belied her size, and Colin, as though half expecting as much, and who had made every move as if it had been his last, offered no resistance.

Standing silently now beside each other, Rosaleen was the first to speak. But before she did, Colin, watching her intently, looked at her as she reduced her weakened state by sitting down at the foot of the great big tree that had stood solid witness to her previous state, and feeling its supportive strength now behind her, he saw her gather her dress about her in a gesture of girlish modesty.

Crouching down beside her, he had to bend his head to see her face and to hear her voice, which was hardly more than a whisper.

"I'm sorry, Colin," she said slowly and softly. "I don't know what you must think of me. But I have never done anything like this before." Pulling his brows into a puzzled frown, he asked her,

"Well, then, why did you, if you knew

that it was going to bother you beforehand?" Throwing him a quick glance, as
though half-expecting him to know the
answer to that more than she, Rosaleen
answered.

"I didn't know. Please believe that.
What I thought would happen was that
we would kiss and, then, start to enjoy it
more and more, you know . . . " and she
looked away, toying with the hem of her
dress. " . . . the caresses, and all. I
thought we would reach a point where we
could talk and tell each other things, and
. . . kiss some more . . . "

"And the rest?" Colin interrupted her.

"Oh, that."

"Oh, that?" Colin asked. "Is that all it
meant to you that you can refer to it as,
'Oh, that'?" He looked away from her for
a moment and then, "It doesn't quite
work the way you think it does, Rosaleen.
You can't just turn it off the way you just
did." Looking at him, Rosaleen gave him
a steady gaze, and her voice rose in tone
to meet its level.

"Look, Colin, all this is probably old
hat to you, but it's not something I talk
about as a matter of course. It's a very big

step for me, but one I don't think I can go beyond, you can be sure of that."

"Wait a minute," Colin said, giving her a solemn look. "Back up a minute. What do you mean by 'this is probably old hat to me'? What kind of person do you take me for?" Turning away from her for a moment, he then looked at her. "Sure there's a lot of it around. I never have to go looking for it. But after a while, it becomes all the same; you can't tell where one leaves off and another begins. You forget what one girl likes and another doesn't, and believe me, it can get you in a whole lot of trouble . . ." Seeing the sudden change in Rosaleen's expression, Colin broke off, and raising a hand to his face, he groaned behind it. "Oh, Rosaleen, you must know what I'm talking about." Then lifting his head to look at her, studying her face, he gave her a long, steady look. "So alright, all girls are not the same. Some of them go for this sort of stuff and some don't. You don't, and maybe that makes you different, but, baby . . ." This endearment from Colin's lips, never ceasing to make her blood rise under any circumstances, caused Rosaleen to look away, but not before Colin saw that it brought a certain look to her eyes and a blush to her cheeks, " . . . you're special too; you're special to me and I would have kept hands off forever, if you had asked me to; but I thought you were ready." Looking away again, Rosaleen asked,

"Colin, what would you have done if I hadn't stopped you?" Looking at her in disbelief, Colin said,

"Don't you know?" Getting no immediate reply, he tilted his head to look at her face.

Even without looking into her eyes, Colin could see the innocence in her, yet not mistaking it for naivety, and definitely not for vulnerability, for they were not to be confused: he thought of the many he knew who, while making themselves so readily available, had lost that part *believed* to be innocence, while, in truth, their real innocence did not disappear with one swift act, but, rather, with each fleeting moment they submitted their wills, without question, and without thought of consequence, and that, though it be committed a thousand times, became *that* many times their real loss of innocence, and, if not restrained, reduced them to a state in which the soul is deadened and the body becomes mindless, and that definitely was not Rosaleen. No, her innocence was eternal and could never be destroyed; not even by force. For whatever it was she believed in it had made her strong, and this strength that he saw in her, he had yet to find in anyone so young, boy or girl.

Reaching out his hand, he stroked her head.

"C'mon," he told her tenderly, "I think it's time we went home."

On the way back, as though hit by sudden inspiration, Colin interrupted their journey before they were even halfway home, and, much to Rosaleen's great curiosity, they got off the bus.

Taking her hand, Colin led her up through the treelined avenue to a large building site. Upon seeing the scaffolded, red-brick edifice, Rosaleen recognized it as the new church which had been under construction for some time and she looked quizzically at Colin. Without a word, he proceeded to lead her to the very front of the site and there, looking out onto the main road, was a large billboard sign which read:

BUILDING UNDER CONSTRUCTION
CHURCH OF THE SACRED HEART

and within the list of names of the various contractors,

JOINERS:
WILLIAM P. MURDOCH & SONS

stood out.

Rosaleen gasped, as she saw the name, and then she saw the unconcealed pride on Colin's face.

"Oh, Colin! I read about it in the paper when they laid the foundation stone, and you told me that you were a joiner, but . . . but . . . was that . . . is that you?" she exclaimed.

"Well, just one of them is; I have to give my brother *some* of the dues."

"Oh, Colin," Rosaleen said again, still awed by the significance of the whole thing.

"It's our first big job, and what a break

for the old man — for all of us."

"Oh, I'm sure it'll be beautiful, it looks beautiful already, even before it's finished."

"C'mon," Colin told her. "You haven't seen anything yet."

He led the way across the not-yet leavened ground to a little side door, waving a hand to the day watchman, who was sitting outside his hut smoking a pipe.

Once inside, Rosaleen breathed in the smells that always accompany a new building, such as those bequested to the air by cement and new wood and which managed to cling forever till they become part of the atmosphere: they immediately reminded her of the new school wing that had been unveiled two years ago, particularly the science room, where sister's numerous jars of formaldehyde, containing their little dissected specimens, could not erase the newness which seemed to prevail, almost sacredly, to caution the students and to command their respect as to the ominous cost of such surroundings.

Walking with Colin down the aisle,

though it could hardly be called one, since the church itself was without pews, still, it portrayed the semblence of an aisle for directly ahead of them, at the other end of the church, was an entire wall architecturally sketched with the markings of where the high-altar was going to be. But before coming to the end of it, Colin paused, and crossing over to his right stopped in front of one of the church's very first furnishings. Rosaleen watched as he bent down and took the end of a heavy dust canvas and proceeded to roll it up, revealing, as he did, a massive and magnificent pulpit. Throwing the entire roll of canvas up and over the top, he then held out his hand to Rosaleen.

Going to his side, she looked as he ran his hand over the fine oak grain, and touching the narrow panelled inserts of carved arabesque as though familiar with every intricate detail, he traced with his fingertips for Rosaleen variances in wood tones which, at first though difficult to detect, became highly distinguishable when viewed with a knowing eye and he told her,

"See these markings that are slightly

offset from the rest, well, if you look carefully and pay close attention to the direction of my finger, you'll begin to see definite lines form and you'll see letters appear that were not visible before." Then, as much as he seemed familiar with it all, his astonishment seemed to renew itself in sharing it with her. "Look, look at that! Did you see that? That was a fish I just traced. Now let me see if I can find you the snake and the four mice." Rosaleen, smiled at his enthusiasm, watched as he brought the animals forth, presenting each to her as it materialized in order of his promise.

"Isn't that fantastic?" he said, and, as though he were a magician pulling a real live rabbit from a hat, he gave her an otter with a fish in its mouth. Completely taken by this boyish pleasure in him, Rosaleen moved closer and tenderly placed a hand on his shoulder. "This is called illumination," he told her, watching intently for something he might have missed. "But you'd be surprised at the people who don't see anything; all this is just a bunch of carving to them." He broke off, suddenly, and brought to light with his forefinger the letters CIFIXEBANT. "I don't know what they stand for but I'm going to ask Monsignor Connolly the next time he comes . . . " he broke off, hearing Rosaleen's voice soft and gentle-like next to his ear.

"Then there were two thieves crucified with him; one on the right hand, and another on the left." Turning, Colin looked down at her, his eyes light with surprise, and, Rosaleen, nodding towards the panel, told him, "It's Latin, and it's a page from the *Book of Kells*: Matthew 27: Verse 38. It's all there," she said, nodding her head again.

"Well, well," Colin said, turning to her full face. "What do you know. Now where did you get all that from?" And Rosaleen, with the ghost of a smile in her eyes for him:

"They do teach us something in school, you know."

Colin looked at her and saw for a second time that day yet another side to her, and the light in his eyes grew even brighter as he, himself, smiling, responded.

"You're perfectly right. These panels were done in Dublin; they're exact replicas of pages from the *Book of Kells*." Then, turning back to the pulpit, looking at the overall structure of it, as though studying it for flaws, and, then, positive there were none, he told Rosaleen,

"Six months it took to make this; and that didn't include the panels; we had to wait for those to arrive before we could even cut, as everything had to be hand-cut to the minimum of a hair, in fact, I spent an entire fortnight on that alone. And, can you imagine, it took twelve coats of finish to get it to match exactly to the panels. You should've see the shop; everything came to a standstill because, while the actual applications were given, you couldn't even as much as sneeze for fear of getting a speck of dust on it. And there was no way to protect it with a cover, since the finish was highly tenacious. So the shop virtually shut down for the entire time," and he smiled, suddenly, bringing that period to mind. "The old man had a fit every time the new finish dried and it still didn't match. He still hasn't given the monsignor the bill for this yet, and I'd hate to be around when he does." He gave Rosaleen a long, tender look as he finished, and, she, smiling at him, brought her eyes filled with pride, to rest on the pulpit.

"Oh, but it's so beautiful, Colin. You couldn't really put a price on it. I mean, it's a treasure, and just like all treasures, it's priceless. It's truly a beautiful piece of work. You must really have great hands." Throwing her a quick glance, Colin caught her eye, then, clearing his throat, he added smilingly,

"Yeah, that's what they all say." And Rosaleen, though still filled with mis-givings about the afternoon, yet seeing the humour in what she had just said, smiled anyhow.

15

FOR Rosaleen, Tuesday night couldn't come fast enough. Since leaving Colin on Sunday night, she hadn't been able to get him or the afternoon they'd spent together out of her head. Over and over, she had relived his kisses, his embraces, and, to a certain extent, his caresses, but more than any of these, and above all else, she had relived the happiness of just being with him, of talking with him, seeing him smile and sharing his thoughts. So it was with a joyous heart and high spirits that she went up to the school to meet him.

Surprised at not finding him there when she arrived, for he was usually the first at the corner, always waiting for her to come, and when he didn't show up after fifteen minutes, Rosaleen with some concern, decided to go back to the house.

Wondering as to what she would say to her mother, as she was supposed to have gone to see a film with Mary, she ran into

Ann and Phyllis on their way up to the Hibs.

"Aren't you supposed to be out with your beau tonight?" Ann greeted her.

"I was," Rosaleen explained, "but I waited for almost twenty minutes and he didn't show up."

"Well, that's not like him, is it?" Ann attempting to console, "Something must've happened to hold him up. What are you gonna do now?"

"I was just going back to the house. Maybe he'll send a message down."

"Why don't you come on up to the Hibs with us." Ann offered, "If anything, you'll more than likely hear what's happened up there than you would sitting in the house. Besides, that's where he'll probably look for you." Thinking about it for a moment, Rosaleen was inclined to agree, besides, it would save her from having to explain to her mother.

After checking their coats and going up to the ladies room, Rosaleen told the girls that she would see them later as she wanted to have a smoke before going downstairs. Upon being left alone, her thoughts immediately went to Colin and

243

she thought of the irony in not seeing him that night above all nights; her mind having been consumed with him for two days and nights, and she felt gripped by frustration.

About to crush out her cigarette, which had given her a bad taste in her mouth, Rosaleen reached for the ash tray when the girl with the DA came in. Her eyes widened when she saw Rosaleen, and her face broke into a smile.

"Hello, there," she shouted to Rosaleen. "Hey, I hear you and Murdoch are goin' strong. Congratulations. You have succeeded where many a fool has tried and tried." Smiling, Rosaleen looked at this little tough girl she had come to like, and she questioned her shyly.

"You didn't happen to see Colin tonight by any chance, did you?" The girl, starting to comb her DA, spoke into the mirror.

"No, I didn't. Why? Isn't he here?"

"No," Rosaleen told her. "I was supposed to have met him at eight, but he wasn't at our usual place." And then, not wanting to put him a bad light, she added. "I just wondered if you had maybe seen him, or heard anything on your way out tonight, since this is the first time he hasn't shown up."

All the while Rosaleen was talking, the girl had put her comb away and had taken out a dark red lipstick and applied it back and forth across her lips, as Rosaleen looked on.

"He will, don't worry," she told Rosaleen. "Somethin' must've came up." Finishing with her lipstick, the girl then took her little finger and made a slight vertical track down the centre of her upper lip, creating two bright red, glossy half-moons, then, taking the lipstick again, she painted two wide smears, one across each cheek, and, while talking to Rosaleen, again through the mirror, she rubbed the paint into her face.

"But just let me tell you one thing, love. You'd better get a fast hold on Murdoch; he's better off with you than with them friggers he calls his mates. You know, on Sunday night, from about half-past eleven on, probably after they left here, they were hangin' around the corner, carryin' on somethin' terrible. You could hear them all over the neighbourhood. I got home about half-past twelve and found my auld da out in the passage-way in his shirt sleeves. He had been up to the corner tryin' to get them to hold down the noise, and the abuse they gave him was shockin'." She stopped to light a cigarette from the end of Rosaleen's and then, half-leaning, half-sitting against the table, she went on. "He told them he was goin' to ring big McFeely and, as he turned to walk away, one of them threw a porter bottle at him. But, let me tell you," she said, narrowing her eyes and pointing her cigarette, "if that bottle had hit him, I would've killed every one of them with my bare hands, includin' Colin Murdoch," she added.

"Wait a minute." Rosaleen stopped her. "Colin wasn't with them on Sunday night; he was with me."

"Well, he was when Mr Greer went up to them, because when he couldn't get them to keep quiet, he came to our house to tell my da, and he mentioned about how surprised he'd been to see Colin Murdoch there at that hour, seein' how early he rises for work in the mornings, which is more than you can say for some

246

of the others." Puzzled, Rosaleen asked the girl,

"Are you sure it was Colin? Because I was with him all day, and when I left him at half-past ten, he said he was tired and was going straight home to bed."

"Well, he must've met the crowd comin' out of the Hibs and walked home with them. All I know is that there was a lot of drink goin' around, 'cause there's a club around our way where they can get it at the back door. So maybe, again, he just stopped and had a bottle or two." Now standing in front of the mirror the girl, her cigarette clenched between her teeth, tucked her blouse into her skirt, turned up the collar, and nodded to Rosaleen, "Are you comin'?"

There was a slow dance going on as they emerged from the lighted hallway into the dance-hall, and letting their eyes get accustomed to the dimness, the two girls paused momentarily by the door. Suddenly, from around the corner, but out of sight of them, came a voice proclaiming in insolent tones.

"Well! Well! Well! If it isn't Mary Magdalen and Virgin Mary together.

Now isn't that a sight for sore eyes." Rosaleen didn't have to look to see that it was one or other of Colin's mates; the ones she now knew were referred to as 'Chancer' and 'Bopper', but she turned around anyway and saw the two of them in the corner.

"Don't pay them any attention," she heard the girl beside her say. "They're only out for their usual kicks, which, for them, is always below the belt." The dance was coming to an end just then and the girl went off and Rosaleen walked over to where Ann and Phyllis would be under the record-box.

The rest of the night passed quietly, but despite Ann's predictions, Colin did not come looking for her. And so it was, that filled with the awful uncertainty of not knowing why he stood her up, or when she would see him again, Rosaleen's thoughts became morose and foreboding.

It was within the depth of this mood that towards the end of the night, about the third to the last dance, a young fellow, who Rosaleen knew by sight, asked her to dance. But no sooner had she reached the floor than she wished she hadn't accepted. For starters, her mood became somewhat ludicrous, for the record which was playing was Fats Domino's 'Blueberry Hill', and it, while being effective and conducive to a more memorable train of reverie, caused a paradox with her already present train of thought, and, on top of this, forced her into the arms of someone other than Colin, wherein she was stung by the double ambiguity of her situation.

Coming around the floor, the fellow struck up a conversation, with him doing most of the talking, and Rosaleen listening only half attentively, for her thoughts were completely filled with Colin and hardly on what he was saying, they passed in front of the doorway. For a few seconds their forms were clearly visible in the rectangle of light made by the open door and, just as they passed on, the sound of voices, singing along with the record, rose to greet them.

Rosaleen's partner, completely engrossed now in his part of the conversation and oblivious to anything else that might be going on, paid not the slightest heed to the two standing in the shadow of the corner, just beyond the light from the doorway. But Rosaleen, not so impenetrable to anything that might in the least possible way concern Colin, the littlest of which at the moment were these two mates of his, gave them the benefit of her gaze by looking in their direction.

Standing shoulder to shoulder, each with an arm about the other, they struck a pose that bore the suggestion of an innocent duet; except, in passing them, Rosaleen heard something other than what was supposed to be, for instead of singing the proper words to the song, these two had substituted those of their own, and loaded with brazen insinuations — with references to Sunday afternoon on the Cavehill, the chorus of the song spilling out like filth, concerning the intimacies she had shared with Colin — they were deliberately aimed at her.

The words were a death knell to her. She felt the blood drain from her entire system, which left her weak to the point of nausea.

Beyond earshot of them now, the

fellow she was dancing with, apparently either not hearing them, or pretending he didn't, carried on with his story. But Rosaleen, unable to wait for a suitable break in the conversation, said in the steadiest voice she could muster up, "Would you excuse me," and, then, leaving him there on the dance-floor with a look of complete surprise on his face, she walked away.

The hardest part for her now was to pass the corner with the two of them standing there, and she had to do it in such a way that would give them the least satisfaction; she had to do it with as much deliberation and calmness as she could find within herself at that moment. So walking towards the door, she fixed her eyes on the light, the one single, solitary light in the hall, and with steps that felt like her feet had been nailed to the floor, she walked slowly and painfully past them.

On down the narrow hall she walked, feeling their eyes in her back like spears, and even though it took but a second for the boy in the cloakroom to hand her her coat, it was long enough for the raucous laughter to reach her ears from the corner of the dance-hall.

Managing to give the boy a weak smile, she purposely remained outside the cloakroom until she had both arms in the sleeves of her coat, and when she had it fully buttoned, then, and only then, did she go down the stairs.

Taking one step at a time, she was finding it more and more difficult to see the stone substances under her feet, for they kept coming at her like big grey waves, with each one coming closer and faster than the one before, until it was as if she were running from the water's edge into the deep, with the power of the mighty ocean before her to swallow her up. But taking hold of the wooden banister with both hands, she managed to hold on, and upon reaching the last step, she pulled open the big, heavy, wooden door, and feeling the immediate rush of cool air on her face, she rushed headlong into it in an effort to thwart off any and all effects the whole experience had wrought on her.

Wednesday at school passed in agony; Wednesday night, about half-past seven, a little girl about eight years old, came knocking on the door, asking for her.

"Rosaleen," the child said, "A man up at McCluskey's corner sent me down to tell you he wants to talk to you."

Rosaleen brought her height down to the level of the little girl's, and putting a hand on her shoulder, she spoke earnestly into the child's face. "Elizabeth, you be very sure and tell the man up at the corner that Rosaleen's not home and that you don't know where she is. Will you do that?"

The child nodded her head and smiled shyly, and Rosaleen, looking into the little face that Colin had just looked upon, and would look upon again in a minute or so, kissed her ever so lightly on the forehead, and through closed eyelids, said to her, "That's a good girl." She then went in and closed the door shut.

Thursday, Mary invited Rosaleen home for dinner and to which they went directly after school. Grateful for the opportunity to relax a little without having to worry about a knock on the door, for, as of Tuesday, she felt that she could never look Colin Murdoch straight in the face again, Rosaleen attempted to shed some of her heavy mood.

Besides the splendid dinner, there was one other highlight of the evening which gave Rosaleen some joy and warmed her heart in a very melancholy way.

Seated with Mary, her parents and one of her brothers in a very stately drawing room, they were served tea, wheeled in on a tea-server, by the uniformed-maid, who poured the tea from a silver tea-service and passed around fine pastries on multilayered silver-rimmed china. After tea, Mary went to the piano, and after several pieces of her own choosing, to loosen up her fingers, her mother invited Rosaleen to make a selection.

There was nothing more Rosaleen would rather have her friend play right than a composition first introduced to her by her own father, when she was just a child, and one which she had had an affinity for ever since, the hauntingly beautiful Handel's *Largo*.

Not sure whether or not it was her own mood that produced the effect, but Rosaleen had never heard Mary play so overwhelmingly emotional, and the effect was heightened even further when Mary's brother raised his violin to his shoulder and accompanied her, and the mood which resulted, Rosaleen thought, must have been acutely in sync with the composer's own state of mind when he had been creating it.

Sitting there, letting the music encompass her, she could no longer prevent the thought of Colin from creeping in, and even though she had struggled with the attempt to keep it from her mind for two whole days, along with the self-promise never to think about it again, their afternoon on the Cavehill. And she resigned herself to the fact that no matter what vulgarity he may have found in it, to her, it had been beautiful: it had been her first real awakening to love; it had been her first real response as a woman to a man, and she wasn't ashamed of neither what had happened, nor what had not. For while she had gone as far as her conscience had allowed her, and while it had not been physically consummated, she knew in her heart that all of the gestures that had taken place between them; the kisses, the embraces, the touches, the caresses, the endearments — the passions themselves — all the individual sensings of love-making had been hers; what matter that she had not experienced them all in one single moment, she would remember all of them as they had come to her; slowly, gently, tenderly, caringly, lovingly, and passionately, at least by her record of it, and these would be the memories of her first love, forever.

Thanking Mary's parents and saying goodbye to them at the door, Rosaleen walked with Mary and her brother to the bus stop, and waving to them from the platform, she saw them wait until the bus disappeared from sight.

With her friend's recital still in her head, Rosaleen was followed by Handel as she got off the bus at Northumberland Street and cut through the narrow, winding side streets, rather than big busy Albert Street.

As she walked, she couldn't help but draw comparisons between her neighbourhood, with its treeless pavements and tiny, little row houses without gardens, and the one she had just come from. But these were her streets, she had been born on them, had grown up on them, and she loved them, every last one.

Walking along, and without making a sound on the pavement, she followed her shadow, which, with the moon behind her, was cast before her, long and distant-like, almost separate from her, as though it were not hers; that it didn't belong to her; that it was just there by coincidence, leading the way up one street, around the corner, and down another. Then, becoming pre-occupied with the odd contradiction of it, and as though needing to convince herself that, indeed, it did belong to her, she began to look for something in it with which to identify.

For two or three blocks, Rosaleen couldn't find one, single common factor that could associate her with this shadowy image which walked the pavements ahead of her; that is, until turning one corner, when the light of the moon, shifting in angle, suddenly, as though presenting her with a claim-check to her own shadow, revealed, above all things, the one thing which made her sure that this had been her own and not anyone else's that she'd been following all the while, and it was nothing more than the insignificant length of her school uniform, which being ridiculously short, merely prompted her to consider that within a few short weeks, she would be able to discard it for good.

Coming towards her own street now, turning the corner, whereby, normally, being with Colin, she would turn right and in the direction of the school, but tonight, and alone, Rosaleen turned left, in the direction of home. Attempting not to notice the sudden pang of remorse, she looked once again to her shadow, but realized, too late, that with the new direction she'd taken, the moon, with its light, was now ahead of her, and her shadow, which had previously gone before her, had now been discarded to secondary position, where it followed, sight unseen, behind her.

Of the few times that Rosaleen had unexpectedly come across Colin, in the relatively short time she had known him, none of the encounters had ever thrown her, nor had they unsteadied her as much as this one right then. She came upon him completely by surprise; but it was no surprise to Colin, for he had been waiting for her.

Hearing her name come out of the darkness at her in a voice that, to her, might just as well have come from heaven itself, with the total unexpectedness of it, caused her to jump and brought her heart to her mouth and drained her veins of everything but the adrenaline that was flowing from the pit of her stomach to her head, where it was pumped with such velocity throughout her entire body as to make her head spin, that she had to stop and compose herself before finding it possible to co-ordinate her walking ability with her runaway emotions.

Colin, standing before her, towering over her, her slight frame diminished even more so by her school uniform, looked down at her, and with eyes looking like they had just been set alight, and with a sudden smile to his lips, as his gaze swept over her, and in a voice, which, if she didn't know better, she would acknowledge as an affectionate tone.

"Well, well," he said, his smile broadening, as his gaze deepened. "I see you're wearing the old Celtic colours." And with eyes encompassing her entire figure, his visual response reflecting in his voice, "Let me say, miss, that you do them more justice than most of the footballers I've come across on the field."

At some other time and on some other occasion, Rosaleen might have readily warmed to his teasing manner; even revelled in it, for practically everything Colin Murdoch said and did had a provocative ring to it, something which she knew could only be captured by one such as himself, to be woven like thread into the web of his personality, only to magically reappear as charm to captivate even the most wary, such as she herself who, from the very beginning, had fallen prey and who, with the mitigated suspect of the fly, had crept deeper and deeper along the strands towards the heart, where they were held together. Only too late had she discovered that that which she'd hoped would sustain her, had merely served to ensnare her and hold her for such times as the host itself would see fit to unravel her with the benefit of his presumptuous wit, which never failed to touch and arouse the deepest of her sensitivities, all of which, even now, in spite of her reserve, were racing to the surface in obeisance to his tantalizing tone.

"You know, if I didn't know better, I would take you for just another little schoolgirl."

She, who for four days and nights, had endured no end of remorse as a result of his arrogant suggestiveness, concerning the afternoon they'd spent on the mountain, was now reminded of it as he confronted her with the exact same titillating insinuation, and she was languished by the memory to which he alluded.

Now completely caught off guard, she felt herself swept up in his embrace and her lips seized by his in what she hopelessly wanted to believe was his way of abating four days of growing hunger — it certainly would be hers.

Lessening his hold on her just enough to move away from the light of the street lamp, he pulled her into the protective shadow of the wall and looked down at her with eyes that were like blue fire in the night, and his hands about her shoulders seemed to be pushing her into the ground, as though their owner wanted to root her there.

"Where were you?" he said, in a voice that equalled his eyes, "I've been waiting for hours."

Finding it hard to say anything, Rosaleen threw him a look which, along with a tone in her voice, quenched the fire within him, and she watched it die. "You needn't have bothered. I have nothing to say to you."

Looking at her in disbelief, Colin's voice came alive with another element. "Rosaleen! Are you mad at me for not showing up on Tuesday night? Look, that's what I wanted to tell you, to explain to you, that I had an accident at work on Tuesday just before quitting time. Look," he said, holding up a bandaged thumb, and in a softer tone, "Eight stitches, that's what you cost me."

Rosaleen repeated his pronouncement and almost choked on it. "*I* cost you?"

"Yes", he confirmed. "I was thinking about you at the time it happened, and not about what I was doing. It happened so fast that I didn't even feel it until I saw the blood; but that was because I had just put a new blade in the electric saw that made it such a clean cut."

Rosaleen's face tightened at the thought of him being injured, but she had well prepared her defences in advance and there was nothing he could say or do anymore that would ever cause them to weaken.

"I'm sorry you got hurt," she said, her apology dry and cold.

Either not noticing her tone, or thinking everything to be alright between them, Colin replied, "Oh, this is nothing. It happens all the time on the job. But I just wanted to let you know the reason why I didn't show up; I'm just sorry there wasn't enough time to let you know then. I didn't get home till after eight, and with the sedatives, and all, they gave me, I was half asleep before I even got into the house." Then with his eyes and voice warming to her, he took a step closer. "I hope you didn't wait too long, besides, I had an idea that you'd go on up to the Hibs." And, pausing, he waited for her to reply, but not getting any, he asked her,

"Did you go to the Hibs?"

Without keeping him waiting any longer, she answered, looking at him coldly, seemingly unaffected by his new warmth, or by his nearness. "Oh, yes, I went to the Hibs, alright."

Throwing his good hand out in a gesture of regret, Colin reproached himself. "See! I knew I should've sent word down with one of the mates; they were just heading in that direction when we passed them on the road." But, then, having second thoughts, he added. "Oh, well, maybe it's better this way. I don't like having messages delivered by a go-between; things tend to get built up out of proportion. By the time they got to you, I'd have lost an arm or something." He started to smile, but lost it halfway, as he saw the look on Rosaleen's face, and before he could ask what the matter was, she got her say in first.

In cool, clear, pointed tones, she poured her voice over him, her words spilling out like cold, hard ice. "Do they, Colin? Do people really exaggerate?" But the ice cracked, as Colin, stung by the sudden effect, turned pale. "Or do they tell it as it is; exactly the way it has been told to them?"

With a hurt, but puzzled look in his eyes, Colin asked in an unusually low, quiet tone, "Rosaleen, what are you talking about?"

The ice, completely melted now, but, running with the emotional turbulence of having been prematurely evoked. "Oh, you know very well what I'm talking about. You went straight to them on Sunday night, after leaving me, and you stood at the corner with them, drinking and telling them about us; where we went; what we did."

Colin's jaw dropped, his face taking on an expression of disappointment, of hurt and bewilderment, sadly changed to remorse, and Rosaleen, seeing all of this, interpreted it as guilt at having been caught carrying tales, and she accepted it as final confirmation. And, thus, feeling now as though they had come to a dead end, tears started to well up in her eyes, but determined not to break down, she halted them and held them back and they remained there, glistening under the street lamp.

"There's only one thing I regret, Colin," she told him, when she was sure of a steady voice, "and that is of not finishing it with you. At least you would have been telling the truth, you wouldn't have to lie about it."

"Rosaleen!" The strength and volatility behind the tone brought Rosaleen up short and she stood there frozen to the spot, forced to stare at him. "Now, I don't know what's going on here, or what you heard, or who you heard it from. But I want you to listen to what I have to say. I did not tell anyone about us — no one — you understand? It's little enough I've had to do to stop thinking about it. I haven't been able to put you out of my mind . . . Sure, I told them that we spent the day on the Cavehill, but nothing more . . . Sure, they slagged me about it, but do you really think so little of me to believe that I would talk to them about us? They are free to think what they like. I can't censor their thoughts or prevent them from forming their own opinions. The hell I care about what they think, and you shouldn't either. Let them believe what they want."

But Rosaleen was having none of it. "Wait a minute." she said, half shouting at him, "Wait a minute. With your track record, who could believe anything else?" With this pronouncement, she saw Colin wince, but determined to get it over with once and for all, she continued, "Or do you deny the fact that you made a ten shilling bet with them the first night you took me home? So sure were you, that you, Colin Murdoch, could have your way with any girl, that you were able to lay down a sure bet on it. Well, it must've broken your heart to lose that money. Next time, don't bet, just go down to the Plaza, I hear there's a nifty little corner where you can buy it, when poor suckers like Blondie don't provide enough of a challenge . . . "

"Rosaleen!" Colin exclaimed, sensing her near-hysteria, and he attempted to grab her hands.

But Rosaleen was too quick for him, and taking one long, last look, she left him standing alone on the darkened pavement, and hurried on down the street.

16

THE week of Junior Exams came at last, but the past three weeks had wrought endless pressure on Rosaleen, the chief one being the absence of Colin from her life. She just couldn't get over him, no matter how determined she was. Everything reminded her of him — first and foremost, herself. Every time she looked in the mirror, she saw the eyes that he'd looked into, the cheeks that he'd touched and the lips that he'd kissed; and when combing her hair, it was the hair that he'd caressed, and on, and on, and on . . . endless things; the clothes that she'd worn when with him, the streets they'd walked together, the very buses they had rode on their dates, and though all of them looked identical, it was this common quality that endeared each one to her as being the one in which they might have sat side by side.

But it was the music on the wireless that disrupted Rosaleen's life the most, for nearly every song that was played on Radio Luxembourg, the top-ten station, kept his memory burning her mind and her heart — and out of all the artists that sang their songs of love, it was Johnny Mathis who taunted her most of all.

With all of this to contend with, Rosaleen wondered how she was going to make it through the exams themselves. No sooner was one over, than she could barely remember what it was about. The entire week was just one long, endless continuity of entering the exam room with its row upon row of desks, each with a personally assigned four-digit number pasted on the top, left-hand corner; a number that was to be her identity for the entire week: 8530 was what she wrote on every sheet of paper she used and on every printed exam page, over and over.

8530, the number branded itself into her brain so that when she slept, she heard it throughout her entire dreams where it became an enigma to her, and that, along with other things, caused her nights to be filled with anguish, just like her days:

"Where is 8530?" demanded the booming voice of Bopper the Bailiff, and the question resounded through her room, shaking her bed with its impact.

"She has gone to be with Napoleon again," offered Chancer the Prosecutor, introducing the evidence.

"Then cut off her arms," came the high order from Bopper, Colin's number one Magistrate, passing sentence before Chancer, Foreman of the Jury, handed over the verdict.

"8530 has been found guilty."

The Magistrate sneered,

"Then cut off her arms so that she will never go there again," and the sneering became a roar, "WHEN THE WEEK IS OVER, CUT OFF HER ARMS."

"But 8530 cannot dance without her arms," implied the deceitful voice of reprieve, and the courtroom rose in one voice.

"Stitch them! Stitch them!" and the number one Magistrate, beckoning the favour of the majority, malevolently pronounced, "Eight stitches

give her . . . only eight."
And his voice, with an appeasing tone, emptied the nightmare with the finality of a gavel.

Every night it was the same, and every morning Rosaleen had to sit and see that number on the corner of her desk. Once, she almost stopped in the middle of the exam to write a letter to Colin, begging him to forgive her and telling him how she really felt about him, and she was simply going to sign it, Yours truly, 8530. He would never know who sent it.

That was how overwrought she was. Under normal circumstances she would never entertain such a notion. But she was willing to try anything just to get word to him that somebody cared for him, he didn't necessarily have to know that it was her, it would be enough just for her to know that he knew somebody really cared about him, despite all of the cruel things she had said. If only she could erase that look from his eyes, and stop the pain that had marred his beautiful features in their last moments together, and which had become cemented into a mask before her eyes, and one that she couldn't get rid of.

And then, too, she had the pressure against failing the exam, because she had been told in advance by her mother that if she didn't pass, she would have to take it over again the following year, which would mean another whole year at school, repeating everything all over again. She could never do that.

And then came the last exam and the number 8530 was peeled from the desk, leaving behind a formidable blank: the official tag was to be placed with her final test papers and sent to the Ministry of Education at Stormont, wherein whose files the number 8530 would live immortal — no other student would ever be branded with it.

The exams over; the nightmares stopped and Rosaleen went to confession.

Two weeks passed and it was a Saturday afternoon when Rosaleen got word that the exam results were out. Filled with such painful anticipation and unable to wait for the post, she went to a telephone kiosk that same afternoon and telephoned the school. Ann, who was with her, stood quietly by her side as she held the line, waiting while the sister looked up her results.

The sister who had answered the telephone had never had Rosaleen as a pupil and she was very precise and abrupt as she came back on the line, which didn't help Rosaleen who, holding the receiver in a vice-grip, felt her palm moist with perspiration, created by the anxiety of the moment. Now, hearing the receiver being picked up on the other end, she brought her other hand to her eyes and she closed them tightly, as if, in doing so, she could shut out the inevitable. The sister's voice was exact and cool, as it came through the wire.

"The results are not listed in order of the students' names. I will have to have your exam number. Do you remember what it was?" Drawing the necessary breath with which she needed to reply, Rosaleen said,

"Yes, sister, it was 8530," and with her hand over the mouthpiece and casting her eyes to the ceiling, she murmured, more to herself than to the girl at her side, "How could I forget."

Now with a mixed expression of both

hopefulness and hopelessness, she turned to Ann with her fingers crossed. But there was something within her that Ann didn't see: it was the silent prayer in her heart that she wouldn't have to go back to school, that she could get out into the world and get a chance to spread her wings.

She heard the receiver being picked up once more and she heard the sister draw in her breath before saying,

"8530? Yes, you have passed the examination. You will receive an official notification from the Ministry of Education. It should be in the post on Tuesday."

"Thank you very much, sister," Rosaleen said in an almost inaudible whisper, "Goodbye."

Gently cradling the receiver, she let loose with a scream. There was no need to put it into words for Ann, but Rosaleen did so in an excited voice.

"I passed, Ann. I passed. Oh, thank God, it's all over," and as she received a congratulatory hug from Ann, she felt the emotions which she had been suppressing, rise slowly within her and come to rest barely beyond the protective gleam in her eyes.

"Hey, Rosie," Ann's voice broke in on her pensive mood, as they walked back home, "why don't we go to the Plaza tonight." But seeing the negative look on Rosaleen's face, she knew that it was going to take a lot of persuasion on her part. "Look, we'll go and celebrate your having passed the exam." She got nowhere. "Just think, Rosie, no more school work! You're as free as a bird." Nothing. Ann knew that it was going to take more than mere persuasion, so she approached with a new weapon — out and out sneakiness, and she knew it. But she also knew that Rosaleen hadn't been out of the house in five weeks, apart from school, and so she was willing to try anything. She now slung her last shot, knowing she was hitting below the belt and knowing perfectly well how much it was going to hurt. But she'd rather see her friend in pain than see her continue to feel nothing at all; more than once she had come across Rosaleen looking like death warmed up. "Oh, for God's sake, Rosaleen," she flung at her, "if it's Colin

Murdoch you're afraid of, forget it. You've no chance of running into him. He's been going with a girl from the Shankill this past month; I hear it's pretty serious too," and throwing Rosaleen a side glance, "What with her being his own kind, and all, you know, Protestant. So you're only wasting your time worrying about him." And then, as an aside, "We didn't want to say anything to you before this."

It was the 'we' bit that grabbed Rosaleen and she lashed out retaliatively.

"'We'? Who's the 'we'?"

"Oh, everybody," Ann told her firmly. "Everybody knows you two broke it off, besides, he goes everywhere with . . . ah . . . Marian . . . I think that's her name. Lovely wee girl she is too." Rosaleen threw her a look.

"Oh, thanks a lot, Ann."

"Sure," Ann threw back at her, "what else are friends for?"

17

THE Plaza was jam-packed, which was always the case on a Saturday night, and whatever it was that provoked Rosaleen during the time between the afternoon and then, she was feeling somewhat lightheaded and unusually giddy and she was enjoying herself in a reckless sort of way; a feeling, she knew, that came with the utter freedom of being out of school. And so it was with this carefree attitude that she went so far as to accept a dance from a man much older than she, and, who was sporting a 'Clark Gable' moustache. Then she went one further by going back to the EL MOMBO ROOM with him for coffee.

But it was here, sitting amongst so many memories, that reminded Rosaleen of the last time she was here; the night that had been the 'crossing over' in her relationship with Colin, and she was suddenly filled with a great longing for him. Now barely able to remain with this older 'Lothario' for one moment longer, she got up to leave, and he followed her out.

Coming into the ballroom, Rosaleen saw that the dance had reached the request period of the evening, for many of the dancers had crowded around the bandstand, and the debonair bandleader was smiling broadly towards the ball-room and, with arms widely spread, he beckoned those still sitting at the tables to come forward. Rosaleen felt 'Clark Gable' steering her to the front of the crowd, and she cringed inwardly, as she felt his hands go about her shoulders.

"Well, ladies and gentlemen," the bandleader addressed the floor, "as you all know by now, this is request time. Anything you want to hear, just come on up and whisper in my ear, especially the ladies. Everything is on me; my band, my vocalists. So don't be shy; I'm not. Look, I'll even break the ice for you by making the first request," and turning to the vocalists; a handsome young male singer and a pretty female brunette, who were standing by the microphone. "Hey, Jim," the bandleader called to the young pair, "How about a nice ballad for all the young lovers here tonight."

Now standing just a few feet away from the singers, Rosaleen covered her ears as the requests came flying over her head like stones. The male singer, feeling the avalanche, withdrew from the line of fire, as he tried to bring some order to the chaos. But it was the girl singer who, taking the stand, managed to bring some calm, if not total order, to the proceedings, and she looked down into the crowd. And, as was now their show-business practice, it was she who performed the female requests, and he, the male, and so it was to the girls that she looked for requests.

Suddenly Rosaleen felt a great compulsion sweep over her, and she heard herself saying, as she caught the singer's eye,

"Wild is the Wind!" Not sure of what prompted her to make any request at all, never mind that particular one, all Rosaleen knew was that it was a Johnny Mathis song, and that it had been released the week just before she and

Colin had gone to the Cavehill: it was also the one she had heard him singing to himself on the way home on the bus that day, as they'd sat in the last seat at the back, having the entire top of the bus to themselves. It had been after he had taken her to show her his work, which had created a special closeness between them, and she had smiled at him in an encouraging way, and he had brought his arm across her shoulder and pulled her nearer to him, and he had sang softly in her ear.

In the weeks that followed, when she knew that she and Colin were finished for good, every time she heard that song on the wireless, she'd had to run upstairs and close the bedroom door, for through the song she'd relive, moment by moment, that day, from the second they'd met, until they had kissed good-night; that is, until she'd had a talk with Father Hanlon, and she hadn't dared think about it again.

Now standing there and listening to the opening of the same song; the beautiful instrumentals alone, without the assistance of the even more beautiful haunting words, was enough to receive the memory of it all over again. Only now, instead of Colin's arms embracing her, she felt the unfamiliar hands of the stranger she was now with, and so, with heart like lead, and arms and legs like dead limbs, she closed her eyes to shut him out, and did her best to envision the feeling that only one man in the whole world could awaken in her.

Like someone dispossessed of her body, Rosaleen was far removed from the Plaza. She was on a hilltop thick with gorse and tall trees touching the sky. There was a cliff hanging over into nothingness. There was a stillness interrupted by nothing but a soft breeze blowing on her face, and through her hair, and, once in a while, playing with the hem of her dress, and carrying it above her knees. There was a man, whose eyes were deeper than the sky and warmer than the sun, with arms more sturdy than the strongest tree, with lips much softer than the breeze, with hands so powerful, they could shape her destiny.

And then, as the words came alive, Rosaleen felt their intensity with deep yearning. And now it was all gone; her deepest yearnings would never be fulfilled, for Rosaleen knew that she had loved and lost. Colin meant everything to her, but she was nothing to him. He had caught her off guard and had played with her emotions for his own amusement. But he would never do it again.

The song was finished and the applause was loud and long, and now, as only performers can, who are completely in sync with their audience, the vocalists started to kid around, while still holding each and every one in the palm of their hands.

"I don't know what kind of magic Johhn Mathis holds for all you young people out there," quipped Jim, "but I do hope it's catching. I have a request here," he continued, "Now although this is not a blackout dance, this song is enough to make you want to take the one you love close to your heart. It is a love song, and I want you to listen to the words, as well as to the beautiful melody, they seem to say a whole lot." And as the first instrumental strains were heard, he added in afterthought, "By the way, this is also a

Mathis number. It's called 'No Love'."
And he shook his head slightly, as if to
reinforce his own admiration for the man.

Something began to stir in Rosaleen,
which was at the same time both exciting
and upsetting. Because of the fact that
the male vocalist was singing, told her
that the request was made by a man, and
because Johnny Mathis was her favourite
artist — something that Colin knew —
and that this particular song was one of
the first ones they had danced to on that
memorable night when they first met,
and, lastly, it was one that she had
expressed as being particularly beautiful,
and one of her favourites. With all these
individual surmises rushing in on her,
they came together to form only one
conclusion — that it was Colin who had
made the request.

The immediate suggestion of such a
thought created a ball of congestion in
the centre of her chest and it increased in
size as the thoughts started to build in her
mind, but not so much as with the
obvious, for as the final inference struck
her, the ball swelled all out of proportion
and burst upon her with the realization

that Colin was there at the Plaza, and she panicked.

The first emotion to manifest itself upon the acknowledgement of Colin being there was fear. His presence alone meant that he had heard her request, and knowing that she had made it would enable him to draw all sorts of conclusions, especially one that would tell him that she still thought about that day on the Cavehill and that it had meant something to her. She couldn't take that, and she felt that she would rather die first than let him know that.

Secondly, her thoughts flew to remind her that he was going with someone else now. Then this being Saturday, it could only mean that he was here with *her*. The notion of her seeing Colin with someone else had an immediate, painful effect, which deepened the more she thought about it, because she felt there was only one thing that could be worse than that, and that was of Colin knowing that she had seen him with another girl; she couldn't let that happen. But in order to avoid it, she had to know where he was. Dancing there in the midst of so many, her mind started racing through the crowds. Where was he? Could he see her? Was he watching her?

As she danced she could feel his eyes burning into her, following her wherever and whichever way she turned, just like the words of the song, which, she knew, would be a mockery to her if she saw him holding someone else in his arms. So with heart pounding every time she saw anyone who might even remotely resemble him, she closed her eyes against the possibility of this happening.

With eyes shut to all visual threats, she wished she could shut out the rest, for the words and the music were playing havoc with her emotions. Listening to them, she knew that deep down inside she was longing — aching — to see him, even from a distance. So there she was; hoping that she wouldn't see him, and, again, hoping that she would, and dreading the thought of either.

It was in this frame of mind, then, that she heard his voice breaking in on her thoughts, saying, "Excuse me, mate, I believe this one's mine."

Upon being taken by the hand from the

man she had been dancing with and into the arms of Colin was, for Rosaleen, like being swallowed up by a tidal wave while imagining to be merely paddling in a shallow stream; the after effects would be the same: gone was the ground under her feet, bringing with it the panic that prevents the breath and lightens the head and gives the sensation of never again reaching the shore.

The words and music, starting all over again, were at first stones around her neck, pulling her down, as she fought to keep her head above the water. But, then, all her old familiarities of Colin; the touch of his hand on hers, the warmth of his body against her, the magnificent magic he created with his eyes when they looked into her own, swept over her and she succumbed altogether.

With every last stone dissolved, the words and music became the heavenly song that one must hear upon awakening from the trauma of death, into a bright and wondrous world.

The singer told of a certain love, the kind that creates a flame in the heart, replaces fear with strength, and changes destinies; the singer told of a certain love that was thrilling and exciting and that would last beyond a lifetime; the singer told of a certain love that was greater and deeper than any other and that *no love* could ever touch his heart the way that this one could.

The dance ended, but the song continued on in Rosaleen's heart, and it was all there in her eyes for Colin to see — and she knew it, because she could see it reflected in his own as he looked down at her, but which, instead of accepting it as was, only led her to believe that there was more to it than that. For as much as she'd been open with him, which was a lot considering that the situation did not call for, nor was it one that should normally evoke the depth of a response such as she'd given him — even though it emerged against the control with which she'd fought to retain it — he had merely shown her that even with all the pain he had caused her, with all the suffering she had gone through, that no matter what differences of opinion they may have, she was still capable of arousing this passionate tendency in him — but then, with

Colin, so was any girl.

Now with a voice as soft as his eyes, he said to her, "What have you been doing with yourself lately, Rosaleen?"

But looking away so as not to give him the chance of captivating her anymore than he already had, she told him casually, "Well, as you know, I've had a week of exams, and that required a lot of studying. But that's all over now, thank God."

And then, bringing her face around to look at him, embarrassed by the awkward candidness between them, she met his eyes. But what she saw there was nothing like what she herself was feeling, for there was nothing awkward about his look; it was long, and steady, and very warm.

"So, you've hung up the old Celtic colours, and you're not a little school-girl anymore," he said, drawing her around by the shoulders to meet him full face, and giving her the benefit of his complete look, he added, "How does it feel to be a woman of the world?"

Feeling the sensations arise from every facet of her being and charge upon the crumbling strength of her once-solid resistance, Rosaleen summoned the aid of every muscle within her possession, which, under her direction, fought back the enemies of her soul until, when the war-cry had ended, and the battlefield quiet, she heard herself say, in a matter-of-fact tone, "And what about you, Colin? Has your work been keeping you busy?"

But Colin, being nobody's fool, had seen the blush that had captured her cheeks, and the strong glow of woman-hood that so steadily affixed her eyes to his own, and he was enraptured.

"As always," he told her. "In fact, we're up to six days a week, now that the weather has warmed."

Nurturing every minute of their being together with conversation, lest any projected silence threaten to take them apart, Colin continued to look at her, hoping to see still burning in her eyes, the answer to his yet unspoken question.

And she, while attempting to avert his look, his tone of voice, his stance; in fact, his total presence, was failing hopelessly, and as though this were a battle of the senses — hers — with every weapon being on his side, he now gathered reinforcements as the music began to start up again for the next dance.

Not knowing if his lingering with her like this meant that he wanted the next dance with her, and not sure if it would be too final a gesture just to walk away, Rosaleen gave him a quick look, as the couples surrounding them started to move around the floor. But, in doing so, Colin caught her eye, and made a move to put his arms around her.

"Rosaleen . . . " he started to say, but breaking off, he took her by the arm, and making his way through the intervining couples, he led her to the edge of the dance-floor.

Standing under the arc of a tiny, golden-yellow light, and hidden somewhat by the protective mass of one of the ball-room's giant pillars, Colin looked down at her, the top of her head not quite reaching his chin, and he discovered the trick imagery that one's eyes can play.

Blending with the deep brown curves of her hair, were little off-shoots of light that hid and then revealed themselves with every move of her head, and even when they vanished, as she tilted back her head to look up at him, they suddenly reappeared within the depths of her eyes, like little golden specks of light, which increased as her gaze deepened and became like stars themselves in the darkness of a night sky, and Colin wondered if this was what it was like on top of the Cavehill, on such a starry night.

"Rosaleen." His voice commanded her eyes to remain fixed where they were on his, and he felt the urge to place his hands on her shoulders as though to evoke the right response from her. "I want to talk to you," he said, hesitating, then, "Let me take you home."

His voice had come down softly to her as she stood there between the shadow of the pillar and his own, and while she was still deeply affected by all that had just taken place within her and, despite her strong resolve, she drowned now completely in his eyes, and looking back at him, she wished with all her heart that if it were within her power she would make him feel, just once, what she was feeling right then, and she told him, "I'll have to tell Ann. Wait for me here."

Walking away from him, she could feel his eyes follow her until she was lost from his sight by the couples on the floor.

Seeking out Ann, and telling her of her intention, she went and got her coat, and then ran to catch the last bus home.

18

WITH the month of June running into July, Rosaleen's mother and father, as by way of a present in passing her Junior Exam, put off any immediate plans that she might have had in looking for work. So with several weeks of summer ahead of her, she accepted an invitation to spend a fortnight at a relative's place in the country.

Having many cousins her own age, both male and female, who had also been invited, and which turned the entire holiday into one big family reunion, provided Rosaleen with the emotional break she needed, whereupon returning to Belfast, she was calm, cool and collected.

Even when invited by Ann to go to the Hibs that same Saturday night, she accepted without even as much as an argument, much to Ann's surprise and delight, since she, herself, had not been there much since Rosaleen's absence, now that Phyllis was going steady with Jimmy.

Almost immediately, upon entering, Rosaleen knew that something was going on, for the atmosphere was charged with excitement. It wasn't long before she and Ann were told the reason — it was the night that the jiving contest was to be held. Everybody was there; 'wee' Andy, 'Dirty Eyes', his hair now grown back somewhat, Manuel, and all the rest of the jivers, and Colin.

The contest was very informal, with no special rules or format; the dancers simply got out onto the floor, boy-girl, and as the records were played, starting with a slow dance, and proceeding into slow, then fast jiving, those who tired left the floor and were automatically eliminated. But partners were permitted to split; a girl could leave the floor and be replaced by another, with the other taking over where she left off, but once the girl left, she couldn't come back on to the floor, neither to the same partner nor to any other.

Rosaleen was both excited and anxious

at the prospect of seeing so many good dancers on the floor at the same time, and of seeing who would outlast who. Taking seats that would give them full view of the floor, she and Ann then sat back to watch, as the first record started, and, although most of those participating had apparently prearranged everything, two young fellows tried to persuade the two girls to join them on the floor, but Ann and Rosaleen, smiling, both declined, their smiles widening into grins, as the fellows turned their backs.

The first record was Jim Reeves' 'She'll Have To Go', and every one destined for the contest was on the floor, and the girls though anxious to see who was dancing with whom, passed the word between them in subdued and discreet tones.

It was Ann who first spotted Colin, and when she saw who he had as a partner, she couldn't refrain from giving Rosaleen a dig with her elbow. Rosaleen didn't need to know why, she just had to look and see Colin coming around the floor, and with none other than Maisie Boyle, from Beechmount. Maisie was a nice looking girl, and one Rosaleen admired both for her quiet manner as well as for her beautiful face, her long auburn tresses, and for her magnificently proportioned body: nobody, but nobody, wore v-necked sweaters better than Maisie; they were invented for her, and Rosaleen did not come to this conclusion by herself, it was very obvious in the way that every man turned his head and looked. Everybody liked Maisie and the very fact that she was Colin's partner made the whole ordeal of having to sit there and watch him that much easier for Rosaleen, and it heightened the excitement for her as well, because she was curious to see them jiving together — what with their individual styles, they were bound to make a very unique couple.

Without stop, the second record was played, and hearing that it was a Buddy Holly number, there was a burst of cheers and whistles and applause. The record was 'Party Doll', which was good for a slow jive, and which, because of its moderate constant monobeat, the spectators were infected and they accompanied it, and instead of the applause dying out, it merely slowed in pace to the music, until everyone's hand clapping was in sync and the entire hall was filled with one, slow, rythmic beat.

From Buddy Holly to Paul Anka to the Everly Brothers, whose 'Wake Up Little Susie' started to liven things up a bit, and with the beat, the jivers' feet started to pick up, which, in turn, caused a current of excitement to run around the room, at first, like little waves, touching those who were closest to the floor, and, then, building in crescendo, it swept up the people who had filled the benches that surrounded the walls and soon had the entire place rocking in motion.

From the Everly Brothers to Fats Domino and his ever-loving 'When My Dreamboat Comes Home'. At which point, the spectators went into a roar, and as cat-calls and whistles and shouts of 'Yeah, Fats,' were hurled about the room, several of them, unable to contain themselves any longer, got up and joined the contestants on the floor.

Amongst those who had just gotten up were three girls, who, going into the corner, proceeded to dance, all three together. With one in the middle setting the beat by working up a pattern of laborious steps, she handled the other two with great dexterity, displaying with ease a talent of co-ordination so brilliant, that it would have put most people doing less to shame.

The others who had gotten up consisted of two couples, who, although very good dancers, had apparently, for one reason or another, denied themselves the chance to compete, because, now, coming around the hall was Louie, an A.O.H. member, and he was determined to rid the floor of the late-comers, and the two couples, who after just getting their systems in gear, were frustrated now in being forced to sit down.

Not so the three girls; not by a long shot. For the one in the middle, the co-ordinator, as soon as she saw the man coming, moved herself and her two comrades around the floor, and she kept moving, always on the lookout, as if she had eyes in the back of her head, eluding the club-member, step by step, and without missing a beat.

After successfully defeating the man for

the completion of Fats's record, the trio drew a roar from the crowd, and as the little one in the centre, looking like a miniature Bridget Bardot, with her bushy ponytail and her French Bardot bangs and kisscurls, raised her arms, and bringing her hands together above her head, acknowledged the wild applause she had created, and then went on to repeat her victory in the very popular 'My Blue Heaven', also by Fats.

Now, this time, in order to waylay Louie, her pursuer, from seizing her bodily, and throwing her off the floor, for he was livid with rage at having been outwitted and of being made a laughing stock, she manoeuvered her two partners into the centre of the contestants, to where she had wisely perceived the man wouldn't dare follow.

Little Anthony, taking over from Fats, and thus enticing the girls to stay, threw Louie into convulsions, for in seeing that he'd have to go through the contestants to get to them, amongst those being, Manuel, 'Dirty Eyes' and 'wee' Andy, he decided his task to be more difficult than he thought. Thus, finding it impossible to carry out his duty by himself, he looked up at the record-box to Gerry, the jockey who was on duty, and he tried to get his attention. But Gerry, looking down on everyone and everything, except Louie, suddenly found himself preoccupied within the box itself, and he disappeared from sight. Still determined to take matters into his own hands, Louie took the next step and went to ascend the ladder to the record-box to turn off the music himself, But, in doing so, he was greatly perturbed in finding the ladder missing, and standing there in the spot where the feet of the ladder would normally rest, he swung around suddenly as bursts of applause and laughter shook the hall, and he was just in time to see little 'Bridget Bardot', the last of the trio, disappear out the door, but not before she threw him a wave of her fingers and a smile, that made her look like butter wouldn't melt in her mouth. The spectators grew wilder, and Louie, seeing the destiny of his duty filled with frustration, went over and kicked the wall.

Little Anthony, bowing out, gave the

floor to Jackie Wilson, who handed it to Pat Boone and his 'Be-Bop-A-Lulu'. On the ninth record, the music started to speed up, and Bill Haley's 'Rock Around the Clock' was another one that brought applause from the spectators.

With this, things really started to get hot, and the jockey kept it coming with a straight line of them; the first and foremost of which threatened to wreck the crowd, Little Richard and his 'Long Tall Sally'.

After this, several contestants dropped out, as though they had been biding their time, just waiting for this particular record. After the eleventh record was played, the twelfth was given as a sort of consolation, and the dancers got a breather. As soon as the first notes sounded, Rosaleen could tell what the song was going to be; appropriately enough it was 'The Twelfth of Never', one of the first Johnny Mathis records to which she had danced with Colin. In fact, it had been this very record that had gotten Jimmy Reed into hot water with the A.O.H. members for having exceeded the limited number supposed

301

to be played in one set.

Now sitting there, Rosaleen thought of the irony of it all. There was Jimmy and Phyllis dancing together as though they were the only couple on the floor, and rightly so, since they were going to be engaged within the next few months; and then, here she was, sitting alone while Colin danced with someone else, Maisie Boyle, and apparently thrilled with her company, for he hadn't even acknowledged her presence; he hadn't even looked her way once, since she'd entered the Hibs and, as far as she was concerned, he probably never would again.

Supposedly refreshed after the 'interval', the contestants were now introduced to a true test of stamina, as the records brought out now had been chosen mainly for their speed and provocative beat, and which, after about a half-dozen or more, there seemed to be more spectators than dancers.

Still, Rosaleen didn't know who to watch, as the contestants on the floor now created a dance-lover's paradise, and her attention was divided amongst them all.

First there were Jimmy and Phyllis, who, although not eligible, with Jimmy being an A.O.H. member, were just dancing for the fun of it, and to whom Rosaleen didn't give too much more time before they dropped out, because their real interest was in each other, and not in the contest. Still, she liked to watch Jimmy's style. Then there was Manuel and his little blonde partner, Bernie, 'Dirty Eyes' and his partner, Delia, and there was 'wee' Andy and Deirdre — and then, there was Colin and Maisie, and although Rosaleen's attention was diverted between all of them, she found Colin and Maisie the hardest to watch, but they were also the best, and she felt herself drawn back to them, time and time again.

Looking like they were born to dance together, they made every move look simple, yet Rosaleen knew just how intricate and complex the steps really were to perform, and she was secretly hoping that they would be the winners — if their endurance held out.

Now, as the real hard drive continued, the contest became a true test of endeavour, and as contestants now left the floor, the spectators, more subdued, since the seriousness of it all was beginning to take its toll, could do nothing other than give them a nice round of applause.

Of those making up the couples on the floor, Rosaleen saw that most of them were the pros; the Hib-hoppers who were known for their jiving ability; the girls as much as the fellows, and almost none of them were 'sweetheart' couples, except Jimmy and Phyllis — who had now just decided to call it a night, and who left the floor to a surprising thunder of applause, that would make one think they had just won the 'Decathlon'.

Never having witnessed this kind of contest before, Rosaleen was finding it not only exhilarating, but downright intriguing, for she wondered what the line-up was on the two benches opposite her across the room. For one thing, she knew that they were not ordinary spectators, for they were too tense, with all of them having an air of expectancy about them. She didn't have to wait too long to find out for as 'wee' Andy's partner,

Deirdre, showed signs of waning and slowing down Andy's steps, a girl, sitting on the edge of one of the benches, got up and took her place. There was a little applause as Deirdre, tired and dejected looking, stumbled out into the hallway. Rosaleen's curiosity was aroused and she waited in anticipation for the next move.

The second jiver's partner to drop out was Terry Malcomson's, neither one of which Rosaleen expected to last too long, and, right away, she, too, was replaced by a girl from the other bench. And, then, on the heels of that one, Manuel's partner was replaced by a girl from the same bench.

Just then, Jerry Coogan's partner, Sally, who Rosaleen had also been watching intently, not simply for her style of dancing, but because she had been driving a hard bargain throughout; first with the high-heel shoes she was wearing, which were inappropriate for a long-term contest, and, secondly, Rosaleen felt that she had been pushing too hard; she and Jerry had chosen too many exertive steps, which had tired them prematurely and that, added to Sally's too-strong determination, had created problems for them, and now, in her exhausted state, she had thrown an ankle. Oddly enough, Rosaleen saw that Jerry had no one to replace Sally and he had to follow her off the floor, thus eliminating himself. Of course, his departure was met with cheering applause, but, as they came and sat beside Rosaleen and Ann, she could see the disappointment in Jerry's face.

"That hardly seems fair," she said to Sally, as the girl limped down onto the bench beside her. Gratefully accepting a lighted cigarette, that had been handed down the bench to her and Jerry, and looking at Rosaleen through the haze of smoke that she blew through her nostrils, she asked breathlessly,

"What's not fair?"

"That line-up over there," Rosaleen said, nodding in the direction of the benches, "It makes the whole thing look like a conspiracy." Shrugging her shoulders, the girl replied,

"What do you expect? They're popular fellows," and then, she added, "That's their privilege."

"But you know who's going to win," Rosaleen said, "Hand's down, it'll be Andy, with that collection he has over there." But all she got was another shrug from the girl. But she couldn't let the matter drop. "Do you mean to tell me that everybody knows that it'll be Andy; that everybody knew before this all got underway exactly what he had going for him?" But all Sally gave was a discouraging smile.

Now Bo Bo Gillen was following his partner off the floor, and there was very little applause, and Rosaleen saw that it was diminishing, almost as if the crowd could tell that the end was near and that they were saving their victory applause for the winner.

Now came Frankie Falooney, followed by his partner; it was he who had given up and she, with no other choice, had to follow.

The contestants left on the floor were down to a few, and these included Manuel, 'Dirty Eyes', Albert McGahy, one of Colin's friends, 'wee' Andy and, of course, Colin. But, there was another fellow who Rosaleen had seen only a few times, but really didn't know, who had been jiving in the same spot since the contest began. He and his partner were not really doing anything spectacular, as far as jiving went, but they were holding their own. Oddly enough, too, they seemed to be the only couple who had managed to keep a conversation going between them the whole time, and, as this became more obvious to Rosaleen, she noticed that it was the fellow who was doing most of the talking, and constantly, although barely visible and hardly audible, except to the girl. He appeared to be blowing the words over his bottom lip, like bubbles, and she, catching them, bursted them open with her eyes, as though they contained the encouragement she needed. This fascinated Rosaleen because what they were doing was mere repetition more than anything; she could hardly call it good dancing, and yet, they stood a very good chance of winning; in fact, even more so than Colin and Maisie, for despite their earlier exuberance, they were both beginning to show signs of wear. Whereas before, Rosaleen had been admiring Maisie's ability, her rhythm, the way she held herself when she danced, the certain response she provided to fulfill Colin's persuasive gestures, all of which had goaded Rosaleen into feeling proud of Colin because he had shown good sense, as well as good taste in choosing her, she was now worried about the slight slump in their performance. But this wasn't because she was afraid that they were going to drop out; but because of the fact that Colin's two companions, Chancer and Bopper, holed up in their usual corner, were expecting them to.

Looking at them, they reminded Rosaleen of vultures, waiting for the last breath to expire from their prey, for they were watching Colin and one of them was throwing furtive looks at the watch that the other was holding on his wrist, as though, any minute, they could begin the countdown.

Although Colin's back was to Rosaleen, he appeared to be every bit as tired as Maisie, and she surmised that from the way Maisie was looking at him, that he was giving her some form of encouragement, but, that Maisie, try as she may, could not deliver. With one last compassionate look at Colin, and, as though she had intended it that way, she stopped dead in her tracks, just as the record ended, and, in the midst of scattered applause, which was a mixture of polite acknowledgement and sombre regret, she walked off the floor.

But before Maisie had even time to reach her destination in the corner, the applause suddenly changed in tone, and, whereas Maisie's departure had dashed the hopes of those who had been riding on both her and Colin, the unexpected appearance of a new figure on the floor brought the dejected spectators to their feet and, with them, an arousing applause, filled with the magnitude of a newly inspired hope. Colin was both surprised and stunned; first, by the newly charged emotion of the spectators, and then, by the sudden appearance of Rosaleen at his side.

Recovering from the initial shock of seeing what and who had aroused the crowd to such a state, Colin was taken aback by the sheer gall of it. Being mindful of the fact that it was she who had walked out on him, the last time he had seen her, and still smarting from it, he'd sworn that she'd never walk away from him again; yet, here she was, back again, and of her own free will. What had possessed her to come to him voluntarily like this? It wasn't like her; her with her secondary school mannerisms, and all the airs that went with them. Or was it?

Colin didn't need to be reminded; he knew only too well the discerning way she had of getting what she wanted, and how much, yet, when she wanted to back off, he'd always been the one who was left in the uncompromising position of not only having to worry about his own sensitivities, but also those of hers, which he had been wary of offending in the first place, and still, with all that, he always seemed to end up feeling like the big, bad villian, who'd been out to threaten her virtue.

But what did she want from him now? He knew what she needed; something that she should have gotten a long time ago, and that was to be put over somebody's knee; except it was too late for that, she was a big girl now, yet, there was enough of the child still in her — well, anyway, that really wasn't his concern, besides, it was the woman in her now that needed tending; it wasn't his fault that she'd been spoilt growing up.

The next record was starting and Colin, who had been knocked slightly off balance by the sudden appearance of Rosaleen, and her nearness, was fired awake now with Little Richard, and the energy he was currently giving out, and he grabbed it with both hands, along with the silver platter on which he'd been handed the golden opportunity of not only evening the score with this 'little girl', but of getting one step ahead of her, and on *his* terms now — and he intended using *everything* in his power to attain it.

Looking over at Rosaleen, his thoughts fleeting momentarily to Maisie, he felt a new surge of excitement take hold, and he discovered that what he'd been involved with up to this point had been tame compared to what he was faced with now. And as the record spun to fill his senses, so did the sight of Rosaleen, along with the one or two memories she'd given him cause for.

Seeing Colin looking at her, but with no hint in his eyes as to what he was thinking, Rosaleen could only surmise that, at the very least, he must still be angry with her. But that was something she could worry about later, and God knows how she'd worry about it later; this probably being the last time she'd ever be this close to him.

But for now, and, as though she suddenly realized the enormity of her predicament — the stiff competition she had to face — she realized that it wasn't the girls she had to outlast, because there were more than enough replacements, it was the men; the likes of Manuel, 'Dirty Eyes', and 'wee' Andy. And filled with the anticipation of her overwhelming odds, she kicked off her high-heel shoes, and, as she warmed up rhythmically opposite Colin, some spectator graciously removed them from the floor.

Following Colin's foot movements, which were deliberately slow-paced in order for her to set her rhythm, motion and tempo in sync with his, she unconsciously pushed the sleeves of her white sweater up to her elbows, and she pulled it neatly and tightly down at the waist, down over the top of her black straight skirt, and coming slowly for the first of the hand to hand confrontations, which would indicate the follow-up steps, she moved towards Colin.

While every second brought the two of them closer together, Colin made no effort to acknowledge her, but, instead, continued to maintain his warm-up pace, and he waited for Rosaleen to get right up to him, until he and she were eye to eye.

Looking down at her, he could read his name in her very expression, and then, when they could get no closer, he could see it silently on her lips, urging him to make his move, and, then, just to make sure that she knew what she was in for, he prolonged the moment, just long enough, to catch her off guard, and then, and only then, did he reach for her hand and, in a vice-like grip, he tightened it within his own. Still looking down at her, he pulled her to him with such uncharacteristic force, she was compelled to look at him.

Gone was the tiredness that appeared

to have marked his progress when he'd been dancing with Maisie, and in its place was an air about his behaviour that was new and fierce, a side to him that Rosaleen had yet to see.

With the tempo of the music slowing somewhat with another Fats Domino record, Rosaleen felt the tension of Colin's hand relax on hers, and she moved away for the breakaway.

Now separated from him, with about four feet of space between them, and with room to breathe, Rosaleen, while faithfully following his lead in the first step, saw that the second step was one which she hadn't perfected yet, and Colin knew it, and while she glanced up at him in reproach, he looked away.

Still, in keeping a cool exterior, yet with heart pounding within, she managed to follow and finish at the same time he did.

Although it was not within her grasp right then to try and understand his conduct, or of whether he was deliberately or unwittingly making it difficult for her to follow him, she was aware of the one saving grace, which was, that

315

whatever the reason, it was his own proficiency in the steps, themselves, which enabled her to keep up with him. This became more evident in the next step, which was also unfamiliar to her, but which, nonetheless, even with difficulty, she performed to the end.

Now anxious to see what his next step was going to be, she was thrown another unexpected curve, for, instead of the customary three steps, followed by the bounce — which was to jiving what the chorus is to the song — a succession of swift, little jumping-thumping movements — reminiscent of someone digging into the ground with the balls of their feet — and performed after every three steps, Colin skipped the third step and went directly to the bounce itself, with a record that was long and arduous to dance to, because it evoked sensuous gesticulations in the dancers both with its provocative lyrics and equally provocative, intrinsic beat.

"Come over here, baby,
I wanna see you dance
The way your body moves

316

Puts me in a trance
There's not another, sugar,
That can match your skill
You set my heart thumpin'
An' you always will . . .
With your shakin', shakin', shakin',
Your shakin', shakin', shakin'
Sets me shakin', shakin', shakin',
That's it, honey, let me see you
shakin', shakin', shakin',
You're shakin' it real good, sugar,
Come on, keep it up now . . . ”

For longer than what was called for,
Colin continued the bounce.

“ . . . Now, shake again, honey,
And this time for real,
Now, here we go,
Come on, start it shakin', baby,
That's it, nice and slow,
Faster now, honey — Wow! . . . ”

Rosaleen couldn't believe what he was
doing, or what it was he was trying to
prove by doing it. If it wasn't for the fact
that she came to help him out and to help
him get something which he apparently

317

wanted, she would not have been a part of this.

" . . . The way you shake it, baby,
Gives me such a thrill,
I love the way you move it
And I always will
So shake it up, honey,
That's my one desire
Shake it some more,
Wow! My heart's on fire . . . "

Seeing that he had no intention of giving up the bounce, and thinking him crazy for it, Rosaleen wanted to stop, but, then, knowing how it would look, leaving the floor just because she didn't have the expertise to follow through, especially when she had come out voluntarily in the first place, she kept it up right along with him.

" . . . With your shakin', shakin', shakin'
Your shakin', shakin', shakin'
Sends me shakin', shakin', shakin' . . . "

Attempting to concentrate her entire energy on what was going on, the irony of the whole situation caught up with her and she felt, with sickening realization, that Colin was putting her to a test of his own creation; she knew now that she was not competing with Andy or any of the others at all; but with Colin himself.

Feeling weak at the first suggestion that he would do such a thing, confirmed in her mind, once and for all, the feelings with which she was constantly struggling: and despite the tender entanglements she'd had with him, when her defences were down, she now saw him exactly as the kind of person he was; arrogant, boorish, and totally self-centred — along with all the other things that Father Hanlon had talked to her about. This reckless display of complete disregard for her right then was the deciding factor that would settle her emotional attachment to him once and for all. After tonight, she wouldn't see him again. She would make sure of it.

But for now, he was not going to get the better of her. Despite the fact that he had the upper hand, as every move was his lead, and she to follow, she was determined to match him every step of

319

the way, beat for beat; bounce for bounce.

"... Come on, honey, let me see you shakin', shakin', shakin',
Come on, keep it up, baby ... "

Even though there was no need to watch him, as she could predict his obstinacy, keeping this going for some time to come, she still looked at him and, Oh, God, if she couldn't help but find something pleasingly disturbing in his attitude and in the way he was looking at her, all of which mounted along with her accompanying anger.

Therefore, tearing her eyes from him, she was brought almost deliberately to a complete stop, as she was confronted by the drooling countenances of the vultures, Chancer and Bopper, who, having lost their original prey, had now taken the ambiguous position behind Colin to watch, and wait, and whet their gullets for the female of the species. And that, which was intended to halt her in her tracks, instead, caused her to pause long enough to catch her breath, which gave birth to a new determination, along with a glimmer of light which clarified their predatory traits to be completely self-indulged, and in no way sanctioned nor condoned to any rightful place within the human breast.

" . . . shakin', shakin', shakin',
shakin', shakin', shakin',
shakin', shakin', shakin',
shakin', shakin', shakin' . . . "

By now, seeing something take place that was out of the ordinary sphere of the rest of the jivers, some of the spectators gathered around, more or less, out of sheer curiosity, and then, watching Colin, who, starting to sweat profusely, removed his jacket and went into a third round, his movements becoming faster and faster, building an exciting momentum between himself and Rosaleen, professed loud admiration, causing others to come to their feet to watch.

" . . . Your shakin' gets me shakin',
I'm shakin', shakin', shakin' . . . "

With the recording starting to wind up, but without any sign of letting up, Colin loosened his tie and undid the top button of his skirt, watching Rosaleen intently, as he did so.

" . . . I wanna see you shakin',
I love to see you shakin',
Your shakin' sets me shakin' — Wow!
I'm shakin', shakin', shakin',
Help me, baby, I'm-a-shakin'
Wow! baby-I'm-a-shakin',
I'm-a-shakin', I'm-a-shakin',
I'm-a-s-h-a-k-i-n' . . . "

The crowd went into an uproar, as the record came to an end, and, as though Colin had foreseen what was coming and had prepared the way for it, the crowd grew even wilder, as the first Elvis record marked the highlight of the contest.

As though infected with the very excitement, which he was arousing in the spectators, and completely unexpected to them, and more so to Rosaleen, Colin began to halt momentarily between bounces — something, which, if performed with practice and to a

322

pattern, was difficult enough, but to introduce it under such circumstances rendered it almost impossible to perform, because of the fact that the 'leader' himself did not have a set timing to follow, although he could determine one. As with Colin, now, once into the rhythm, he felt himself carried by the automation to which his feet had become adjusted, though he was still not consciously deliberating the pauses themselves. Yet watching Rosaleen, for although she had no way of knowing exactly when he was going to pause, he saw that she still carried it out with the uncanny knack of anticipating his every move, thus creating a game of cat and mouse between them.

Finding the challenge to defeat her irresistible, Colin, the excitement continuing to mount, hastened the process and, with it, heightened the emotion both in himself and in the crowd of spectators, which had grown considerably around the benches and floor surrounding them, and, although they had no way of knowing exactly what was at stake, they were, nonetheless, impressed with what they were witnessing, and they showed it in a burst of applause.

Fast becoming tired, and not knowing how much longer he intended keeping it up, Rosaleen didn't know how much longer she could last, or Colin, for that matter; it could all be over in a matter of seconds at this pace. She could no longer feel her feet or legs, for they seemed to have gained control from some outside source other than herself, and all she could sense was the numbness this dispossession spread throughout the rest of her body.

Then, as though the fate of the contest no longer rested on what either she or Colin, or any of them, did, the record changed, and with it, the tempo which seemed to have held this phenomenon together, and the noise which the crowd made was a mixture of both recognition of that fact, as well as with excitement for the new record which dictated the change and compelled Colin to close in on Rosaleen and take hold of her for the customary swing that pronounced the fresh beginning.

As the space between Rosaleen and

Colin shortened, so too did it between them and the spectators, and, at close range now, Rosaleen caught sight of 'Dirty Eyes', Manuel, and Colin's friend Albert McGahy, the latter wiping his face with a handkerchief and looking on in disbelief, not so much at what Colin had endured but at Rosaleen herself.

Now Rosaleen saw that the other fellow, the whisperer, and his girl, too, had left the floor, only to have disappeared from sight, for there was no sign of them amongst the spectators. The thought that it was all now between her and Colin and 'wee' Andy, while not even considering his partner, since she could be replaced, filled Rosaleen with a new acceleration of excitement, which she also sensed in Colin, though of a somewhat different nature, for every time he caught her hand his hold seemed to convey it. And that wasn't all; there was something else in his grasp which caused her to look up at him and, in doing so, she saw in his eyes the all-too-familiar sparkle which she had come to recognize as his hallmark, foretelling that he was out for something, which told her that he was not going to give up.

The spectators, as though professing to know Colin's mood as well as she; as though sensing his unwillingness to give up, now opened up to swallow 'wee' Andy and his fresh new partner, and Rosaleen, glancing at her, could only guess what her own dancing form must be like compared to this new burst of energy. And, again, as though by some magical thread of mental telepathy connecting the dancers with the spectators, several of them standing near Rosaleen started to clap her supportively and one fellow called out, "That-a-girl, Rosie, c'mon."

And a girl's voice behind her said, "That's the style, Rosie. Keep it up."

Smiling, but more to herself than to anyone else, she silently acknowledged their support, and she felt that they must have known intuitively that she had started out doing this for Colin, as surely as he should have known himself. In looking up at him, she found too much present in his eyes to enable her to know definitely whether he had come to realize that or if he still felt the need to wear her down. But she didn't have to look in his eyes for any answer, for no sooner had this thought crossed her mind than he, showing signs of completing the swing, pushed her into another set of intricate steps. Then, as he widened the gap between them, for what Rosaleen knew for sure was going to finish her off, he caught her eyes and held them, while starting into the first steps.

Seeing the determination stronger than ever in his eyes, and deciding that if it meant so much to him, egotistically, to wear her down, then she would gladly let him suffer his pride because she herself knew that in the long run he was only cutting off his nose to spite his face, for, while in defeating her, he would, in turn, be losing to Andy, and the realization that this was exactly what Colin Murdoch wanted, Rosaleen decided to give it to him; it would be no skin off her nose, since this was the last time she was ever going to be with him.

Still looking at him and feeling the strength of his gaze on hers, she was just on the verge of calling it quits, but, while trying to muster up the courage to do so, she saw his eyes leave her own and fall all over her, in one long look.

Feeling her cheeks flush, Rosaleen continued dancing and she fixed her eyes on his, so that when he next looked at her face, he was met by a steady gaze. But, in the temperament of the old Colin; the one she'd first met, he continued to look at her, caressing her with his eyes, and Rosaleen, holding her own to meet his gaze again, felt the impetus to quicken her steps and to keep not one second behind him whereas she'd be following his lead, but right on beat with him, her timing matching his own.

Sensing this, Colin brought his eyes up to her own, and finding her gaze as steady as ever, and she not at all unnerved, he threw her a questionable look. And Rosaleen, her expression remaining unchanged, looked at him right back, which, in turn, brought a smile to his lips, telling her that despite the brave front she was putting on, he knew exactly how disturbing it all was to her.

Suddenly, sensing something happening around them, Rosaleen saw Andy bowing out, much to her surprise and amazement. Amidst much applause, and without further ado, he casually waved to the crowd and went out down the hall to the billiard room. Now, with the last remaining pair holding all that applause, Rosaleen couldn't imagine why he would suddenly concede like he did; there was no visible sign that he had to.

With this question still occupying her mind, she was suddenly aware of Colin close beside her and of the crowd gathering around them with congratulatory pats on the back, and she felt him reach down and take her hand and pull her closer to him, and she felt the pressure of his hand tighten around her fingers.

Breathless and overheated and exhausted from the whole experience, the realization that they'd won, they'd actually won the jiving contest, swept over Rosaleen and she looked at Colin.

Already the centre of attention, Colin shared her breathless, excited state, but Rosaleen, neither being in the same frame of mind as either the crowd or him, could only think that it was no thanks to him that they'd won, the only ingredient that he had supplied had been his downright audacity, and then, as if the thought alone was enough to bring the blood rushing to her cheeks, she pulled her hand from his.

Bringing her hand to her face, and feeling it hot under her palm, the fresh flush hidden by the high colour already there from dancing, she saw Colin looking at her. Not wanting him to read anything in her face, she immediately looked away, yet even in the instant of their eyes meeting, he managed to convey that he had something to say to her.

Moving out from the midst of the crowd, Rosaleen pushed her way through the room to look for her shoes and upon finding them, and without even taking the time to put them on, she picked them up and ran out of the door and up the stairs.

In the ladies room, though hearing the hub of voices all around her while not really listening to it, she attempted to refresh herself with some cold water from the tap, but, upon turning the knob, all she got was the grating noise of the threadbare plumbing, and then, a slow, somewhat, less than clean, lukewarm trickle. Seeing Ann come in, she then suggested going over to Moloccos and, going downstairs together, they left the Hibs.

19

WHILE waiting to cross the street, heavy at this hour with Saturday night traffic and filled with the noise and music blasting across from Moloccos, Rosaleen heard Colin's voice from behind, and then a roar of laughter, followed by Chancer and Bopper winding their way through the flow of traffic. Watching their antics in the middle of the road, Rosaleen and Ann, remaining at the curb, watched as Bopper, who, with an authoritative wave of the hand, summoned the traffic forward and onward, wringing it faster and faster through the air until the line of cars and buses, speeding beyond their normal measure, were brought suddenly and unexpectedly to an abrupt halt by Bopper raising his palm and, then, nonchalantly stepping in front of the still-moving cars, all of which caused havoc all the way down the line, as each driver, respectively awakened to the unforeseen obstacles, screeched to a braking stop; and Chancer, performing equally as bad on the other side of the street, spotting a girl he apparently knew on one of the buses, yelled her name through the window to get her attention, and, being obviously ignored, chased the bus as it started to move off, and running, he grabbed onto the open window and hung by the fingertips, continuing to shout at the girl and flinging her several backhanded compliments. Rosaleen and Ann, exchanging a look of contempt, hesitated to cross the street while the two of them still loitered there. But, then, seeing them move off, they looked for a break in the traffic and were just about to step off the curb when Rosaleen felt Colin's hand on her arm and heard his voice saying to her,

"I want to talk to you."

Turning around to look at him, Rosaleen told him abrasively,

"Well, I don't want to talk to you." But instead of Colin releasing his hold on her, she felt it tighten into a grip, and ignoring what she had just said, he directed his next statement to Ann.

"If you don't mind, I have something to say to this one."

This remark was all Rosaleen needed, because to her it was merely a continuation of how he'd been behaving towards her during the contest, and so, with the determination and strength not to prolong it, she tore herself free and stepped out into the traffic.

"Rosaleen!" Colin's voice followed her into the road, but she continued to walk without even as much as a glance backwards. But, upon crossing the street, Colin reached the pavement at the same time she did and he grabbed her arm again, and spinning her around to face him, he told her,

"Didn't you hear me? I said I wanted to talk to you."

Hearing the angry tone in his voice alerted Rosaleen to look at his face, and when she did, she found all trace of his former audacity gone from his eyes and it was replaced with a harsh stillness, and she knew he had something on his mind.

Looking at Ann crossing the street before saying anything, her expression apparently momentarily appeasing Colin to let go of her arm, she said to her as she got near them,

"Ann, this won't take too long. If you want, you could get us a booth in Moloccos. I'll be in a couple of minutes." But Ann, looking from one to the other, told her,

"No, that's alright, Rosie. I think I'll go on home. I'll see you tomorrow."

Waiting for a second or two while Ann walked away, Rosaleen turned to look at Colin, waiting to hear what he had to say. But, without a word, he started walking up the block, turning to look at her only to answer her unspoken question.

"I can't talk to you here."

Walking past Moloccos, with its juke-box blaring, he led the way across the street, which ran down the side of Moloccos, and over to the park where, under the trees that stood inside the dark green palings, he turned to her.

Believing that he was going to start reproaching her for what she'd done to him at the Plaza, Rosaleen searched for something to say to him herself. But standing there outside the park, with the unaccustomed scent of fresly-cut grass escaping from between the palings and onto the treeless, city street; the trees inside the park, like big halved-umbrellas over their heads, blocked off the busy Falls Road traffic, both pedestrian and otherwise, and let in the street lights just a little at a time, and, regardless of the length of time she'd just spent dancing with him during the contest, she felt the nearness of him now too close for comfort, yet, with all this, she dared to lift her eyes to look at him

Drawing a silent breath, Rosaleen saw Colin's eyes pouring down into her own and, seeing something come alive in them, she could hardly release the breath from her body, and, so, standing there beside him so close, she felt the night air trapped like a still fire within her breast.

"Now, do you want to tell me what the hell you were doing tonight?" Colin threw at her unexpectedly, and Rosaleen, trying not to notice the effect he was having on her, standing in the shadows like that, the lights, coming through the trees, casting enough of their glow to catch his hair and reflect in his eyes, asked him,

"What are you talking about?"

"I'm talking about you taking over from Maisie. What gave you the idea that I needed any help from you? There were plenty of other birds that I would have preferred to you, so what made you think you had that priviledge?"

Taken aback, both by his tone and by the implication of his words, Rosaleen knew that she'd been right in thinking that he'd had a certain fierceness about him throughout the contest, but, for whatever reason, that did not excuse his behaviour towards her then, or now.

"Privilege?" she practically shouted at him. "What privilege? Who do you think you are, Colin Murdoch?"

As though hearing the sound of his name from her lips, on top of everything else concerning her tonight, had a profound effect on him, Colin pulled her against him and kissed her mouth.

Recovering from the shock of his sudden movement, Rosaleen pulled her face away from his, but was unable to free herself from his hold.

"That's not fair," she told him, her voice filled with determination, but reaching him in a whisper that was packed with emotion, which only seemed to affect him more. Still holding her and looking down at her, he asked her,

"What's not fair? That I get what I want, or you make me look like a fool in the Plaza?" And without waiting for an answer, "Seems to me that we're just about even." And pulling her to him even tighter, he told her, "Except now, it's my turn," and he brought his mouth, now passionate and exacting, down on hers. Rosaleen felt in him the need and demand that was far beyond anything she had yet to witness and in an immediate attempt to push him off, she fought to free her mouth which was crushed helplessly beneath his own.

Startled and momentarily caught off guard by his audacity, Rosaleen was still very much aware of having been subjected to an entire evening of his arrogance, no matter how discreet it had been, and she was not about to become party to his insolence now, neither willingly nor otherwise. But feeling the power behind his lips, and sensing the drive behind his kiss, that had created it, she found no trace of that discretion now, much to her concern. And much more to her concern was the memory of the first time he had ever kissed her. He had been a complete stranger to her then, she knowing nothing of him before that night; according to her knowledge of him he hadn't even existed, and yet, even then, she had found her resistance hard to sustain. Yet, here she was again with him, much in the same situation as she had been that first night she met him, but she knew that it was a far cry from then, because, now, she knew him; she had spent time with him, and enjoyed him; she had spent time apart from him, and had missed him insufferably, and more than then, she knew exactly what it was that her resistance had to withstand, and she fought all the harder.

Striving with every fibre of her being to free herself, her hands pushing against his chest in an effort to break his hold on her, Rosaleen's endeavour was gradually diverted by the slowly decreasing pressure on her mouth, and with a feeling of expectancy, as though one had a direct effect on the other, her own resistance began to wane, as she waited for him to subside altogether.

Finding the urgency disappear from his kiss, Rosaleen was relieved, but, still his mouth remained on hers, and she unwittingly had yet to contend with his lips. Feeling them now searching her own for the response she was unwilling to give, she sensed the sudden, momentary pauses, the consequences of which, intermittently, brought an arousal, and subsequently, left her waiting for more. Although she had no way of knowing exactly when he was going to bring his lips back to hers, she anticipated each moment with longing and she responded to each new arousal until she was fully awakened by his lips. And then the moment when she felt the fear of her own emotions, rather than of the unknown, and she knew that she had to stop at once, or there would be no turning back. But Colin's mouth on hers and his arms still tight around her refused to let her go, and, once again, she struggled to free herself.

Keeping his arms firm in their hold, but lifting his head to look at her, he took his mouth away from hers and, in a

Checkout Receipt
Castell Central Library

Title: The divided heart : [a
Belfast love story]
: 39065050185956
Date due: October 17, 2017
11:59 PM

Total checkouts for session:1
Total checkouts:1

To check your card and renew
items, go to
www.calgarylibrary.ca
or call 262-2928

manner mindful of his hold, his voice, matching in vocal power the physical strength of his arms, his words, more alarming than his kiss, while forcefully tying her with their provincial implication, purposely incited her heart to heights of rebellion, murmured,

"Now what do you think of that, Celtic?"

On the other side of the street and around the corner in Moloccos, the Hib crowd had carried their mood with them across the street and continued where they had left off, with a succession of rock and roll records. But for the past few minutes the jukebox had been silent, and it was during this interlude that his words had come to her. But, instead of disappearing into the night, they hung there in the darkness, the air resounding with them, taunting her with the impact of their intimation, "Now what do you think of that, Celtic?"

Over and over she heard them repeated until, mercifully, the words were pushed to second position in her thoughts by those of a song now reaching them from Moloccos, and to which Rosaleen clung as though each word were a life-preserver, and she using every one to pull herself further and further up out of the depths into which Colin had taken her.

"You're the only one
who can make me fall in love
The stars in your eyes
say that we're in heaven . . . "

But not so he, for now, without loosening his hold on her, he removed one of his hands from behind her, and Rosaleen, still feeling the strength of his remaining arm across the small of her back, felt his free hand reach up and touch her.

Struggling now against his grasp on her, which was hard and demanding, she heard again the strongly provocative, "Now what do you think of that, Celtic?" Then, as if to convince her of her real feelings, Colin softened his grasp, his hand, now gentle and caressing, was filling her with very tender memories of the first and last time they had been together like this, and her heart, aroused and titillated further, was beyond even its former measure by the softly ardent, "Now what do you think of that, Celtic?"

She then became aware of the strength of his hold lessening, enabling her to break free — if she wanted to.

But it was a move that was as subtle as the impact of a double-decker bus, for inasmuch as he had released her physically, he now bound her to him emotionally, and the words to the song, which had previously been an aid to her, now shifted loyalties to help him do it.

" . . . You're the only one who can do the things you do
Right or wrong, no one thrills me quite like you
When you touch me, and I feel the flame
Right or wrong, the feeling's just the same
— and is my poor heart to blame? . . . "

And all Rosaleen could do for the moment was take her lips away from his and hope that the act alone would stand to subside the roaring tide of emotions within her. But the loss of her lips merely seemed to increase his desire for more of her, and he brought his own to her neck and to her throat.

As he bent over her, pulling her closer, they were emotionally nearer to what they'd almost had on the Cavehill, and Rosaleen, because of having suffered the long and painful separation from him in the intervening weeks, now found herself somewhat weaker, having lost much of the constitutional strength that her soul had borne that day. And yet, while her outward senses were gratified and elated, she still felt an inner sense stirring, and opening her eyes, she searched wildly and helplessly for an answer to all of this.

From where she was standing she could see into the park, and over Colin's shoulder and through the trees, against an oddly white night sky, she could see the form of the dome that topped the big circular, yellow fountain where she used to play as a child. Always filled with rainwater, it was dirty and crawling with microscopic life, such as the dreaded blood-suckers that couldn't be seen with the naked eye, only detected when one or more came in contact with a child's bare flesh, and which caused perpetual flights to the emergency room of the great, big Royal Victoria Hospital, that was just across the street, on the other side of the park, and of which Rosaleen had childishly believed was there solely for the purpose of detaching blood-suckers. But although she had hated to think of these unseen creatures, who hid within the rainwater's depth, they never stopped her from taking off her shoes and socks, nor from tucking her dress in at the thighs, and wading out to the big, ornately handsome, gazebo-like, stone structure under the dome, with its well, which was said to have no bottom, whereupon, if a child fell in, it would automatically end up in hell, devoured, no doubt, by the giant gargoyles whose images surrounded the structure and threatened one and all with their stone-fiery countenances.

Yet all of this had failed to keep Rosaleen from the excitement of climbing on top of the well, which she loved, nor from peering down into the depths of 'hell' itself, which terrified her.

And now, the big dome over the well looked to her like a citadel in the night sky, one she could run to and lock herself away from all these emotions that were tearing her apart; emotions such as she had never expected nor created, yet as they soared within her now, she heard the chiding voice of Father Halton, and she heard the penances he had given her for atonement.

Feeling Colin's lips, again, seeking hers, more eager now than even before, and completely overwhelmed by her feelings and by her old longings for him, her warmth, her senses, her very passions far surpassing his own because they accompanied a depth he didn't even know about, she was awakened again to the stirring of a stronger emotion, something which made these frail desires, which only left her weak and willing, pale by comparison, and she remembered all the resolutions she had made both internally to herself, as well as externally in confession.

Then, too, she was reminded of Colin Murdoch's arrogance, and of his association with the likes of Chancer and Bopper, and freeing her mouth from his, and without looking at him, she said,

"If this is all you wanted, why didn't you just go home with one of your so-called 'birds'?"

With these words Colin's hand froze, and withdrawing it, he brought his cheek against hers and holding her tightly in his embrace for several moments before speaking and then in a voice, filled with so much emotion that Rosaleen didn't recognize, he asked her, "Do you think that's all I wanted? Do you really believe that this is all I want you for?"

Keeping her voice free of her own rising emotions, she asked him, "Well, isn't it?"

"Rosaleen." She heard her name fall from his lips as soft as petals falling from a rose. "If you don't know any better than that by now, how am I ever going to convince you?"

Her eyes now closed against the well of emotions that had gathered there, Rosaleen's voice, though steady, was barely audible. "Convince me of what?"

Pressing her tighter to him, but with a slightly reticent tone, he told her, "You know, of the way I feel about you."

Swallowing a breath, Rosaleen pulled

back to look at him. Without saying a word, she met his eyes, waiting for him to say more.

In a tone not common with his usual flippancy, and with a look far distant from the characteristic sparkle, he continued, "Oh, Rosaleen, you're far different from any other girl I've ever met. There's nobody I want to be with more than you."

Looking away from him, and trying to get her heart aligned with her head, she told him, "You have a funny way of showing your feelings." Looking at him, and then, looking away again, "What was all that about just now?"

Turning her face towards him, and looking into her eyes, Colin said, "I'm sorry, baby. You know I wouldn't hurt you for the world."

"And in the Hibs tonight," Rosaleen stirred his memory, "during the contest?"

Colin looked at the ground, as though searching for the answer there, and then, looking directly at her, he told her, "Look, Rosaleen, sometimes it's hard getting through to you. You wouldn't talk to me; you left me waiting for you all night in the Plaza." and his tone took on a paradoxical softness, "Right there in front of everybody, Chancer and Bopper . . . "

"How did *they* know you were waiting for me?" Rosaleen asked, her voice noticeably rising in demand.

"I told them." Colin told her.

Greatly taken aback by the directness of his statement, Rosaleen acknowledged that this was the first admission of any direct reference he had made to them concerning her, and now, wanting to clear the air further of some of his shortcomings, the result of which she had been painfully harbouring, she retorted, "You see! That's exactly what I'm talking about, Colin. You take everything for granted. You know, you have a very egotistical streak about you . . . and . . . it was painted all over you tonight . . . when we were dancing. And by the way," she interjected, knowing this to be her last opportunity, and not wanting to leave anything unsaid, which would bring regret later when she would be reflecting on all of this, she went on, "the reason I took over from Maisie was because I thought it was important for you to win, but you . . . " Suddenly overcome with the overwhelming experiences of the entire night, she struggled to keep her emotions in check, not daring to let them come out, but her eyes were shining with unspilt tears. " . . . but you just showed your arrogance in that Colin Murdoch manner you have . . . going out of your way to make me feel uncomfortable."

"I didn't though, did I?" Colin said, not having missed a thing, and Rosaleen saw some of his former seriousness begin to disappear in a tone of renewed flippancy. Then, leaning against the palings, he pulled her around to face him and looking down at her, he said, "You're getting to be a big girl, now that you're out of school. Does it not bother you to see me looking at you?"

The air hushed all around them, and Colin's remark, coming through the stark stillness to warm her, resounded with priority, as though it required the most deliberate of considerations, and Rosaleen, feeling the blush come to her cheeks, said nothing.

Looking at him through the darkness, her heart roaring like a fire within the breast that contained it; itself burning like a hearth before it, Rosaleen began to see something for the first time: Helplessly warmed by the very characteristics that rendered their relationship hopeless, she understood the terrible ambiguity of her entire situation, the weight of which sat heavily on her chest like a burden; the irony of which reached into her heart and twisted in it like a knife.

"It doesn't bother you, does it?" she heard him repeat, and she felt the blush deepen, and she looked away. But Colin, putting a hand under her chin, brought her face back to his, but not yet her eyes. "Rosaleen?" His voice softly brushed the silence, looking for an answer, and receiving none, he determined to find it himself.

Closing her eyes so as not to see him, she sensed that he might just as well be touching her for all the turmoil he was causing within, not only emotionally but also conscience wise, and the tears unshed behind her lids were a mixture of the joy and the pain created by both.

Then Colin, raising his eyes to her face, opened her own with his lips, awakening in them a response, and looking in them, he saw exactly what he had hoped to find, and he put his arms around her and enclosed her in his embrace.

With his lips now against her ear, his whisperings were both tender and sensuous. "Oh, baby! My baby. My Rosaleen. You're beautiful, you know that? I couldn't keep my eyes off you when we were dancing. You're the most beautiful girl I've ever laid eyes on." Then gently circling the rim of her crew-neck sweater with his forefinger, he added, "I love how you look in that white sweater."

Feeling the tip of his finger caressing the front of her throat and feeling the warmth of his breath against her cheek and like a soft breeze bearing the impact of a hot, tropical wind down into her ear itself, Rosaleen knew what she had to do.

Pulling away from him, she said plainly enough, "Colin, I have to go now."

Colin, reluctant to release her, kept her near him for several more minutes. Caressing the top of her arms just below her shoulders, and letting his eyes take in all of her features, he then brought them to rest on her own.

"Yeah, I suppose it is getting late," he said, and then, deepening his look, he asked her, "Where are we going tomorrow night?"

Looking at him, Rosaleen told him, "Nowhere, Colin," and then looking away, she added, "I can't go out with you anymore."

Looking surprised, Colin straightened himself up from the palings. "What do you mean you can't go out with me anymore?" he asked, looking down at her, and Rosaleen, seeing the question in his eyes, and feeling the strength of his gaze, couldn't trust herself to look at him anymore, and she looked away.

"You're kidding, aren't you, Rosaleen?" Colin pursued, but without success, and once again, he forced her to look at him. With his hand warmly cradling her throat and his thumb sensuously tracing her bottom lip, he said to her in the tenderest tone he had yet to equal, "Tell me now you can't go out with me."

Rosaleen, attempting to turn away again, but he, refusing to let her, was forced to say to him, "You're making this very hard for me, Colin."

And he, in answer, said, "Look, Rosaleen, maybe my judgement is all wrong or something, but I thought . . ." he broke off, then gently stroking her cheek, he said, "What's the matter, don't you like me?"

"That has nothing to do with it," Rosaleen told him.

But Colin, bringing her face closer to his, told her, "Oh, I think that has everything to do with it."

Feeling herself slipping backwards emotionally, yet unable to look away from him, she gave him the benefit of her full gaze. "Colin, I . . ." she began, then stopped, taking her eyes from him.

Colin, sensing her genuine embarrassment, realized that she had something specific on her mind, and he put a finger to her lips. "You don't want me looking at you while you tell me, is that it?" and he took his arm from about her.

And Rosaleen, watching his profile, as he leaned his hand against the paling and looked past her down the street, started to tell him something of which she never thought she would ever hear herself talk to him about. "Colin, I went to confession," she began softly, "and I told the priest about that day on the Cavehill."

Colin turned his head and looked down at her and then looked away again to let her continue. But the words were slow in coming, as though unsure of his understanding the gravity of it all.

"Colin . . . " she said, still holding back, almost as if she were ready to jump off a cliff and that once doing so there would be no turning back. "I . . . started by telling him about . . . the . . . passionate kissing . . . "

Again, Colin looked at her and this time his eyes remained, ponderous and serious looking, and Rosaleen, sensing him sympathetic to her plight, continued.

" . . . I thought he would give me absolution and that would be it, but he started asking questions, such as where we went, and why, and how long we stayed there and . . . " she paused, looking down, her voice dropping to an even softer tone, " . . . he asked if you

355

had touched me, and whether or not I had deliberately encouraged you.

"He was furious that I had gone with you to the Cavehill. He said that it was obvious that we wanted to be in a lonely place." Stopping to draw a breath, she went on, now looking at him, "He asked me how far we went. Oh, Colin, it was awful having to tell him; having to put it into words. I nearly died from the embarrassment of it all."

Touched by the ordeal he knew she had suffered, Colin brought his arm around her shoulders and pulled her to him and buried her face against his chest.

Taking a minute to compose herself, Rosaleen continued. "When I had finished telling him, he wanted to know, step by step, how we had gotten so far, and why I had let it." And taking another deep breath, she said, "He, then, asked me if I had wanted to go further. Oh, Colin, it was so confusing, I couldn't even think straight. For days after that I tried to think about it clearly, only it became worse. I felt as if I had told him a whole pack of lies, on top of everything else."

Stopping for a minute now, she then went on in a saddened sort of tone. "And then, after all that, I couldn't even bring myself to go to Communion."

In an attempt to comfort her, Colin hugged her to him. "Oh, my little Rosaleen," he said, soothing her and stroking her hair and kissing the top of her head.

Looking up at him, her eyes now wide and trusting, acknowledging the fact that he had been there; he knew exactly the way it had been, he could be her witness before God Almightly that what she had not done had not been intentionally sinful, she went on to tell him more.

"He asked me if you were a Catholic. When I told him 'no' he almost hit the roof. He wanted to know where I had met you, and he called the Hibs 'a den iniquity', and said that it should be closed down, and then . . . "

Hesitating, and looking away from him, she cast her eyes across the park. But it was darker now, and nothing was visible except for the lights of the Royal Victoria Hospital, which stood like a sentinel over the fountain, its little squares of light, ever ready, remaining through the night, waiting . . . But there were no children in the invisible fountain, and the blood-suckers had disappeared with the rain, and the well had a false bottom, and the gargoyles had been rendered harmless.

" . . . he said that we have a very dangerous relationship, and that he could see how things had gotten so out of hand, because, you, being a Protestant have a different set of morals than we do." Looking down, she went on, "He asked me if I was still going with you, and I told him 'no'. Then he said that under no circumstances was I ever to go with you again, because, he said, you were an occasion of sin to me."

She looked up at him, but Colin looked away. "Colin," she said, her tone retrieving his eyes, "I could be excommunicated if I ever went with you on a continuous basis." And then, her own eyes taking leave, she murmured, "And, after to-night, Colin, I can see what he meant."

There was a long moment between them in which Colin put his head against his hand on one of the palings, as though searching for words that would make everything right for them. Then, lifting his head, but looking down the street, he said, "He said my morals are different from yours?" And then, looking directly at her, he went on, "You know, Rosaleen, you may not believe this, but I do have a conscience."

"I'm not saying you don't, Colin. I'm only telling you how the Catholic Church feels about these things. It is very strict as far as mixed religions go. It believes in Catholics sticking to their own kind."

"Oh!" Colin said, and with a note of sarcasm in his voice, "And what if I was a Catholic, would that make it all the less 'sinful'?"

Detecting his tone, and in a raised voice, she told him, "Of course not. There are rules even for Catholics going with Catholics."

"Oh, is that right!" he said, maintaining his tone, "Tell me about them."

Rosaleen looked at the ground without saying anything.

Colin looked at her long and hard. "So, tell me about them," he repeated his tone.

"Do you really want to know?"

"Yeah, I want to know,"

"Well, as far as the Catholic Church is concerned, two people should only see each other on a steady basis if they are seriously thinking of marriage. The Church believes that two people should be able to determine their true feelings about each other within the first six months of their meeting. After that they should publicize their intentions by becoming engaged. During that time, they are expected to attend the sacraments of confession and Communion on a regular basis."

"Wait a minute." Colin stopped her, and feeling his anger rise, he let it get the better of him. "Are you telling me that the Church says that two Catholics could fuck it up every night, just so long as they're both Catholics and they go and report it every week?"

"Colin!" Rosaleen called out his name, shocked by his attitude. "That's a terrible thing to say."

"Oh, is it?" He said, taking hold of two of the palings, his knuckles white, as though from the strain of pulling them apart, and he looked through them into the park. "Well, what you've said to me isn't all that 'nice' either." And looking at her, he asked her, "How do you think I feel being told that I have no conscience; that I'm a dangerous person to be with?"

He looked away from her and back to the park, and then back to her again, and then, turning his back on the park, he leaned against the palings. "Do you honestly believe that showing someone how much you like them is a sin? Do you really believe that?"

Rosaleen looked at him and paused before answering, "But you show it to so many, Colin."

Stretching his hands in a helpless gesture, Colin's tone lightened. "I happen to like girls," and, he added, "A lot."

"That's why it's so hard to take you serious," Rosaleen said, feeling a familiar sting at his pronouncement. "Every girl is the same to you; you told me that yourself. How do you ever know where to draw the line? Where do you stop?"

Leaning his head back against the palings and looking up at the sky for a long time, "I could say I stop here," he said, with an almost serious note back in his voice.

"Is that supposed to be a compliment?" Rosaleen asked, in a light, level voice, afraid of sounding serious.

"Sure," Colin answered; and looking over at her, he added facetiously, "When you've tried all the rest, you stop with the best."

More than sensitive to the duplicity in his statement, Rosaleen felt the blood rush to her face, and turning from his incorrigible attitude, she started to walk away.

But Colin reached out his arm and pulled her back and up to him. Then, looking down at her, the jest gone entirely from his voice and from his eyes, he told her, "Don't be confused, little girl, about someone who cares about you and someone who is only out for a good time. If you can't tell the difference, then there is no difference."

He paused for a moment before continuing, "Is what we did so sinful, or was it beautiful? I don't happen to see anything wrong with it, when it's done for the right reasons. *I* know it's not good when it's done for kicks and" he added, gently squeezing her shoulders, "I've never looked for that in you, not after I'd gotten to know you. If I had, I'd never be standing here talking to you like this. So, c'mon, why can't we go on seeing each other like this, and to hell with everybody else, including that priest. What does he know about it anyway?"

About to ask a question, and knowing only too well what the answer was going to be before she asked it, Rosaleen determined to let his answer be the concluding one for both of them. "Oh, does that also include your mates, Chancer and that other one? Is it 'to hell' with them too? Is it really to hell with everyone and everybody except us, Colin?"

"What are you talking about, Rosaleen?" Colin asked her, surprise in his voice, as well as in his eyes. "What do my mates have to do with this?"

"Everything, Colin," Rosaleen said earnestly. "You know, you're judged by the company you keep, and I wouldn't want you as a link between them and myself."

"You're kidding, Rosaleen. Chancer and Bopper are harmless. They just enjoy life, that's all."

"Sure!" Rosaleen exclaimed, "At everybody else's expense." And then, proceeding to see it through, she continued, "Well, do you want to go out with me that much that you would give up going around with those two?"

"Are you giving me an ultimatum?" Colin asked in disbelief.

"It's no more than you're giving me," she retorted.

"Well, to tell you the truth, I'm not about to turn my back on two people I've known all my life; fellows I've grown up with."

"But you expect me to turn my back on something I also happen to 'have known' all my life, and 'have grown up with'?" And Rosaleen laughed at the idea of it, but it was filled with irony. "God, look at what we're bargaining with: the Holy Roman Catholic Church and the likes of your two so-called 'friends', Chancer and Bopper. Colin, I'm sorry, but the odds aren't exactly even. I'd practically be throwing my life away just to go out with you, and here you are clinging to what . . . ? Scum?"

"Hey, Rosaleen!" Colin pulled her up short, angry. "Who the hell are you? The Virgin Mary?"

Recoiling from his statement, the familiarity of it striking her like a slap on the face, she turned on him, her hurt pride choosing her words. "You're just like them." Then, repeating it for her own emphasis, "You're no different than they are. Oh, God!" she cried, choking back her rising emotions, "How could I have been so stupid in thinking that you were any better than them." And then, her remorse giving away to anger, she hurled at him the peremptory condemnation, "You could never give them up, Colin Murdoch, and you know why? Because the two of them are like scabs on your soul, you all belong together, you deserve each other."

Unable to face him any longer, she started to walk away and her step was hurried, and Colin made no attempt to stop her, except to get in one last word, and he called after her, and his voice stopped her dead in her tracks.

"You know, Rosaleen, when you made that confession, I bet there was one thing you didn't tell the priest." And then, coming to her, he put his hand on her arm, and turning her around to face him, he said, looking straight at her, "I bet you didn't confess to the priest about how much you enjoyed everything on the Cavehill that day — every bit as much as I did." And his tone hardened, and with it his eyes, "But, then, how could you when you can't even confess it to yourself. And you know why? Because you're too f . . . . . proud to admit that you're human — just like the rest of us."

Making no sign of removing his hand from her arm, Rosaleen felt his fingers digging into her flesh, and closing her eyes against the intensity of it all, she opened them to see him still looking at her, and then Colin, without anything further to say, suddenly released her, and watching as she walked away, and waiting for her to turn the corner, he went up the street in the opposite direction.

20

WITH the jiving contest marking the end of the crowded nights at the Hibs until the end of summer, Rosaleen needed no excuse to avoid Colin; not that she intended running into him again, for she had started going out with someone else.

A fellow who Rosaleen had known for years, a Patrick Brennan, who, in fact, came from her own neighbourhood and with whom she had much in common, and who, for all appearances, was more right for her than Colin Murdoch could ever be.

Slightly older than Rosaleen, Patrick Brennan had just completed his secondary education at one of Belfast's top Catholic schools and had just received his Senior Certificate. With the option open to him of either going to the Teacher's Training College or accepting a post as a clerk in one of Northern Ireland's largest breweries, where his uncle had been the head night clerk for fifteen years, and which offered someone like Patrick one of the best opportunities a young man of his distinction could possibly receive, he chose the latter.

During the first couple of weeks that they were going together, Rosaleen and Patrick had a lot to talk about, as, in fact, he was one of the fellows who used to go to the ceilidhes, and still did; and who wore the perennial grey-flannel trousers and navy blazer, and still did; and who had actually been in the Gaeltacht, in Donegal, the same time as Rosaleen herself, except, during the times she'd run into him, he always appeared to have looked at her rather disdainfully, but when Rosaleen reminded him of this, he didn't seem to remember. In talking about old times, having had common scholastic backgrounds, they both discovered that they had shared or heard of many similar and funny experiences, all of which filled Rosaleen with a certain nostalgia, but which also helped make their dates pleasant at least, if not totally pleasurable.

Living just a few streets from Rosaleen,

Patrick Brennan had grown up on the Falls, yet he knew nothing of the Hibs; a thought which occupied Rosaleen's mind during most of the film that she had gone with him to see on one of their Friday night dates. Knowing that Patrick must have passed the A.O.H. hall hundreds, even thousands of times, during the course of his life, just as she herself had done, she visualized him entering it for the first time, and on a Saturday night, and of going up the stairs: she thought about him being confronted, first and foremost, with the patrons themselves; the congestion of so many Teddy Boys and Girls in one place; with the likes of Little Richard and one of his screaming recordings, such as, 'Rip It Up'; with the form of dancing; in fact, with the whole place in general. And she thought about how it had been for her the first time she'd entered it all, and how she'd felt; it had been another world to her, and yet, she'd had the intervening Martin Specky's to pave the way. Patrick Brennan, she knew, would be thrown, head first, into cultural shock.

But, in the end, all that this conjecturing

had done for Rosaleen was to remind her of Colin and to set her thinking of him for the rest of the entire evening, all of which put her in a very receptive mood for their meeting — or rather — their seeing each other the next day.

Saturday in Belfast, if not the shopper's paradise, was, then, the sports fiend's fury: between the greyhound racing (the dogs), horse racing (the bookies); football (Windsor Park), Linfield and Glenavon; football (Cliftonville Park), Cliftonville and Distillery; football (Celtic Park), Belfast Celtic and Sarsfields; and, in the local parks, where everybody played; 'Balaclava Street', 'Roumania Street', 'Raglan Street', and, on this particular Saturday, 'Broadway', with its star centre forward, Colin Murdoch.

Patrick Brennan didn't care much for 'English soccer', being strictly a Gaelic League football fan himself, and he suffered the indignities of having to pass the players coming off the fields, as he and Rosaleen walked through the park, on that warm, sunny afternoon. Passing through the midst of the various coloured jerseys of the team members; the red and white stripes of 'Balaclava Street', the gold and white of 'Roumania Street', and, in the fashion of old Celtic, itself, as with many other regional teams, the green and white of 'Raglan Street', nearly all of whom Rosaleen knew, she saw, in the distance, the colours of blue and white.

Although knowing that they, like the Celtic colours, were popular, in their various shades, with many teams, they were also Colin's team-colours. Getting closer to them, each player anonymous behind the uniform, it wasn't until she got close enough to recognize Colin's distinguishable walk did she know for sure it was him, the anticipation of which created all the old breathlessness and blood racings and adrenalin flows, which had become as familiar to her as her daily breath, but which she would never get used to. But there was more to it than just a girlish response, for she knew of the many who had probable cause to feel the same way she did; it was coming upon him like this, having not seen him in over two months, that gradually made her aware of her very serious state; the cause of which she had diagnosed; the symptoms of which she had yet to recognize, having nothing with which to compare them: there had been a void within her breast, which the passing days, spent without him, had hallowed out into a skeletal depth of emptiness; until now, in coming closer and closer to him, his presence, reaching out to her and touching her like a warm sun; his radiance, spilling over her and filling her with its regenerative powers, aroused something within her, and she felt her breast come alive with something of hers, which, the last time she had seen him, had turned white from fear of never seeing him again, and, since then, had started to decay with the dread of having to live without him, and it began to beat, slow and unsure at first, and then, steady and strong, and she knew how the leper felt to be cured; the little one who had returned to give thanks. For she had experienced, in one moment, a truth which had started with the beginning of time; its two hundred century-old message, which had begun to unravel back when her ancient ancestors had sought the answer to it in their idolatry gods of bronze and stone, and would continue long after she was in her grave; long after the hazzlewoods had begun to shrivel and die, and the gorse no longer existed, and the sun had settled on the Cavehill for the last time.

Colin was with several other fellows and two girls, and, although it was hard to tell which of the fellows the girls were with, Rosaleen had a good idea that one of them was with Colin, for as she and he approached, their eyes on each other, watching, as every step narrowed the distance between them — something which one of the girls couldn't help but notice — and, in the moment of passing, just when it all seemed to Rosaleen that they were here for some perfunctory sort of exercise, which caused them to ultimately cross each other's path, and, in the duty of which, it seemed plausible that they should each shine their eyes into the other's heart and whisper, 'I love you', she heard the girl say, and in a redundant sort of way,

"Colin, what time will I meet you tonight?" A question, no doubt, spoken mainly for her benefit, with the echo of it sitting like a lump in her chest, replacing the fleeting joy of but a few minutes ago.

Later that same evening, while the waning sun still clung tenaciously to the Divis Mountains, the western range of which ran aloft the top of the diminutive little Falls Road streets, it appeared almost reluctant to give up the day much like Rosaleen herself, who was standing in the shadow of her own street corner with Patrick Brennan, and while he was the respected object of a few passers-by, who nodded their unacknowledged courtesies his way, he was by no means the reason for Rosaleen's not wanting to see the sun go down.

Feeling tired now, both physically and with the company of Patrick, with whom she'd been since early afternoon, and, besides, wanting to be alone with her own melancholy, she told him goodnight. Then he bent his head towards her, and she, bracing herself for his customary goodnight kiss, was suddenly confronted with the advancing familiarity which comes with the assumption that two or three weeks of dating was considerably long enough for the right to proceed with the ultimate: for, during his very polite kiss, which was painful enough in itself, he then placed his hand on her breast; not because of any innate desire of his own, but, plainly and freely, just because it was there.

If the past three weeks had been long enough for Patrick Brennan to consider that he had 'rights' with her, they had been too long for Rosaleen not to know when she was being patronized, for she had come to learn that with all his gentle mannerisms, his polite kisses were not merely lacking in passion, but were downright condescending in nature, and that he had chanced touching her merely because it was the thing to do; while Colin Murdoch, for all his arrogance and insolence, had never once made her feel anything less than what she believed herself to be: whereas Patrick Brennan kissed her politely because she was a female; not passionately, like Colin, because she was a woman, Rosaleen discovered the danger of being patronized to be far greater than that of being seduced, so she, then, firmly and politely, and because he was such a gentleman, removed his hand, and in none too ladylike terms, told him quietly to take himself off, and bade him a final goodnight.

With the days and weeks falling away into autumn, Rosaleen saw Colin one more time and, like the time before it, it was quite unintentional.

Working now in a dispatch office downtown for a leathergoods manufacturer, the locale of which Rosaleen considered to a downright affrontery, because, not only was it just around the corner from the Plaza, but the name of the street in which she spent nine of her waking hours, five days a week, was Joy Street; the irony of which hit her every morning at half-past eight and dragged behind her all day until half-past five, with all the time in between anything but joyful. For not only did she dislike her job, but she was finding it difficult to be anything but less than happy, having to contend more and more with her memories of Colin. She saw everything around her, while innocuous to everyone else, to stand as remembrances of him, and which threw her into a state of anguish that could last from one day to the next.

But as much as there were daily reminders to keep her spirits low, there was also a daily practice which Rosaleen had begun to adapt; one that had been her mother's for as long as she could remember, and which soon began to directly offset the misery of Joy Street, and this was the exercise of attending six-thirty morning mass at the monastery.

Awakening with the first sound of the monastery's carillon, the music of which stirred the morning air with its melodious quality of early songbirds; loud enough in its calling to those who wanted to get up, yet gentle enough so as not to intrude upon the sleep of those who did not, and laying there quietly, and contemplating the serenity of the gradual consciousness that separates sleep from wakefulness, Rosaleen waited for the monotone bell of the six o'clock angelus before getting up to face the new day.

In the beginning, walking along in the still-night, the anxiety of early October daylight preceded the way: painstakingly and unmercifully, it pierced the darkness upon reaching the top of Balaclava Steeet, and growing in strength around the streets opposite the A.O.H. hall, it boldly and shamelessly illuminated the way across the Falls from the park and Moloccos, slightly demurring just before the big gates of the monastery itself; until, with the mild, early autumn shifting in gear for the approach of winter, the morning route to the monastery was intercedingly darkened, with the morning stars alone lighting the way to the very gates of the monastery, gradually relaying the pitch-blackness of the sky to an early light at the first 'In nomine patris' and relinquishing it as though on direct dismissal at the 'Dominus vobiscum, ite missa est' which, by then, emerging with the sun, was the renewed-found solace for the return route homewards.

More able now, Rosaleen's entrance into Joy Street was a little more affable, with the paradox of it all not nearly so gruesome; until that is, towards the end of October when the imminent occurred, which made all remembrances of Colin to date appear as pale derivatives in face of the source and which destroyed any and

378

all of the progress she had been able to make and which set her right back to where she'd been in the beginning.

Returning home from mass one morning with her mother, and stepping off the pavement at the crosswalk, Rosaleen absentmindedly looked at the van which had stopped to let them cross, only to see Colin behind the wheel. His father and brother next to him, strangers, if she didn't know better, but neither of them more so than Colin, for in the moment it took her to realize that it was him, and to look away again, he offered no sign of acknowledgement, or of even knowing her, but looked at her with a driver's concern, and, as soon as she and her mother were out of his path, he took off down the road just as he would if she had been just another pedestrian: except, if she were, she wouldn't have been left with her heart yanked clean from her breast and dragged along behind, all the way to the building site of William P. Murdoch & Sons, where one of the sons, with the craftsmanship to build and create, had, with the very same hands, pulled apart her life and destroyed all

379

chances she may ever have had of being happy.

It was only natural that the sudden unexpectedness of seeing him like this should play havoc with her emotions; it was later, when the shock had diminished and all the memories had time to flood back and settle in once more, that her emotions reaped the wild harvest of his having sown the expression of his eyes into her soul. For gone were her good intentions of getting over him, and for days she slipped back into her former state of misery. But there was more; for she was becoming aware that every vehicle that suddenly idled behind her, or beside her, caused her considerable concern in thinking that it was Colin; the time, the day, nor the place making no discrimination, which, in a city the size of Belfast, was often enough to create a certain feeling of paranoia, and Rosaleen knew it, and, right there, alongside to encourage it, the same old ambiguity of hoping it to be him, and again, of hoping it not to be, and dreading the thought of either.

After this, Rosaleen knew, without a

doubt, that the only safe route to take from then on was away from Belfast altogether; away from the joylessness of Joy Street, with the Plaza like a beacon on the corner; away from the school, with its doorway of memories; away from the park and Moloccos and the A.O.H. hall. And away from Colin himself. And so, by the end of that same week, Rosaleen started thinking seriously about leaving home.

21

THE week of her sixteenth birthday came and went and soon the Christmas season was in evidence everywhere. But not half as much until the week just before Christmas, when it started to snow. All that week, practically without stop, it kept coming down until all the streets in the neighbourhood looked like a white wonderland, filling everyone with genuine Christmas spirit. But none more so than Phyllis and Jimmy, who had planned to become engaged at Christmas, and now, with just a few days to go, they were going to make it of official.

Rosaleen and Ann were both very happy for their friend and looking forward to the party; that is, until Phyllis told Rosaleen that Jimmy had invited Colin, which created a lot of mixed feelings in her. Yet, not wanting to saddle Phyllis with any unnecessary unpleasantness, she assured her friend that it wouldn't cause any problems for her.

But now the thought of seeing him again, of being under the same roof with him, of sitting in the same room with him, perhaps even talking to him, filled her with both excitement and anxious anticipation, and caused her no end of worry when getting dressed the night of the party.

Having promised Phyllis's mother beforehand that they would help with the preparations of the tea and sandwiches, Rosaleen and Ann were there at the house before anybody else arrived. While Ann was in the kitchen setting up the glasses, and filling the cigarette cases, Rosaleen went into the back room, which was being used to serve the teas. Finding everything laid out for her, she closed the door, glad of the privacy to be alone with her thoughts.

Spreading a large white linen cloth over the table, and then arranging the bone-china place-settings according to each chair, Rosaleen felt her heart leap every time she heard the front door open and the arrival of new voices, listening for the one voice that would cause her insides to go all to pieces. Yet, as time passed and she didn't hear the one she had been wanting to hear, a new kind of anxiety began to take hold and she couldn't bear the thought of going through the evening without seeing him.

As more and more people began to arrive and the house started to fill up, it took on the atmosphere of a real party, and, with the combination of the Christmas spirit and the festivity of an engagement all mixed together, everybody was in the best of moods. Even Rosaleen couldn't resist the capers of some of the fellows, as one after another used the mistletoe for an excuse to grab the girls; any girls, even Phyllis's mother, Mrs Donegan, was not excused, as she passed in and out of the kitchen doorway, carrying trays loaded with bottles of porter and stout. And Rosaleen, herself, was grabbed for the third time by one of Phyllis's older brothers, Billy, who had used no end of excuses to get her through the doorway, until, laughingly, ignoring his request for a bottle of stout, she shouted at him, as she eluded him, ducking into the scullery with her arms loaded with empty bottles.

"Hey, Billy, why don't you help yourself. You know where everything is better than I do." Which was the wrong thing to say to a fellow like Billy Donegan, for Billy was the type who didn't need any encouragement, nor any mistletoe, for that matter, to go after a girl, and he lunged playfully after her, teasingly, adding,

"Aye, right you are, love, nobody knows where everything is better than me," and grabbing Rosaleen in the scullery, bottles and all, he playfully bit at her neck, not in the least put off by her protests or threats.

But his mother, coming into the scullery, and seeing the way her son was behaving, scolded him in the way only a mother could, whose son was too old to be reprimanded, yet old enough to know better.

"Catch yourself on, you big blout and leave the wee girl alone," she shouted at Billy and caused him to release Rosaleen, and he muttered under his breath in retort, only the way a son could, who was old enough to get away with it.

"Jesus, ma! Your timing is perfect. And me just about to get a free feel." Receiving a too-well-known, meaningful look from his mother, and anticipating her right swing, which had an empty porter bottle in it, Billy ducked accordingly and then bounced back to throw at her, before going out of the scullery,

"It was her, ma. That wee innocent girl seduced me into coming in here with her, didn't you, Rosie, love?" Rosaleen smiled, as Billy ducked out, but his mother didn't show her humour, and with a dry wit she told Rosaleen,

"I wish to God they were all getting engaged tonight, maybe there'd be peace in this house. Look, Rosaleen, if that bugger bothers you again, just let him have this over the head, maybe it'll knock some sense into him," and she shook her head in futility, all of which made Rosaleen smile even more, as she went to dispose of the empties in the back yard.

Putting the bottles back into the crates which they had originally come in, and feeling the snow on her face and hands as she did so, Rosaleen stepped gratefully back into the warmth of the scullery, as Mrs Donegan called her over.

"Rosaleen, love, do me a favour, will you? There's a nice looking big fellow in there, over on the settee, he's not drinking, but he's asked for a glass of wine. Be a good girl and bring it into him. He's the one at the end, near the fire. Thanks, love," she said, handing Rosaleen the little wine glass. "Now I can start getting out the sandwiches. Would you mind coming back to give me a hand." And as Rosaleen was about to turn away, Mrs Donegan added, by way of apology, "It's not much of a party for you, love, is it? But maybe we'll be doing this for you someday soon." Saying nothing, Rosaleen turned her back, as she went to bring the wine to the guest.

Someone had gotten the party rolling by putting some records on the radiogramme, and as Rosaleen pushed her way through the standing crowd, she felt a strong pull of nostalgia, as she heard the opening strains of a song which was an instant reminder of her nights at the Hibs, and as the familiar voice of the singer filled the room with his mellow tones of remembrances, his words ultimately filled Rosaleen with a sense of total despair.

"Evening is falling
And the sun has set
It's time to be with you
Night is descending
like dark curtains of velvet
Oh, my darling,
it's time to be with you . . . "

Standing in the midst of so many, with the tiny, little wine glass in her hand, Rosaleen looked helplessly about her in the hopes of finding at least one other person in whom she might recognize the same kind of constraint she herself was under. But again, with so many surrounding her, she looked around and there was not one face with which to commiserate: all about her people were doing exactly what they were supposed to be doing: talking, laughing, telling jokes and anecdotes, with one couple over in the corner engaged in a long kiss, without regard to the mistletoe, or to the people around them: and now some of those around her had started to dance, their bodies, all close together, swaying, and all touching, due to lack of floor space, and Rosaleen, alone, standing by herself in the middle of them, feeling like a lost little island in a moving sea of humanity, tightened her hand around the wine glass.

" . . . The shadows deepen
And the day is gone forever
Night is upon us
And soon we'll be together . . . "

Sensing her voice evolving from a lump somewhere in her throat, Rosaleen declared her presence in a tone, which, although inaudible to her own ears, managed to break through the wave of dancers. "Who was it asked for the wine?"

And the voice coming back, carried to her by the same wave, reached her ears. "Over here, love."

And, upon that command, the little island was no more, for the sea had swallowed it whole.

Floundering in their midst, Rosaleen felt the nearness of the bodies suffocating;

the density of it all bringing a deafness to her ears, and then, the thundering silence was heightened by that single summons: "Over here, love", resounding . . . resounding . . . resounding.

Wanting to get out from under the depression, and still mindful of the wine, not wanting to spill a drop, she found a small opening in the wave, and holding the wine before her, she managed to get through before it closed up again. And now, out of the sea, the face was there to meet up with the voice, and again the words, varied but little, the tone the same, reflecting the provincial term of endearment, reserved by the Ulster by degree for the stranger; and by the user by decree for platonics.

"Thanks, love," Colin told her, as though she were as familiar to him as the hand he was holding out to her; the pain of which killed her, aided and abetted, no less, as she met his eyes and his touch at the same time, and she felt her hand tremble, and to make matters worse, he brought his other hand over it to get a steadier grasp on the glass, and all this did was send the trembling to her knees.

And now as he looked up at her, she was sure he must have heard her heart beating. But, if he did, he showed no sign of it, for he merely smiled and continued the conversation he was having with the two other fellows who were sitting with him.

Going straight back to the scullery, to where Mrs Donegan, busy at the table, had her back to her, Rosaleen escaped into the yet empty tea-room. Grateful for its solitude, and going over to the window that looked out on the small enclosed yard, she found the coolness of the glass a welcoming balm to her flushed face, and touching it to her forehead, she found a calming relief in the gentleness of the snowflakes falling softly against it.

From the other room, over and above the noise of the party, the record continued, the familiarity of it deepening her mood.

" . . . Here in the darkness your kisses fill me
With a love completely new
That I dream of night-time, darling, just to be with you . . . "

"Jesus! I must say, Rosie, you carried that glass of wine through the room as though it was going to the altar to become the blood of Christ himself!"

Shocked awake from her reverie by the booming voice of Phyllis's oldest brother, Malachy, whom she hadn't heard come into the room, Rosaleen spun around and saw him standing by the door.

"No! Malachy. I didn't realize it was for . . . " Too late, she realized her mistake, and Malachy, coming across the room to her, holding on to a bottle of porter, his bold venture apparently emboldened by its contents, who was known only to Rosaleen as a quiet man with a gentility towards his native tongue, which he had gained as a political prisoner during the early fifties, and which he spoke fluently, now approached her with it, his voice somewhat subdued, both by the language and by her mood.

"Caidé atá cearr leat, a Róisín?" He asked her what the matter was, his eyes softening at the sight of her standing by the window, and he repeated the question, slower now so she could understand him, addressing her now with the title that embellished all of Ireland. "An bhfuil gradh atá ort, a Róisín Dubh? . . . Unrequited love, no doubt, by the look of them tears in your eyes. Here," he said, taking one of the linen napkins off the table, and holding it out to her, he spoke slowly, his mellifluous tones coming from under his great ginger beard, "Ní feidir leat a' iarraidh do ailleacht, mar atá cailín faoi bron le culrá sneachta . . . What more beauty could you ask, but the snow for the background of a maiden's sorrow; nor riches, as yet, but linen on which to dry her tears. Oh, never let the one you love see you crying, for it only gives him the upper hand." And bending down to peer into her face, as she attempted to dab the tears from the corner of her eyes. "So it's the big fellow in the corner, is it? Oh, he's a good-looking one, alright." Then, straightening up to take the last drink from the bottle, he drained it, and placing it carefully on the table, as though he were balancing it against the odds of the question that was on his lips. "Ná hinis dom. Nac bhfuil seans ar bith, go bhfuil Colin Murdoch an tainm atá air, nac bhfuil? An bhfuil mé ceart?"

Throwing him a quick look, Rosaleen blurted out in English, "How do you know that, Malachy? Did Phyllis tell you?"

Falling himself into the English of his own Ulster dialect, he told her seriously, "Ach, Rosie, you don't live on the Falls Road and not have it known that you're courtin' a Protestant. It's no secret."

"No . . . well . . . I haven't seen him in a long time, it's just the shock of seeing him here tonight, that's all."

"Oh, that's not shock that I'm seein' there in your eyes, Rosie; it looks more like love to me."

At that the door opened, and Mrs Donegan came into the room, and believing Malachy, like Billy, to be teasing Rosaleen, she held the door open for him and motioned for him to leave. "You, too? I swear to God, you're worse than Billy again. Sure, you'd think you'd have more sense than to go botherin' the wee girl. Away out to the yard and bring in another case of porter, before it turns to ice in this weather." And then, throwing Rosaleen an apologetic look over her shoulder, she followed her son out of the room.

Left alone, Rosaleen waited a minute or two and then, sure that her face didn't betray her emotions, she pushed her own way out of the room to help with the making of the sandwiches.

The party was in full swing, as the second sitting got up to leave the tea-room, and Rosaleen watched as Ann put a hand to her frizzled brow before starting to clear away the dishes, for she knew exactly how she felt.

"Twenty-four teas, Rosie," Ann noted, "and about a thousand more to go."

"That's forty-eight, Ann, if you're counting seconds."

"Who's counting? It could be a million by the way I feel," Ann answered her.

"Well, don't you worry, love," Mrs Donegan said, coming into the room unnoticed behind them. "My two sisters are here for the official engagement; they'll be takin' over for you after the next lot so's you two can go inside and have some fun."

Throwing Rosaleen a guilty look, Ann

followed Mrs Donegan out to the scullery.

Alone in the room, and with a fresh set of dishes before her, Rosaleen was just about to re-set the table, when she heard a familiar step enter the room, and she knew his presence only too well to know that he was behind her, and she felt her hand freeze around the cup she was holding, when she heard his voice.

"Hello, Rosaleen."

Oh, God! How long she had waited to hear her name on his lips again, and she felt the painful ecstasy of it as she turned to look at him.

"Hello, Colin," she said, and then, for all the waiting, and for all the longing, and for all the agony, all she could do then was to proceed with setting the table, which she had to do in as casual a manner as her impatience, her desire, and her aching heart would allow.

"I'm sorry I didn't get a chance to talk to you before," he told her, coming to stand beside her, and placing one foot on the rail of one of the chairs, he began to watch as she continued with the dishes, "but one of the blokes was in the middle of telling me something and I didn't want to interrupt him. And, then, you've been so busy here yourself," he said, running his eyes over the table, and he added, "And I must say, everything is going great. You make a great little hostess." And his eyes, leaving the table, came to rest on her.

And she felt them on her, which disconcertingly caused the simple task at hand to become the most difficult she had ever had to perform. Yet, as much as he had thwarted her own attempts to appear casual, Rosaleen was very much aware of his own casualness, and she then tended to making her tone colder by comparison, and so she asked in an off-handed way, "Are you having tea?"

And he, in a light manner, smiled back, "Are you serving?"

"That's what I'm here for," she told him, moving around to the other side of the table to disperse the silverware.

"Have you had yours yet?" his voice followed her, and Rosaleen, surprised by his concern, answered matter of factly.

"No, no I haven't even thought about it."

"Well, then, why don't the two of us have ours together," and seeing her hesitate, he quickly added, "Look, you can sit with me over there; they look like two comfortable chairs. What do you say?"

But Rosaleen hadn't gotten by 'the two of us', and was still caught up with these words when the second phrase, 'you can sit with me', caught up with her, and she wished that he would be a bit more careful in choosing his words.

"Well, I'll see what the arrangements are for this sitting," she told him. Then, as the people started to crowd in around them, Rosaleen moved aside to let them get seated, and she heard Colin say,

"Look, I'm going to reserve those two seats, so hurry in."

Pouring the teas as the cups and saucers were handed around the table to her, Rosaleen could hear Colin engaged in conversation with several others around the table, and she heard him laugh, but not being able to concentrate on what was being said, neither was she able to discern what he was laughing at, but she did feel his eyes on her from time to time, and she wasn't sure why. So it was not with joy that she silently acknowledged him, but with pain; a dull, thick ache that she knew there was no cure for right then, but she was shortly going to have an answer for what ailed her, and she was counting the days until it came.

Pouring the last of the teas, and with Ann carrying in the plates piled with sandwiches, accompanied, no less, by the running commentaries and humourous jestings of some of the male guests at the table, and while she accused them of 'biting the hand that fed them', which only brought further comments, sprinkled with a few mild conjectures, Rosaleen slipped quietly into the chair beside Colin.

Sipping her tea, and waiting for everyone to finish eating before lighting a cigarette, Rosaleen made an excuse of one small sandwich. Feeling Colin's arm go across the back of her chair, and seeing him lean towards her, she heard him ask, for the second time,

"What's the matter, Rosaleen?"

And, as the insensitivity of his question

stung her, she could do nothing but smile and tell him, "Nothing, Colin. Everything's alright."

But the second time Colin was not about to be put off. "C'mon, Rosaleen," he said, "you've hardly eaten a thing, and you're never this quiet. Something's bothering you."

Turning away from the intensity of his gaze, Rosaleen concentrated on the remains of the tea in her cup, which she swallowed in one mouthful. But its taste had disappeared and in place of the strong, hot brew, which she'd poured herself, she found a weak, cold solution, which left its unsavoury flavour on her tongue, and on the roof of her mouth, and even down into her throat itself, and as though she had expressed all of this, which she didn't, for she had been more than careful not to display anything that he might read on her face, Colin reached over, and taking the fresh pot of tea just recently placed there, he filled her cup.

"C'mon now," he continued, "you can tell me, can't you?"

Never getting used to this way he had of making her want to openly declare everything she had ever thought or felt about him, she had the strongest urge to say to him, "Well, you see, Colin, there is this fellow that I met, oh, about a couple of hundred years ago, and for a while he makes me happier than I've ever been in my whole life, but, then, something always seems to go wrong, and I end up feeling miserable and dejected, and this time it was awful and there is just no way back, and I don't know what to do about it. So what do you think, Colin? Maybe you could tell me what to do."

"You can tell me, can't you?" Rosaleen looked at his gaze, at those eyes that never wavered, that never met doubt, that never reached an indecision; always reflecting that he was right in everything he did, no matter what anyone else might think, and feeling choked by the irony of it, she thought, that out of all the people she knew, Colin was probably the one who could help her solve her problem; that is, if the problem lay between her and someone else, not between the two of them.

"You can tell me, can't you?" Oh, what a warm and assuring statement, Rosaleen thought, "And, oh, the things I could tell you, Colin; the things I could tell you." But, instead, she said, rather ruefully, looking up at him,

"Oh, I think I'm just suffering from pangs of remorse, you know, when friendships start to break up — like Phyllis getting engaged — you just know that things are never going to be the same again."

"And what about you, Rosaleen? I suppose you'll be the next to go?"

Sitting there next to him, his arm across the back of her chair, she listened to his words as they came to her like a death sentence. How could he? How could he talk to her like that — like some big benevolent brother — after all they'd been through. And the thought of how he really felt about her made her feel sick to her stomach.

Sitting there beside him, and he looking at her, she had seen the warmth in his eyes, felt it, too, in his attitude and concern for her, and she had read something into it. But, now, just minutes later, she realized that he was this way with everybody; Colin Murdoch warmed to everybody, and everybody warmed to him: and that other side to him? She alone in this room knew *that* Colin Murdoch. Yet, how different he seemed tonight. In fact, how different he had seemed that morning when she had seen him on his way to work; and the time before that, in the park; there was a somewhat quieter air to him, and yet, basically, there always had been, he just seemed to be more sullen, more serious looking lately than she'd ever known him to be. And Rosaleen thought that maybe he had changed; maybe the old Colin was gone, and then, suddenly realizing her thoughts, she began to think of that old Colin and of never seeing that side to him again, and she felt a great, sudden sadness settle around the pre-nuptial feast.

"By the way, where's your boyfriend? Isn't he here tonight?"

His words broke into her thoughts and scattered them, leaving a big empty void, and rummaging for something with which to fill it, she looked at him questioningly.

"Oh!" she said, suddenly realizing his inference, "you mean Patrick Brennan?

Oh, that was nothing, just one of those things, you know, more friendship than anything."

"And us, Rosaleen? What are we?" She heard his words, low, and meant just for her, and she felt pale, except he added to them, "I'd like to think that we'll always be friends."

Like a natural reflex, she turned from him immediately, as though his tone were a deathly repellent, and she some creature he wished to dispose of.

Unable to return her eyes to his direction, she fixed her gaze on the window and looked at the falling snow. Sitting there, and with her emotional state being what it was, she looked at the hurried, whirling little snowflakes falling about the dark glass, and she felt like she was in one of those little glass balls; the kind she had seen so many times, that could be picked up and shaken and turned every which way until the scene is filled with fallen snow, with the little people inside having no jurisdiction whatsoever over their plight, as they stand pinned to the ground outside their tiny house, waiting for some unmerciful hand

to turn their world upside down —
something, which Rosaleen felt, she
would never do again, and, then, turning
back to Colin with her answer, she said,
"Sure," and smiling at him, she added,
"Why not," and she got up to clear the
table, with everything inside her frozen
and numbed to the core.

Dreading now the moment when
Jimmy and Phyllis would announce their
engagement, Rosaleen kept more or less
to the background, and even though her
help was not needed so much since Mrs
Donegan's sisters had arrived, she kept
herself busy in the scullery. Then, as the
moment itself arrived, standing just within the doorway between the two rooms,
she watched the ceremonious placing of
the ring, and she saw the joy and
happiness shining on both Phyllis and
Jimmy's faces.

Feeling genuinely happy for the couple,
Rosaleen heard the announcement of
their wedding date as being sometime in
June, and she heard the cheering
response of the wellwishers. But, inside
her, she heard her own voice screaming,
"Why? Why was it that some people were

automatically happy, without even a cloud on their horizons?" And she thought of how the love between Phyllis and Jimmy had grown without even as much as an argument between them. "Oh, how lucky Phyllis was, never to have been subjected to anything but Jimmy's trust and love, never to have had to put up with raucous nor crude friends, never to have had to be condemned by a priest, a stranger, for daring to let her emotions run free, just once; nor to have been put in the position of having had to chose between her faith and her love, both of which held for Rosaleen the deepest of human needs a soul would ever need in his life."

"Phyllis, I wish you all the luck and happiness in the world," she heard herself saying, as her former thoughts materialized, and putting her arms around her friend, the girl she had known since early childhood, she hugged her to her, and trying to hold back the tears, she took Phyllis's fingers between her own, and looking at the delicate little band, with its setting of five little diamonds, their brilliance offset even more by her own glimmering emotions, she told her, "Your ring is just beautiful, Phyllis," and, in an effort to dispel her sobriety, she said, "Looks like somebody's making it big around here." And, then, putting her arms around Jimmy, she offered him her best wishes. "Congratulations, Jimmy, and the best of luck to both of you."

Kissing her on the cheek, Jimmy said aloud, "Thanks, love," but into her ear, he told her, "Don't let him get away from you, Rosie, for this is the greatest thing that can happen to anybody," and then, giving her a firm pat on the arm, he swung around to accept someone else's congratulatory handshake.

Trying to keep out of things for the rest of the night, Rosaleen was at the sink rinsing out some glasses when Mrs Donegan came up behind her, and handing her a towel, she forced her away from the sink and out of the scullery and into the heart of the party, much against her own wishes.

The singing session, very popular at house parties of all kinds, was under way, with Billy Donegan as master of ceremonies. Standing by the scullery door,

Rosaleen waited for the present singer to bring her song to an end before taking a seat beside some people, who she knew to be friends of Mrs Donegans', but, who she didn't know well enough to have to worry about making conversation.

Seated a safe distance from Colin, she lit a cigarette and concentrated all her attention on Billy, who, taking his allotment as m.c. very seriously, was standing in the middle of the floor listening to Joe Ward from Balkan Street, and Stan Skelly from Belgrade Street, the time and intensity of which all three employed, it might very well have been the Crimean Conference itself, and which, upon hearing the outcome, Rosaleen considered that it might just as well have been.

Now, in his very best master of ceremonies voice, the tone of which brought a smile from everybody, Billy related to the party, "Alright, alright now. I have just been informed that we have here on the premises, a singer, who can put to shame, Dean Martin, Perry Como, and Al Martino all rolled into one," and bowing slightly in Colin's direction, he said, "Now, Mr Murdoch, what's your pleasure?"

Colin, himself smiling during Billy's introduction, was taken by surprise and he broke into a laugh, and not admitting that he had a singing voice, he declined. Rosaleen, in casually looking over at him, was surprised to see that he was actually embarrassed.

"C'mon, Murdoch," Joe Ward shouted, "Give us the one you got six months for," at which the whole house laughed, and Colin, seemingly more relaxed by the outburst, quipped in return.

"Well, how about the one Johnny Mathis got twelve months for?" at which, between the fresh outburst of laughter, and applause, Rosaleen threw him a quick glance, and, feeling slightly stung by his statement, she knew that he could have been more diplomatic in his choice of songs.

"Okay, here goes," she heard him say. "Now, since most of the songs have been dedicated to the happy couple, of which I don't begrudge them one, this one is for those of you who happen to like Johnny

Mathis, and, if you don't, then just take it for what it is."

Remaining motionless, and not daring to look in Colin's direction, Rosaleen wished that she were anywhere in the room, any corner, but there in full view of him, for she was not up to sitting through his Johnny Mathis song. And she thought of how typical it was of him to attempt to taunt her, either with the song itself or with the implication of it, and so, fixing her eyes on a spot between the floor and the opposite wall, she inhaled on her cigarette, and exhaling slowly, she hoped, at least, that her tenseness, which she felt was obvious, would lift and disappear with the smoke. But as Colin began his song, and realizing that it was one that she hadn't heard before and therefore bore no significance to their past relationship, she permitted some of the tension to escape and was able to relax a little and pay considerable attention, not just to the song, but to the singer himself.

The song was 'When I Am With You', and listening to Colin singing it, Rosaleen couldn't help but be impressed by the deep quality of his voice, and she could tell that the others felt the same way by the silent attitudes being communicated towards Billy, the m.c., in that the singer hadn't been oversold, and she even felt a smile on her lips at Billy's own response, for his expression was heavy with complacency, which not only said that he agreed with their opinion, but it tended to back up his own good judgement, that he knew before they did, exactly how good the singer was going to be.

Feeling more sure now that her semi-relaxed mood would not betray her by conveying any involuntary emotions, Rosaleen looked over at Colin, only to find that he had been looking at her. Meeting his eyes, and finding it unbearable to have to look at him with about as much feeling as the elderly woman sitting next to her, she was finding it even more unbearable to have to look away, and so, letting him hold her eyes with his own, she felt his song filling her heart right to the very brim.

She knew that there was no colour left in her face, for she had felt it slowly drain away under the power of his gaze, and

411

she knew she was trembling, and she knew, too, that he probably was aware of it just as much as she, and, as he finished the song, he continued to look at her, and amidst the applause, in which she took no part, she knew that he saw her exactly the way she felt. But feeling a hand on her arm, and a voice coming across the woman beside her, Rosaleen tore her eyes from his and brought them to meet the voice which was speaking to her.

"Aren't you the wee girl who was serving the drinks? Do us a favour, love," the voice was saying, "and get Ginny here a wee brandy. She's feelin' a wee bit lightheaded with the smoke an' all."

Getting up out of her chair, and going for brandy for the woman was the last thing Rosaleen wanted to do; what she really wanted to do was scream; scream at Colin for being who and what he was, and scream at the woman with the 'light head'. Why should she have to get her brandy? What about her? She had a heavy heart. Who's getting her anything? Who even cared? Did that woman care? Didn't she know that she'd been sitting there with more than a light head? Couldn't she see? Couldn't any of them see how she felt? Colin Murdoch saw it, but did he care?

Going through the scullery and into the now deserted tearoom, Rosaleen bent down to the cabinet where Mrs Donegan kept the liqueurs, and reaching in to move the wines aside, in order to reach the brandy in the back, there was a sudden outburst of song from the next room. Upon hearing it, Rosaleen knew that Phyllis and Jimmy, who had been upstairs opening their engagement presents, had just now returned to the party, and, that at any minute, as was customary, would lead the guests back up to the front room, where all the presents, accompanied by their little gift-cards, would be on display.

But first there would be the traditional theatrics, which always preceeded the custom. Like every party, regardless of what the celebration, there was a song to suit the occasion — engagement parties, not to be outdone, had their very own signature tune, and one which called for the participation of the intended groom as well as the party guests. And, now, as

413

Rosaleen poured the brandy, she knew the theatrics to be well under way, for she could hear only too well the boisterous, though happy, voices of everybody singing in unison, with Jimmy doing his bit on his own.

"Jimmy, you say you wanna get
    married?"
"That's right, preacher, I wanna get
    married"
"Don't you wanna think it over?"
"No, I wanna get married"
"But she's too young, Jimmy, think of
    that part"
"But she's not too young to have
    captured my heart . . . "

Having to go back into the room with Colin being there was chore enough for Rosaleen, but having to go back now in the midst of all the partying was more than she could bear.

" . . . C'mon, Jimmy, an' think it over
She may not be the girl for you
Jimmy, if you think it over
You'll find another just as true . . . "

After pushing her way through the merry-making, she gave the brandy to the woman, and, on turning away, saw Colin talking and laughing and thoroughly having a good time with the rest of the party-makers, and so, deciding against sitting down again, she pushed her way back through the crowd and headed for the scullery instead.

" . . . Why does our love upset you? Why do you cause us pain . . . "

Jimmy, reaching out his hand to Rosaleen as she passed, grabbed her and pulled her into him and put his arm around her.

" . . . You just say we can't get married But I know what you really mean . . . "

"How're you doin', Rosie, love?" Jimmy asked, alternating his question with the line of the song, and Rosaleen could see that he'd had a little too much to drink.

" . . . We just wanna get married . . .
Hey, everybody, this here's wee Rosie.
. . . We don't wanna tarry . . .
She's the one that made youse your
tea.
Isn't she just a great wee girl?"

and then, accompanied by the response
of cheers and applause,

" . . . But she's not too young
to mend my broken heart . . . "

Turning the entire song over to the
others, Jimmy gave his full attention to
Rosaleen.

"Hey, Rosie, d'ye see who's here?" he
said, a little too loud, "D'ye see who I
brought with me?"

"Yes, Jimmy," Rosaleen said, taking
him by the arm and towards the scullery
and away from his prominent position in
the middle of the room. And in order to
pacify him, she told him, "I spoke to him
earlier on, Jimmy, when he was having his
tea."

"You know, Rosie," he said, turning
to her and with a sudden shift in

416

conversation, "this is my engagement party, an' you've been workin' your fingers to the bone for Phyllis an' me, an' I just wanna say that I appreciate that very, very much . . . "

"That's alright, Jimmy," Rosaleen said quietly, "I was . . . "

"No, no that's not alright. I just wanna say thank you, Rosie, that's all I wanna say." And looking down at her, he continued where he had left off. "Hey, did you see who I brought with me? Here! To my engagement party."

"Yes, Jimmy, I know."

"D'ye know he's crazy about you?" Rosaleen looked away, and Jimmy, suddenly realizing the spot they were in, said, "Hey, Rosie, how about a kiss under the mistletoe for a man's who's engaged to be married?"

Just to appease him, Rosaleen gave him a light kiss on cheek.

"O-o-o-o-oh," said Jimmy. "It's not me you wanna be under here with. I bet you wouldn't kiss big Murdoch like that." And seeing Rosaleen look away, he bent down and said against her ear, "D'ye want me to go and get him for you so's you can kiss him under the mistletoe . . . ?"

"Jimmy!" Rosaleen panicked, pulling on his arm. "Don't you dare."

Then, Jimmy, talking to her in a firm voice, for one who was supposedly inebriated, said, "Rosie, what is it with you two that you never seem to make a go of it? Is it because he's a Protestant, because I know you were brought up strict an' . . . "

"No! No, Jimmy," Rosaleen said quickly, adding, "It has nothing to do with that, not really . . . somehow I wish it had've been just that."

"Had've been?" Jimmy pronounced, repeating her inference to the past, "Well, then, what for God's sake's ailin' you? Whenever the two of you are around each other, an' I see you lookin' at him, an' him lookin' at you, Jesus, I see sparks comin' out of both of your eyes, an' I think to myself, 'Well, this is it. Now it's this time for sure.' But then, before you know it, it's all over again." Then, giving her an earnest look, he said, "Have you not told him you love him yet?"

"Jimmy!" Rosaleen looked away.

"Maybe that's what's ailin' you both, Rosie."

Looking at him, her expression was filled with the condemnation that such a statement could only be attributed to either his inebriation or to his own newly acquired happiness, or both. But Jimmy continued.

"Away and tell him how much you love him, Rosaleen. You know, you wouldn't be losin' nothin'. You wouldn't even be losin' your pride."

Back in the scullery, Rosaleen heard the singing liven up again with Jimmy's participation, and she heard it get louder, with Jimmy's voice being the loudest of all.

" . . . But she's not too young
    to mend my broken heart"
"But, Jimmy, she's way too young . . . "

Rosaleen didn't stay for the rest, for taking her coat from the back of the tearoom door, she went down the scullery and out into the yard, and crossing it, she pulled on the door that led out into the entry. But the door, being very seldom

419

used, if ever, was warped and banked up by snow, and she pulled on it with all her strength, and she felt the old wood splinter and break away under her fingernails. But rather than go back into the party, she persevered, until everything that had held the door shut for years gave way, and dragging it open as far as it would go, she squeezed through and went out into the entry. In total darkness, and only able to feel her way along behind the long rows of walled-in yards, which created the narrow entry, it was conceivable that there was one emotion within the human breast that was far greater, and which went deeper, than all the rest, even more than fear itself. Because this entry, like all the others in the district, while bearing semblance to the streets it paralleled, both in distance and availability, was but a mere shadow of them, for lacking the brightness of the street lights, and without space, not even a crack, between the attached houses to let in as much as a glimmer, ran sullen and deep, not exposing itself at night, but preserving its anonymity, like all the others, for ulterior motives: and while running up the back of two adjacent streets, rather than separating them, like some jagged chasm, it joined them instead, like a column of spinal nerve, which transmitted the sensation of all and anything that took place there, for, while not only affecting the spot in which it occurred, it stigmatized, through association, the reputation of the streets around it, the houses from which the streets are comprised, and all of the people who live in the houses; with this particular entry being the foremost and fiercest in creating nightmares, avoidance, and wariness in the children, young girls, and women of the neighbourhood.

Feeling the snow on her face, and her hands now numb from the cold, Rosaleen picked her way over the snowcovered debris; the whiteness of the snow, itself, showing through the blackness of the night, being her only comfort.

With about a hundred feet between Donegan's house and the end of the entry, which opened out onto an adjoining street, it had taken her twice as long than if she had come by way of the street. And, now, upon reaching the corner, and glancing up the street in passing, she saw Donegan's house ablaze with lights, the only solitary one of the otherwise darkened street.

Upon reaching the next block, and pausing for a moment in the snow, trying to detect where the pavement ended and the road began, she crossed over and, while doing so, she looked up at the street lamp on the other side, and seeing the swiftness and density of the racing snow reflected as it fell to the ground, she saw that it was coming down harder than ever.

Now reaching the other side and directly under the street lamp, she heard her name being called, and turning around, she came face to face with Colin.

Breathless, his skin glowing from the cold air, he caught hold of her arm, as though half expecting her to keep on walking, and telling her something that would hold her there, while he let go of her, he said, "Rosaleen, I have something for you," and drawing in deep breaths of air, and reaching into his inside pocket, he brought out a small brown-paper package. "Here," he said, putting it into her hands. "I wanted to give you some-thing for your birthday. I've been carrying it around with me everywhere, just in case I'd run into you, and I guess tonight's as good a time as any. Who knows," he breathed, and pausing, hur-riedly added, "when our paths will cross after this."

Numbed by the cold, but more now by his words, Rosaleen couldn't tear her eyes from his face.

"Well, aren't you going to open it?" she heard him saying, and she saw him smiling, and feeling the paper wrapping between her fingers, and although unaware of having moved her lips, she heard her own voice saying,

"What is it?"

And again, she heard his voice, "Open it and see."

Removing the gift from its wrapping, Rosaleen found two small boxes. With one being smaller than the other, she opened the first, and taking the contents out, and holding it between her fingers, she admired the perfect delicacy of the fine, gold heart-shaped locket and chain, and, upon seeing its fragility catch and reflect the light from the street lamp, even in the face of the driving snow, she looked at Colin and then back at the locket.

In looking at it the second time, Rosaleen noticed that the little heart had an almost invisible catch, which caused it to spring open at the slightest touch, and while it lay there in the palm of her hand, opened in two, with nothing to protect it from filling with falling snow, she closed it softly, without making a sound, and looked at Colin.

"Thank you, Colin. It's just lovely. I'll wear it always."

Seemingly embarrassed, but with an air of outwardly excitement, Colin urged her to open the other box. Unsure of the contents, due to its bulk, she heard him tell her as she opened it, "Come on over by the light more and you'll be able to see it better."

Holding it in her hand, Rosaleen could see that it was a powder compact, but a very unusual one. Flat and shiny black, she learned from Colin that it was black onyx. But it was the lid of the compact itself that fascinated her, for right in the centre, cut into the onyx, was a little inlaid oval covered with raised glass, and under the glass, lying in a bed of white satin, was the form of a little red rose.

"Oh, Colin," she said, without taking her eyes from it, "I have never seen anything more beautiful in my whole life," and caressing the glass with her finger tip, she told him, "I can almost smell its fragrance it's so real looking. How did you ever find such a beautiful gift?"

"I was told that Rosaleen meant 'little rose'," Colin said, looking down at her, "so when I saw this, I knew there was nothing more appropriate that I could give you."

Looking up at him, her eyes soft and shining under the light, she said to him, "Thank you, Colin, from the bottom of my heart. I'll always treasure it; both of them." And then, with a slight inflection in her tone, she continued, "These are just the things I'd like to have with me when I go to the States. I'll always treasure them in remembrance of you."

Surprised and greatly taken aback by what he had just heard, Colin looked at

425

her hard and long. "The States?" he asked, his own tone changed. "You're going to America?"

"Yes," Rosaleen replied. "I have my papers away. It's just a matter of getting my visa." And then, matter of factly, she added, "It shouldn't be any longer than a week or two now."

"You mean you've been thinking about this all along? Why did I not hear about it before now?"

"I haven't told anybody yet," Rosaleen said, looking down, "Maybe I'm superstitious, but I always feel that when you talk about something, it never seems to work out."

"Well, this is a surprise," Colin said, leaning against the lamp-post. "I just never imagined you leaving Belfast, Rosaleen."

"There's really nothing here for me, Colin," she said, looking off into the snow, and she felt it catch on her lashes and melt in her eyes. "Even with the little extra education I've had, I didn't find any golden opportunities waiting at the end of it."

"And what are you going to be doing

in America?" Colin asked, straightening up. "You're not going for good, are you?"

"Oh, I don't know what I'll be doing later on, but as far as starting out, I have a position with a family with two small children. I'll be a sort of nursemaid and governess to them for about a year. At least that's the period of time stated in the contract I signed . . . As for coming back," she said, looking around, "I don't imagine that one does come back," she said, looking at him, she added, "No one around here ever seems to."

There was a long moment of silence between them, as they both stood there looking at each other, until Colin said, "Will I see you again before you go?"

"I don't think that would be a good idea, Colin," she said, looking down again. "It would be sort of like saying goodbye twice, wouldn't it?"

Taking a deep breath, Colin said, "Well, I guess this is goodbye, then, isn't it?" And looking at her standing before him, holding the little gifts that were to be her remembrance of him, he said to her, "What will I have to remember you by, Rosaleen?"

Looking up at him, her eyes blinded by the snow, her ears numbed by the cold, and her lips frozen by the utter desolation of it all, she was unable to speak, and he, moving closer to her, and reaching over, touching her on the collar of her coat, and searching along her left lapel with the thumb of his left hand, felt the little white shield with the red heart, which she wore, invisible now under the snow.

"If I take your pioneer pin, it won't mean that you've broken your pledge, or anything, or that you'll be hitting the American bars every night, will it?"

Feeling the light pressure of his thumb and forefinger just below her shoulder, the effect of which enabled her to answer him accordingly. And Colin, seeing the ghost of a smile on her lips and the slight movement of her head, reached out with his right hand, and brushing away the snow, brought it to the underside of her collar and removed the pin. While Rosaleen watched, he pinned it to his own coat, but out of sight, under his right lapel, and then, raising his eyes, he met hers.

Looking at her, he saw her pale and

stiff under the street light, like a colour-less little rose frozen in the snow. Then, once more, bringing his hands back to her, he finished where he had left off, brushing away the snow from her collar, and turning it up, he gently pressed it closer to her neck and throat. Then, unwilling to take his hands from her, but unable to prolong touching her, he removed them, and pausing for a moment, he held them bare to the cold whiteness of the snow, then, no longer needing an excuse, nor wanting one, he brought them beneath the fold of her collar and gently rested them at the nape of her neck, and then, letting them fall to her shoulders, he whispered to her, "Is this goodbye, then?"

Feeling the strength of his hands on her, bringing her warmth, and giving her life, Rosaleen looked at him, and then, letting her eyes fall from his face, she said, "It looks like it is, Colin."

"All right, Rosaleen, I'll be seeing you," he said, "All the best."

Looking at her, he heard her tell him, "I'll see you around, Colin."

Remaining under the street light long

after she had gone, Colin felt the tears well deep down in his chest; the same tears he sensed Rosaleen had carried with her; tears which he would never in his life see. Then looking down to where she had stood beside him, he saw her footprints, the last part of Rosaleen that he could reach out and touch, but even they were fast disappearing in the falling snow.

Letting herself into the house, grateful for the very late hour, everyone having gone to bed, Rosaleen walked through the silent house. Closing the glass door which would shut her off from that part of the house over which the bedrooms were located, she went into the little extension off the scullery. And there, under the glow of the night light, she unclasped her hand from her breast and looked at the crude, brown-paper wrapping that she'd been clutching to her ever since she'd first removed it from the gifts. But, now, the life had gone out of it, and it was damp and limp from the snow, and holding it once more to her breast, she went over to the back door.

The upper half of the door contained a stained-glass window which bore a picture of two bluebirds, one on each side of a rose, with both appearing to be taking flight in opposite directions. But one of the panes had recently been broken, the missing one being a wing of one of the bluebirds, and standing there looking up at it, it was not the broken pane that Rosaleen saw, but beyond it, to the night sky, and to the falling snow.

Looking at the snow for a long time, she thought of the encompassing nature of it. Watching it, she saw it as it fell over the little yard outside, over the old iron mangle, rusted from disuse now, in one corner; over the pile of coals, heaped in another; over the honey-suckle bush with its roots in the big wooden tub outside the door: and she thought of it as the same snow that was falling around the A.O.H. hall, around at the top of the street, around the Cavehill; upon the rocks, and upon the gorse, and upon the hazel trees: and she saw it as the same snow that was falling around the Dunville Park, and upon its big yellow fountain: and she saw it as the same snow that was falling around Colin, as he walked home; upon his hair, and upon his lashes, and she called out his name to it, as it fell to the earth: through the missing wing of the little bluebird, she called it, again and again, until, unable to call it any more, she fell crying against the door, clutching the brown-paper wrapping tighter than ever to her breast.

22

COMING out of work on Monday night, with only four working days left before Christmas, Rosaleen listened while the other girls talked about the imminent four-day holiday. Walking along Joy Street, one of the girls, suddenly realizing that she needed cigarettes, decided to stop at the little shop in Hutchinson Street. But Rosaleen, preferring not to wait, as the other two only went with her as far as the City Hall, where they both got their buses, and which was only a few blocks away, said goodnight to them at the corner, and walked down Joy Street alone.

Feeling the remains of the snow under her feet, or rather the slush, for the mildness throughout noon had melted the day a little, Rosaleen walked the remaining block, her own private thoughts few and far between, as she sullenly surveyed the surrounding pavement. The city traffic had turned the streets a dirty brown and grey: hardly Christmas colours, she reflected, letting her mind slip to the past several days, when the city would have been more receptive to the coming feast. She viewed the pavement before her, seeing what the city sweepers had done, not only to this street, but to the others surrounding it; they had deemed fit to bring in and dump the excesses of slush from the main thoroughfares, the piles of which formed mountains on the pavements and, which, the now-cold, sunless sky had carved into dark, crusted over-like volcanoes, brooding in their bulk, as though about to erupt any minute.

But further along, getting closer to the city lights, as though their brightness shed an equal warmth, the mountains dissolved into embankments, their dissolution running like little rivers along the street.

Now coming to the end of Joy Street, the atmosphere ahead seemed more in keeping with the approaching feast than the dismal tone behind. The distant voices of carol singers, and the equally distant sound of Christmas bells, were cast even further by the sudden interjection of the nearby tolling of St Malachy's angelus bell. Simultaneously, and just seconds behind, the chiming of the city's big custom clock began ringing the sixth hour; its volume and tone akin to its relation at Westminster, and every bit as ominous, it reached into every corner of downtown Belfast, which belied its position where it stood way off from the heart of the city. Striking discord now, and subsequently at all three angelus hours, it caused a sabbath of disharmony with the area's entirety of churches, reminding one and all of its presence, every hour on the hour, and midway through the hour, and, then, halfway through that again, its two-faced countenances looked out over the city from its big, black tower.

Standing at the intersection and waiting for the traffic to clear, Rosaleen looked to the source of the celebration, to Donegall Square, wherein Belfast's huge, palatial-like City Hall stood alight, its great Byzantine, green dome illuminated to the point of transparancy brought its four multi-directional thoroughfares into prominence, and she looked towards those who had faced the chilling air to bestow the glad tidings of Christmas upon the workers now leaving their jobs: God knows, she needed something to touch her right now, as she never needed anything before in her life.

Feeling nothing these past two days, but hurt, bitterness, and a deep resentment towards everyone; her family, her co-workers, and, most of all, towards Colin, Rosaleen, for the first time in her life, had lost her ability to pray. Unable to turn to anything spiritual, she had knelt through two masses and had come away with the same coldness with which she'd entered. Greatly fearing that her resentment had extended to God, the result of which she knew would be a loss of faith and the ultimate death of her soul, she had uttered one request, though hardly in the form of a prayer, for she had felt nothing and had thought of nothing during its utterance; she had simply stated in her mind that she would rather die than go through life unfeeling the way she was, especially the new life, which awaited her in America.

And, now, unable to face even her own family, and, in fact, not wanting to go home at all, she started to cross the street and, without intention, without even the effort of making the decision, she knew that she would walk around Donegall Square: without stopping, she would walk, until the tiredness took hold of her legs; at least, then, she would begin to feel something.

Aware of others behind her, rushing alongside her, anxiously hurrying to get to wherever they were going, Rosaleen deadened her own pace and let them pass by her and onto the curb. Sensing it, more than seeing it, she slowed to almost a full stop to let an approaching vehicle pass, and, when it didn't, she was just about to cross in front of it, when she heard Colin's voice calling her name.

Looking at the van stopped at the curb, she saw Colin get out, and coming to meet her, he walked with her to the curb.

"I thought maybe you'd want a lift," was all he said, explaining his presence.

Totally surprised and confused at seeing him, especially in this end of town and at this hour, she could think of nothing to say, except to ask him if he hadn't been working.

"The site had become too muddy on account of some of the snow melting," he told her. "We got a lot of it up there, being so high up, and as the new terrazzo vestibule and floors were recently laid . . . " Seeing the look on her face, he broke off, saying, "C'mon, get in out of the cold." Holding the door open for her, she got into the van. Watching him, as he walked around to the driver's seat, Rosaleen began to feel sorry she accepted his offer, because, now, it would only mean having to painfully leave him one more time.

Sitting there silent and looking straight ahead, she heard him ask,

"Are you expected home at a certain time?"

"Usually I am," Rosaleen answered, "Why?"

"I'd like to take you somewhere," he said, looking at her. "That is, unless you'd rather go home."

Slightly stunned by these unexpected turn of events, Rosaleen looked at him, her expression giving him the leeway to go either way, and taking her up on it, he pulled out from the curb, and turning the van around, he took off in the opposite direction from the one in which she lived.

Leaving the downtown area behind, Rosaleen found them heading for a part of the city she had never been to before, and finding it strangely unfamiliar, she asked him,

"Where are we, Colin? Or where are we going?"

"To the Lagan District," he said, referring to the river on which the city is built, and looking over at her, and seeing the curious look on her face, he smiled. "That's where my father grew up. My grandmother, granny Murdoch, lived there all her life, until her death about nine months ago," and he looked at her again, "Just about the time I met you, or just before it. Anyway, her death came just about a year after my grandfather's, and, because it was so sudden, she'd never been sick a day in her life, it caused the family a lot of thought before doing anything about the house. You see, my father and all my aunts and uncles had been born in it, so you can imagine how they must have felt about giving it up."

"Don't you have any relatives, cousins or somebody, who could take it over?" Rosaleen asked, looking over at him.

"That's easier said than done. I have two cousins, from different families, both married this year, but, one is an engineer and built his own house out at Glengormley, the other married an English bloke, and although he'd worked in Belfast for years, a damn good job, too, when it came to the bit, he decided Belfast wasn't good enough to raise a family, so he and my cousin went to live in London."

"And the house is just sitting idle?"

"Yeah," Colin said, momentarily distracted, as he concentrated his attention on a sudden patch of fog, then, getting back to the subject, he told Rosaleen, "I have an aunt who lives over here, my Aunt Rita. She's lived all her life practically next door to her mother, well, a couple of streets away. In any case, she only had one daughter, but she went to Canada four years ago; married a Canadian, and seems to be doing very well. In fact, that's where my aunt and uncle are now; they went to spend Christmas with their daughter and their son-in-law and their two grandchildren; twins, who they hadn't seen yet. And that's as far as it goes concerning all the eligibles, except for my brother and myself, that is," and he smiled, "I'm always telling him he better grab it before I do, for I might just live out my entire bachelor days in the old homestead."

Rosaleen felt the atmosphere thick between them, as she stared straight ahead, and not daring to break it, she kept her eyes fixed on the road before them, or what was to see of it, for it was pitch black outside and the headlamps of the van fell like two golden pools in front of them leading the way.

"You're very quiet tonight, Rosaleen," Colin remarked, just when Rosaleen was about to scream with the suspense of it all. Why did he ask her to come out here with him? What was the purpose of him telling her all this? Why? Why? Why? Will the questions surrounding Colin Murdoch never cease to taunt her? And then she heard him say, "But you're always quiet. That's one of the things

I've always liked about you."

Looking over at him, his face barely visible to her, she caught his eyes, nonetheless. A few more moments of silence, and then, pulling out of the darkness, he drove onto a stretch of road well lighted with tall stately lamps.

"Over there," he said, pointing to the right, "is the park by the river. It's really very pretty there, Rosaleen. You should see it in the summer. There's a towpath that runs right along by the river, with trees on the side closest to the water, and on the other side, great big flowering bushes, rhododendrons, I think they're called, all in different colours."

Listening to Colin talk, Rosaleen couldn't help but get the feeling that he was happy about something. It had been a long time since she heard him talk like this, and she found herself warming up to his tone, as he continued.

"I used to come here for two weeks every summer. God, we had such great times here. It beat going down to the country." And changing his tone a little, he told her, "You know, Rosaleen, this old city has a lot to offer; you just have to know where to look for it."

Rosaleen heard the slight break in his voice, almost as though a touch of melancholy had been added to it. But then, she thought: Colin Murdoch melancholy? Never in a million years. But she felt his old mood continue, as he told her,

"We used to ride our bikes along the towpath, and, towards evening, before the sun went down, we used to hide in the bushes, bikes and all, and spy on all the young lovers who used to come and sit on the benches." Smiling at the memory of it all, he went on, "One kid, who I used to hang around with . . . what was his name . . . ? I can't think of it," and he started to laugh. "I wonder if he still lives over here? Well, anyhow, one Saturday night, we got into one of the bushes just before this couple took over the bench, and Raymond . . . yeah, that's his name!" Colin laughed again, upon remembering it. "Well, Raymond got pretty close to that bench, and he started writing down everything the poor fellow said, and, then, when the couple got into a clinch, the bold Raymond got right up behind the girl and started whispering in a deep voice all of the affections that her boyfriend had previously said to her. The girl never batted an eye. But thank goodness her boyfriend was a decent sort of fellow and didn't say anything too far out of line, or else Raymond would have been in deep trouble.

"Now picture this, Rosaleen," he said, looking at her, "Here I am, completely hidden in the bushes, but still able to see everything that was going on, and Raymond, crouched down behind the bench, rhyming off the phrases to the girl. He was so busy reading that he didn't see the fellow get up and go around the bench, and there being no way I could help, I had to stand helpless and watch the whole thing happen. Anyway, the fellow grabbed him by the scruff of the neck and by the seat of the pants and lifted him bodily off the ground. He made Raymond go around the bench and apologize to the girl. Raymond was mortified, especially when the park ranger happened to walk by, and the fellow told him that Raymond was a troublemaker and a pervert, and he threw Raymond out of the park altogether." Again, Colin laughed at the memory of it, and he added, "But I ended up getting the worst of the deal, because I had to stay in the bush for two whole hours. I was too frightened, or too embarrassed to move; one of the two, but did those two hours ever seem like an eternity. I couldn't wait to get out of there. I was busting to go to the toilet, I was hungry, I was tired, and it started to get cold. When they left, I must've rode my bike about ninety miles an hour to get home, and then, I got it from my grandfather for staying out so late." Shaking his head, he laughed all over again at the thought of it. "Barred for life, Raymond was. Do you know that to this day, he can't go to that park, even if he wanted to."

Feeling the smile break out all over her face, Rosaleen asked him,

"What age were you, Colin, when all this happened?" And Colin, looking at her replied,

"Seventeen." At which Rosaleen felt the beginning of a laugh in the pit of her stomach, and was overcome by it by the time it reached her throat, and Colin, looking at her, said, "I was old enough to appreciate the things that fellow said to the girl after Raymond left," and, as an afterthought, he added, "Maybe I didn't make out too bad after all." And for no explicable reason, Rosaleen felt her old sobriety take hold of her again.

Back onto a dark part of the road again and, after a little bit, Colin made a left and, then, after two more turns, pulled into a little street that seemed quiet and unobtrusive.

"Since I was sixteen," he told Rosaleen, "I've had a key to granny Murdoch's house. In fact, all of her grandchildren had. She used to encourage us to come anytime and not to leave visiting her and my grandfather to any particular time or day. Her greatest pleasure was to come home and find somebody here." And, as he pulled up to the last house on the row, he said, as he looked at it, "I only wish I had done it more often."

Feeling shy in a strange neighbourhood, Rosaleen waited until Colin was out of the van before she opened the door on her side. Then, feeling awkward, she waited by the van while he opened the door of the house.

There was no sudden flood of light with which to enter the house; instead, Colin held out his hand to her, saying,

"It'll only take a minute to get a light on in here," and Rosaleen, feeling his hand close around hers, followed him into the house.

In total darkness, she sensed him taking matches from his pocket, and, upon hearing him strike one, she saw the small flame go up above her head, and she heard the gentle hiss of air being released, and, suddenly, it dawned on her what he was doing.

"Oh, Colin, gaslight?" she said to him through the darkness, and, as he appeared to her in the palest light she had ever seen he turned to her.

"Yeah, my grandfather couldn't bear to have it changed over, he loved to read by the mantle. He used to say that electricity was too hard on the eyes and that gaslight had a softer glow . . . " and, looking down at Rosaleen, he said, "And, you know something, I'm inclined to agree," and leaning down he kissed her, his arms loosely around her at first, and, then, pulling them tighter, he clutched her to him, and his kiss got harder, and all he said, by way of excuse, was her name.

"Colin, don't," Rosaleen said, pushing him away, looking at him.

"You didn't think I was going to let you go away without kissing you goodbye, did you?"

"I wish you hadn't, Colin," Rosaleen said, "Anyway, not like this."

"What was I supposed to do? Kiss you goodbye at the corner the other night, in the middle of a snow storm?"

"It would have been appropriate enough."

"Not for me it wouldn't. You know, you took the ground from under me, when you told me you were going away, I couldn't even think straight, never mind kiss you goodbye."

Then, as if to change the mood they'd gotten into, he said to her,

"If your eyes have got used to this now, I'll turn it up," and seeing her nod, he reached up and turned the mantle higher.

Deeply affected, both by his kiss and by his sudden embrace, Rosaleen felt herself

448

trembling, and looking at her, Colin said,

"I'll have the fire going in a couple of minutes, and then I'm going to make us some tea. So, if there's anything you want, just help yourself, I'm sure you'll be able to find your way around. I don't think these houses are that much different from the ones on the Falls."

Feeling a slight tinge on her cheeks, Rosaleen felt like screaming at her own shyness. Sure she'd be able to 'find her way around', but in front of Colin? She couldn't bring herself to be that obvious. Instead, she just stood where she was, watching him, as he went about setting the fire.

Watching as the rolled-up newspapers took light and caught hold of the sticks and set them crackling, Rosaleen, upon hearing that one familiar sound, released her first relaxed breath, since entering the house, and, with the beginning of the fire warming the hearth, she felt it pick up her spirits a little, and she felt them begin to thaw.

Straightening up after putting the coal on the fire, Colin said,

"The house will be warm in no time

449

and you'll be able to take off your coat." Then smiling at her, he reached out playfully to touch her face, with hands all blackened from the coals, and, as she pulled back from him, he gave her a reassuring wink, as he went out of the room.

Left alone, Rosaleen watched the fire, and, as she heard Colin in the scullery, she heard the sound of running water, the clang of the kettle on the stove; she heard the noise made by cups being put onto saucers; she heard all the familiar noises that she had heard all her life, and, suddenly, she thought of Colin's grandmother who had spent fifty and some odd years in this house, day after day, year after year, decade after decade, her business in the scullery creating these very same noises, all of which had been heard from this room, where she now was, but only by different ears. Yet, having never met his grandmother, she thought of her own, who, living in a little house just like this one, bearing and raising so many children, working hard in the house all day and looking for her husband to come home at night, and she realized that there was very little difference between them. Thinking about it all made Rosaleen not feel like such a stranger, the thought of which invited her to sit before the fire and to hold her hands out to the flame.

Coming back into the room, Colin looked at Rosaleen sitting before the hearth, the fire bright enough now to catch the colour of her hair and illuminate her face, and calling her name, he saw the flame from it reflect in her eyes as she turned to him.

"There's a shop just about two blocks from here," he said, bringing himself down beside her, "So I'm going to run out before it closes and get some things that will do you for supper. Is there anything in particular you'd like?"

"No, Colin," Rosaleen said, seeing his face closer to hers than she thought she'd ever see it again. "I'm not hungry. I'd just like a cup of tea."

"C'mon, Rosaleen. You missed your dinner. Can't I even get you some fish and chips? That's just the thing you need on a night like this."

"No, honestly. I don't feel like eating

anything right now."

"All right then, maybe later. There's a place not too far from here that stays open to eleven." Then standing up and taking his coat from the chair, he told her, "I'm going to go out anyway, as we need milk for the tea." Then, looking at her, and seeing her tense and drawn, he asked, "You'll be alright, then, till I get back? I'll only be a couple of minutes." Nodding, and giving him a bit of a smile, she watched the door close behind him and she heard the van pull away from the curb.

Now left completely by herself, Rosaleen's thoughts turned strictly to Colin, and how she felt about him; she knew how she felt about him without having to think about it; what she wanted to know was how he felt about her. She knew that he felt something as sure as she knew that he wouldn't have given her a present, not even a birthday present, if there hadn't been something there, for she knew he wasn't the type to casually give someone a gift like that if there wasn't a genuine fondness to go along with it.

A fondness? Was that it? Well, she

knew he liked her; she could see it in his manner and in the way he looked at her when he talked to her. But what about the way he kissed her? *That* said a lot more than fondness. Well, then, why had their relationship not developed into something more substantial? Why had it always floundered — and wasn't that the very reason why she was going away? Well, then, what was it? Had it just been a physical attraction? Could that alone have kept him coming after her? But what did he get from her? Nothing! Absolutely nothing. Which was a whole lot less than he could have gotten from somebody else, say, somebody like Blondie, who was not only beautiful, but who appeared to have a lot of fun in her, much like Colin himself. So it just didn't make sense that he preferred her company, for she felt herself to have been much too serious most of the time, especially when she'd been alone with him. How could he have put up with her tone then, when his was the exact opposite? And why did he? How many times she wished she could have been different; had even looked for changes in herself, but had found none.

She knew she couldn't change, and, yet, again, she had asked herself why she should have to. Colin had known right from the start how she had been. So, why had he pursued her? Why had he kept coming after her those first few months of their meeting? Was it because he knew how she would eventually feel about him? He must've known how all the others he went with felt about him. *Was* she just a challenge to him? He certainly wasn't to her; it was inevitable that she should end up feeling for him the way she did.

All at once, Rosaleen felt a resurgence of the resentment, bitterness and pain that had plagued her for the past two days. And she nursed it for a while. Then, suddenly, the thought came to her. It wasn't just the physical part of Colin that made her feel the way she did; that was just part of him. It was the whole person, Colin Murdoch, she had responded to; not just the man. The physical part could not be separated from the rest. Colin could no more purposely make her feel something she didn't want to feel, any more than Patrick Brennan could; it had been Rosaleen herself.

Thinking about this, Rosaleen was beset with the thought of how she made him feel. Oh, she had evidenced that several times, and the memory of it now brought warmth to her cheeks. But she had always been so concerned about how she was affecting him as Colin Murdoch, she had never given any consideration as to how she was affecting him as a man.

Thinking about her own emotions, which, although were hers individually, were not hers specifically; every woman on the face of the earth possessed the same senses, the same feelings of sexuality; it was just the depth and height to which these feelings went that made the difference; not the feelings themselves. And were men's that much different?

The thought shook Rosaleen, as though it were a new form of language she was learning and that it was being revealed to her in one instant, as she realized, that, man or woman, every single person shared the exact same basic emotions, that they were not all that different; their bodies, yes, for the obvious reason, but, basically, their drives, their desires and their needs were one and the same; it was only the way in which they were displayed that made the difference.

Then, as exploratory as her line of thought had been, she suddenly felt herself blushing. Right there, with no one else even near her, she felt her cheeks stinging, as she thought for the first time of Colin, not as Colin Murdoch, but as a man, having the exact same sensual spots as she herself. Beyond her initial embarrassed acknowledgement of the fact, Rosaleen realized how self-centred and selfish she had been in not realizing it before.

"Well, so much for that," she mused, "I'm sure Colin Murdoch will appreciate the conclusion I have drawn; it was kind of late for self-realization, or even for self-recrimination, for that matter."

Hardly believing that this was all happening now, she stared into the fire. There were so many questions on her mind, now, as to why she was here, but she gave thought to none of them. The time for questions was gone; any she had, she should have asked before she got into the van.

Hearing the sound of the kettle boiling,

she realized that it had been for some time, and getting up from the hearth, she went into the scullery, and lowering the flame, she, at once, set to preparing the tea.

Touching and handling the objects in the little scullery that had belonged to someone else, made Rosaleen feel oddly strange. Sure, she'd done the very same thing at Donegans' the other night, and she'd helped out at wakes on many occasions; once even staying for three entire nights at a friend of the family whose brother had died, making tea for the mourners, but she'd never felt like this. At least, before, she had known the person to whom the objects belonged, but, now, she looked on these — the oriental tea-cannister, the little teapot, the china cups and saucers, and the tea-spoons, with their heavily decorated designs — not just as objects, but as someone's treasured possessions, and here she was, a total stranger, invading the intimacy of that domain, and she wondered if she had the right to.

The sound of Colin coming in chased Rosaleen's anxious thoughts and sent her looking for a tea-strainer, but it was with a feeling of helplessness, until, in what was almost a reflex action, she pulled out the little drawer in the scrub-table, which filled the space between the sink and the stove, the same which was at her grandmother's, and, upon finding it there, she then picked up the teapot and began to fill the cups.

"I see you've been busy," Colin said, coming into the scullery beside her, his height making it even more diminutive by comparison. "There's a tray in that lower cupboard," he told her, "We might as well bring everything into the fire, the house will warm up faster if we keep this door closed," and picking up the teapot, he went out ahead of Rosaleen, leaving her to bring the rest.

Putting the tray down on the little card-table that he had set up by the side of the fireplace, Rosaleen felt the heat from the fire to be much stronger, and, before sitting down in one of the armchairs that Colin had pulled closer to the hearth, she took off her coat.

A little more relaxed, now, while drinking her tea, with neither of them saying too much, Rosaleen let the atmosphere of the room settle in on her. Sitting across from her, and leaning towards the hearth, his cup cradled in both hands, and staring into the fire, Colin seemed to be engrossed in thoughts of his own, but sensing Rosaleen looking around the room, he lay back in the chair and looked at her.

Watching her eyes, as she took everything in, he could tell each and every object she was looking at without having to look himself, and he let her discover everything in silence. But, Rosaleen, suddenly aware of him watching her, broke the silence by remarking on the beauty and antiquity of everything. Then, Colin, his own eyes joining hers, took her on a visual tour of their surroundings, making her second time around more interesting by providing all sorts of little anecdotes, which not only enlightened her as to their origin and history but succeeded in amusing her and brought a smile to her face.

"You see that vase," he said, sitting forward again, and resting his elbows on his knees, and letting his empty cup dangle by the handle, he nodded to one of a pair of brightly coloured Chinese vases that decorated each end of the dark, highly-polished sideboard, which flanked the wall adjacent to the door. "Well, if you look close enough, you can see a lot of little fine lines in it that the other one doesn't have," and he went on to explain.

"About six weeks after my father was born — he was the third baby in a row, and my grandparents hadn't even been married three years yet — anyway, my grandmother had put in a terrible day between one or another of the babies. My grandfather, who worked on the docks then, had taken on some nightwatch duties there for a friend of his who had taken sick. Which meant, that for about a week, he was working from six in the morning to midnight every night. Well, this particular night, his friend showed up unexpectedly and ready to take over his job again. But my grandfather, instead of coming on home, went with one of the blokes he worked with, whose wife apparently gave him his dinner and then sent him to lie down for a while, telling him that she'd waken him in time to catch the last tram home. But, she didn't; instead she let him sleep, and, the next day, he had to leave straight from their house to go to work.

"In the meantime, my grandmother, who, every night that week, had waited up for him, keeping his dinners warm, had sat up the whole night, afraid to close her eyes for a minute for fearing the worst had happened to him. Finally, at a quarter past five the next morning, a man from down the street, who worked along with my grandfather, and who used to catch the half-past five tram with him every morning, came knocking on the door for him. Well, by this time, my grandmother was frantic with worry, and she told the man that my grandfather hadn't been home all night. Well, from the way I heard it, the man said, as casual as you like,

'Well, now, isn't that a wee bit peculiar, because I saw Robbie with my own two eyes catchin' the tram with his work-mates from the Falls *Loney* last night around a quarter past six.'

"That was all my granny had to hear," Colin told Rosaleen, smiling, "What with

461

contending with the three youngsters all day, sitting up all night, and having his dinner stick to the backside of the pot.

"The way my grandmother told it, that was the worst part for her, having to throw his dinner out. She was ready to light into him by the time he came home that night. In fact, she was more than ready, for when she heard his foot in the hall, she had the vase in her hand, ready to let him have it as soon as he came through the door. And she did. Only it wasn't my granda; it was the man from Society Insurance, and the vase came in contact with his skull before he'd even put a foot in the house.

"Well, that was the last straw. On top of everything else, my poor granny went into convulsions crying. She was so upset, she couldn't even help the poor man. Just then, my granda came in, and finding my granny in tears, and the society man with blood all over him, and the Chinese vase lying in smithereens on the floor, he just didn't know what to think. Anyway, after the poor man was all patched up, and my granda got my granny calmed down, he was able to get the whole story from her.

"For days after that, everytime he thought of 'his Rachel' throwing the vase at the society man, he would go into hysterics over it, and just couldn't bring himself to throw away the broken pieces. It took him weeks glueing it all back together again. And," Colin said, ending the story, "I don't know how the society man felt seeing it sitting there all in one piece the next time he came collecting, but," he continued, "my granda told him that 'that was what he called taking the job to heart', he'd been right there on the spot insuring my granda from getting hit on the head with a Chinese vase."

Looking at Colin the whole time he'd been talking, her eyes never leaving his face for a moment, Rosaleen found his mood exhilarating, and it showed. And Colin, seeing signs of it in her eyes, and in her laugh, said to her,

"Do you know what age they were at the time this happened? My grandfather was all of twenty and my grandmother barely eighteen." Then taking a deep breath, he added, "I think the point my grandfather was trying to make by telling us the story, Rosaleen, was that no matter

463

how bad anything becomes, it can always be put right again."

Without a word, Rosaleen refilled their cups from the teapot which had been sitting warming on the fire range, and, then, leaning back in her chair, she looked for a long time at the big ornamental brass boots that adorned the hearth, and she quietly told Colin.

"There used to be a woman . . . my mother always referred to her as a girl . . . although at the time I never knew why . . . and she lived a few doors from us, and she had come up from the country to live in Belfast, oh, long before I was born. Her name was Mary Jane, and she never married. But she lived in that house for forty years, and always kept to herself. She worked in one of the warerooms downtown, and she never wore a coat, just a big black shawl, and she had the blackest hair I ever saw.

"Going to work in the mornings, and coming home in the evenings, she would never stop to talk to anybody, and she always wore the shawl, even in the summer, no matter how warm it was.

"But one Sunday night, it was very

late, and I was coming back from a *feis*, and who should get on the bus and take a seat at the front, but Mary Jane. She was alone, and she wasn't wearing the shawl, but had it draped over her arm. I was sitting at the back of the bus with the rest of the dancers and our teacher, and I kept looking at her from time to time, and thinking to myself how handsome she was — a word my sister later laughed at, as she said it was only men who were handsome, and although I didn't know myself why I chose the word, it was the only way I could describe her — and she must've been well over fifty then; yet there wasn't a trace of grey in her hair.

"All the way home, I kept looking at her, as I could see her face in the glass, but all she did was stare out of the window. When we got to Oxford Street, she was the first to get off the bus, so I didn't think she even saw me. But, a few days after that, towards evening, coming home from work, and just as she was about to put the key in the lock, she called me over.

"First, she asked me to go to the shop and get her two ounces of cheese. Then, when I came back, she brought me in: it was the first time, I think, that she had ever invited anyone into the house; any visitors that she had, although they were few and far between, were country people. Well, anyway, she gave me tea and some bread and cheese, and she sat there by the fire and ate her supper. I was admiring the house, as it was the cleanest house I had ever seen, not to mention the quietest, and she told me that all the stuff she had there she had brought from the country, and that it had belonged to her dead mother.

"Oh, there were so many lovely things around. There were great big dishes with blue willow patterns, a huge, big bone-white soup tureen, and delft vases, and china dogs, and the little cherry-boy. Oh, so many things, and they filled the sideboard and several little tables, and she even had shelves on the walls, something which I had never seen in any of the houses around our way, and they were filled, too. But it was so odd seeing them all around like that, like they were on exhibit, or something.

"Then, I don't know why it was, but

my attention was suddenly brought to the mantlepiece. Maybe it was on account of the chiming of the clock, it broke through the silence like thunder, but up there on that huge, big mantlepiece, stood the two loneliest objects in the whole house." And looking down at the hearth, Rosaleen said, "They were a pair of brass, high-heeled boots. They were separated from all the other things in the room, and they stood apart, way up there on their own, and not even together as a pair, separated by the clock ticking away between them.

"Then, as we were having our tea, she told me how surprised she'd been to see me down in that part of the country, and she asked me if I had seen her friend when we had come along the lane to the bus stop. I was embarrassed, as I didn't know whether to say I had even seen her. And she must've seen it on my face, for she then asked me if I had heard anything that was said between her friend and herself. I just came right out and told her that I hadn't seen her until she'd gotten on that bus. And then it came to me, that the raised voices that I had heard in the lane, just before we boarded the bus, must've been those of her and her friend, but I didn't say anything. Then she asked me again if I was sure I didn't hear her friend make a remark as to my hair and such, that it was just this remark that had brought my presence there to her attention. I told her, I didn't, and I became curious, and I asked her what she meant. But she was very quiet after that, and she hardly spoke to me again, and she never invited me in again.

"Several years after that, after she'd retired, no one ever saw her, except running out to early mass on Sunday and home again, with the black shawl up over her head. That was all. She seldom ever opened the hall door; it remained shut, summer and winter.

"The only other times that I ever saw her was when I'd be playing in the street outside her house. I used to see her at the window, but way back, and no sooner would I look, than she'd move away.

"Then, one day, I think I must've been about fourteen at the time, some people came up from the country and took all her stuff away. As they were carrying it

468

out to the car, someone asked what the matter was, but all the people said was, that Mary Jane had died.

"No one ever found out how she died, or where, or how they had found out down in the country. Before I knew it, the house was taken over by new people, it was completely renovated, and there wasn't a trace of Mary Jane having lived there," Then, looking at the brass boots at her feet, Rosaleen said, "Mary Jane kept hers on top of the mantlepiece, where they looked so hard and cold, she should have kept them in the hearth, close to the fire, they look much warmer with the flame reflecting in them."

Looking at her long and hard, though unable to catch her eyes, and wanting desperately to see them, Colin went on to say,

"Well, there seems to be a story behind brass boots because this pair has a uniqueness of its own," and he continued,

"When my grandmother was growing up, her family lived next door to a Catholic Family. There was a girl about granny's age, and they became like sisters. But then," he said, "at that time, about nineteen hundred and eight, I think it was, there was some terrible street fighting broke out between the Catholics and the Protestants," and he shook his head, as if finding it hard to conceive of the year or the drama that took place then. "The Catholics got burned out of their houses, and then the Protestants, who tried to help. After a while, nobody knew who was burning who out; everybody was running for their lives. Anyway, granny's friend and her family moved away before any trouble came to their door, and they went to the south of Ireland to live. I think that's where they were from originally. After the troubles died down, the girl started writing to granny, and they remained good friends through their letters. She came back to Belfast for granny's wedding and after the birth of each of her first three children. But then came World War One, and, right on its tail, the Black and Tans . . . well . . . " Colin said, looking over at Rosaleen, " . . . granny and her friend lost touch with each other, and for about fifteen years there were no letters.

"Then, one day, a letter came with a Dundalk postmark; it was granny's old friend. The letter said that she had been working for a milliner for years but that she'd met a man and they were going to be married, and she wanted both my grandparents to attend the wedding. But, granny was in the family way, the eleventh, and last of the brood, and her confinement was too close to the wedding date, so she decided to surprise her friend by going to visit her right there and then.

"So off she went to Dundalk, taking with her a pair of brass, high-heeled boots as a wedding present. As she told us, they were very popular then, but also expensive. Anyway, when granny's train was stopped at the first border, the one on the Northern Ireland side, and the customs men came on board, granny had stuffed the boots inside her coat, and the customs men didn't know whether to search her, or rush her to the maternity ward. Well, she got the boots through.

"But, at the second border, she was too sure of herself, and she even stood up as much to convince the guard she was 'clean' and had nothing to declare. But, one of the boots fell to the floor. Granny acted nonchalantly and offered to pay the duty tax, but the guard wouldn't hear tell of it, said he would lose his job, and all that. Granny told him they were for a very dear friend, but he wouldn't listen, and she started to cry. But, still, even in spite of her condition, the guard confiscated them.

"Granny was in a terrible state. She didn't want to tell her friend what had happened in case it sounded too ridiculous. So, for the rest of the train journey, she was trying to find a better excuse as to what had happened to her wedding gift. But, by the time she arrived in Dundalk, she'd already decided to buy another present in order to save the embarrassment of having to explain. So she did; a tablecloth, or something, which only upset her more, for she had her heart set on giving the brass boots; a lifetime gift. She felt that Irish Linen was too common a wedding gift. Anyway, she gave it and it was well received, and the two of them talked all evening. Just before dinner, granny went to lie down for a bit. When she got up again, and came into the parlour, she found that her friend's fiancé had dropped in to give her *his* wedding gift to her; something she'd always wanted . . . " He didn't have to finish, for seeing Rosaleen's face, he let her do it for him.

"A pair of brass boots? Oh, Colin, that must've been awful for your grandmother."

"Well, my grandmother felt worse for her friend. Naturally, she didn't say anything, but the fiancé looked kind of green around the gills. All of it was enough to have knocked the heart out of the visit, and granny came back the next day. But, funny enough, she never heard from her friend after that. She tried to write to her, but all her letters were returned as address unknown."

But Rosaleen, looking at the boots in the hearth, was just about to ask the inevitable, when Colin, reading her expression, provided her with the answer.

"About five years ago, a package was delivered to the door. I mean hand-delivered, no name, no address, no postage, no explanation, nothing; just the brass boots inside a cardboard box.

Granny was upset for days over it; she just didn't know what to think. And," Colin went on to explain, "that's when we came to learn the story behind the boots in the first place."

Letting out a long breath, as though it was she who had been telling the story, Rosaleen bent down and picked up the boot closest to her, and turning it slowly in her hand, as though half-expecting to find the answer in its brassy sheen, she then put it back in the exact same spot she'd found it. Then, looking around her, drawing everything in with her gaze; every object, complete with all that Colin had told her, as though storing it all away for another time, for when the need arose, she could recall each item individually and go over it, inch by inch, and word by word, until the object, itself, would become visible to her.

Colin looked at her as though by the expression on her face, he was able to read her thoughts, and Rosaleen, finding his eyes on her, looked around the room once more.

"The house is kept so nice, Colin. Everything is so polished," and nodding in the direction of the fireplace, "And the grate is beautiful, I mean, black-lead must catch the dust so easily." Noticing the fire come alive in her eyes, Colin told her,

"That's because my Aunt Rita comes around a few times a week," and then, he told her, taking his eyes from the fire, and holding them with his own, "and, once in a while, I sleep over on a weekend night, just to light the fire; you know, to keep out the dampness." Losing his hold on her eyes, as she suddenly looked away, he brought them back to him, telling her, "Rosaleen. I've never had anyone else here, if that's what you're thinking," and with his eyes intensifying their hold on her, he added, "Never."

Looking at her, and watching her reaction to what he had just said, and, whether consciously or unconsciously, in what seemed like a gesture of abandoning his statement to hopeless redundancy, she brought both hands to her eyes and, then, drawing them along the length of her cheek bones, she sunk into the chair, and leaning back her head, she fixed her eyes on the wall behind him.

Continuing to watch her, Colin saw her stretch and cross her feet in front of her, and she, resting her head on the back of the chair, was suddenly slightly at odds with herself to find her feet touching his own. Not wanting to appear obtrusive, yet thinking it too obvious to abruptly pull them away, and preferring to remove them gradually, she let them remain where they were. But, upon closing her eyes, she immediately opened them as she felt her left foot gently prodded, and without moving her head, she looked at Colin, and saw him looking at her.

"Why don't you take your boots off and put your feet up on the fender. You'll be much more comfortable." Then, before she had time to take him up on his suggestion, she felt him lift, first, her right foot and remove her boot and, then, the other; her left foot remaining in his hand, as he set the boots aside.

Feeling the warmth of his hand closing around it, she heard him say,

"Your feet are freezing, Rosaleen," and, while she felt him massage some life into it, he said to her, "Come on over here and I'll warm them both up for you." And, as he released her foot, he held out his hand to her, saying, "C'mon, Celtic, you'll find it much warmer over here." And Rosaleen, reaching out her own hand, felt herself gently drawn up out of the chair and over onto his knee.

"Now isn't this better than you sitting way over there and me sitting here by myself," he said, enclosing her in his arms, and cradling her against him. Then, his eyes, going from her face to her hair, came to rest on her own, and he kissed her.

Without words, without excuse, without even gentility, his kiss captured her mind, and clearing it of any and all thoughts that might prevail against it, left it free to think of nothing, but what his lips were telling her.

And his hand in her hair, and on her face, and around her throat, destroyed altogether the remnants of doubt in which had previously and securely been wrapped all kinds of misgivings and guilt, and whose ability, now, had seen better days.

And his caresses put a stop to all

would-be trespassers and arrested them on suspicion of intrusion, and of causing personal pain.

And his words, soothing, and reassuring, and comforting, prepared the way for tranquility:

"Rosaleen, it's you. Oh, baby, it's only because it's you."

And his nearness, dominating her sense of equilibrium, combined all of her other senses and united them with the strongest and most urgent of all.

And in the joy of their union, the *child* in Rosaleen went out, and with it went all the resentment, and bitterness, and hurt. And only the love remained.

Feeling weightless in his arms, and having the sensation of ascending, the path before them open, with a faint light from behind, but growing dimmer the higher they climbed, Rosaleen found herself in total blackness, and her arms around Colin tightened, and she heard him whisper next to her ear.

"It's all right, baby. It's all right."

Then, feeling herself being lowered from his arms, she felt the solid comfort of softness beneath her; its delicious coolness encompassed her, yet, upon seeing the emerging quilt under the spreading gaslight, the glow from which spilled like liquid gold across the room, its mellow yellow charmed the colours of brown and yellow and orange, which came alive and warmed her. But not so much as when Colin came to sit on the edge of the bed, and brushed her hair with his hand, and asked her, as he bent over her.

"Are you alright?" and, upon seeing her nod her head, he bent closer to see the smile in her eyes, and he said, "Did I make you happy, baby? Was it as wonderful for you as it was for me?" And seeing the smile break out on her lips, he heard her tell him,

"Yes, Colin. Yes. It was more wonderful than I ever dreamed it could be. You've made me happier than you'll ever know." And Colin, seeing the smile fade from her lips and from her eyes, and seeing it replaced with a seriousness which was in keeping with her whole nature, he caressed her face, and he filled his eyes with the sight of her, until his arms went around her, and he told her,

"This time, baby, we're going to take our time; we're going to take it slow, because I want to get to know you, and I don't want to miss a thing." And he felt her arms go up around his neck, and he felt the pressure of them tighten, pulling him down for his kiss, and reaching for the buttons on her sweater, he began to undress her.

Now with the first urgent demand gone from their lovemaking, Rosaleen experienced a whole new different approach. For now Colin's moves were slower and more deliberate than before, and, unable to take her eyes from his face, she watched, as he gently undid each button. Sensing the anticipation mounting in her breast, she saw it present in his eyes as he looked at her, and in the slight touch of his hand as it brushed against her, and she watched his look turn to a very deep tenderness, when, at last, all obstacles removed from his sight, he looked at her for the very first time.

Time stood still for both of them in the endless duration of the first, glorious look. For Rosaleen, it was the joy expressed so deeply in Colin's eyes that made her happy; an expression that grew deeper, as his hands touched her bare shoulders and he held her at arm's length.

Warmed immensely by his gaze, Rosaleen, then, felt the intensity of that warmth sweep her entire body as his hands reached out for her and took hold of her bare breasts.

As soft as his touch, his voice enveloped her with its tenderness and emotion as he told her of his admiration for her. Giving adulation to the beauty of her breasts, Rosaleen had to smile, wondering if whether some form of magical transformation had taken place under his touch, and she told him so. But Colin stopped the words on her lips with his own, and, then, bringing his mouth to her ear, he told her that he'd always thought she had magnificent breasts, but that even with that, he had greatly underrated her. And Rosaleen, the smile completely gone now, succumbed altogether to his touch.

Aware for the first time of the physiological changes that do take place under a lover's touch, the knowledge of which, along with his now deep caresses, made her wish that none of it would ever have to end.

Seeing the glow in her eyes outreach anything he had yet to witness in another, Colin saw it turn to fire as his hands continued to caress her. Feeling the tips of her breasts tingle beneath his finger-tips, he was at once overwhelmed, not only by her response to him, but, by and large, because most of the girls he had known had grown insensitive to these gestures, their wants becoming more demanding, almost to the point of nausea. But Rosaleen? Aaah, Rosaleen was different. She was exhilarating — and, God, what an innocent heart she had behind such a sensual bosom! Then, almost forgetting his own intentions of postponing any rising demand he might have, he held back, not so much for his own sake, as for hers, because it was all so new to her.

But any intentions he may have had of prolonging things were soon waylaid, because Rosaleen raised her lips to his, and he felt her unbuttoning his shirt, and he felt the nakedness of her breasts against his own, and he felt his senses soar.

Unable to keep from touching the rest of her any longer, Colin's hands dropped to her hips, to the base of her spine, and, as though touching the very core of her being, he felt her entire body come alive. And, as though before had been a mere run through, even as magnificent as it had been, he felt every nerve, every sensual fibre in her body awaken anew, and his hands fell to her thighs.

Supple and taut as the flesh on her breasts, and just as sensuous, Colin felt his heart roar within his own breast, as he traced and retraced these lines of her body: then, although gentle at first, his hands smoothed the warmth and pliancy of her abdomen, until, hearing his name from her lips, his touch became more demanding, and, like nothing he ever experienced before, he felt her beneath him, against him, arousing him, leading him, soaring him; her body complying with all of his gestures — this girl, this Rosaleen, unwittingly demanding — no — commanding of himself more than he had ever given anyone before: this . . . woman, the most sensuous of all the others combined, yet with the purity of a child, and, with a happiness that was almost sacred in its intensity, he went to her, knowing that never again would he ever want to go to anyone else.

* ★ *

Knowing it to be very late, but having no way of telling for certain, since all the clocks in the house had been stopped, Rosaleen, half-dressed by now, picked up the rest of her clothes, and going around to the side of the bed, towards the direction in which Colin's head was turned on the pillow, she stood there, and she watched his sleeping face. Then, knowing that she couldn't put it off any longer, she went to him, and kissing him on the forehead, she let her lips remain against the smoothness of his brow, until she could no longer bear it.

"Goodbye, my love," she whispered almost to herself, as she took one, long, last look, then clutching her belongings to her, she went quietly out of the room and down the stairs.

Stopping only for as long as it took her to put on her boots and coat and to look around at the surroundings wherein Colin had, at last, become her very own, she breathed it all in with her eyes, shutting them immediately lest one tiny detail should escape.

Remembering the direction from which they had come, and the two turns, which Colin had made from the main road, Rosaleen began to walk in the direction of the lights, and, upon turning the corner, was relieved to see some people, about a half a block away, waiting for a bus.

Not caring, now, about what time of the night it was, just so long as she could get to the Castle Junction, she could always walk from there, Rosaleen stood quietly apart from the small group gathered under the transit sign and waited for the bus that would take her away from East Dunbar Street, and out of the Lagan District.

23

THE following morning at the usual six-thirty mass with her mother, but with it now over, the priest leaving the altar, Rosaleen leaned over to tell her mother that she was going to stay on for a while, and her mother, nodding to her, left the monastery without her.

Rosaleen waited for the people around her to leave, and then, going up the side aisle of the church, she passed the altar of the Mother of Perpetual Succour, with its splendid surround of golden gates. She genuflected before the high altar and then walked over to the left, to the altar of Saint Joseph the Worker.

Normally there would be a mass going on at this time, as the monastery was renowned for its daily offering of successive masses. With one mass starting as one ended, meant that, from six-thirty each morning until ten o'clock, there was a continuous rotation of masses going on at the seven altars; a practice which brought people from all over the city of Belfast, and, as a result, various sections of the big, old church were filled respectively according to which altar the mass was being said at. But this being the holy season of Christmas, Saint Joseph's altar had been utilized for the erection of the Christmas manger. With huge, tent-like, canvas structures, the whole area had been converted, with very effective results, into a stable.

Through all the years that Rosaleen had been coming here, she had always been overwhelmed, both by the significance of this Christmas scene, and by its simplicity. She had never seen one that had come close in comparison anywhere in the city. But, now, today, her feelings were not aroused by the atmosphere which this Christmas scene inspired. For, as she looked to the innocence of the face on the baby Jesus and to the sculptured countenances of Mary and Joseph, as they humbly knelt on the straw before the King of Kings, she was not filled with the joy which the birth of this baby brought, but more with the pain in which he died.

When she had left Colin last night, Rosaleen had carried with her a very great part of him; which was the light of his eyes, which had brightened her soul; the warmth of his smile, which had set fire to her heart; and the security of his embrace, which had strengthened her way. But awakening this morning, and long before the monastery carillon had sounded, she had lain there alone in the dark, remembering him, thinking about everything he had said to her, all the wonderful things he had told her, and she had loved him to the fullest of human capacity. But of everything that Colin had given her, he had not given her the one thing she really hungered for, and that was his love. As splendid as the kiss was, which had inspired the rest, so, too, had been the fulfillment of the promise which it had held; the physical part of it humanly satisfying to her, but not spiritually. And she couldn't imagine what it would have been like if she didn't love him. Would the joy, and excitement and fulfillment still have been there? It seemed to have been present for Colin.

Then, was that how it was for men? They must not need love to accompany their desires. But then she began to think of the girls who did the very same things, and she thought of herself at being painfully at odds with the world. Because if she didn't love Colin, she could never have made physical love to him, and she would trade that part of it if she could turn her head on the pillow and hear him say right now, 'I love you, Rosaleen.' And then, suddenly, she had become aware of the tears streaming down her cheeks, and turning her face into the empty pillow, she had let them come.

Having slept but little after her release of tears, and upon awakening the second time, the thoughts she'd been having earlier renewed themselves afresh in her mind, and, as she was getting dressed, the thoughts had deepened, bringing with them a new kind of anguish.

All during mass, Rosaleen's mind had been filled with how much she loved Colin, and, then, she had begun to think that perhaps she had been better off yesterday, and the day before, feeling nothing at all, and that it was better to be numb from everything than to feel the pain from an intensifying love that could have no future.

Now, kneeling before the little manger, Rosaleen began to understand the agony in which Jesus had hung on the cross. She had a sense of the source from where the real pain came from. She knew now, although she had heard it a thousand times, that it wasn't merely from the nails in his hands, nor from those that had joined his feet, nor from the thorns on his head; nor was it from the spear in his side.

"Oh, God, no," she breathed into her hands that covered her face, "It was the love that mankind refused to give you; it was from the pain of your own heart that you suffered the most. Oh, Jesus, combine my pain with your own that I may have some of your courage, your hope, and your obedience to the Divine Will of the Father; that I, too, will be able to bear the love that is not to be mine."

After what seemed like hours, Rosaleen raised her eyes to the statue of Saint Joseph in its place high on the wall above the stable. Looking first to the overall profile of a man so great as to inspire this image in the mind of the sculptor, Rosaleen then looked to the details, not only of the stone mason's chisel, but of the life of the man whose simplicity had led to his magnitude: to his garments, her eyes went, and she examined the crude, brown cloth, the type of which Joseph himself wore wrapped around him; to the course, rope sandals he wore on his feet. And then her eyes went to his hands, rough and work-torn; she looked long and lovingly at these, and to the tool, which he held in his left hand; the symbol of his labour, a carpenter's square, and, in the other, a simple, white lily; the symbol of purity: a seemingly paradox, these two objects, yet to Joseph, one was simply synonomous with the other.

Without moving her lips, Rosaleen invoked Saint Joseph through his image, for a very special intention:

"Oh, Dearest Joseph, I beseech you with all the power in my heart, to look after Colin for me. Watch over him night and day; help him in the company he keeps, and protect him in his labours that nothing ever happens to him. Dear Saint Joseph, do this as a special favour for me, and I won't ever ask you for anything again, except for one last request: Help Colin to find someone who will love him as much as I do, and who will make him happy always. Amen."

Then, lighting a tiny candle at the side of the altar, Rosaleen left the church.

Coming out into the courtyard, she pulled at the ends of her scarf and tightened it around her ears to keep out the cold, December frost, then coming through the big, black iron gates, she was out of the courtyard and into Clonard Street.

Due to the season, the street, and many others surrounding it, was filled with people both coming and going to the monastery; all sorts of people. There were uniformed nurses on bicycles, men with lunch boxes under their arms, old women, old men, women walking with their children, and others with their children in their arms, and young altar boys, swinging their satchels, as they walked along in twos and threes.

Seeing daylight for the first time that morning, since it was still dark when she went into mass, Rosaleen, eyes downcast against the rays of the winter sun shining through the leafless branches of the trees which lined the pavement outside the monastery, suddenly found her path blocked by someone coming in the opposite direction. Without having to look up, she knew that it was Colin.

There was a long moment of silence between them, as though there was no need for either of them to speak, and when it was broken, it was done so by Colin.

"Hello, Rosaleen," he said, looking at her with eyes as intense as the night before. Shading her eyes from the sun, which was directly behind him, she looked up at him, her eyes filled with surprise at seeing him.

"Colin! What are you doing here?" And in a voice that was just as intense as his eyes, he said,

"I could say I just happened to be in the neighbourhood, Rosaleen, but you know better than that."

And the two of them, standing there on the crowded pavement, creating an obstacle for those coming in opposite directions, caused not only those closest to them to alter their course, as they had to stop and go around them, but the slight detour, as insignificant as it seemed, affected the entire length and breadth of the street, and Rosaleen, seeing the annoyed expressions on the faces of some, felt Colin's hand on her back, as he changed her own direction and led her back up the street and past the monastery.

"I was waiting for you at the corner of the Falls," he said, his speech interrupted, as one or another came between them, separating them for a short part of the way, with others blindly following through to keep them apart even further, "and when I saw your mother coming by herself, I thought you had stayed home this morning." And gently taking her hand, to make sure that no one came between them again, he held it between his own, as they continued to walk.

"You know, today is the first morning I missed seeing you . . . oh, in weeks," he told her, keeping his eyes straight ahead, and, as Rosaleen threw him a quick look, he added, "I usually find you going down the Falls, but, this morning above all mornings," he said, looking at her, "you weren't there. So I had to stop and ask your mother where you were."

Sensing his ominous tone, along with the fact that she hadn't been aware that he should even recognize her mother, she turned to him, wide-eyed.

"You spoke to my mother?"

"Sure, why not? She seems like a very nice woman." And Rosaleen, her curiosity rising, asked him,

"Did she not ask who you were, or why you wanted to see me?"

"Oh, I think she had a very good idea who I was. And, no, didn't ask me any questions." And Rosaleen, looking ahead now, felt him looking at her. "I think she knew that her daughter would know the answer to that." Rosaleen felt her cheeks grow warm, despite the cold, morning air, and, not daring to ask the inevitable, she continued in silence.

Feeling Colin's presence beside her rather than seeing it, she realized that this was the first time that she had actually seen him in his work clothes, and, as she continued to look straight ahead, she held the mental image of him before her: Wearing the kind of clothing, which his outdoor, winter work required, he had on a heavy woollen, navy turtle-neck sweater, dark blue jeans, a fleece-lined, brown jacket and construction boots. And she was very aware that he had disrupted his workday to come looking for her like this.

Seeing that their walk had taken them to the quiet, little street at the back of the monastery, Rosaleen knew that their direction had been intentional, and, as they continued on by the single row of garden houses, they followed the street to where it wended its way into a dead end.

Beyond the sight of the houses, and hemmed in by two adjacent walls, one of which was flanked by the priest's burial house and the underground crypts of the monastery, the snow still lay pure and even; undisturbed by commercial venture, its depth and softness more fully revealed by the imprints now left in it.

All the while they'd been walking, and beyond the walls of the monastery, a special mass, being sung in honour of the coming savior, had followed them, and Rosaleen, recognizing it as Handel's *Messiah*, now heard the dual-toned voices of the servers and the choir spill the *Kyrie* out over the stillness, and the penitential fugue of 'Lord have mercy; Christ have mercy' instead of detracting from it, mysteriously added to it, and she felt the atmosphere surround them like a blanket of solitude, while she waited for Colin to speak.

"You're alright, then, after last night?" His question came sudden and straight to the point, and, as he turned to look at her, his right hand went against the wall behind her, and Rosaleen, taking it as it came to her, raised her eyes to his, and seeing the deep and genuine concern present there, answered him.

"I'm alright, Colin."

"Then why did you run off the way you did?" And now, taking her eyes away, and looking directly in front of her, she told him,

"Colin . . . I," she began, and, then, looking to the ground beneath her feet, " . . . I thought you'd understand the reason." Bringing his other hand to the wall on the other side of her, Colin bent his head towards her, and Rosaleen, lifting her face, met his eyes, as he told her,

"Rosaleen, it's little enough that I do understand your reasons for doing some of the things you do, but last night was the climax." Then, stopping for a moment, he studied her face in silence, before adding, and with his voice softening, "I wanted so much to wake up with you beside me. For the first time in my life I wanted the girl to be there when I woke up. No. Don't look away, Rosaleen," he said, turning her face back to him, "I'm not proud of what I've done, but we can't change what's behind us, can we?" and leaning closer to her, his eyes piercing hers, his mouth almost touching her own, "I wanted you beside me so badly that it hurt."

Feeling a lump rising in her throat, and attempting to swallow it, Rosaleen felt it double in size, as it came back, and bringing with it a stinging sensation to her eyes that was just as hard to blink away, and Colin, touching her with his lips in the gentlest kiss he had ever given her, continued, "You didn't give me a chance to say half the things I wanted to tell you."

Unable to bear it any longer, Rosaleen pushed him away, and walking a short distance from him, stood with her back to him, and raising her eyes to the sky in front of her, she let the cold air bite into them and cause them to freeze behind her lids and, as though in recompense, she let out a breath, giving warmth to the air around her.

Remaining where she was, not daring to look back at Colin, she looked beyond the burial house to the big, stone edifice of the monastery, and to the two tall steeples, whose grey spires were all but lost in the grey, December clouds, as though renting them to let in the *Hosannah en Excelsis Deo.*

Not wanting to breathe while the choir raised its earthly praise; its voice filled the vacuum which she had created between her and Colin, 'GLORY TO GOD IN THE HIGHEST AND PEACE ON EARTH TO MEN OF GOOD WILL.' Forced to relieve the pain that the cold air had produced within her, she felt Colin's hands on her shoulders from behind, as she let her breath out.

Purposely taking in a deep breath, and filling his lungs with the morning freshness, Colin exhaled a stream of air that was visible against the cold, and Rosaleen felt its comfort against her cheek.

"I'm glad the snow stopped," she heard him say, and she felt the pressure of his hands increase, as he drew her into him, bringing his jaw in line with her temple. "It caused us to lose some time on the job, but not too much . . . " She felt his smile against the side of her face, and it suddenly came to her that these casual-like conversations of his that always seemed to madden her whenever her own mood had been just the opposite, were not just unconcern, as she'd always thought, but rather, most of the time, they were a shift from the obvious whenever she'd been hurting, and she started to see that Colin understood her better than he knew, or maybe cared to admit. " . . . just enough for Monsignor Connolly to get all excited at the thought of having to delay the opening dedication ceremonies in May. But I think we'll finish in time without a hitch," and, pausing for a moment, he straightened to his full height, and she felt his chin brush the top of her head as he came around to face her, and he, looking at her, her features illuminated by the stark whiteness of the wall at the back of her, then added, "Though I must say it was pretty while it lasted."

Feeling his eyes remaining, Rosaleen brought her own up to meet his gaze, and a moment of eternity passed between them. But it overwhelmed her with its intensity, and she had to look away, then, knowing that his eyes hadn't left her face, she dared to look back.

Closing the single space that separated them, Colin told her, "You know, when I first started seeing you in the mornings," and he took an end of the knot at her throat between his fingers, "I'd been noticing how you look in these; especially the blue one," then, with the other hand, he took both ends and untied them, and said to her softly, "But you don't know how much I wanted to see your hair." And, as the scarf fell about her neck, he gently smoothed her head with the palm of his hand.

Not sure of what his intentions were, nor of why he had brought her here, Rosaleen only knew that she was filled with all of her old longings, and looking at him, she felt his name on her lips. But seeing that he was more composed than she, she swallowed hard and hid the emotions in her eyes by watching him caress the ends of her hair between his fingers.

"Rosaleen . . . " she heard him suddenly start to say, and looking up, she saw the very serious look in his eyes. " . . . I've had a long talk with Monsignor Connolly," and reading the question in her eyes, he said, "About you."

"What about me, Colin?"

"Well . . . " he started, and breaking off, he then started again. " . . . I was working inside the church, one day last week. I was alone at the time and feeling kind of overwhelmed by the amount of work that still had to be done before completion . . . I stopped what I was doing, and standing there at the back of the church, just looking around, I suddenly noticed that, during the day or so we'd been knocked off on account of the snow, the big crucifix, that was designed for the wall above the altar, had been hung in our absence. I was standing looking up at it, when the monsignor came up behind me. I didn't hear him come in, and I didn't know he was there, until I heard his voice. He asked me what I thought of the figure of Christ; that it had been formed from marble by an Italian sculptor, who had used the face of *The Pieta* as a model, and he invited me to take a closer look at it. The two of us walked up the church and, then, while we were standing beneath the cross, looking up at it, I heard myself ask him if there really was such a thing as miracles within the Catholic Church. He assured me there was, and asked why I wanted to know. I told him that I was looking for one for myself."

Feeling herself grow pale, Rosaleen saw that Colin's own face was drained of colour, with his eyes dark and sombre, like two liquid pools, their depth going all the way to his soul, and he continued, as

503

though looking into her own soul.

"We started to talk after that, oh, it must've been for an hour or so, and by the time we'd finished, I had told him everything: Everything! Rosaleen. About you and me, and about what the priest had said to you in confession."

Rosaleen, her mouth and throat void of moisture; her lips parched, listened dumbfounded, as he continued.

"He didn't seem to think that what we had was sinful, but that we had found something that was very special. He said that the most serious sin would be to throw it all away; although he suggested that we be more prudent." Then putting his hands lightly on her shoulders, she saw, again, the depth in his eyes. "Incredible as it might seem, but that's one of the things I wanted to tell you last night. But, I don't know, Rosaleen," and his hands left her in a helpless gesture, "God knows, I didn't plan anything else to happen; it just happened; it seemed like the most natural thing to do." Then taking her by the shoulders again, he bent down and said into her eyes, "You're not sorry that it happened, are you?"

But Rosaleen, unable to speak, was barely able to move her head for fear she'd shake every last tear from her eyes.

Straightening up, and holding her against him, she felt him rest his chin gently on her head as he went on.

"Because, when I was talking to the monsignor, I told him how you affected me, about how I never stop thinking about you, about how you are in my thoughts every minute of my waking hours . . .

" . . . I had been hoping for a long time, Rosaleen, for us to get together again. But I know how standoffish you can be, and I didn't want to stir up another occurrence of hard feelings between us. I thought that if things had time to cool, then, just maybe, we could start all over again.

"Then I saw you in the park that time, coming towards me with that big, blond fellow. Well, at first, I saw red, but yet, I somehow knew that it wasn't going to last, and, in fact, Jimmy told me a few nights later that you had broken it off with him," and looking at her, he said, "I sort of hoped that I had something to do with it. But then you never came back to the Hibs, and I guess that sort of told me something.

"Still, I was going to make it my business to go and see you. But that morning you passed in front of the van, you looked at me as if I had been a total stranger; I mean, not even a smile; you were as cold as ice.

"But I never stopped thinking about you, and, when Jimmy invited me to his engagement party, I thought that this was the opportunity I'd been waiting for. I thought that maybe, if I didn't come on too strong, that we could at least get on the same footing and sort of take it from there: and I swore to myself, Rosaleen," he said, holding up his hands, "that I was going to be on my best behaviour. I wasn't going to do one, single thing that would rile you. But again, you were as cold as ever, and I just didn't know how to reach you, and I realized that things had cooled too much on your part.

"Still, I was going to chance asking you to go out with me just one more time. I thought that if we could just talk, with no strings attached, then, maybe, we could start all over again. But, when I went to look for you, I realized that you were gone. I didn't know what to think and my first thought was that maybe you weren't feeling well. So I asked Phyllis. The next thing, Jimmy came over to tell me that, 'Wee Rosie was love sick.'

"That's all I had to hear, and so I went after you. But, then, that's when you dropped the bombshell by telling me that you were going to the States." Taking her in his arms again and holding her head against his chest, he told her, "After talking to you, in fact, after you had left, I said to myself, 'Not with them tears inside you, you're not.'" And then looking down at her, he saw them, and he clutched her to him.

Feeling his arms tighten about her, binding her to him, her head just beneath his chin, Rosaleen felt the pounding of his heart and the tremor of his voice against her temple as he told her,

"I love you, Rosaleen," and burying her head in his chest, he told her again, "Oh, God, how I love you."

Holding each other in that little snow-filled street for what seemed like endless time, Rosaleen waited while his words washed over her, bathed her, refreshed her, and brought new life to her spirit. Then feeling completely reborn by his love, she told him,

"I love you too, Colin. With all my heart." She lifted her face, which was wet with tears, to his, and she felt his wet, too, with his own.

Touching her face now with his fingers, he caressed the area around her mouth, as he heard her tell him,

"I think I've loved you from the first moment I saw you."

"Then why the tears?" he asked, now smiling through his own. "I thought it would make you happy hearing me tell you that I loved you."

"Because I wanted to tell you I love you, more than anything in the world."

"Well, why didn't you?" he said, looking down at her. "Well?" But seeing her eyes fill up afresh, he shook her gently by the shoulders, and said, "C'mon, tell me now."

"I love you."

"I didn't hear you too well," he said, holding her against him, "You'd better tell me again." And feeling her arms go up around his neck, he heard her saying, "I love you, Colin."

"And I love you too, baby," he said against her ear. "That's why I picked you up last night, so I could tell you in so many words: that's what I wanted to tell you when I woke up, only to find you'd run off on me again."

"And the reason I did, Colin," Rosaleen said, bringing her head back to look at him, "was because that's what was missing, and I had to know that more than anything."

"I sort of thought that was the reason. But it took me all the way home and then half the night to figure it out. And here all the time I thought I'd been making a fool of myself with you because you know how I felt and still would have nothing to do with me." Rosaleen felt his arms tighten their hold on her. "But that's the last time you're ever going to run out on me," and suddenly pulling her tighter, "Do you hear?" Then, his hand on the back of her head, he brought her face up for the first kiss of their newly declared love.

Finally, upon releasing her, he said, "I'll pick you up from work, then?"

"No, I better go home first," she told him, "I'll meet you up at the corner at seven o'clock."

"Can we make that a quarter to seven?" he said, stroking her hair, "We still have an awful lot to talk about."

Seeing the light in his eyes, Rosaleen nodded her head. Then, as he touched her lips once more with his own, she heard the first choruses of the *Alleluia* verse fall like thunder about their ears: "Praise ye the Lord . . . "

24

PUTTING the key in the lock and turning it, the door being stiff from disuse, Colin put a little force behind his weight and pushed it back into the quietness of the empty house. Then reaching for Rosaleen's hand, he brought her in as before, only this time, he pulled her to him in the darkened hall, and shutting the door tight behind them, he leaned against it.

Having driven over in almost complete silence, there being no need for either of them to have spoken, they had both been saving their thoughts for this moment, and, now, Rosaleen, her face next to Colin's, and he, with his arms securely holding her, the past twelve hours that had separated them, dissolved away in one long, sweet, and impassioned kiss.

"Do you want tea?" he asked, sudden, but soft, from behind the kiss, and Rosaleen, smiling against his mouth, shook her head.

"Well, then, I'm going to light the fire upstairs, so if you'll come with me and help me to find my way . . . " He broke off, and pulling her head back by the hair, he looked deep down into her face.

With the help of the little bit of streetlight coming in through the fanlight above their heads, he studied her features.

"Did I ever tell you that you have eyes like a cat?" Rosaleen, smiling, looking up at him, shook her head.

"Well, you do, you know," he said, pulling her head back further. "All silent, and watching, and cool, and never being taken off guard; they've fascinated me since the first time I ever looked at them."

"Oh, you're wrong about that, Colin," Rosaleen told him, bringing her head up as he slowly released her hair. "I've been caught off guard since the moment you walked into my life, and besides," she told him openly, "I don't like cats; they terrify me."

"Well, I like them," he told her, his voice matching the darkness surrounding them, deep and penetrating, "I always have. I like to hold them and to stroke their fur, and to watch them lie there, so beautiful and mysterious; they knowing every move you're going to make, and they let you, as long as it pleases them. But, try and anticipate what they're going to do, and they just look at you with all the secrets of their species hidden behind their deep, green eyes, and they don't give you a clue as to how or why they ever let themselves become domesticated; they go about their haunts on silent feet, taking to the entries at night, needing neither sun nor light to guide them, and they spring to heights of freedom; their characters providing them with the ability to watch down on everyone and everything that follows in their path." And with his hold tightening once more on her hair, he pulled her head back and kissed her eyes, her mouth, and her throat, and he whispered against her ear, "C'mon upstairs, Celtic. You can warm up the bed, while I light the fire."

Looking around the room, which Colin had brought to light with a low flame in the gas mantle, Rosaleen surveyed its shrine-like sanctity with the same reverent courtesy she would display upon entering a church that she wasn't familiar with. But then, after a few minutes, the gradual recognition seeped in and affirmed the notion that all rooms, like all churches, were alike; they were lived in, and worshipped in; it was only the familiarity of their individual atmospheres which made them appear to be different.

Walking around in her stockinged feet, Rosaleen felt the oilcloth cold and polished against her soles. Yet, it was oddly comforting when she realized that the hands which had last laid a sheen to its surface were now at rest, their earthly toil now finished; their obligations all fulfilled.

Going over to the bureau-like dresser, the height of which came to her chin, Rosaleen looked up at the once-gilt-edged frame, now, brown and discoloured with age, and studied the portrait within its surround.

Unmistakably, it was Colin's grandfather, the remarkable resemblance of the distinctive brows, the setting of the eyes, and the contour of the jaw confirmed it.

Upon hearing Colin coming up the

stairs and along the landing, she turned to look at him, as he came through the doorway.

"Colin, I can't get over how much you resemble your grandfather," she breathed, the disbelief evident in her voice. "If I didn't know better, I'd say this was you."

Walking across the room towards the fireplace, Colin glanced up at the portrait, "That is me," he said, slowly tilting the shovel of coal between the burning sticks. "The Murdochs have a tendency to hide their years well." Straightening up from the grate, he clapped the coal-dust from his hands, and coming to stand behind her, he laid hold of her shoulders. "You wouldn't take me for seventy-four, would you?" he said, looking up at the exact replica as the one which hung in the parlour his own house.

"You had me fooled." Rosaleen smiled, leaning against him, and she felt him kiss the top of her head. "And not only that," she added, "you led me to believe that your name was Murdoch, yet it says here Robert *MacMurtagh*."

"That's because my grandfather came

from Scotland," he told her, "Away west of Inverness again," and putting his hands to her waist, he turned her around to face him.

"He was a true Highlander, then?" Rosaleen asked, looking up into his face, then putting her arms up around his neck, and though still somewhat shy towards their open love, she asked him, "And is that where you got the blue for your eyes, from your grandfather living so close to the skies?"

"Well, if it is, then yours must've come from close to the seas; the deepest and the greenest emerald waters." And, as he went on, he gently caressed her through her coat, "Or from the richest fields, with grasses greener than the seas." And, then, from within her coat, his hands bringing her warmth much faster than the flame from the fire. "Or, maybe, from the mountain slopes, whose great peaks are still humble enough to extend a welcome to the hungry sheep to come up and graze; like my grandfather's home west of Inverness."

"Tell me more about your grandfather," Rosaleen pressed against his ear,

"I'm beginning to like him more and more."

Watching, as he removed her coat, she brought her lips against his cheek, as he lifted her in his arms. And, when he put her down gently onto the bed, he went to lower the mantle.

"Well, he was on his way to America, by way of Belfast," Colin told her, returning across the room, unbuttoning the front of his shirt, "when he met my grandmother; although it was purely by chance." Tossing his shirt across the bottom rail of the bed, he sat by the spot where Rosaleen's feet were resting on the quilt, and, as he took off his shoes, he continued.

"Their meeting was 'within the passing of a shadow', was how he used to phrase it. It seems he had to make an overnight stay in Belfast, and it was just before Christmas. He was passing the time, walking around the town, as his boat shipped out at five the next morning, and being they could start boarding at three, he didn't think that it was worth his while to get a room. But later that night, he was fast regretting it. He was coming around by Corn Market, trying to get out of the wind in High Street, and he ran head-on into a group of people singing Christmas Hymns.

"Now, Robbie Murdoch was never much of a conformist, as far as religions went, but he was open to everything; if a small snowdrop appeared in the ground, that was God, or if a tiny sparrow suddenly took off into the sky, that was God; he just saw God in all creations. But he must've seen him most of all that night; his first night in Belfast, for he never left.

"And, about the singers. He said he liked what they were singing alright, but it was the fact that so many of them standing together like that, sort of acted like a wind barrier, and so he stood as close to them as he dared. Well, as he was standing there, wondering, if perhaps, he looked at all suspicious, he saw this little girl looking at him.

"At first, he took her for the shadow of the bigger one standing in front of her, until he turned and met her full face and when he did, he received the brightest and the warmest smile he had ever, up to that time in his life, seen on the face of another human being. He said he couldn't turn away from it. And, when the singing stopped, he was still looking at her. She took him back with them to the church hall, where they would return at intervals for mugs of hot tea to ward off the cold. After that, she took him on the rest of the rounds, where they sang till midnight, and then, she took him home and asked her father if he could sleep on the sofa, that he had nowhere else to go.

"Well, there's no need to tell you that the little girl was Rachel Butler, my grandmother, who, my grandfather said, filled the need of another human soul with just a smile, and he being a lonely stranger in a cold, dark city, that was all he needed."

There was silence between them, and Colin lay back across the bed and with his hands behind his head, he stared at the ceiling, and after a while, Rosaleen said,

"I envy Rachel Murdoch her warmth."

"And I," Colin said, turning his head to look up at her, "envy Robbie

Murdoch's good judgement. It's fine to receive kindness, but if you don't recognize it as such, what good does it do you? My grandfather spent the rest of his life remembering it," and then he added, "especially when she'd go into one of her tantrums, and, oh, what a temper she had," and Rosaleen smiled, remembering the 'society man'.

"You know, it's sad, Rosaleen, how much we take for granted," Colin said. "When my grandfather used to tell us stories about Scotland, or about his early life here in Belfast . . . you know, he was just turned seventeen, when he was on his way to America. Somehow when an old person tells you about their youth, you tend to think of them as being old when it happened. Anyway, sometimes, when he would be talking, we'd have one eye on him, and the other on the door, waiting for the story to end, so as to get out onto the street to play, and he always knew it.

"Aah!" Colin said, after a noticeable silence, and for the first time since she'd known him, Rosaleen detected a real sadness in his voice. But realizing that he had filled himself with nostalgia, talking about his grandparents, and in their room, she just let him be. "I'd give anything to hear his voice right now, telling us one of his stories."

"What were some of the things he'd talk about?" Rosaleen asked, slipping down to the bottom of the bed where he lay, just to be near him.

It took Colin a while to say something, and, when he did, he was filled with memories.

"Well, like I told you, he wasn't one for the religion, and he never changed; he just went on being himself. Rachel continued being a Methodist and she raised the children Methodists, just as we all were," and he said to Rosaleen, "Would you believe that I used to sing in the boy's choir, when I was a kid?"

"I could believe you." Rosaleen smiled down at him, "You must've taken after your grandmother, then, for if she liked to sing . . . "

"You know," he said, looking up at her, "I never thought of that," and he went on, "It seems to be we just automatically associate ourselves with family members of the same sex . . . but, sure, Rachel loved to sing; but Robbie, he was a talker, and he had the most beautiful speaking voice you ever wanted to hear . . . He used to say the Highlanders got their clear tones from living so high up in the air. Well, he loved history, and he loved anything that had to do with people and nature. But, a lot of the history that he'd brought with him had to do with fighting, and tragedy, and death, so he often started his stories about the Scottish Rebellions, and about Robert Bruce, and the Battle of Bannockburn, and about the terrible Glencoe massacre of 1692; and, as children, we all knew about Culloden Moor, and the awful toll it took on the lives of the people. But he always said that you had to live through the hard times to appreciate the good, and he would always bring the conversations around to the physical beauty and joys of life, and he could talk for hours not only about the Glens, but about what lay beyond them; to the north, it was the Orkney Islands and the Shetlands; and to the west, it was the Isle of Skye and the Hebrides.

"He used to say that there was an invisible chain that linked all of us together and made us all agreeable, but that on account of some people not being able to see it, it became heavy, and, instead of joining us, it weighed us down, like a great, big burden around our necks.

"But you know," he said, brightening, and getting up on one elbow, "my grandfather was a great reader, and, like I said, he loved history, and he loved geography, and he said that growing up in the Highlands maybe gave him an advantage because it gave him a view of the world that many other people missed. He said that standing on a mountain top and looking out over the ocean gave one a perspective on life that shouldn't be argued; it gave him the feeling of being akin to the people on the other side; the people from the Netherlands, and from Bulgaria, and from Siberia.

"He used to say that our history runs in our veins as swift and as sure as does our blood, and that if we stopped to listen to one, we might spill less of the other.

"Oh, God, listen to me," Colin said, laying back again.

"I will," Rosaleen said, "for hours, and hours, and hours."

"And would you not get tired?" he asked, fondling the back of her head.

"Never," she said, and tracing his mouth with her fingers, "And, you still haven't told me why he changed his name from MacMurtagh to Murdoch."

"Well, I think it was because of the pronunciation. After he'd settled in Belfast and started looking around for work, nobody ever got his name right. He ended up either being called Mac, which he detested, or MacMurtig, which sounded too harsh; he said he couldn't go through life with Rachel being referred to as *Mrs MacMurtig*. So hearing a lot of other Anglicized names which he knew to be of Scottish origin, he had his own legally changed to Murdoch, the spelling, he thought, had a soft ring to it."

"I'll say," Rosaleen smiled, looking into his eyes, "And Robbie Murdoch", and she let the name roll off her tongue like a whisper, "sounded like he was a very poetic man."

"Oh, he was." Colin confirmed. "In fact, when we were very young, and used to visit here, he would take one or two of us on his lap, and much like a mother might teach nursery rhymes to her child, sitting there by the fire, Robbie would recite poems from a book, and mostly, Robert Burns."

"Robert Burns? hmmm," Rosaleen said, rolling over on her back, her eyes resting on the ceiling.

"Yeah! But not just because Robert Burns was Scottish, because, back in the Glens, Burns not being a Highlander, they looked more to their own poets. But my grandfather looked to Burns because he was a self-educated man, much like himself, and because he never let his pride climb to equal his aspirations. My grandfather always looked for a bit of the *everyday* in everything he read. He was a very enlightened man, and yet he was the most down to earth person I ever knew."

Letting the silence remain between them for a long moment after Colin had finished, Rosaleen asked, "Why do you suppose he ever left the Highlands, Colin?"

"I think it was mainly because he couldn't find anyone to read Robert

Burns to," he smiled, looking at her, and then, suddenly, looking serious, he said, "I really think it was because, after a while, it was too confining for him; too provincial. I often heard him say that the worst illness to befall a person was a narrow mind. I think he found Belfast to be more of a metropolitan place to live than the Glens."

"Oh, aye! Being a stranger to it, he might see that," Rosaleen said, giving a laugh, "He should have made the rounds with me, when I was looking for a job."

"Well," Colin said seriously, "maybe it was the fact that he received a smile from a stranger. I don't know, Rosaleen. I think anyplace in the world, no matter how large, still has its share of narrow-mindedness," and after a moment's pause, he added, "I mean, look at the States."

Getting his inference, Rosaleen looked away, but she felt Colin's hand on her chin.

"Hey," he said, softly, and she turned to look at him. "I know Robbie would have liked you very much. He would have taken great pleasure in reciting Robert Burns to you."

"Oh?" Rosaleen said in a whisper, "Then I would have enjoyed listening to him." And putting her hands on Colin, and feeling her senses come alive, with her fingers touching his hair, his face, and his neck, she said, "But it would be more gratifying to hear it from his grandson's lips."

Seeing everything in her eyes, Colin filled her present need by bringing his mouth on hers with a long and satisfying kiss. Then lifting his head to look in her eyes again, he saw that, far from stilling the demand in them, he had merely stirred it to the ultimate.

"I'm not a poet, understand," he told her, stroking the hair back from her face, "but, when I'm here like this with you, you could ask me to do anything, and nothing would be impossible." And feeling the softness of her cheek against his lips, he said to her, "This may have been written in the eighteenth century, and I must've heard it a hundred times or more, but it never held as much meaning for me, until I met you," and brushing her lips gently with his own, he looked again into her eyes. "You are my little rose, aren't you?" and seeing the gentle nod of her head, he added, "Well, Robert Burns must've had twentieth century vision, when he wrote:

'My love is like a red, red rose
That's newly sprung in June
My love is like a melody
That's sweetly played in tune
As fair as you, my bonnie lass,
So deep in love am I,
And I will love you still, my dear,
Till all the seas run dry.
Till all the seas run dry, my dear,
And the rocks melt with the sun!
And I will love you still, my dear,
While the sands of life shall run . . . '

Colin's voice fell silent, as, looking at Rosaleen with all the tenderness and emotion of their new found love, he recognized the deep need she had for him, for with one simple gesture, she had conveyed to him, the necessity of fulfilling all the things that had been left unsaid and left undone the night before, and that they had to be fulfilled before either of them would realize the complete extent of their love.

Undaunted neither by her own shyness nor by her awkwardness, he watched as she unbuckled his belt, and, as she took him in hand, she looked at him, and saw for the first time, the glorious symbol of his manhood, and then, stroking him, exploring him, exciting him beyond all measure, he felt his great need for her surge and swell relentlessly within. And he began to completely undress her.

Looking at her, the complete lines of her body softly silhouetted beneath the mellow glow of the gas mantle, he saw one knee raised slightly above the other, her pose unwittingly inviting him, entrancing him, enchanting him out of the physical world, that they both appeared to be in, and into an unseen world, where nothing existed except the two of them and the immense love that had brought them both here, and he went to her.

With more feeling than he had ever experienced in all of his life, he went to her, and entering her body he felt the joyous tenderness enclose him, but then, swift and sharp, as though being carried through the air, on a winged charger, but one without reins with which to secure himself, he knew that the journey would be all too short, and, in an attempt to delay the climax, in which he would be flung from the bare flesh of such a magnificent creature, he fastened his hands beneath her arms and held on for dear life.

But, he felt her embrace telling him to succumb, and he let his voice intrude upon this fantastic journey, hoping that it would waylay the moment of the two fleshes becoming one.

"Easy. Take it easy, baby," he told her, his voice penetrating the silence that surrounded them, and feeling the gradual relaxing of her limbs beneath him, he withdrew momentarily from her. Yet, wanting her even more, his hands reached for the soft, sensuous flesh around her navel, until, feeling below it, he sought the physical centre of her womanhood, and he began to caress her.

Consenting, and complying with each and all of his gestures, Colin found her lovemaking the most ardent, the most generous, the most genuine of anything he had ever hoped to experience, and, with his mouth against her ear, his voice warm with emotion, his words immensely pleasing to her, he made verbal love to her.

"Baby, I've waited all my life for you. If I had known that there was someone like you, I'd never even have looked at another girl." And kissing her, but at a momentum in keeping with his desire to make everything last, he then told her, "You have the most beautiful body in the whole world, baby." And, then, taking in every part of her with his eyes, he then told her, "You are the most beautiful, the most exquisite woman I've ever laid eyes on." And seeing something come alive in her eyes, he told her, close to her ear, "Oh, yes, you're a woman, alright, and you're my woman, aren't you?"

And with the slight motion of her head in assent, Rosaleen felt his lovemaking intensify. Slowly at first, then fast and purposeful, until she was no longer aware of anything but the overwhelming joy of his deep and penetrating caresses. Until, with a tremendous sense of floating, she experienced an odd kind of disembodiment; her soul was no longer trapped within her physical form, and, as she soared, she felt beyond all limitations of physical boundaries, and beyond all control of whatever it was that kept her human body and her spiritual being together.

With the blackness of another worldly dimension enveloping her, she had the fleeting experience of having united with the source from which all love sprung, and she succumbed to whatever it was that had beckoned her there, and, which, she could only surmise, was a gaining of paradise itself, through a form of simulated death.

Having been lost for so long within
the depths of darkness and despair,
she finally came upon the light;
the warmth and brightness of it
like wings on either side of her soul,
and chasing the anguish from her heart,
it suddenly lit upon her face,
and made her spirit whole.

Still within the ecstacy which had momentarily taken her from him, Colin saw the residue of it filling her eyes, as she opened them slowly and looked at him: and it was on account of her own joyous experience that brought him very close to the brink of what she had just been through, and in a loving embrace, his arms pulling her to him, he, once more, entered her body.

Never happier, never more at peace, Rosaleen welcomed her love with the fullness of her embrace, but, as he sought her mouth with his own, for the kiss that would lift him off the edge of the earth, she gently reminded him that he hadn't finished Robert Burns for her.

Feeling her smiling mouth beneath his own and pulling her even closer to him, her body yielding to his, enabling him to penetrate her to the fullest extent, he whispered to her.

"Now how could I refuse you anything, baby, while we're together like this."

And Rosaleen, feeling his arms encompass her entire body, felt the full magnitude of his own body, and she listened to the passionate voice against her ear.

" . . . And fare you well, my only love
and fare you well a while!
and I will come again, my love
Though it were ten-thousand mile!"

Hearing his voice lull against her cheek, she placed her fingers in his hair, and softly kissing his face, she drew his head to rest against her breast.

★　★　★

Upon awakening into the ever-present stillness that surrounded the house, her eyes heavy against even the low flicker of the mantle, Rosaleen heard Colin's voice.

"Are you awake, baby?" And she answered him by reaching out for his hand.

Feeling him take her fingers between his own, and by the strength with which he did, she knew that his mood was a serious one, and laying there close by his side, she heard him ask.

"What are we going to do about your notion of going to America?"

Not answering immediately, Rosaleen lay there, her eyes watching the light in the mantle flicker, looking like it was about to extinguish itself any minute; low, lower, lower still, until, suddenly, it picked itself up again and kept going as before, then, through watching it, and drawing in her breath, she answered.

"It's more than a notion now, Colin. My papers came in this morning's post. They were waiting for me, when I got home after leaving you."

"And what do you intend doing with them?"

Waiting again, before answering, she told him, "Well, as it stands now, the affidavits are only worth the paper they're written on. I have to take them to the American Embassy before they become legal documents."

"Would you find that more appealing than, say, becoming Mrs Murdoch?" And he said the name softly, rolling it off his tongue like a whisper.

And Rosaleen's lips broke into a smile, as turning to meet his eyes, she reached up and touched his face.

"It's all settled, then," he said, pulling her over and onto him.

Looking at her long and lovingly, his

look deepening with every feature he looked upon; her hair, her eyes, her mouth, and back to her eyes again, and in a tone more serious than she had yet to hear him speak, he told her,

"I've wakened up just this one time with you beside me, and, baby, I could almost taste the sweetness of it. I just don't know how I'm going to put in the next six months."

"Six months?" Rosaleen repeated, "What six months?"

"You know, the six months that the Catholic Church gives you to get to know someone. Well, I'm going to use that period to take instructions."

"Colin! What are you saying?"

"I'm saying what I didn't get to tell you this morning. Monsignor Connolly says that if I start now, not only can we be the first ones married in the new church, but that I will probably be the first convert from it."

Getting up from the bed, and pulling her coat around her, Rosaleen crossed the room to the fire. Suddenly chilled, she huddled up to it for warmth.

"Hey, what's the matter, baby?" Colin

asked, jumping up and coming after her, and bringing himself down to eye-level with her, he said, "I thought all of this would make you happy."

Looking at her hands, as though they had previously held something precious but had now lost it, Rosaleen told him, "Colin, wait a minute. You're going way too fast for me," and she stopped, drawing in her breath. Then, steadying her thoughts, she looked at him, saying, "I don't want you to change."

"You don't want me to convert?"

Putting her arms around him, Rosaleen pulled him against her, and too confused right then to put what she was feeling into its proper perspective, she let out a breath.

But it sounded like a sigh to Colin, and standing up, he brought her up with him, and with his hands remaining on her shoulders, he looked down at her, and he pulled her against him, and holding her tightly, he said, "All right, baby. Maybe we have moved too fast these past few days." But, shaking his head, he added, "But it really wasn't fast enough for me." Releasing her, he held her at arm's length. "Not after the months I've put in longing for you and not being able to get hold of you."

Breaking into tears, Rosaleen threw herself back into his arms, and Colin, stroking her head, told her.

"I'd give the world, right now, to be able to turn out the mantle, and turn down the bed, and to say to the entire city of Belfast, 'Goodnight, one and all, Mr and Mrs Murdoch are now retiring for the night.' But, instead, we have to get ourselves together and get away to the other end of town, and I have a pain in my gut just thinking about it, Rosaleen. Now, can you understand why I'm in such a hurry?"

★ ★ ★

There was silence in the van until they were out of East Dunbar Street and onto the dark section of the main road, and it was Colin's voice that reached Rosaleen first, and its bluntness caused her to turn and stare.

"My father says that this is a terrible town for a couple with mixed religions;

he said that we'd be better off if we didn't have any at all; that we would be more acceptable."

"Colin! You spoke to your father about us?"

"Well, I couldn't very well have Monsignor Connolly suddenly spring it on him out of the blue, that his son had been talking to him about getting married." And looking at her, he added, "Needless to say, my mother knows about us, too."

"You spoke to them before you even talked to me about it?"

Regardless of whether it was a question or a statement, Colin knew it was a fact, and he told her, "Rosaleen, I knew you were for me the first time I ever laid eyes on you." Looking over at her and meeting her eyes, he went on. "I didn't know it then, but you had something that I needed desperately."

"That can't be right, Colin." Rosaleen said slowly, not looking at him, but, rather, keeping her eyes determinedly on the windshield in front of her, "Sure, I didn't even give you a smile."

"You didn't have to, Rosaleen, for I

was no stranger. I knew my way around only too well; that was the whole trouble. It was your restraint that had touched me. I think I had had my fill of smiles up to that time."

Breaking her eyes loose of the windshield, Rosaleen turned her face and looked out into the night as they sped past it, and choked back the tears: for being tears of joy, she didn't want to lose them, but wanted to keep them for herself where they could remain forever locked up within her.

"I'll never forget that night as long as I live," Colin told her. "Even though it took quite a while to catch up with me." And reaching across, he took Rosaleen's hand, and pressing it tightly within his own, he let it remain there, and he said to her softly, "I love you, Celtic."

His words came to her like 'a melody played in tune', the last one being the sweetest note of all, since it carried a whole new meaning.

25

NEW YEAR'S EVE at the Hibs wasn't only as crowded as Rosaleen and Colin expected it to be; it was jam-packed, and only for the fact that they were known by the A.O.H. member at the door, they would have been turned away along with all the others.

It had started to snow just before it had started to get dark, and for several hours it had continuously fallen cleaning up the streets and purifying the air for the coming new year.

Without even bothering to look for seats on the crowded benches that lined the walls, Rosaleen and Colin pushed their way directly through to the dance floor and into each other's arms. Oblivious to all and everything around them, they had eyes only for one another; their surroundings merely the setting in which they had both chosen to say goodbye to the old year, 1956, and to bring in the new, with its promise and hope of togetherness and happiness for a whole lifetime ahead.

Having Colin so close to her, Rosaleen was still filled with the wonder of what his presence could do to her. For now, even after having had his total love, the physicality of it, though numerous now in its display, had not detracted one single sense from the mystery of it all; the spirituality of it, though endless in its rewards, still continued to add to the eternal power of it all.

Dancing so close to him, knowing that she had his love, feeling the commitment of it in his embrace, Rosaleen was glad that nineteen fifty-six was coming to an end. For inasmuch, as it had brought her Colin, it had also wrought heartaches and pain; the kind of which came with the unknowing and uncertainty of youth, but, which, once overcome, could never go quite so deep again.

Looking around the little A.O.H. hall as she danced, it all looked so oddly familiar to her; a paradox, to be sure, because, as it still looked the same, it felt different. Yet, there were all the old familiar faces she had come to know: 'Wee' Andy, still looking the same, still immaculately dressed in black; 'Dirty Eyes' and Manuel, still hanging around together, looking no different, now that 'Dirty Eyes' had his beautiful, full-head of hair back; and all the others were there too; Jerry Coogan, Terry Malcomson, big Albert McGahy; she saw, too, the little girl with the DA, and also Maisie, she looking like she had a new boyfriend and still looking as wonderful as ever in her v-neck sweater.

And then, coming around by the door, she saw Colin's old companions, Chancer and Bopper; they still looking the same, yet having somehow aged because it all seemed so long ago now since they had been the thorn in her side, and the spear in her heart. Still, she closed her eyes against them, but unfortunately she couldn't close her ears and she heard their conversation, though more like an argument, spewed with their own brand of innuendoes and gutter language, which she had come to hate.

Pressing closer to Colin, as they left these two to their harassing whatever poor creature they had picked on, she was startled to hear one of them yell out Colin's name, and she felt his hand leave her in a gesture of acknowledgement. Then she felt it come back, twice as firm, twice as secure, and very reassuring. But, no sooner had they passed by than there was the sound of breaking glass; a porter or whiskey bottle, no doubt, Rosaleen thought, and she got a tighter grasp on Colin. But whatever dispute had arisen, it seemed to have blown over as fast as it had come.

Closing her eyes to all but the closeness of her love, Rosaleen was very aware of Colin's hand at the small of her back; right there at the base of her spine, where he had revealed to her in a very compromising way, and very pleasantly, the spot where relayed sensations to every part of her being, and she felt the pressure of his fingers there, bringing her attention to a very familiar voice, and who, to Rosaleen, seemed almost like an old friend. It was Johnny Mathis. Pulling her closer, Colin held her hand against his heart, and she felt the beat of it against her palm, and she heard his voice against her ear, singing, softly, the words to the song, 'I Want You With Me All The Time.''

Lifting his head to look down at her, she raised her face to his, and seeing the smile in her eyes, he said,

"Do you like that?" and seeing the nod of her head, he then said, "You want me to sing you to sleep with it tonight?" And suddenly, he saw the smile disappear from her eyes, and in its place a look that he had come to know so well, and bringing her head against his chest, he said, "Yeah, I wish it was time to go, myself."

Feeling his heart beat faster now beneath her palm, Rosaleen raised her face once more to his, telling him softly, "I feel like I have your heart in my hand."

"That's impossible," he told her, just as softly, "How could you, when you're wearing it on a chain around your neck."

Without letting go of her hand, he reached for the little heart-shaped locket he had given her, and touching it at the base of her throat, he lifted it up with one finger. But Rosaleen, bringing her hand out from under his, closed her fingers around it and squeezing his hand within her own, she pressed it against her.

"Oh, no, Colin. That's not your heart," she told him. "It's more like mine was before I met you; cold and hard and empty of everything; that is, except pride. But from the minute you came into my life, you set a fire in it that has never gone out since: and the more I love you, the more fuel for the flames. And now, my love, it will never cease to burn."

Pulling her again to his chest, he told her something that was meant for her ears alone, "I'm glad we have the whole night together, Rosaleen, for when the mantle goes out, you're going to see a heart on fire with so much love, you'll think that Belfast, itself, is in flames."

And Rosaleen, touching her lips to his ear, whispered, "I already have, my love," and, again, "I already have."

With the record coming to an end, and while waiting for the next one to begin, and with their two shadows cast as one upon the crowded surroundings of the other dancers, Colin, with one hand around her waist, holding her as close to him as he dared, and, with the other lost within her hair at the back of her neck, bent his head close to hers, and asked her, "Did you put those papers away like I told you?" and he saw a soft gleam come into her eyes, as she told him.

"Well, not too far away, Mr Murdoch. You know, you're good for a year, and suppose I suddenly get the wanderlust, they'll be awful handy to fall back on."

"Oh, I don't think I'll have to worry about you wandering too far from my side," he said, "Not as long as I can keep that look in your eyes. Besides," he added, "I'm going to make a frame, myself, for those papers and hang them right over the mantlepiece in East Dunbar Street, right alongside our marriage licence." Then, as the next record began, he brought both his arms around her waist and playfully hugged her to him. "Now what does the future Mrs Murdoch think about that?" And Rosaleen, in answer, reached up and kissed his cheek with her smiling mouth.

Dancing so close together, their mood deepened further by the song that was now playing, Colin said to her,

"Do you suppose they knew we were coming here tonight? Seems like old times, doesn't it?"

Without answering, Rosaleen thought to herself, 'not quite', and was glad of the fact that it wasn't. Because, even though it was her favourite Mathis song, 'The Twelfth of Never', that was playing, it was the one that had caused her the most anguish during the time when she had broken up with him, and now it played to provoke that memory of how it had been without him. But that was all behind her now, and she pushed the thought from her mind, and she let the words and music carry her thoughts to the future; a very bright future, because Colin would be part of it.

No longer aware of the other dancers around her, nor even feeling the floor beneath her feet, Rosaleen was suddenly and overwhelmingly filled with the sensation of Colin's breath soft and warm against her ear, his now all familiar scent, his nearness, his heartbeat; all of him, flooding her being with all the memories he had ever brought her: the first night she met him, their first kiss, the day on the Cavehill, the night he gave her the gifts, the declaration of his undying love for her — and the consummation of that love — and all the wonderful times they had shared since then; including their making plans for the future together — all of these beautiful experiences came together in one glorious moment for Rosaleen and she felt that she could never love him more than she did right then.

Through the midst of her heightened sensation of him, the realization that the record was not the only music she was hearing, gradually descended on her, for along with its melody came the euphony of *Roisin Dubh*, played on the strings of some old instrument, and, with it, a composition that was hauntingly beautiful, Handel's *Largo*, and the individual choruses of his *Great Messiah*; the *Kyrie*, the *Gloria*, the *Alleluia*, and, now, each and every piece of music she had ever shared with Colin, all of it playing harmoniously at once: and through the divine symphony of it all, she sensed the words of the poetry of Robert Burns, the most dazzling, the most sensational of all, 'A Red, Red Rose': and blending with these seraphic tones were colours of red and yellow; brown and black; gold and orange, and many, many shades of green and blue; but none of them separate; all of them contained in one magnificent, celestial, solid colour, the likes of which Rosaleen had never seen: all of this, combined with her intense, heartfelt love for Colin, came together in one glorious moment of ecstasy for her, and there was an immediate awareness of the relevancy between the earthly joys of this life and those of the world to come: and then, hearing, again, the words and music to which she and Colin were moving, she knew that what she had just borne witness to was one fleeting moment of eternity, though swift in its encompassment; its utter joy completely overwhelming and totally unrecountable and unretrievable.

Suddenly the crash of broken glass intruded upon her thoughts. Much louder than the last one, it disrupted Rosaleen to no end and caused a great deal of turmoil within her, as though a moment of eternity itself had been pervaded.

Someone close to Colin and Rosaleen got the relayed message that somebody's head had gone through a window. After that there was more of the same kind of noise and it was the sound of porter bottles against glass, endlessly being flung against the windows, until every one on the far side of the room had been smashed in. Then there was quiet.

A more pathetic and ironic scene Rosaleen had yet to see, as the crowds deserted one half of the hall to come and see the results that the contraband porter had wrought on the premises of the little A.O.H. hall. Streams of tiny snowflakes were fluttering in through the window gaps left by the broken glass and were landing on the floor to mix with the spilt porter, as the record continued to play.

Turning to one another, some with complacent looks, others with concern, the dancers re-engaged themselves for the dance, as it appeared that the trouble-makers had been removed.

Then, like the calm before the storm, all hell let loose from the direction of the gent's toilet, just outside the hall, and the fierceness of it numbed Rosaleen with fear to the point of paralysis. Sensing someone screaming out Colin's name, she saw Chancer pushing his way towards them and grabbing Colin by the arm.

"Ah, Jesus, Murdoch, they're killin' him in there. There's four of them, I'm tellin' ye, there's goin' to be bloody murder."

"No!" Rosaleen shouted at the top of her voice to the drunken and disarrayed state of someone who was less deserving of anyone's help, much less theirs. "No, Colin!" she demanded of him, moving in between the two of them, as she attempted to put a distance between themselves and Chancer, as though this would be enough to put him off and to make him leave them alone. But, she felt Colin's hand on her arm.

"Wait a minute, Rosaleen," she heard him saying, "the fellow's in trouble . . . " and she was aware of being taken by the arm and removed from the path between him and Chancer, and, as she grabbed hold of him, she felt him being pulled from her. Fighting to keep him with her, she pleaded with him not to go.

But through it all, and over and above

her own voice, came the unmerciful screams of pleading anguish, and Chancer's own begging tone.

"They've got the f . . . door locked. Jesus, I'm tellin' ye, they're murderin' him."

As though from a distance, Rosaleen heard Colin's voice telling her,

"Rosaleen, I have to help him. You stay here. I'll be back in a minute."

"Colin!" Rosaleen screamed his name, making one final demand. "Please don't go! Let somebody else help him! Please, Colin!" and she flung herself into his arms.

Feeling the strength of a force that belied all physical law, Colin was unable to move. Then seeing her tear-filled eyes, he was reminded of their own recent and prolonged anguish, and taking her arms in one last, desperate attempt to release himself, he nodded to a couple nearby to take care of her, and he ran with Chancer to the door.

No sooner had Colin gone from her side than the record changed, and, in the heat of a fast and loud rock and roll number, the floor was soon filled with jiving couples, all warming up and getting into spirits for the approaching new year.

Feeling strange arms around her, comforting arms, but not Colin's arms, Rosaleen told the couple that it was alright, but the girl and the fellow, choosing to stay with her, each lit a cigarette, and gave one to her.

Through the terror of not knowing what was happening, came the sound of heavy thuds, and, suddenly Rosaleen was aware of the little girl with the DA, telling her that the A.O.H. men had everything in hand and not to worry, and that John, himself, had broken down the door to get at the troublemakers.

Feeling a little of the anxiety subside in her, Rosaleen drew on the cigarette, and, then, as if to break the tension further, someone over in the corner, under the record box, laughed, and it was a single, solitary laugh, and it stayed with her, hanging there in the middle of the room, as the dancers revolved around it.

Sitting there, while a conversation went on between the couple who had stayed with her and the girl with the DA, the thought of Phyllis and Jimmy suddenly entered her mind, and, and in the midst of this waiting period, she thought of them in terms of herself and Colin, and, for the first time, she realized that there were as many approaches to love as there were departures from it: she believed that hers and Colin's had been given a longer trial of patience, and, that having borne it had only made them that much stronger in their love.

Emerging from her train of thoughts, Rosaleen was met by shouts coming up from the street, and seeing those who had generously stood at her side going to the window, and believing it to be some unrelated incident, she remained where she was, and, with her eyes on the door, she waited for Colin to return.

Gradually becoming aware of a buzz of conversation going on around her, Rosaleen saw many people milling around the door, blocking her view, which would prevent her from seeing Colin when he came back into the hall, and she wished that they would move.

Then, suddenly, the room went black, as the door to the hallway was shut, closing out the one bright light. The people who had been forced back into the dance hall against their wills were not pleased, and, as recompense to their having been shut off from the action, they flocked to the gaping windows, splashing their way through the porter filled with snow flakes. Rosaleen, sitting silently by herself, watched them and she heard them yell down into the street below.

Wishing that Colin would come back so they could leave, Rosaleen had lost the desire to bring in the new year surrounded by memories; she would have much preferred to celebrate it in the quietness and solitude of Colin's company and in the little house in East Dunbar Street, in the Lagan District.

But all at once that little house seemed so far away; hurled even farther by the growing buzz of voices, and by the sound of someone crying, and by the harshness of that one laugh coming from the corner. Rising from the bench, if for no other reason than to be near someone, she walked to the window, the one to which the little girl with the DA, Colin's next-door neighbour, had gone.

As she approached, one girl, seeing

her, nudged another, and the buzz died a little, and someone said,

"Sssh. Get her away."

And another one said, "Don't be saying anything."

And Rosaleen, feeling confused, looked at all of them. Then, out over the heads of the crowd, the voice of Colin's little neighbour reached her, and though while not understanding her tone, or why everyone should look away, she heard her saying,

"What the hell's wrong with all of you? What do you think she is; a friggin' child? She needs to be with him more now, than standin' around here."

Rosaleen saw the girl appear out of the crowd, and she felt her take her by the arm and guide her towards the door.

"C'mon, love," she said firmly and without hesitation, "Colin's been hurt. I don't know how bad, but I'm sure to Christ Almighty, he needs you with him." And then, as both of them pushed their way out through the door, Leo, the A.O.H. member, who had been keeping the crowds from becoming spectators, let them through, and he shut the door quickly in their wake.

"C'mere, love," the girl pulled Rosaleen back from the stairs, "You can't go out like that," and nodding to the boy in the cloakroom, she lifted the wooden counter as he held open the half-door, and Rosaleen, taking her own coat, took Colin's also, and then ran down the stairs.

Upon reaching the bottom hallway, the girl, having put on her coat, took Rosaleen's and put it across her shoulders as they ran outside.

With the girl in the lead, and Rosaleen following, but not knowing where, they ran across the Falls. As they ran past Moloccos, Rosaleen was suddenly confronted by Malachy Donegan, Phyllis's brother, who, driving slowly along on the snow-filled Falls, had seen Rosaleen running from the A.O.H. hall, and leaving his motor running, had run to meet her, as she, and the girl with her, turned into Dunville Street.

"Rosie!" he shouted, grabbing her arm, "Is there something wrong?"

"Oh, Malachy!" she cried, releasing the first of her tears, "Colin's been hurt."

As Malachy ran back to his car, he backed it up a bit, the little Austin sending up a flurry of snow, as he turned into Dunville Street. Following the girls, his pace was much slower than theirs, on account of the frozen ground beneath his wheels.

Running the full length of the block opposite the Dunville Park, Rosaleen followed the girl into an entry, and pushing her way through the small crowd that had gathered, she looked to see Albert McGahy sitting with his back to one of the yard walls, with Colin cradled against him.

"He's alright, love, he's alright," he told Rosaleen, as she got down beside Colin.

Taking one look at his pallor, she quickly wrapped his coat about him, feeling him cold under her touch.

"What happened, Albert?" she asked, not taking her eyes off Colin, and in a voice that was heavy with tears, she controlled it to the best of her ability, "Where is he hurt?"

"We don't know yet, love. We didn't want to tamper, or even move him. John, here," he said, nodding in the direction of an older man, standing nearby, "has already rung for an ambulance. It should be here any minute."

Feeling someone get down beside her, Rosaleen recognized him as the A.O.H. man with whom she had seen Colin talking on a certain night, so long ago, now, and she heard the man's gentle voice beside her now, talking in low tones, not meant to be overheard.

"I rang for St John's Ambulance to take him to the Mater," he told her, "He'll be properly taken care of. Do you understand?"

Rosaleen, looking at Albert, who nodded agreeably, felt Malachy's hand on her shoulder.

"It's alright, Rosie," he told her, immediately grasping situation. "They'll take good care of him for you, love." feeling the reassuring clasp of his hand, she heard him say, "Sure, he's going to be alright."

But Rosaleen, understanding none of what seemed to be passing between the three men, was perplexed as to why he wasn't being taken to the Royal Victoria

Hospital, just across the park, on the other side. But before she had time to question this, a man's voice from behind, said in a loud whisper,

"That frigger, Louie," he said in reference to another A.O.H. member, "just went and rang Springfield Road . . . they have an ambulance on the way from the Royal."

"Ah, dear, dear," said John, shaking his head, and looking way off up the entry, his eyes, bearing a look of unpleasant anticipation, brought a tone to his voice that confused Rosaleen even more. "Sure, that's just what we've been trying to avoid."

"Look," Malachy Donegan cut in, "I have my motor running, why don't we just go ahead and take him to the Mater."

But Albert McGahy, apparently disturbed by this suggestion, interrupted. "No. I wouldn't advise that. Jesus, he's in bad enough shape as it is."

Whitefaced and shaken, Rosaleen looked at Albert and meeting his gaze, her eyes fell to Colin again, and gently lifting the coat from his chest, she noticed for the first time that Albert had been pressing something tight against him, just above the ribs on his left side.

"It's okay, love. It's okay," he told her, almost pleading with her to take his word for it. "It's only minor, it's not that bad. It just looks worse than what it is."

Feeling like a knife had just pierced her own side, Rosaleen felt the tears come: starting deep down in her chest and welling up, she felt them fill her eyes, burning and stinging, as they spilled from her, and struggling to keep the long, hallowed sobs from doing the same, she held them back, saying to Malachy, "Take him to the Royal, Malachy," and gently replacing his coat around him, she took Colin's hand between her own, and, in doing so, missed the look of concern that passed between Malachy and John.

"I'm afraid we can't do that," John told her. "You don't know what the *boyos* will do to this story when they get their hands on it: it'll put the Falls Road in an awful bad light; it could stir up a whole lot of unnecessary trouble."

Unable to contain herself, Rosaleen let loose on him. "Look at him!" she cried, her tears coming along with her voice.

"Look at my poor Colin!" she beseeched, looking at his deathly pallor. "Don't you think he's got troubles? Malachy, if you don't take him to the Royal, I will, should I have to carry him there myself."

Just as Malachy was about to move, Albert said, "There's no need to, here's the ambulance now."

"Oh, thank God!" Rosaleen breathed, pressing Colin's hand, first to her cheek, and then to her mouth, in reassurance to both of them, that, now, everything was going to be alright. Then, pulling his coat up closer to his face, she bent over and kissed him gently on the forehead.

Hearing the hurried footsteps coming along the entry, Rosaleen, tearing her eyes away from Colin's face, turned expectingly, and looking over her shoulder for the ambulance team, found, instead, the black-uniformed figures of the Royal Ulster Constabulary, crunching their way over the snow. With the aid of huge flashlights, they descended upon the group surrounding Colin.

"Here come the *boyos* now," John said, under his breath. "Now, we're going to have some fun, alright."

Without getting up, Rosaleen remained where she was, still holding Colin's hand between her own, as two of the lights shone directly onto them.

"Is this the fellow that has been stabbed?" one of the uniformed policemen asked, stepping between the beams and nodding in Colin's direction.

His words, falling on Rosaleen, wrenched her heart from her body and met with total silence, and, then, turning to his left, he threw a curt nod to his immediate superior.

The policeman, then, coming closer to where Colin was lying, asked in cold, crisp tones, which froze Rosaleen more than the snow she was kneeling in, "Which one of you will be responsible for questioning? We cannot move the victim until we know a few particulars," and then raising a clipboard, while another policeman stepped forward and shone a large flashlight over his shoulder, he licked the point of his pencil.

Clearing his throat, and with his eyes bearing down on the four who were around Colin, he cleared it again, as he looked from one to the other. Then, not sure who to direct his questions to, he fixed his gaze on Rosaleen.

"Miss . . . ?" he said, short and dry, and seeing the slight nod of her head, he took a few more steps in her direction, the flashlight following, and he stood immediately perpendicular over her slumped form.

Upon receiving Colin's name and address, and writing them both down, the policeman, followed by the flashlight, proceeded to his superior, while the other two policemen, standing stiff and rigid, like two lamp-posts, aimed their flashlights at the small group on the ground, as though holding it there with their beams.

Numb to everything but her anxiety for Colin, Rosaleen slowly became aware of a hand at her shoulder and of a voice at her ear, and turning her head to Colin's little next-door neighbour, she heard her saying,

" . . . it would be awful to hear it from the police, so, if you want me to, I'll go and ring them now. I won't say anything, except that he's hurt."

"Tell them to come to the Royal

Hospital," Rosaleen said, "Don't let them know that he's here."

Running down the entry to telephone Colin's parents, the girl almost collided with two men coming into it, with one of them broad-voiced and loud, and, more or less, leading the other. Upon reaching the police, the loud one, Louie, pushed his way amongst them and directed himself to the one in charge.

"Sergeant," he said, "I'm the one that rung youse up." And turning to his companion, he told them, "This here's Christy McLarnon from the *Tally*." And then, sniffing, he added, his voice taking on an air of acknowledged awareness, "As I'm sure youse have met before, considering the line of work youse are both in," and, going on, he said, "Terrible *bizness* this; terrible *bizness*, altogether." And he looked in the direction of Colin, but rather than seeing the people gathered on the ground, his eyes passed over their heads to the other end of the entry. Then, upon hearing what the policeman with the clipboard had to say to the sergeant, he brought his head back quickly, as though it had just been snapped into place.

"You see, sir," the policeman told his superior, "this is an address outside our jurisdiction, therefore, it will be necessary to place a call through to Broadway and to get someone down here at once."

"H'mmm," the sergeant replied, and Louie said,

"I coulda told youse that!" and sniffing again, he brought a note of importance to his tone. "Oh, he doesn't live around these parts at all."

"Well, then," the sergeant said, taking command, "Place a call through to Broadway and get someone down here at once." And the policeman, followed by the flashlight, went to relay the superior's order.

"Malachy!" Rosaleen's voice had an urgent tone, as she turned to him. "Please get them to hurry up."

Rising to his feet, Malachy went to talk to the sergeant, who, standing with his hands burrowed deep into his pockets, his great black military coat flung slightly back, revealed the awesome gloss of the black belt and soldierly buttons of his militaristic-styled black tunic; and Malachy, who, since the early fifties, had had a residue of built-in political hatred for the uniform, and, being this close to it, felt something rise inside him. But, clenching his own hands inside his pockets, he said, in a quiet voice,

"The fellow's in a bad way over there. Could we get a move on."

The sergeant, maintaining his pose, and remaining silent, threw a look over his shoulder, and seeing his man return, the beam of the flashlight behind him lighting the way, watched while he came up the length of the entry, and, without turning at all to Malachy, he held his frozen face towards the light, until it was directly beside him.

"Broadway says to get the fellow to the hospital; that they will get the particulars there."

"Let's do it, then," Malachy heard the frozen face pronounce. "Let's get the fellow to the hospital."

Hurrying back to Rosaleen, and putting a comforting arm around her, he told her, "They're taking him in now, love," and patting her on the shoulder, he said, somewhat bitterly, "Though I must say, by Christ, that they've taken their bloody time about it." Then, looking anxiously about for the stretcher to appear, Malachy saw Louie, his back to them, talking rapidly to the policeman with the clipboard, who, with the full beam of the flashlight behind him, licked the point of his pencil, listening intently, as though the light shining over his shoulder was the interrogatory beam eliciting truths from Louie that had to be written down.

And, right alongside them, the man from the *Tally*, although in a somewhat more proficient hand, tooled by his trade, taking everything down, word for word, as though all that was spilling from Louie's mouth was the gospel truth.

" . . . Like everybody knows, the Hibs is strictly for our own kind. Ye know, we *niver* encouraged outsiders to come in. God knows, we've our work cut out for us caterin' to our own, with them always tryin' to sneak in the drink." Sniff, "That's one thing that was *niver* allowed. Definitely taboo with the youngsters, 'cause they don't know how to handle it. Then we *git* in these outsiders," sniff, "now no offence, mind youse," he said, laying a hand on both the policeman and the man from the *Tally*, "but youse understand how it is. They come luckin' for trouble, and they got it." Sniff, "Youse can see the results yerselves, over there."

"Then, what you're basically saying," said the *Tally*, "is that this is nothing more than the usual Protestant-Catholic thing?"

"Aye, that's exactly what I'm sayin'." Sniff.

"H'mmm." The sergeant turned to the *Tally*, and, in a voice that melted his frozen austerity by half a degree or more, ordered: "Put that in your report. It will sit well with the press."

"And what about the ones who did it?" asked the *Tally*, pencil poised, "Do you know who they are?"

"Aye, I do." Sniff, "As well as I know the back of my own hand."

Upon hearing the dry cough of his superior, the policeman with the clipboard turned in his direction, and, immediately, bringing his attention back to Louie and the *Tally*, he took the former by the arm, and led him a little way down the entry, and handing him over to one of three policemen, who had been standing in a trio, facing the street, since they had first arrived, he said,

"This man has a statement to make. He will give you all the particulars." And then, in a lower voice, he told him, "See that he signs it."

And Louie, going off with his escort, threw him a nod, saying, "Aye, right youse be."

Returning from making the telephone call to Colin's parents, his little neighbour, coming back along Dunville Street, saw the ambulance from the Royal Hospital parked alongside the curb. With still half a block to go before the entry, she then saw the arrival of St John's ambulance coming alongside the street beside her, and in the opposite direction from which the other one had come. Watching, as it overtook her, it reached the entry before she did, and coming up to the other vehicle, it stopped in front of it, each one facing the other, nose to nose.

With the motor still running, the

volunteer team of St John's emerged from its ambulance, their dark uniforms visible against the snow, as they hastened towards the entry.

"Hey! Where do youse think yer goin'?" The voice of the Royal Hospital ambulance driver pulled them up short.

"We have an emergency to attend to." A tall, well-spoken young man told him.

"Not yere, yees don't," the driver, a small, balding man, with a cigarette butt between his teeth, told him. "We're here ourselves on official business; police business, that is," he finished, looking up into the young man's face.

"Well, you take care of your 'official business'," the young man told him back, "and we'll take care of the emergency." And running on into the entry, he was followed after by the rest of the ambulance team.

"Jesus! The cheek of some people, these days," the Royal Hospital driver said, "Well, we'll soon see about that!" and going to the back of his own ambulance, he slammed twice on the doors with his fist.

"H'mmm," the sergeant said, hands

still in his pockets, as he was confronted with this new dilemna, "And who did you say rang for you?" he directed his question to the young man from St John's, yet, without looking at him, he stared past him, his eyes ice-watery in his frozen face.

"Look, the devil I care who rang," the young man said. "You have an injured man over there, and we're here to take him to the hospital."

"And where do you propose taking him?" asked the policeman, clearing his throat, his clipboard now under his arm.

"Ahm . . . to . . . the Mater . . . I suppose," answered the young man.

"And suppose we inform you that the victim is not a Catholic . . . ?" the policeman told him coyly, withdrawing his information from underneath his arm.

"Look! You just said the key word," the young man from St John's told him, and heading towards Colin, he said, "Come on, fellows, I can see there's been enough time wasted here as it is." Followed by his team, he hastened to Colin's side. "I'm sorry, miss," he said to Rosaleen, taking her gently by the shoulder, "but we need all the room we can get," and motioning to the men, he bent over Colin.

"Now, just a bloody minute!" the voice of the Royal Hospital ambulance driver cut across the entry. "We've been sittin' out there freezin', these past five or ten minutes," he addressed the sergeant. "Don't tell me yer goin' to let them take him in?"

"Look, Ernie," a man from the same ambulance said, "What's the difference who takes him in. What does it matter . . . ?"

"It matters to me," the ambulance driver said, shrugging off his co-worker, "By Christ, it matters to me."

Turning to the young man from St John's, her pallor nearly equalling that of Colin's, Rosaleen said to him quietly, "His family has already been told that he is at the Royal." Then directly to the sergeant, she said, "Please get him there right away."

Working as fast as they could, the Royal Hospital ambulance men, co-ordinating their efforts as a team, while the driver went off to start up the motor, prepared to take Colin from Albert's arms and place him on a stretcher.

Watching them from a few feet away, the policeman, with the aid of his perennial torch-bearer, cleared his throat, as he reached out with his clipboard and used it as an obstacle to prevent one of the ambulance team from folding Colin's coat across the bottom of the stretcher.

"Just one moment!" he said, managing to flip back the lapel of Colin's coat with the bulk of his board, and he enquired, more to himself, than to anyone in particular, "What's this?" Then throwing a curt nod to his superior, he took the coat from the attendant, and turning away from everyone, and with the aid of the flashlight, they both examined the little white shield, with the red heart in the centre.

"What do you suppose this means?" mused the policeman, clearing his throat, again.

"H'mm," his superior answered, giving him a frozen look, and buried his hands further into his pockets.

"That's something that the Catholics wear when they stop drinking . . . "

the *Tally* broke in, and then broke off, just as sudden.

"What do you make of it?" the policeman asked hurriedly, using his clipboard as a privacy shield between himself and his superior and the little group to his right.

"I must say, this complicates things," said the sergeant.

"I'll say!" the *Tally* spoke up, "Now what am I supposed to do? I already have my report filled out."

"H'mmm."

"Well! What is he?" the *Tally* demanded, "Is he a Protestant, or isn't he? For Christ's sake, make up your minds. I have a deadline to make."

His voice carried across the entry, and Rosaleen, unable to bear it anymore, left Colin's side for the first time, and coming over to them clustered about his coat, she screamed.

"He's a human being! But if you have to know his religion before you can save his life — he's a Methodist." And through her tears, breaking loose, she cried, "Now, for God's sake, will you please get him into the ambulance."

With a look of relief in the ice-watery eyes, the sergeant turned to the *Tally*, his face melting further by half a degree or less, and told him, "You may keep your report as it is," and then, turning his entire frame to the waiting ambulance men, he gave them a stiff nod of his head.

Hurrying even more now, the Royal Hospital team, bringing Colin out to the street, expertly placed him into the ambulance. But Rosaleen, about to climb in behind, found her way blocked by the clipboard.

"Just one moment, miss," the policeman said, "Only immediate family in the ambulance."

Looking at him through an expression of disbelief, Rosaleen knocked the clipboard out of his hand, and, as it fell to the ground, she told him, "I am his immediate family; I'm his wife. And, mister, if you don't get him to the hospital this minute, without any further delay, I'm going to hold you personally responsible for anything that happens to him."

The bells, bringing in the New Year, and ringing out the old, were heard throughout the city, and, as the ambulance entered the hospital through the main gates on the Grosvenor Road, Rosaleen, holding Colin's hand, gently squeezed it, and bending over him, she softly told him, "Happy New Year, sweetheart." And believing to have seen a smile on his lips, she said even softer into his ear, "Well, you didn't think that I was going to spend New Year's Eve with Robbie MacMurtagh's grandson and not get to sing *Auld Lang Syne* with him, and bending her head, she kissed him gently on the lips, and raising her eyes, she looked at his face and said to him, "Just for old time's sake."

★ ★ ★

Sitting in the cold sterility of the hospital corridor, Rosaleen had found a little niche containing a wooden bench and a solitary bubble-glass window, which gave her the solitude she so desperately needed, and she sat there, with her head leaning against the wall behind her.

"Rosaleen?" the voice broke in on the

silence surrounding her, and she opened her eyes, from what seemed like an eternity, to see Colin's little neighbour.

"Do you mind if I sit with you?" And upon seeing the consenting flicker in Rosaleen's eyes, she sat down on the bench beside her.

Taking Rosaleen's hand, and finding it as cold as ice, she placed it between her own, and holding it there, wanting to give the young girl some of her own warmth, she started to fill her in on some of the details of what had happened to Colin — at least the part which had been told to her boyfriend, by someone who had witnessed Chancer and Bopper's part in it.

"Apparently they had gone to join in the celebrations at the 'big clock'. They had gotten there sometime in the afternoon and had spent the rest of the day in one of the nearby pubs. When they left to join the crowds that had already gathered in High Street, they had a load of drink with them.

"Apparently they had been their usual rowdy selves, and goaded along by the drink they'd become even rowdier and had picked on everybody and anybody that had looked in the least bit defenceless.

"Most of the people had ignored them, but there was one young fellow with his girl who didn't take too lightly to some of the comments they'd been making. So, taking his girl home, he had left them still shouting insults after them all the way down High Street.

"But the young fellow was from the local area, and he got some of his mates to come back with him to the clock. There were about six of them, and Chancer and Bopper were lucky to have gotten even as far as the Hibs, for the fellow was in vengeance. He had acted like he wanted to kill the two of them with his bare hands when he had left them at the clock; it was him who had brought the knife, intending to use it when he came back to look for them."

She then went on to tell Rosaleen, firsthand, what she herself had witnessed at the Hibs.

"When Colin had gone to help Bopper, he had been the first to do so; no one else had made the move, but as soon as Colin had become involved, 'Dirty Eyes', Manuel, and big Albert McGahy had all gone to help him. They had all helped John to break down the door in the gents' toilet and had gotten Bopper out. But, by then, he was in a state of panic; having met his match, he hadn't been able for them. He just wanted to get away from them as far as possible, and once having been freed in the Hibs, he had run blindly across the Falls and down into Dunville Street, with Colin after him.

"The fellow, who had been out to get either one or the other of Chancer or Bopper, or both, had been watching them closely. But Chancer was shrewd and had kept well within the crowd at the Hibs; but Bopper was careless and had gone into the gents' one too many times. And the fellow and his mates, who had somehow managed to get by the man at the door, had been waiting for him. Well, they gave him a terrible going over, and then there were the stab wounds; I heard he got cut up about the face and arms, but nothing serious; and then the fellow followed him from the Hibs, with the intention of finishing him off."

Numbed, and silent throughout it all, Rosaleen listened as the girl went on to tell her about what had happened in the entry. Without going into detail, she told Rosaleen that the fellow had made a lunge at Bopper, and Colin, unfortunately, had gotten in the way.

Keeping silent for a few minutes, the girl then told Rosaleen, "You know, love," she began, smoothing the back of Rosaleen's hand, "I always hated to see Colin with those two. I often wondered what he could possibly find in their company; they were always a bad lot. But, you know, love," she repeated, "I finally came to realize, as did a lot of other people, that it wasn't so much that they were bad for Colin as it was that he was good for them. He, more or less, kept them in line. They weren't half as bad or rowdy, when he went around with them." And looking at Rosaleen, she said, "I know that might seem funny to you, but I've seen them at their worst, and believe you me, they are none too pleasant. These past couple of months, everybody in the neighbourhood has been complaining about their behaviour, and," she said, adding the pressure of her fingers to Rosaleen's hand, "that's because Colin wasn't around any more."

Remaining quiet now, the girl sat in silence at Rosaleen's side, until, a few feet away, and just beyond the corner to their right, there came the sound of voices; one slow and precise, the words interrupted by the intermittently clearing of the throat; and the other, though loud by nature, was somewhat subdued by circumstances. Looking down the corridor, the girl saw the policeman, bereft now of both his superior and his clipboard, and Chancer, who, for the first time in his life, had a serious expression on his face.

As the two of them spoke, one asking the questions; the other answering, the volume of their voices filled the corridor and swept past Rosaleen and the girl, sitting unseen in the alcove, and it caught them up, making them unwilling listeners to what was being said.

"What were you and your companions doing on *that* part of the road anyway?" the policeman asked, a patronizing tone creeping into his voice, "You were in the wrong neck of the woods, wouldn't you say?"

"Naw," Chancer told him, "We always hang around down there."

"But why?" the policeman asked, laconically, "You have a much more, shall we say, compatible social environment within your own neighbourhood."

"And where would that be?" Chancer wanted to know.

"Why, right there on the Donegall Road. I'm sure there are more than a few nice spots for you youngsters, instead of having to go to the . . . Well then, what about over by Shaftesbury Square, or the Lisburn Road . . . ?"

"Naw, too far," Chancer said, "We always liked the Falls better."

"Oh, I see," the policeman said, changing the subject. "Well now, it seems like we have our work cut out for us for the coming new year. What can you tell us about the fellows you were fighting with? It seems that our men are having a difficult time tracing them."

"Nothing." Chancer said, "We never saw them before in our lives."

"Come now. Surely you must have

seen them at that hall before. You said so yourself that you've been going there for a number of years."

"Oh, they weren't from the Hibs." Chancer told him, "We ran into them down the town — at the 'big clock' — they followed us up to the Hibs from there."

"You mean to say that they were not residents from the Falls Road?"

"I don't know where they were residents from," Chancer told him.

"Why, I was led to believe that they were . . . Did you happen to get any of their names . . . or perhaps the name of a street, where they might live . . . ?"

"Jesus, mister, you have to be kiddin'! Them fellows had blood in their eyes, we didn't think to get their addresses."

"Well, that's understandable, I suppose. But tell me, how did you manage to elude them for so long? I mean, this would have been just the case for Hasting Street to handle, since the downtown area is their beat."

"Oh, you mean how did we manage to duck them? We came up through the side streets hopin' to lose them, 'cause we

585

knew they weren't from the Falls, an' we thought if they didn't know the area, we might have a chance. We were doin' alright, until we came to Cullingtree Road barracks. We tried to get in there, but there seemed to be a party goin' on, an' nobody would open the door . . . "

"Cullingtree Road, too? . . . mmm. Go on."

"Then, when we saw them gainin' on us, we ran up all the rest of the side streets, hopin' to get to the front of the Falls before they caught up on us. We thought we might stand a chance there. But it was a bad night, what with it snowin', an' bein' New Year's Eve, an' all, there was hardly anybody about.

"As we came into Servia Street, we thought we heard some celebrations goin' on in the direction of Belgrade Street, but we were mistaken; Belgrade was deserted. We didn't know where to turn. Then we thought we heard the celebrations again, this time comin' from Roumania Street. So we ran along Servia, but when we reached it, Roumania was deserted too. We didn't even stop. We just kept on runnin'.

"Along Servia, we ran, cuttin' up Bosnia, we took the hill up past Plevna and into Balkan — headin' all the time for the front. We kept Balkan, followin' alongside Raglan all the way forward, up past Osman, then, changin' direction even more to the front, we followed Garnet and met Raglan, and changin' direction again, furtherin' our advance we followed Raglan and headed for Balaclava. Then suddenly I couldn't run any more, an' stoppin' to draw my breath, I looked over my shoulder an' there they were, gainin' on us even more. My mate shouted for me to come on, but I couldn't move. I had my arms around the lamp-post an' I just didn't want to let go.

"'Come on!' my mate shouted to me through the snow, an' then, comin' over to me, he took my arm, but it was my legs that were frozen, an' then he said to me, 'Come on, it's only half a block.' An' it worked, an' he said again, 'Come on, half a block, half a block, just half a block more.' And we went up to Balaclava, followin' Raglan all the way.

"But, God, it was desolate, not a soul

about, except them behind us. We could hardly see where we were goin' — it was snowin' to the right of us, it was snowin' to the left of us, it was snowin' in front of us. When we reached Balaclava, I looked behind me one more time, an' that's when I saw the knife. The fellow waved it above his head, an' I caught the glint of the bare steel under the light of the street lamp. 'God help us!' I cried out, 'Jesus help us!' I cried, as they started to charge. I'm tellin' you, mister, it was hell . . . "

"Yes," the policeman said, interrupting, "Tell me about the fellow with the knife."

At this the girl got up from the bench, but as she came near them, she saw a doctor approach from the opposite direction, and she heard him say to Chancer,

"I'm afraid that your friend's wounds are not as superficial as we first thought. I'm sorry to say that he was ripped up very bad on the left side of his face," and, as Chancer made a move down the corridor towards the emergency room, the doctor put a hand on his arm, telling him further, "and I'm sorry to have to tell you this, but we are going to have to remove his eye."

"Oh, God!" Chancer cried out, all the anguish in his voice evident upon his face.

And still, the policeman wanted to continue his line of questioning.

"What can you tell me about the fellow with the knife?"

And all Chancer could say was, "Oh, God!" over and over again.

"Look, mister," the girl said to the policeman, "Don't you have a place on the Springfield Road for this sort of thing? A hospital corridor isn't exactly an interrogation room." And going over to Chancer, she put a hand on his arm and pressed it tight within her grasp.

"Rosaleen?" The sound of her name coming from the stranger's lips commanded Rosaleen to look up immediately, and the big sandy-haired doctor, seeing that he had the right person, reached down, and taking hold of her hand, bent over her.

"Mr and Mrs Murdoch told me your name, and I wanted to talk to you myself, Rosaleen." Sitting down on the bench beside her, he tightened his grasp on her hand in his own massive one and looked at her solemnly.

"I'm very sorry, dear, to have to tell you this, but your young man's gone."

Listening to his voice, but not quite hearing the words, Rosaleen turned to him full face. The doctor sensed her confusion before she asked the question.

"What do you mean, gone . . . ?"

Leaning his elbows on his knees, avoiding the searching look in her eyes before it turned to pain, he told her, "There was nothing we could do. He was already dead when the ambulance brought him in."

Following the short lapse of silence, as his words sank in, he heard the beginning of a long, tormented sob, somewhere inside her. And this big doctor, who had seen so much of life and death, had never, even at the peak of his war experiences, ever witnessed anything as earth shattering in its poignancy, as the cry that escaped from the young girl at his side, and placing an arm around her, he gave her his shoulder for the support she so desperately needed.

But it only took a moment for the

professional in him to determine that the girl was on the verge of hysteria and that unless he did something fast, he was going to have another emergency on his hands.

Picking her up in his arms, the young body already in the throes of danger, with all the control over her emotions gone, he ran with her down the corridor, shouting above her anguished screams for Colin, for his nurses to prepare a sedative, and to get in touch with her parents immediately.

★   ★   ★

Exhausted, and worn, and pale, without a trace of life in her face, Rosaleen was not even aware of the doctor coming into the room, nor of him seating himself on the edge of the bed. Taking her hand between his own, he felt it cold and limp.

"Rosaleen," he said her name softly, so as not to startle her out of her reverie. Then, because he thought that she must not have heard him, he leaned towards her, saying her name again. But, in looking at her, he immediately recognized the symptom of something deadly in her glazed expression. Speaking to her in a stern voice, he rapped the back of her hand with his knuckles, commanding a response from her; anything, except that God-forsaken expression, which had been so prevalent on the shell-shocked men he had tended during the war, and from which he had never known one to emerge.

"Rosaleen!" he shouted, the suddenness of which caused the nurse to jump, but nothing from Rosaleen. Then, tapping her on the cheek, first one, and then the other; his actions bringing a slight tinge to their surface, but nothing else.

"Damn it!" he cried, slapping her harder. "Rosaleen!" he shouted, as he kept on hitting her. But getting nowhere except to bring tears to the nurse's eyes, he knew that he'd better change his tactics.

And so once more he called her name, and immediately following, he said, "It's me, Colin." And leaning closer to her, he repeated, again and again, "Rosaleen, it's Colin," until, finally, he saw the tiniest flickering of her eyelids, but nothing more. Then, in a renewed determined effort, he slammed the metal locker with his fist, shouting at her, "It's Colin, Rosaleen. Do you hear what I'm telling you? It's Colin."

And then, in the softest whisper, he heard her say, "Colin's dead."

Running his hand through his hair, perspiring from the strain of it all, he said to her, "That's right, Rosaleen, Colin's dead." Then, leaning over the bed, he said into her face, "Colin's dead, Rosaleen. Cry for Colin. Cry for Colin! Rosaleen! Colin's dead. Damn it! Rosaleen, cry for Colin. For God's sake, cry for Colin."

The air broken, not only by his shouting, but also by the nurse's sobbing, and, underneath it all, the doctor heard the ghost of a whimper.

Screaming for the nurse to get out of the room, he turned to the girl in the bed.

"You call that crying? Rosaleen, you don't cry too much for Colin. Rosaleen, Colin's dead! Why aren't you crying?"

And again the whimper, but louder, and he leaned closer and said, "That's the girl, c'mon, cry; cry for Colin."

Upon hearing the sob escape from the motionless form in the bed, he began to cry himself. And as one sob followed another, the body of the girl began to shake, and as the head nurse came into the room, followed by her now distraught subordinate, the doctor, laughing, yet with the tears streaming down his face, told her,

"She's crying! Rosaleen's crying," and putting his arms around her, and hugging her in a fatherly fashion, he told her, "That's just fine, Rosaleen. Now you cry for Colin all you want."

* * *

Getting dressed to go home, Rosaleen turned wistfully from the window, as Doctor Kerr came through the doorway.

"Rosaleen," he told her, giving her a serious look. "I don't want you to go to the funeral, or even to go near the viewing. Do you hear me?"

Not answering immediately, and drawing a deep breath before she did, Rosaleen slowly shook her head. "No, I'm not going to." And then, her tone getting softer, almost inaudible, she said, "I always want to remember him the way he was."

Letting a deep sigh escape him, the doctor told her, "Rosaleen, you know Colin was dead when you came in with him; and he was dead a long time before that." Coming to her, and placing his hands on her shoulders, he told her, "My dear child, Colin Murdoch died the instant the knife touched his heart."

Turning away, and with a break in her voice, Rosaleen told him, "That's alright, doctor. I thought he was alive the whole time; I believed him to be, and that's all that matters."

Sequel

ON the evening of the third day after the New Year, the following letter appeared in the editorial section of one of the city's leading newspapers.

3rd January, 1957

Dear Readers:

During my most recent visit to your city of Belfast, from which I shall have made my departure by the time this letter goes to press, I was abhorred and horrified by the tragedy which took place during my brief stay. Therefore, I feel it is most necessary that all of us awaken to the awful state in which humanity finds itself. Nowhere do I find this better said, than in a poem by William Wordsworth, and which I would like to share with you, because it is as much a reflection of life today, as it was when the words were written, more than a hundred years ago.

"I heard a thousand blended notes
While in the grove I sat reclined
In that sweet mood when pleasant
     thoughts
bring sad thought to the mind.

To her fair works did nature link
The human soul that through me ran
And much it grieved my heart to think
What man has made of man.

Through primrose tufts in that green
     bower,
the periwinkle trailed its wreaths;
And 'tis my faith that every flower
Enjoys the air it breathes

The birds around me hopped and
     played
Their thoughts I cannot measure
But the least motion which they made
It seemed a thrill of pleasure

The budding twigs spread out their fan
to catch the breezy air;
And I must think, do all I can,
That there was pleasure there.

If this belief from heaven sent
If such be Nature's holy plan
Have I not reason to lament
What man has done to man?"

(Professor) Morris B. Harrison
(English Dept.)
Kent College, England

On the thirty-first of January, a month to the day of Colin's death, the editor of the same newspaper received (name withheld upon request) the following for publication.

In Memory
"Is life nought but a troubled plan?
The tearful destiny of man?
Though if it be for me to say,
I'd smile and look the other way.
Though sorrow breaks the joy we know
And sadness streaks the plans we sow
And parting thwarts the love we grow,
Then what becomes of man?
Within a city dark and cold
With winter's bite December-bold
Another's smile did warm my day
Another's eyes did light my way

Another's heart reached out to say,
What man has done to man."

Rosaleen kept her American visa until two days before it was due to expire, and on the twenty-first of December, nineteen fifty-seven, she left for the States.

She left Belfast just ten days before Colin's anniversary, but carrying with her, always, his little gold locket with his photograph, his compact with the rose, and most of all, his memory.

From the day he was laid to rest, all bitterness went out of her. She saw Colin as a true gift from God, who, for all his young nineteen years, had brought her a love of such intensity that it could only come once in a lifetime. Yet the memory of it mellowed enough for her to love again.

In a way she felt that her prayers to St Joseph had been answered, for she has always felt that Colin's death had been timed; that even if she had never met him, the end would have been inevitable, but that he had died after having known a true, pure love. For Rosaleen that was answer enough, for he would carry that love with him through all eternity, as part of the treasure trove he had gathered for himself here on earth.

And yet for Rosaleen, Colin is as much alive as ever; she has only to return to Belfast, to the Church of the Sacred Heart, and see the fruits of his labours; she has only to return to the Cavehill on a spring afternoon, and see the sight of him on every leaf, gorse, and tree; and she has only to listen to the treasury of songs by Johnny Mathis, to bring back his scent, his smile, his touch. Yet she returns to none of these, for she has only to look into the one place that contains the strongest memories of all, and that is her heart, for that is the place where his memory goes deepest.

Afterword

And be assured that everyone who has been within a relative distance to me, both socially and educationally, since the fifties until the publication of *The Celtic Heart* has inspired, influenced and contributed, in one way or another, to the writing of it. To each and everyone of you I give my warmest and sincerest thanks because you have all deeply touched and enriched my life. This gratitude is especially extended to include the musical artists to whom I give mention in the story, those whose lyrics I have used in the text, and all those who helped bring about *the* most exciting era of the twentieth century. I loved you all.

TO FIGHT THE WILD
Rod Ansell and Rachel Percy

Lost in uncharted Australian bush, Rod Ansell survived by hunting and trapping wild animals, improvising shelter and using all the bushman's skills he knew.

COROMANDEL
Pat Barr

India in the 1830s is a hot, uncomfortable place, where the East India Company still rules. Amelia and her new husband find themselves caught up in the animosities which seethe between the old order and the new.

THE SMALL PARTY
Lillian Beckwith

A frightening journey to safety begins for Ruth and her small party as their island is caught up in the dangers of armed insurrection.

THE WILDERNESS WALK
Sheila Bishop

Stifling unpleasant memories of a misbegotten romance in Cleave with Lord Francis Aubrey, Lavinia goes on holiday there with her sister. The two women are thrust into a romantic intrigue involving none other than Lord Francis.

THE RELUCTANT GUEST
Rosalind Brett

Ann Calvert went to spend a month on a South African farm with Theo Borland and his sister. They both proved to be different from her first idea of them, and there was Storr Peterson the most disturbing man she had ever met.

ONE ENCHANTED SUMMER
Anne Tedlock Brooks

A tale of mystery and romance and a girl who found both during one enchanted summer.

CLOUD OVER MALVERTON
Nancy Buckingham

Dulcie soon realises that something is seriously wrong at Malverton, and when violence strikes she is horrified to find herself under suspicion of murder.

AFTER THOUGHTS
Max Bygraves

The Cockney entertainer tells stories of his East End childhood, of his RAF days, and his post-war showbusiness successes and friendships with fellow comedians.

MOONLIGHT
AND MARCH ROSES
D. Y. Cameron

Lynn's search to trace a missing girl takes her to Spain, where she meets Clive Hendon. While untangling the situation, she untangles her emotions and decides on her own future.

NURSE ALICE IN LOVE
Theresa Charles

Accepting the post of nurse to little Fernie Sherrod, Alice Everton could not guess at the romance, suspense and danger which lay ahead at the Sherrod's isolated estate.

POIROT INVESTIGATES
Agatha Christie

Two things bind these eleven stories together — the brilliance and uncanny skill of the diminutive Belgian detective, and the stupidity of his Watson-like partner, Captain Hastings.

LET LOOSE THE TIGERS
Josephine Cox

Queenie promised to find the long-lost son of the frail, elderly murderess, Hannah Jason. But her enquiries threatened to unlock the cage where crucial secrets had long been held captive.

THE TWILIGHT MAN
Frank Gruber

Jim Rand lives alone in the California desert awaiting death. Into his hermit existence comes a teenage girl who blows both his past and his brief future wide open.

DOG IN THE DARK
Gerald Hammond

Jim Cunningham breeds and trains gun dogs, and his antagonism towards the devotees of show spaniels earns him many enemies. So when one of them is found murdered, the police are on his doorstep within hours.

THE RED KNIGHT
Geoffrey Moxon

When he finds himself a pawn on the chessboard of international espionage with his family in constant danger, Guy Trent becomes embroiled in moves and countermoves which may mean life or death for Western scientists.

TIGER TIGER
Frank Ryan

A young man involved in drugs is found murdered. This is the first event which will draw Detective Inspector Sandy Woodings into a whirlpool of murder and deceit.

CAROLINE MINUSCULE
Andrew Taylor

Caroline Minuscule, a medieval script, is the first clue to the whereabouts of a cache of diamonds. The search becomes a deadly kind of fairy story in which several murders have an other-worldly quality.

LONG CHAIN OF DEATH
Sarah Wolf

During the Second World War four American teenagers from the same town join the Army together. Forty-two years later, the son of one of the soldiers realises that someone is systematically wiping out the families of the four men.

THE LISTERDALE MYSTERY
Agatha Christie

Twelve short stories ranging from the light-hearted to the macabre, diverse mysteries ingeniously and plausibly contrived and convincingly unravelled.

TO BE LOVED
Lynne Collins

Andrew married the woman he had always loved despite the knowledge that Sarah married him for reasons of her own. So much heartache could have been avoided if only he had known how vital it was to be loved.

ACCUSED NURSE
Jane Converse

Paula found herself accused of a crime which could cost her her job, her nurse's reputation, and even the man she loved, unless the truth came to light.

BUTTERFLY MONTANE
Dorothy Cork

Parma had come to New Guinea to marry Alec Rivers, but she found him completely disinterested and that overbearing Pierce Adams getting entirely the wrong idea about her.

HONOURABLE FRIENDS
Janet Daley

Priscilla Burford is happily married when she meets Junior Environment Minister Alistair Thurston. Inevitably, sexual obsession and political necessity collide.

WANDERING MINSTRELS
Mary Delorme

Stella Wade's career as a concert pianist might have been ruined by the rudeness of a famous conductor, so it seemed to her agent and benefactor. Even Sir Nicholas fails to see the possibilities when John Tallis falls deeply in love with Stella.

MORNING IS BREAKING
Lesley Denny

The growing frenzy of war catapults
Diane Clements into a clandestine
marriage and separation with a German
refugee.

LAST BUS TO WOODSTOCK
Colin Dexter

A girl's body is discovered huddled in
the courtyard of a Woodstock pub,
and Detective Chief Inspector Morse
and Sergeant Lewis are hunting a
rapist and a murderer.

THE STUBBORN TIDE
Anne Durham

Everyone advised Carol not to grieve
so excessively over her cousin's death.
She might have followed their advice
if the man she loved thought that way
about her, but another girl came first
in his affections.

PREJUDICED WITNESS
Dilys Gater

Fleur Rowley finds when she leaves London for her 'author's retreat' in the wilds of North Wales that she is drawn, in spite of herself, into an old tragedy.

GENTLE TYRANT
Lucy Gillen

Working as Ross McAdam's secretary, Laura couldn't imagine why his bitchy exwife should see her as a rival.

DEAR CAPRICE
Juliet Gray

Clifford Fortune married Caprice but his brother, Luke, knew the marriage was a mistake. He could allow himself to love Caprice blindly but that would be betraying his own brother.

IN PALE BATTALIONS
Robert Goddard

Leonora Galloway has waited all her life to learn the truth about her father, slain on the Somme before she was born, the truth about the death of her mother and the mystery of an unsolved wartime murder.

A DREAM FOR TOMORROW
Grace Goodwin

In her new position as resident nurse at Coombe Magna, Karen Stevens has to bear the emnity of the beautiful Lisa, secretary to the doctor-on-call.

AFTER EMMA
Sheila Hocken

Following the author's previous auto-biographies — EMMA & I, and EMMA & Co., she relates more of the hilarious (and sometimes despairing) antics of her guide dogs.